TRIUMPH TO TRAGEDY

Book Three

*The Fall of Toussaint and the Rise
of Dessalines in Saint Domingue*

DANIEL J.D. BAYARD

Illustrations by Dian Triyasa

Cover by Carl Craig
In Collaboration with Jean-Bernard Bayard

L&D Publishing

SAINT DOMINGUE
Present Day Haiti
in the
Late Eighteenth Century
N
Môle-Saint-Nicolas
Jean R
Île de La Gaonave
Grande Cayemite
Dame-Marie
Jérémie
Port-de-Nippes
Miragô
Liburon
Front d
Nègre
Les Cayes
Île a Vache
Port-Salut

La Tortue
Port-de-Paix
LaBorgne
Limbé
Gros Morne
Acul
Plaine du Nord
Cap Français
Fort Liberté
Fort Dauphin
Dondon
Plaisance
Ferrier Rouge
Ennery
Marmelade
Ouanaminthe
Dajabòn
Saint Raphael
Gonaïves
La Croix
Ravine à Couleuvre
Estèr
Hinche
La Crète'a Pierrot
Petit Riviére
Verrettes
Banica
Saint Marc
Artibonite Valley
Mirebalais
Elias Pina
Arcahaie
Sources Puantes
Croix des Bouquets
Port-au-Prince
(Port Républicain)
Léogane
Grand-Goâve
Plaine de
Cul de Sac
Petit-Goâve
Jacmel
Bahoruco
Cote Espanol

Daniel J.D. Bayard

**Triumph To Tragedy
Book Three**

First Edition

Copyright © 2023 by
Daniel J.D. Bayard and L&D Publishing

All rights reserved.

First Printing, 2023
L&D Publishing

Email: Author@TriumphToTragedy.com

Paperback ISBN: 978-1-961297-14-2
Hardcover ISBN: 978-1-961297-15-9
eBook ISBN: 978-1-961297-17-3

www.TriumphToTragedy.com

Dedicated to the strong women in my life:
My loving wife Lily
My sisters Marie-Denise and Mica

With Wonderful Memories:
Mom, Dad and Jackie

To my children;
Laura, Daniel III, Phillippe and Brock

And my Grandchildren;
Bianca, Calista, Daniel IV, Andre, and Julien

Special Thanks for Support,
Critical Input and Encouragement:

Jean-Bernard Bayard
Frantz Ludecke

Parental Discretion Warning

ADULT SEXUAL CONTENT
GRAPHIC VIOLENCE
Not suited for young readers under 18.

For Young Adults under 18 years of age, refer to:

**TRIUMPH TO TRAGEDY
YOUNG ADULT SERIES**

The Cover Artist
Carl Craig

Style
"Symbolic Expressionism"

"My Passion Lies in The Challenge of Capturing the Beauty, the Delicacy and the Fragility of the Human Expression"

Born in Haiti, moved to New York with his family at the age of 15. He served honorably in the U.S. Air Force for more than 5 years. He pursued a Bachelor of Science Degree in Finance and International Business at Florida International University. After a successful career in the financial markets for 16 years, Carl ended his vocation on "Wall Street" and decided to apply his experience and acumen in international consulting.

Despite his successes in the financial markets and as an international consultant, Carl has chosen to walk away from all the power and structure to satisfy his thirst for creativity by unleashing his talent in the arts: painting, photography, and music.

As a self-taught artist, he brilliantly and skillfully projects the inspiration he finds in his models. Since 2008, his work has been constantly displayed on the local and international markets. In 2015 and 2016 Carl was the semi-finalist in the yearly national contest organized by the Bombay Sapphire, The Artisans Series.

Carl is internationally celebrated and has exhibited his works in Mexico by special invitation from Haitian Ambassador in Mexico City. His artworks have also been shown in Cayenne (formerly French Guyana) again, by special invitation of the General Consulate, including many more. Carl's admirers consider him as one of the best Portrait artists of our generation. His critics revere him as the Haitian artist who captures the "Sensuality of the Haitian Woman" like no other. Using Fine Arts By Carl platform, he supports local not-for-profit organizations with the "Philanthropy Through the Arts" program.

Emp. Jacques 1er
By Carl Craig
2023

Carl's belief is that hope lies in the human spirit and, by capturing the balance between delicate facial expressions and body language of his subjects, his message can be conveyed.

    "Koupé Têt, Boulé Kaye" (Cut Heads, Burn Houses) is a phrase attributed to **Jean-Jacques Dessalines**, one of the key leaders of the Haitian Revolution and the first ruler of independent Haiti. It is considered a powerful and symbolic war cry associated with the Haitian Revolution, reflecting the intense and radical nature of the revolt against slavery and colonialism.

    General Dessalines, on his horse, used this slogan to rally and motivate the revolutionary forces to fight against the French colonizers and their allies in order to secure Haiti's independence. The phrase encapsulated the determination and resolve of the Haitian people to achieve freedom, even if it meant resorting to drastic measures.

    The Haitian Revolution, which lasted from 1791 to 1804, was a complex and violent struggle that culminated in the establishment of Haiti as the first independent black republic in the Western Hemisphere. The use of *"Koupé Têt, Boule Kayé"* symbolized the uncompromising stance of the revolutionaries in their quest for liberty and the abolition of slavery.

    Dessalines' leadership and the rallying cry were crucial elements that inspired and unified the revolutionary army, ultimately leading to the victory that resulted in the creation of Haiti as a sovereign nation. The phrase continues to hold significance in Haitian history and is remembered as a potent symbol of the nation's hard-fought struggle for independence and freedom.

Emp. Jacques 1er – Oil on Canvas painting – 72" x 44"
www.fineartsbycarl.com
Editing by Marie-Donald Manigat-Craig

TABLE OF CONTENTS

Daniel J.D. Bayard

PREFACE

Thank you for reading Triumph To Tragedy – Book Three. The series is designed to entertain the reader while providing a detailed account of New World history in a manner that has not previously been presented, and very much ignored.

If you have not yet read Triumph To Tragedy - Book One and Book Two, I strongly suggest you do so before continuing this journey. Your enjoyment and understanding of the characters and series of events will dramatically increase, resulting in a much more rewarding experience. However, if you do not have a copy of Books One and Two readily available, or simply desire a refresher, please read on, but note you will be somewhat limited in complete understanding of the fascinating history of Saint Domingue and the future republic of Haiti.

In 1771, a young Jean-Baptiste Bayard returned home from his studies in Paris to the French Caribbean island colony of Saint-Domingue (present-day Haiti), unsure whether life on his family's plantation suited him. He had long entertained the idea of joining the French military and touring the New World, so he signed up for a multi-year deployment during which he would earn the title of Captain.

On military leave, he falls in love and marries the beautiful Marie Jasmine, beginning an exciting life together—launching a successful business venture, a family, and relocating to the bustling city of *Cap Français*—unaware of the drama, societal upheaval, and revolutionary war on the horizon.

In 1779, Jean was called up to serve as an army reservist to fight in the American Revolution. There he meets Henry Christophe, who over time becomes a member of the Bayard family.

By 1790, the colony of Saint Domingue, the western portion of Hispaniola, had long been crowned *the Pearl of the Antilles*, and its principal city, the bustling seaport of Cap Français, the *Paris of the Caribbean*. Theatre groups, orchestras, and operas would begin their Atlantic tours at Cap Français before any other destination. It was where fashion, high society, and international elites went to play.

At that time, Saint Domingue was undeniably the richest colony on earth, contributing over half of France's revenues from the production of 60% of the world's coffee and half of the world's sugar, amongst other products, and in the process employing tens of thousands of workers to export and process the commodities locally, at sea, and on the European continent.

However, the colony was built on the backs of 500,000 black and mulatto slaves, either born in the colony or imported from West Africa. These laborers served a free population of less than 100,000, equally divided by *Grands Blancs* (plantation owners who were amongst the wealthiest persons on earth at the time), the *Petits Blancs* (white commoners that included teachers, physicians, artisans, government workers, and others), and *Gens de Couleur Libre* (free blacks and mulattos), whom many owned slaves themselves.

The *Gens de Couleur* were racially discriminated against with laws that restricted their movement in the caste system, however, due to their savvy entrepreneurial spirit and work ethic, many were able to accumulate vast wealth and land equivalent to many *Grands Blancs*. This made all *Blancs*, envious, and bitter towards G*ens de Couleur*.

The French Revolution of 1789 introduced the ideals of *Liberté, Egalité, Fraternité*. Later that year, a movement by the *Gens de Couleur* petitioned for the application of these principles, including the right to vote, as had been promised by the ideals of the French Revolution. In a loosely worded proclamation, the French legislature recommended that while the principle of '*Egalité*' ought to be extended to all French citizens, including G*ens de Couleur*, it left the actual implementation of the said proclamation to the local colonial assemblies.

In Saint Domingue, as did elsewhere, the local assemblies quickly dismissed the notion of equal rights to the *Gens de Couleur*. In late 1790, a failed revolt by a group of them, led by Vincent Ogé and Jean-Baptiste Chavannes, were captured along with their colleagues and executed by torture in a rather draconian fashion.

In 1791, restless slaves, led by voodoo leaders Boukman and Cecile Fatiman, revolted in a bloody uprising which was soon put down, but the seeds of the revolt had been sewn, and insurrection continued for some time.

Infighting, backroom politics, deception, and scheming amongst the French, soon had them plotting against each other for control of the colony, leading to an insurrection, by the whites this time, against the French government's chief Commissioner, Léger-Félicité Sonthonax. Worsening the situation, encroachments by Britain and Spain to annex the colony to their own by force had begun in the wake of a disorganized and distracted French government.

In a risky and bold move, Sonthonax unilaterally freed the slaves in Saint Domingue to balance the power on his side believing that these now freed slaves would fight for France. This emancipation prevented the colony from collapsing, though he had no apparent authority to do so.

Meanwhile, leaders of the rebel movement had fled to the Spanish side of Hispaniola and formed the black auxiliaries of the Spanish Colonial Army. They fought the French on behalf of the Spanish, even though Spain was a slave-holding nation. The French legislature ratified Sonthonax's proclamation in 1794, emancipating slaves in all of France's territories.

Toussaint Louverture, then a commander in the Spanish Auxiliaries, performed a *volte-face,* a switching of sides, and he and his soldiers joined the French Army to successfully expel the Spanish and British from the colony.

Toussaint Louverture soon rose to become the supreme power broker by rising to the rank of Governor General and Commander in Chief. Politically, he usurped any French government authority, neutralized challengers with appointments to the French Legislature, subjugated others within his government, or expelled them from the colony.

In 1798, Toussaint chased out Thomas Hédouville, the last French agent with any power to challenge him, but for his final act, Hédouville dastardly appointed Toussaint's subordinate, Colonial General André Rigaud, as supreme commander of the Southern District, causing a rift that led to the beginning of a civil war.

Our story begins here.

.

Daniel J.D. Bayard

BOOK THREE
The Fall of Toussaint
& The Rise of Dessalines in Saint Domingue
1799 - 1804

Saint-Domingue
Present-Day Republic of Haiti

Ay-ti
'Land of Mountains'
The indigenous Taíno-Arawak name
for the entire island of Hispaniola

"Pa gen manman, pa gen papa!
Sa ki mouri? zafe yo!"

Général Jean-Jacques Dessalines

"There is no mother, there is no father
Those who die, it's their problem"

Général Jean-Jacques Dessalines

Daniel J.D. Bayard

One

THE SIEGE OF JACMEL

Jacmel
December 1799

The cool December breeze was salty and fresh. It served to calm the disposition of Alexandre Pétion as he took a deep drag from the cheroot that he had brought to his lips. The shutters of the large windows were open, and he looked out through them from the office he occupied inside the small fort nicknamed La Petite Batterie de Jacmel.

The structure was nearly a hundred years old and built by the Compagnie de Saint-Domingue – a company established by the king of France to stimulate the development of sugar and coffee production in the southern peninsula of Saint-Domingue back in 1698. It is rumored that this city was once the location of a Taíno indigenous village before their extinction by the Spanish in the early 16th century. Death and destruction were no strangers to the local soil.

After the establishment of the Jacmel settlement, the village soon developed into a picturesque bustling harbor town where ship facilities and warehouses were rapidly erected to service the newly minted sugar and coffee planters and traders that migrated to the area. Large estates and homes were built as Jacmel turned into an important international trading port.

Pétion, though from Port-au-Prince, knew of Jacmel's allure but had not spent much time in the city until now. He was there to replace Brigadier General Louis-Jacques Beauvais who had sailed away towards France but perished in a shipwreck on the way. Beauvais had been against the civil war now tearing the colony apart and serving to fuel racial tensions between the whites, blacks, and mulattos.

Beauvais considered the current animosity between Toussaint Louverture and André Rigaud as counterproductive to the stability of the colony. Both leaders had tremendous egos and a desire to rule the colony single-handedly. However, Rigaud wanted a separate domain under his rule in the South whereas Toussaint wanted to rule a consolidated colony. Beauvais knew that both leaders had mothers who were former black slaves from the Dahomey region of West Africa. Toussaint's father was black and Rigaud's white; a family dispute as Beauvais would often protest.

Rigaud and Toussaint both had equal claims of official appointments to their respective positions of power. Toussaint was appointed Governor-General by Commissioner Léger-Félicité Sonthonax. Toussaint, however, later expelled the commissioner from the colony due to lingering disputes.

Rigaud was appointed by Gabriel, comte d'Hédouville, another French agent who had also gotten on the wrong side of Toussaint and was sent running for his life back to France. However, before leaving the island, Hédouville dastardly appointed Rigaud the supreme commander of the Southern region in retaliation for Toussaint's actions.

Beauvais wanted no part of this internal dispute and chose to remain neutral. This drew the ire of his direct superior, General Rigaud since Beauvais was in command of the strategic port of Jacmel. Beauvais argued that his supreme commander was the Governor-General of the colony and that the conflicting appointments needed clarification from the French government before he could take any side.

Fearing retaliation from Rigaud and deciding that his life was worth far more than this political dispute, Beauvais boarded a ship bound for France to report on the predicament and seek direction to his dilemma from government authorities in Paris. Alas, before arriving in France, the ship had mysteriously sunk with many wondering if Rigaud had planted a saboteur amongst the crew. Back in Jacmel, this left behind 750 of Beauvais' loyal troops who were confused by the stalemate and had no appetite for the current civil war.

Rigaud ordered Pétion to assume command of Jacmel. Pétion came marching in with over 5,000 of his battle-tested troops. Local soldiers viewed this as a sort of military takeover of their town but were powerless to do anything about it. Pétion insisted that Beauvais' soldiers fall back into the ranks and follow the orders given them, essentially dissolving their command structure, and reassigning the men to different divisions within his ranks.

Pétion closed his eyes and took another deep drag from his cheroot. He needed to come up with a strategy to get out of his current dilemma. He could count on his 5,000 men who were loyal and would fight to the end with him, but not on Beauvais' soldiers who had no heart in this fight.

Here in Jacmel, he was outnumbered by Dessalines' well-armed forces of nearly 10,000 men who were now besieging the city. He was also well armed, and the fort had cannons, but he had ordered many of those scattered around several well-fortified ledges in the mountains for future use. The cannon would be more effective in elevated locations to rein punishment from on high rather than volleying cannonballs from within the city, especially since his cannonballs and powder were extremely limited. Every shot had to count and being a trained artilleryman, cannons were his favorite weapon of choice.

He opened his eyes and spotted the American frigate, *General Greene*, that now blockaded the harbor. The ship's blockade made it impossible to replenish supplies to his army and the town was growing short on food. The Americans had sided with Toussaint since the economic interests of the United States preferred the trade agreements that Toussaint had negotiated with them. Since the agreement guaranteed the protection of American vessels, Toussaint leveraged this protection against Rigaud and what he called the Rigaudin Rebels.

A knock on the door abruptly interrupted his thoughts. "Entrer" he barked.

A well-built light-skinned mulatto officer in uniform entered the office and stood at attention with a salute, awaiting a response from Pétion.

Pétion saluted "Yes Captain Rocourt?"

"Christophe's army is nearing our eastern front. Louverture is on the march from Grand-Goâve. Général Rigaud has less than 1,000 men fit for combat and is on the southern road near Cote de Fer marching towards Aquin and possibly Les Cayes, mon Général." ,

"Merde!" shouted Pétion as he picked up the box filled with Cheroots and offered one to the captain. "What else have you heard?"

"The Americans are transporting Toussaint's men from different towns to the outskirts of Jacmel," stated Captain Rocourt as he was offered a lit match by Pétion.

"So, this will be our last stand," offered Pétion. "So be it. What other American ships are in the vicinity?"

"The Boston and the Norfolk are operating as shuttles for Toussaint's troops and supplies, mon Général."

Pétion turned toward the window and looked at the *General Greene* with disgust. It was hard enough to keep morale afloat when they would soon be outnumbered four or five to one, but to have the American navy serving Toussaint was something altogether more distressing.

The captain stayed quiet and enjoyed his cheroot as someone knocked on the door.

"Entrer," responded Pétion.

Another officer entered and saluted awaiting Pétion to salute back. As he did so, the young officer said, "We have captured an American, mon Général".

"Did you say, 'an American'?"

"Yes, mon Général, an American sailor."

"What in the world is an American sailor doing in our custody?"

"He was found enjoying the services of one of the houses of prostitution downtown, mon Général. He was arrested by the military police".

"Where is he now?"

"In the office of the prison."

"Bring him here," Pétion ordered as the young officer admiringly looked at Captain Rocourt enjoying his cigar as he left the room.

"Rocourt, who is that officer? I do not recognize him."

Thomas Lamerique. He is one of Beauvais' officers. A captain."

"What is your assessment of our current position here?" asked Pétion.

"We are in a tough spot. We are low on munitions, have little shot for our cannon, and are just about out of food with only rice, beans, dry fish, and cornmeal left to survive on. The men are strong, but the remainder of Beauvais' men riles them up with talk of doubt as to why we wage war against our own people."

"And you, Rocourt? What do you think of the logic of this war?"

"I am a soldier, mon Général. My contribution is not of why, but of how – as in how to defeat the enemy – not why we are in a fight with them."

Suddenly, a commotion could be heard down the corridor with men shouting in Creole and a man shouting in English. "I believe our American is coming near," smiled Pétion.

A knock on the door was heard as Pétion ordered them to enter. The door barged open, and three soldiers were jostling with the prisoner – a young American sailor no older than 18 or 19 Pétion thought.

"I want to be taken to the American Consul immediately!" the American shouted. "You have no right to detain me and certainly no right to throw me in prison!"

The American sailor turned from Pétion and began to make his way to the door and was grabbed by one of Pétion's men and brought back as he attempted to punch one of the soldiers. The officer who had originally come in to announce the arrest hit the boy in the head which forced him to fall to the floor. The two other soldiers grabbed him from either side and stood him up to face Pétion.

Pétion walked from the window to his desk chair and sat down. "It seems, young man, we have demonstrated who is in charge here, henn?" Pétion stated with near-perfect English, albeit with a French accent.

Pétion was born to a wealthy French father and a free mulatto woman which designated him a quadroon – a quarter African ancestry in the French colonial caste system. Like other gens de couleur libres – free people of color – with wealthy fathers, Pétion was sent to France in 1788 to be educated and study at the Military Academy in Paris where he learned his English.

"You speak English then?" asked the young sailor. "I want to see the consulate or an ambassador or something!" he shouted.

"Before we move forward in conversation, you will control your tone and your temper, young man," replied Pétion in English with a calm voice. Then, turning to French he looked at the two soldiers and said "You can leave him to us. Dismissed,"

They both looked at their captain, Lamerique, who gave them a nod and they turned and left the room.

"I can see, Captain Lamerique, that your men have not yet accepted that they are part of my army now," Pétion complained. "I am their supreme commander, not you."

"They are slowly coming to grips with that reality, mon Général"

"Speed up the process, if you please," answered Pétion. "We do not want any confusion in the ranks when we engage our enemy. Now, who do we have here?" he said in English as he looked directly at the sailor.

"I am midshipman Michael McCoy of the USS *General Greene* and I demand an audience with your superior officer," the young sailor stated.

Pétion looked at his two officers and changed his language to Creole and said *"li vle ofisye siperyè mwen"* - he wants my superior officer - as he looked at the two officers and they burst out in laughter. He then picked up his box of cigars and offered one to Captain Lamerique who took one and smiled at Pétion.

"Uhh… excuse me, but do I get one of those?" asked the sailor.

Not acknowledging the request, Pétion said "What are you doing in our city, Mr. McCoy?"

"Exploring the finer things of this French colony," responded the sailor, referring to his visit to the house of prostitution.

"Let me see your visa," Pétion stated.

"They took all my papers," responded McCoy, just as Captain Lamerique extended them to Pétion.

Pétion read the paper out loud; "Michael McCoy, USS *General Greene*. I note that the visa restricts access to several cities and towns, including Jacmel, this one," Pétion stated.

"I demand to see the American consulate!" McCoy said, once again raising his voice.

"For his safety, incarcerate him until we can find this consulate he is asking for. I presume it will be quite some time though, henn?" stated Pétion. "We are at war, you know. Take him away."

Lamerique stood and grabbed McCoy by the arm and yanked him to his feet, dragging the young sailor behind him.

"When you decide that you will speak with me, inform your guards. Or you can await your consulate if we ever find him," shouted Pétion, as McCoy was dragged out of the room in protest.

The military prison was a grim and foreboding place, tucked away in a remote corner of the fort. The air was thick with the oppressive heat of the Caribbean even though it was December.

The atmosphere inside the prison was heavy with tension and despair. McCoy knew he was in a dire situation after a series of unfortunate events had led to his capture by the authorities. It was a fact that he was caught at a house of prostitution but that wasn't his reason for sneaking into Jacmel. However, he now felt happy that it was there he was apprehended.

Michael McCoy was employed by the State Department of the United States with a mission to collect vital intelligence information on the readiness of Rigaud's army to engage that of Toussaint Louverture's forces. He was sent by the U.S. Trade Envoy for the United States, Dr. Edward Stevens, for the clandestine operation and assigned to the USS warship, *General Greene* captained by Christopher Perry.

He was in Jacmel for two days and had been able to ascertain that Pétion's forces were out of cannon balls, low on powder, but plentiful of rifles, swords, and capability. It had been difficult to escape capture, hiding in warehouses by day and sleuthing around at night.

Seeing that he was caught, he won't admit to his superiors that he was enjoying some personal indulgence but instead argue that it was part of his camouflage. The bonus achieved by his apparent partaking in the local pleasures was his capture by the mulatto military police and subsequent audience with General Pétion. He would argue that it was part of his overall plan.

As the rusted iron gate of the prison door clanged shut behind him, McCoy surveyed his surroundings. The prison was a dark and dismal structure, its walls covered in grime and filth. The cells were cramped, and the stench of unwashed bodies and human waste hung densely in the air.

Most of the prisoners were black ex-slaves, probably captured soldiers of Dessalines army, he thought, who had once toiled in the sugarcane fields of Saint Domingue, but now they were here as free soldiers, their spirits unbroken despite their circumstances.

The initial shock of his capture gave way to a sense of vulnerability. McCoy was acutely aware that he was the only apparent white man among a sea of black faces, and he couldn't help but feel like an outsider. The ex-slave prisoners regarded him with a mix of curiosity, suspicion, and indifference.

In the hours that followed, he tried to keep to himself, finding a corner of the cell to sit in and blend into the shadows. The other prisoners spoke in hushed tones in a language he couldn't understand, their eyes filled with a mix of resentment and resignation.

The day following of his arrest, the guards brought food to the cell. A putrid mixture of what appeared to be boiled grass with probably some mud sprinkled in to replace salt and pepper for flavor. Other ingredients would gratefully remain unknown. However, when they handed him a bowl of feed, instead his bowl contained cornmeal topped with a bean sauce and a small ration of meat that smelled like goat.

The men with black faces looked at him with ire and indignation, but before they could act on their anger and jealousy over his apparent feast compared to their disgusting ration, McCoy stood and walked over to what appeared to be a man with severe battle wounds lying in the opposite corner of the cell. McCoy pushed past the crowd, his shoulders unapologetically hitting others in the cramped quarters, as he made his way to the man.

The prisoners looked at him with curiosity and confusion. In the prison world, the slightest infraction of the prisoner hierarchy could get him killed.

McCoy bent on one knee next to the wounded man who looked up at him with surprise, thinking him to be a physician or possibly an executioner about to put him out of his misery. McCoy looked into his eyes and showed him the bowl of food. He helped him somewhat crop himself up and leaned his back against the stone wall of the dark cell.

The man had thick blood that oozed from what appeared to be a gash, probably caused by a sword blade on his torso just under his ribs. He was weak, but McCoy couldn't tell if it was entirely due to the wound or starvation. He put his hand to the back of the man's head and brought his lips up to his other hand filled with some of the cold cornmeal and bean mixture.

As the man took in the food, he closed his eyes to relish the taste and then opened them towards McCoy as if to ask if he could have another scoop. Several men approached and formed a circle to observe the two and exchanged words in what he thought was the island tongue of Creole. It was not French as he had taken some instruction in the French language.

After he had finished with as much as the man could digest, he looked up and handed the unfinished bowl of food to the largest of the black men staring down at him. The bowl still contained about half of the cornmeal and beans and just about all the goat meat. The man took the bowl and looked inside to inspect the food, looked down at McCoy, and then uttered some words to the men around him who chuckled a bit.

McCoy lifted the wounded man's untouched bowl of cold boiled grass and smelled it. It smelled foul and tasted worse. He decided to quickly consume the mixture lest he not feed himself at all. He scooped handfuls, one after another while holding his breath to force it down his throat. After he was finished, he smiled at the men standing over him exposing his white teeth covered with the green slime oozing down his chin.

The big man to whom McCoy had given his bowl of food had taken a piece of meat from it and passed it around to several others who indulged in the meat, cornmeal, and beans as well. They had passed the bowl back to the big man who then handed the bowl back to McCoy. When McCoy investigated the bowl, it contained a single piece of remaining meat. He looked up at the big man and could ascertain that it was a sort of peace offering out of respect for his kindness to the wounded comrade.

McCoy also used his single cup of rationed water to clean the wounded man's ugly gash next to his ribs. He used all of his water except for a final sip he reserved for himself. The next day, the big man passed McCoy's empty cup around to the others who each gave a little of theirs to replenish what he had used for cleaning the wounded man's injury.

Over time his initial fear began to give way to a sense of empathy. He couldn't help but be moved by the stories of suffering and resilience he could hear being spoken without fully understanding the words of his fellow prisoners. They had endured the horrors of slavery, and now they faced the uncertainty of their fate in this wretched prison.

Despite the language barrier, some of the ex-slaves reached out to McCoy with gestures of kindness and even taught him a few words of their Creole language. Slowly, he began to form bonds of camaraderie with some, transcending the racial divide that had initially separated them.

On what McCoy calculated as the tenth day, the man whom he had been nursing back to health uttered some unknown words and offered McCoy a smile. By his general disposition and the gentle hold of his hand, McCoy interpreted that it was an act of thanks for what he had done for him.

"Vini Blanc," said the big black man who appeared to be the leader of the group as he motioned to McCoy.

McCoy came over to him and sat next to the man who put his big hand on his chest and said *"Mwen se Claude, kiyès ou ye?"* – I am Claude, who are you?

It was obvious that he was asking for his name; "I am McCoy"

"Non Blan , di mwen se Mc Coy" – No Blanc, say I am McCoy *"Mwen McCoy"* he repeated as he put his hand on McCoy's chest and insisted he repeat it.

"Moo En McCoy," he repeated sloppily.

"Wi, ou se McCoy," he said as he pointed to McCoy – Yes, you are McCoy.

This began a friendship where the big man named Claude would take a few minutes each day to educate McCoy on the language of Creole. Over time, McCoy began to repeat what he considered his favorite and most useful phrases.

"Ban Mwen" which meant give me. Claude said that if I go to the markets to buy fruits and vegetables, it would be very useful. Point and say 'Ban Mwen'

"Map degaje m" means I'm getting by.

"Kisa wap fè?" – What are you doing?

"Si dye vle" – If God wants, though McCoy didn't venture onto which God he referred to.

In the prison's harsh and unforgiving environment, McCoy learned that the color of one's skin mattered less than the content of their character. Together with his fellow prisoners, he endured the hardships of their confinement, each day bringing them one step closer to an uncertain future. As they shared their stories, hopes, and dreams, McCoy came to realize that their common humanity was a bond stronger than the walls that surrounded them, and it was a lesson he would carry with him long after his time in prison had passed.

Two

THE PRICE OF WAR

Jacmel
December 1799

On the outskirts of the town, Jean-Jacques Dessalines sat in his tent, contemplating his next move. With him in the room were Alix Mercier and Patrick Etienne, two of his most trusted officers. They together had retaken Petit and Grande Goâve from Rigaud but were ordered by Toussaint to stand down and await the army of Henry Christophe for the major assault on Jacmel. They anxiously wanted to take some form of action on their own, especially not wanting to share victory with the Christophe band of the army.

"Let us attack," Dessalines said suddenly. "Doing so is not a violation of any of Toussaint's orders but a test of the enemy defenses in preparation for the main assault."

"What do you have in mind, mon Général?" asked Mercier.

"A full-on attack in the middle of the night'" stated Dessalines. "I want to see how they protect the city after weeks of inactivity. Are they awake or do they take this period of relative quiet as an opportunity to lower their defenses?"

When, mon Général?" asked Mercier.

"Tonight. Get 250 infantry, plus 25 of the cavalry. Storm the front of the city at midnight. Let us devise the plan."

Midnight had cast its dark shroud over the coastal city. The streets were eerily quiet, with only the whisper of the ocean breeze disturbing the stillness. As the clock struck twelve, the moon hung low in the sky, casting a silvery glow on the cobblestone streets and the colonial-style buildings that lined them.

On the outskirts of the city, Dessalines's approaching force moved stealthily on their hands and knees, slowly crawling to keep themselves hidden and using the cover of night to their advantage. They were led by Mercier and Etienne as they cunningly went from tree to tree and rock to rock to sneak up to the outer perimeter of the city's defenses. They were unsure where the mulatto's first defenses would be.

Pétion had erected a series of redoubts, small dug-out areas of ground that gave protection to his soldiers if under attack in front of the city's outer walls, but how many sentries lay in wait within them was impossible to know.

Mercier and Etienne, together at the front of the line, decided to split their forces. Mercier to the left and Etienne to the right, 125 men each. When they reached the small hill of the first redoubt, Etienne gave the signal to the man next to him who lit the end of an arrow with a cloth of humid kerosene and launched the arrow into the air to signal the cavalry to charge.

The clatter of horses' hooves could be heard coming from the distance but still no sound or movement from the defenders of the city. Mercier thought they must feel secure to not have any outer defenses this near the city walls. He could hear the hooves of the cavalry approaching nearer to their location but still no sound from the city walls.

Twenty-five horsemen with swords in the air passed Mercier and Etienne as they rounded the redoubt galloping towards the city. This was the signal for Mercier and Etienne to sound the charge in unison to their men. They all began running as two cavalrymen brought horses to Mercier and Etienne who mounted the animals to lead the charge past the first redoubt. The cavalry

had already reached the second mound when the first shots rang out, breaking the silence like thunder in the night.

Pétion's army had patiently laid in wait with a trap that suddenly roared to life, sending fiery projectiles hurtling toward the attackers from behind the horsemen and the rushing infantry from the protection of their redoubts. The night sky lit up with fiery explosions as the defenders unleashed their firepower and the surprised attackers drew nearer, dropping them mercilessly to the ground.

At the city walls, the defenders grew tense. They knew that the fate of Jacmel hung in the balance, and the specter of a heavy bloody attack weighed heavily on their minds. Torches flared to life along the city's walls, illuminating the determined faces of the defenders awaiting a full-fledged onslaught from the entirety of Dessalines' forces, not knowing that this was a limited test of their outer defenses.

The cavalry clashed with the city's outer sentries in a series of skirmishes that sent echoes reverberating on the walls with no possibility of breaching the city. Dessalines forces pressed forward, undeterred by the barrage. The clash of steel and musket fire filled the air as they engaged the defenders a good distance before the city gates. Both the attackers and defenders fought valiantly until Mercier sounded the retreat, knowing they had entered a trap.

The battle was over within the hour, but the lesson had been well received. The moon bore witness to the chaos and carnage that played out in its silvery glow as Pétions men mercilessly used their swords to hack at the retreat of Dessalines' men. Bodies fell almost exclusively at the expense of Dessalines troops.

At dawn's first light, the remainder of Dessalines' battered soldiers arrived back to camp. Their attempt to seize Jacmel had been expertly thwarted by the resolute defenders. The city had withstood the onslaught without a single attacker reaching its gates. Jacmel's streets were filled with the victorious cheers of those who had defended it and those on the city walls who never needed to fire a single shot. The outer defenses had held.

Jean-Jacques Dessalines now understood the violent and capable abilities of his enemy. He had lost 160 men that night with another 42 wounded. Sixteen horses had not returned. The defenders had prevailed with but a couple of casualties.

The fight for control of Saint Domingue will continue to rage on until we drive these Rigaudins from it, thought Dessalines, as he contemplated the lessons of the night and his next strategy from what he learned.

"I lost some good fighters last night," stated Mercier. "What now, mon Général?"

"Pa gen manman pa gen papa" - There is no mother and there is no father, replied Dessalines *"Sa ki mouri zafè yo"* - those who died, that is their problem.

What made Jean-Jacques Dessalines so effective in battle was his focus on victory at all costs. His willingness to sacrifice his troops for this goal had long been his military strategy. Risk-taking was both rewarded and punished. For tonight, the reward was knowledge of the enemy. *Sa ki mouri zafè yo,* he thought. Others would need to sacrifice for the punishment.

"Three days hence, you attack from the Southwest side. We will test that next and later to the Southeast." Dessalines said. "There is a weakness somewhere and we will continue to test and find it – at all costs."

The prison door opened, and three mulatto soldiers ordered McCoy to stand and follow. The remaining prisoners looked at the mulatto soldiers with a visible sign of contempt as they were taking McCoy away – as if he were truly one of them.

They marched him out to a bathing area and motioned for him to enter a tub to cleanse while one of them held two fingers to his nose to demonstrate the reason if McCoy didn't already understand.

As he gladly immersed himself in a wooden barrel filled with warm water that once held fermenting rum, he could smell citrus and saw sweet-smelling herbs and flowers floating in the water. A fresh set of clean commoner clothes laid waiting in an adjacent chair.

He did as was told, without protest, as he was more than happy to cleanse the stink from his pores. This was the first time he was able to bathe in what he counted as 15 days from his first encounter with Pétion.

When he was finished, he began to gather his uniform in his arms but was told to leave it where it was. They then escorted him to the familiar office where he had first met Pétion. They motioned him to sit in the chair in front of Pétion's desk as they then stood guard at the door.

Pétion entered the room from a door leading to an adjoining balcony and took his seat behind the massive desk followed by Captain Rocourt. "Mr. McCoy. It is so pleasant to see you again," Pétion said in a polite tone. "I trust you have found the accommodations to your satisfaction, henn?"

"It is the best you could do on short notice, McCoy stated. I was hoping this would be a meeting with the American consulate?"

"Ah yes, the consulate. Unfortunately, I have not been able to send word to the American Consul in Port-au-Prince. I am sure you can understand that it would be much too dangerous for me to send a messenger as Dessalines besieges Jacmel?"

"Then what are you planning to do with me?" asked McCoy.

Pétion lifted his finger in the air as an order of silence and said, "Mr. McCoy, it is me who will be asking the questions and you who will be answering them. Is that understood?"

"Understood" answered McCoy.

"Who are you, Mr. McCoy?"

"As I previously stated, my name is Michael McCoy, Midshipman on the *USS General Greene.*"

"Your age, Mr. McCoy?"

"Nineteen last month, sir."

"Your duties on the ship?"

"I work the mid-ship mast, sir."

"Who is your commander?"

"Captain Christopher Perry, sir."

"You were given a healthier meal regiment than the other prisoners. However, my guards have informed me that you have not partaken in our generosity but instead have shared your meal with the other prisoners. Why?"

"You know very well why," McCoy said impatiently.

"Why don't you tell me?" asked Pétion.

"Because you and I know that I would have been killed otherwise. Was that your intent all along?"

"I thought you understood that it is I who is in the position to ask the questions, Mr. McCoy. If that is indeed your name," Pétion said as he raised his big hairy eyebrows and stared at McCoy.

"I do not understand what you mean?"

"You claim to be a mere 19 years old, Mr. McCoy, and a midshipman on the *General Greene*. However, an 18 or 19-year-old boy would not have the intelligence or the reasoning to resist a home-cooked meal over the slop that is served. Don't you think?" asked Pétion.

"I told you I knew that I would be killed otherwise. Have you seen the size and demeanor of your prisoners?"

"I take it you have met Claude Delouse? The big one who is their leader?"

"Yes, I have."

"I understand you and he have developed a sort of, shall I say, friendship?" stated Pétion.

"That is one way to put it, if friendship is indeed the right word?" answered McCoy.

"You have diplomatic skills as is evident by how you have been able to infiltrate and befriend these violent prisoners," offered Pétion.

"So?"

"But yet you contend to be a boy of 18.

I am 19 years old, as I have told you."

"Ah yes, you did mention that. What is your warship doing blocking my harbor, Mr. McCoy?"

"I am but a midshipman sir. I do not make policy. I take orders."

"What has your captain told the crew of his current orders to blockade my ports?"

"I am but a lowly midshipman, sir. I am not privy to those conversations between officers," McCoy replied.

Your Captain Perry has me at a disadvantage, Mr. McCoy. Our countries are not at war so I cannot send a cannon ball his way. To do so would be an act of war which would require him to retaliate and report me to your government as the aggressor."

Pétion pulled out a box filled with cheroots and offered McCoy and Rocourt each one. "What would you do if in my shoes, Mr. McCoy?"

"I am not a general, sir. I do not have the intellect to be one."

"Let us change the subject," shifted Pétion. What do you know of Napoleon Bonaparte?

"Who?" asked McCoy.

General Napoleon Bonaparte who just ended the French Revolution and proclaimed, or had himself proclaimed, First Consul?"

Rocourt stared at McCoy with an uneasy glare as Pétion continued his verbal sparring with the boy. He took a drag of his cheroot and didn't understand why Pétion was investing time in this nobody, this silly boy.

"I am not familiar with French politics, sir."

"Are you a spy, Mr. McCoy?"

"Me, a spy?" laughed McCoy. "What would make you think forever so?"

Alexandre Pétion was a skilled officer. He had been trained in the finest military academy in France. Though his specialty was in artillery, classes in military strategy, sociology, diplomatic protocols, civil society, governance, and espionage tactics prepared him for more than just fighting. He had all the tools necessary for a strategic understanding of who a spy was and how he would conceal his identity.

"For if you were a spy, Mr. McCoy, I could have you executed right here without a diplomatic incident, offered Pétion."

McCoy began to understand that Pétion was way too intelligent and savvy to toy with him much longer. He had to find an exit from the conversation and somehow get it back on track.

"I am not a spy, sir."

"Mr. McCoy, I am not sure I know what to do with you. What would you have done with yourself, be it in my shoes?" Pétion asked.

"I do not follow. I cannot imagine what it is I should do," answered McCoy.

"Let us then speak in hypotheticals," Pétion said as he reached for a flask of brandy, procured 3 small glasses, and poured a swig for him, McCoy, and Rocourt. "Salut mes amis."

"Hypothetically speaking, of course, if you were a spy, I might think to utilize your services and not have you hanged, so to speak," Pétion said.

"Hypothetically, why would you do that sir?" McCoy said as he swallowed the brandy in one gulp, surprised at its excellent quality. He banged the glass on the desk as if to ask for another.

Pétion did not respond to the obvious request and continued, making it a point to slowly sip his brandy as he said, "As an exercise, I would trade something of value to this alleged spy if I thought that he would respond in kind with something of value in return."

"What is it of value would you provide this spy and in exchange for what in return?" asked McCoy.

"Well, hypothetically, of course, let's say that this 'spy' was in your exact position; an intelligent diplomatic officer who had the appearance of a boy 5 to 7 years his younger, was sent here on a reconnaissance mission, pretended to be caught with his proverbial pants down, and found himself in the position to speak with the commander of where he was sent to spy on for information," Pétion said as he refilled McCoy's glass and topped off his and Rocourt's as well.

"What if I could provide this career diplomat information so valuable to his country that it would not only benefit his republic immensely but serve to bolster his career in the process?"

"That sounds like a very lucrative situation for the spy. However, at what price would it extract? Deception, perjury, loss of honor, … treason?" asked McCoy, lingering on the last word to elongate the punctuation.

With that, Pétion was now convinced he had his man. He is indeed a spy or at the very least in contact with one. "No, Mr. McCoy. What I would propose to this representative is an agreement benefiting both parties."

"And what is it you would want from this, hypothetical 'spy'?"

"A chance at a fair fight, that's all. I suffer from a lack of munitions, supplies, and food. The cause is Dessalines who blocks access by roads and your Captain Perry with his *USS General Greene* who blocks my access by sea. All my supply routes are blocked. I need them opened and am willing to trade something so vital to your country in exchange for a reprieve from this blockade." Pétion answered.

"You know I cannot guarantee reciprocity. I am not Captain Perry," McCoy said.

"But I know you have more leverage over the captain than you let on, Mr. McCoy," Pétion answered.

At that point, the cards were on the table. McCoy had all but admitted he was what Pétion said he was – a spy. Now, it was curiosity and intrigue that moved McCoy to engage in this reckless verbal game of chess. "I cannot guarantee, but I can propose, providing the information is as valuable as you say it is," McCoy said.

Pétion opened the top left drawer of his desk and pulled out a pouch. Within the pouch was a stack of documents that he leafed through. He pulled out one page of the document and handed it to McCoy. "Read this, Mr. McCoy," Pétion ordered. "But do so out loud as this is the first time that my Captain Rocourt is hearing it as well."

McCoy held the document up with his right hand and grabbed for the glass of brandy with his left. He couldn't resist again disposing of the fine spirit in one gulp. As he looked at the page in front of him, he could immediately tell that it was the ending of a letter of how many pages unknown. He read out loud;

I congratulate you, my First Consul, on the brilliant strategic plan you have outlined to solidify the interests of France, consolidate her colonies, and annex the fledging country of the United States under the flag of France.

With their current military strength of 16,000 active service personnel, we can quickly… within several months… win a decisive victory. I currently have 60,000 ready soldiers under my command and I can devote 40,000 of them to the campaign combined with the 40,000 you can mobilize. This will serve as not only a significant defeat on their soil but the military can secure the cities and restore and maintain law and order within them.

Additionally, with your current talks with the British that you have outlined in your letter, we will have no significant sea threats as the current strength of the U.S. Navy numbers not more than 3 commissioned warships and a manageable number of commissioned merchant vessels. Your ocean plans show the superiority that we will exercise on the sea.

I have respectfully made some notes on your planning document, enclosed, for your review. You have my full support, commitment, and loyalty to follow your leadership and await your commands.

Your servant in arms,
 Toussaint Louverture

"How did you come across this?" asked McCoy, obviously shocked by the contents of the letter, signed by Toussaint Louverture.

"If you think that is interesting, you should read the first 2 pages prior. Or, better yet, the letter that Napoleon sent to our Governor General and his notes back to the First Consul. That would be very enlightening to the United States government," Pétion responded.

"And how do you suggest we proceed? How can I get those other pages you are now referencing?" asked McCoy.

"That is an important question, henn, Mr. McCoy? But more importantly, what would persuade me to provide you with those documents?"

"What is it that you want, General?" asked McCoy.

"What do I want, Mr. McCoy? That is an interesting choice of words. What I want is to make love to my fiancé Marie-Madeleine. I want to eat a large piece of beef with potatoes smothered with onions, some rice with beans, malanga, and a helping of plantains. I want to bathe in the ocean and rid myself of this stink!" Pétion went on as his voice began to rise.

McCoy looked at Rocourt who was staring at Pétion, obviously surprised by his apparent loss of control.

"I want to ride my horse in the valley at full gallop. I want my men to come out of this ordeal alive. I want Captain Rocourt here to go back to his lovely wife and children in Les Cayes. That is what I want, Mr. McCoy. But right now, what I need is for your frigging warship the *General Greene* to get out of my harbor and allow my supply barges entry. That is what I need Mr. McCoy!" Pétion's voice rose to a crescendo as he stood.

Then, as quickly as his temper had flared, it subsided like a balloon that had been filled with air and suddenly burst as he calmly said; "I am allowing you to go free, Mr. McCoy. You have not been held a prisoner, but merely a guest in our establishment, albeit in not-so-comfortable quarters.

"I thank you, General, for your hospitality and my ability to return to the ship. I hope we can meet under better circumstances on a future encounter?" McCoy said with a sense of relief.

"Should Captain Perry of the *General Greene* desire to possess this valuable and important information for the United States, you can collect it at the port of Les Cayes exactly 7 days from today, precisely at 3 pm at the restaurant Le Recul in the heart of town. Approach the maître d' with the code word 'Simone'".

"And he will remit to me all of the papers you spoke of?"

"Yes. But you and I know, Mr. McCoy, that the decision to proceed lies with you. I am certain that you will be the one ordering Captain Perry to make that trip, henn?"

"And what is it you desire in return, General?"

"The package will only be released if the *General Greene* is in the Les Cayes harbor and no warships are blocking our harbor here in Jacmel three days before that 7th day. Otherwise, there will be no exchange," stated Pétion.

"I see your motivation. Three days is enough time to re-supply the city," stated McCoy.

"Hardly enough time. But it will permit me to get some medical supplies, light arms, and some dry food for the citizens here. Consider it a humanitarian gesture," Pétion responded.

"There is one more small concession that I ask," added McCoy.

"Another concession? Yes, Mr. McCoy, what is it?"

"There is a prisoner who is badly injured and near death. Release him and the prisoner named Claude to carry him from prison and safe passage out of the city," McCoy said.

"You are the diplomat that I have suspected all along, henn?"

"That is the deal. The release of Claude, the injured man plus the papers. In exchange, the *General Greene* will be out of the harbor in four days and no blockade for the following three. You have my word on that," McCoy said with confidence in his voice.

"And how, Mr. McCoy, can I be guaranteed that you will have your warship out of my harbor before the release of my prisoners of war? After all, you have said you are only a Midshipman, henn?" Pétion said as he smiled, knowing he had unmasked the true chess piece that McCoy was and the game of chess he had been playing all along. He had been right from their first meeting; McCoy is a spy, a diplomat, or both.

"You have uncovered who I am, General. I am a man who can pull some strings for both sides of this negotiation," McCoy said as he took a drag of his cheroot and smiled back to Pétion.

Pétion nodded a signal to the two men guarding the door and they opened it. "Take Mr. McCoy to the laundry to collect what should be now his clean uniform and escort him safely to the docks. Have a boat row him out to the *General Greene* to reunite with his comrades," Pétion said.

McCoy stood at attention and saluted Pétion with respect and Pétion did the same in return. He turned to leave the room and looked back at Pétion, smiled, and said, "By the way, my age is 24." He then turned and left the room with the soldiers.

Pétion went back to his desk and poured another brandy for him and Rocourt. Rocourt picked up his glass and said, "Where in the world were you able to capture the letters exchanged between Toussaint and Napoleon, mon Général?

"These are nothing but forgeries, Rocourt, from an artist of the craft. There are no letters exchanged between the First Consul and Toussaint, and no conspiracy that I know of. However, these fakes will open our harbor for much-needed supplies," Pétion confessed.

And you had no reservations leading that young man down the path of deception? It will certainly cost him his career."

"My loyalty is to my men and to the citizens of Jacmel. Phillippe LaPlace, my professor of Espionage and counterintelligence studies at the Military Academy in Paris taught us that the weapons of war are numerous and diversified. We must use every tool at our disposal and that includes espionage, deception, and manipulation right alongside our cannon, swords, and rifles. That is the art of war. And of that, I take no prisoners." Pétion concluded.

Three

HOME FOR CHRISTMAS

Ennery
December 1799

Mars Plaisir, Toussaint's trusted valet, barged into the study with a smile and announced "They are here!"

Plaisir was the only one, except for Suzanne and their children, who could barge in with forgetting to knock on the door of the Governor General and get away with it. After all, Mars Plaisir was more than a valet. He was a trusted confidant who was as loyal as one could be to his employer.

Plaisir was charged with the household finances, inventories, provisions, cleanliness, keeping personnel in line, and just about everything else on behalf of the Louverture family. This gave Suzanne and Toussaint ample opportunities to spend quality time together when he was home and for Suzanne quality time with her sons and gardens when he was away.

Mars Plaisir was indispensable to them both and they treated him like family, as sort of an organized uncle who resided with the household.

Toussaint looked up from the papers he was reviewing and smiled, knowing exactly who Plaisir was referring to. He had invited Dr. Edward Stevens and his wife Hester to join them for the Christmas holidays, and stay through New Year's at his home.

He had already, in a relatively short period of time, grown fond of the young American diplomat and was grateful for the relationship he had fostered with the United States. He had expertly launched the trade initiative dubbed 'Toussaint's Clause' passed by Congress, and enacted by President John Adams this past August.

Even before its inception, trade barriers were lifted and nearly 1,000 ships were plying the waters between America's east coast and Saint Domingue at various ports including Port-Républicain, Cap-Français, and Gonaïves to supply lumber, dried fish, and other manufactured commodities in exchange for molasses, sugar and indigo. Restricted ports of call for all American trading vessels included Jacmel, Jérémie, Les Cayes, and any other port or harbor controlled by the Rigaudins.

By the time Toussaint reached the front door, Mars Plaisir was already at the roundabout awaiting the halt of the carriage to greet it's passengers. Toussaint had sent an honor guard of 10 horsemen to escort the carriage from Cap-Français not only for protection, but for pomp and circumstance for his guest of honor.

The coachman jumped down from his seat and opened the door as the honor guards stood at attention to form a corridor to the front garden of the grand Maison.

First out of the carriage was Dr. Stevens who turned to assist his wife Hester. They both waved and approached Toussaint, with now Suzanne arriving to stand next to him, through the column of soldiers to the fountain at the front of the residence.

"Welcome to our home," stated Toussaint, greeting the weary arrivals. "I trust that your trip has not been too laborious."

I am very grateful for your recommendation to make it a 3-day trip as it was a 14-hour long carriage ride," Hester pleasantly stated. "Your recommended hosts and accommodations along the way were wonderful. Our stops at the Hudicourt home at Haut Limbé and the Lafortune home in Plaisance were delightful. The homes were so beautiful and their hospitality inspired me so," stated Hester. Thank you so much!"

Hester Stevens, since her arrival as the wife of a Diplomatic Trade Envoy, had been remarkably impressed with all things in Saint Domingue. She had initially protested her husband being assigned to the colony instead of a prestigious European post. Her friends and acquaintances would even chide her about going to a colony run by blacks, and with some saying niggers, as opposed to the civilized Saint Domingue once run by white Frenchmen.

But what she found in this colony was surprising indeed. The culture in Cap Français was delightful and she discovered that most of the ballets, operas, orchestras, and other entertainment usually made it here first on tour before reaching American shores, to the delight of multi-racial audiences.

Also, the people she had met, mostly Gens de couleur of black and mulatto descent, with the names of Bayard, Christophe, Bourcicaut, Dorismond, Bunet, Déjean, and Philoctete had made her life entertaining in her new home at Cap Français. They opened doors to meet new and interesting people and helped her in the recruitment of quality staffing, understanding of local protocols, and the administration of her home, which served as the northern American embassy, at Le Cap.

Here she would host parties for important ship captains, local dignitaries, government types, and businessmen who desired connections and contacts with the United States. In a few words, her life had never been more exciting and she felt fulfilled in her new role. She couldn't wait to get back home and boast to the snobs and naysayers who once chided her of the wonderful life in a yes… black run colony!

"As honored guests in our country, Madame Stevens, it is our duty to make it as pleasurable as possible," Toussaint welcomed. "And speaking of that, you must be exhausted from the last leg of the carriage ride from Plaisance. My staff has prepared a warm bath in the room adjacent to yours and Mars here will have your bags brought up immediately."

"Please Governor-General and Suzanne, call me Hester as we are not under the microscope of government protocol out of the official buildings," Hester smiled.

"Of course, Hester, Suzanne said with a smile. "Dinner will be served at 6 p.m. If there is anything you require, anything at all, please let me know," Suzanne said with a smile.

It was two days before Christmas and being the devout Catholics that Toussaint and Suzanne were, the home was filled with holiday décor, a constant assortment of fresh flowers, holiday foods aplenty, and sweet perfumed air. This was Toussaint and Suzanne's favorite part of the year.

They entertained continuously throughout the week with Dr. and Mrs. Stevens relishing it all. They were accustomed to frigid holidays in the north and their first ever Caribbean Christmas warmed their hearts as well as their bodies.

Being the high-level government official that Toussaint Louverture is, there was a multitude of official dinners and parties to attend; Christmas pageants, holiday concerts, children's choirs, and church gatherings that culminated in a New Year party at the government house that the Stevens' would never forget, being the VIP guests of the Governor-General and his wife.

Toussaint made sure that the Stevens would return home with bright memories of their stay in Saint Domingue as he counted on them to broadcast the civility of how a black nation could be to inspire even more diplomatic engagement from the United States.

On January 2nd, the day before the Stevens' would depart back to Cap-Français, Toussaint and Ed Stevens were having a brandy in Toussaint's study when Mars Plaisir knocked once and entered the room. He went over to Toussaint and whispered in his ear.

"Have them escorted here," stated Toussaint. He then turned

to Stevens and said, "There is a contingent of four riders here requesting an audience with you, Ed. I told Mars to allow them entry from the main guard gate."

"I wonder why they are here. My apologies for the intrusion, Toussaint," Stevens answered.

A few minutes later, Mars Plaisir entered the room. "The riders would like an audience with you, Dr. Stevens."

"Have them come in," stated Toussaint. Make sure they have been disarmed by the guards."

"They have," Mars replied. "They are unarmed, but they have requested a private audience with Dr. Stevens."

"My apologies, Toussaint. Would you mind?" asked Stevens. "It may be some official U.S. business."

"Make no mention of it. I want to go up and check on the boys anyway to see how they are enjoying their gifts. Carry on without me," Toussaint said as he got up and left the room.

Two of the riders entered the room and had a meeting with Dr. Stevens. One of them was Michael McCoy who had arrived from Les Cayes. McCoy recounted his entire ordeal at the hands of Alexandre Pétion and produced the scandalous document penned by Toussaint.

As Dr. Stevens was reading the documents, McCoy all but wondered what sort of accolades, elevated status, and possible promotion awaited him personally after this ordeal with Toussaint was done.

He will have saved the new American republic from the invasion of these enemies and possibly sway the American government to side with the Rigaudins as opposed to Toussaint Louverture.

He will have stopped Napoleon Bonaparte dead in his tracks from the treacherous plot he was hatching with Toussaint.

Who knows, maybe the president himself would summon him to his office at President's House in Philadelphia and pin a medal on his vest for bravery. It was a sweet time to be alive and be Michael McCoy, he thought!

"Let us sort this business out immediately," Stevens angrily stated.

"It seems we have uncovered a plot by this government to invade the United States!" McCoy stated.

"We have uncovered a document, Mr. McCoy. As to its authenticity, we do not know." Stevens answered.

I don't think we should go that route," stated McCoy with an air of confidence and command. "What if he is plotting with the new First Consul, Napoleon? We could be at risk of getting killed to keep it secret."

"Toussaint Louverture is a man of honor and also my friend. I will give him the benefit of the doubt and offer him to explain."

Stevens told McCoy to wait with him and had Mars request for Toussaint to join them. In less than 15 minutes, Toussaint had returned to the study and Stevens wasted no time.

"Toussaint, this is Michael McCoy from the State Department. He has been sent here with a document that was intercepted at sea on its way to Paris. You may be familiar with it," Stevens said while handing the document to Toussaint.

Toussaint took some time to read and scan the documents as Stevens, McCoy, and the other rider anxiously observed him and waited. Seconds seemed like minutes and minutes like hours with growing intensity in the room.

Then, all of a sudden Toussaint burst out in a hearty laugh, held the document up in the air, and said, "Obviously a sick joke, Edward, and an obvious fake," Toussaint said.

"Can you verify that it is a fake, Governor General?" asked McCoy.

"Isn't it the responsibility of the bearer of this document to prove its authenticity?" asked Toussaint of Stevens without acknowledging McCoy.

He then looked at the young man and said "Mr. McCoy, what makes you think this document is authentic?"

"It bears your signature and chop, sir," McCoy responded.

"I believe you call my seal a chop? Mr. McCoy. Is that how

easily the State Department of the United States of America can be fooled?" asked Toussaint.

"Your signature, your seal, what else does it need to be authentic?" asked McCoy.

Toussaint burst out in a hearty laugh, part to break the tension and spare Dr. Stevens from further embarrassment. He also thought this engagement amusing as to the naivety of a representative from the American government.

Toussaint walked to his desk in the corner of the study and came back with a document and a magnifying glass. "Mr. McCoy, examine this document that bears my signature which I signed today," ordered Toussaint.

McCoy lifted the document and examined it closely. "What is it I am looking for, Governor General?"

"Is my signature indeed identical to your document?"

"By all accounts, yes it is," replied McCoy.

"Is the seal identical to the one on your document?"

"It appears to be the same chop… I mean seal, sir."

"And you see no difference between the document I have just handed you and the one you claim is penned from me that you came with?"

"The signatures appear the same and so does the seal," stated McCoy.

"Mr. McCoy, now take the magnifying glass and look at this document I have just handed you and compare it with the one you have arrived with. What do you see as the primary difference?"

McCoy carefully examined both, desperately looking to find something, which he knew Toussaint was withholding, but could not decipher the difference in signatures or seals. "Nothing sir," responded McCoy.

"I see your eye is not yet fully trained or developed for such things. That is understandable and forgivable from a young person such as you. Your perception has not yet matured," Toussaint said in a sort of paternal tone.

"The two documents are written on parchment, correct?

continued Toussaint. "Parchment is a writing material made from specially prepared untanned skins of animals—primarily sheep, cows, and goats. It has been used as a writing medium for over two millennia and is my preferred one."

"However, I prefer Vellum parchment for my official correspondence. It is a much finer quality parchment made from the skins of younger animals, such as lambs and young calves," continued Toussaint. "It feels better and lasts longer."

McCoy suddenly realized that he was in unchartered territory as he knew nothing of parchment manufacturing.

"The making of it involves the cleaning, bleaching, and stretching on a frame called a herse. They then scrape the skin with a crescent-shaped lunarium knife," Toussaint continued as Ed Stevens suddenly understood that Toussaint was building up to a conclusion.

"To create tension, the process goes back and forth between scraping, wetting, and drying. Then, scratching the surface with pumice, and expertly treating the hyde with lime or chalk to make it suitable for fine writing can create the final look," Toussaint finished.

Toussaint was clearly enjoying the lesson he was teaching young McCoy and pondered if Ed Stevens was himself being educated in a possible subject he knew little of himself. However, he wanted to uphold diplomatic decorum and not cause too much embarrassment to his friend. "Now, look at the two parchments and tell me you can see the differences, Mr. McCoy?"

McCoy once again looked at the two documents and with the magnifying glass he could easily tell the difference between the parchment he had produced and the finer quality one that Toussaint had handed him.

Toussaint walked to his desk and brought over a stack of a dozen or more documents. "Tell me, Mr. McCoy. Do all of these documents appear to have the same Vellum parchment?"

"Inspecting them will not be necessary," Governor General.

"No, Mr. McCoy, I insist. Please examine all of them, if you so please?"

McCoy scanned each document which took several awkward minutes as Dr. Stevens shifted in his seat at the embarrassment of almost accusing Toussaint of deception by planning an invasion of the United States with Napoleon Bonaparte.

McCoy lifted his head. "All of your documents appear to be written on Vellum, instead of plain parchment," he sheepishly said.

Toussaint was on a roll and he knew it, even relished in it; "So, Mr. McCoy, would you imagine that I, the Governor-General of Saint Domingue, the highest authority of this colony, would send a document to the First Consul, Napoleon Bonaparte, the highest level official of France, on any writing material not deemed to be the very finest available?"

"I would imagine not, Governor-General"

"Do you now clearly admit that the document you have presented is not of the quality that Toussaint Louverture, Governor-General of Saint Domingue would utilize, Mr. McCoy?"

"In that case, it appears to be a fake, Governor-General."

"On behalf of the American Government, I apologize profusely for this error, Governor-General", Stevens sincerely stated addressing Toussaint in his official title. "This is embarrassing to the United States and I pray it does not place a wedge in our relationship for the future of trade and diplomatic relations. Again, my sincerest apologies,"

"Edward, apology accepted. I will leave you and Mr. McCoy with privacy to explore the ramifications of this," Toussaint said.

Michael McCoy was immediately sent back to Philadelphia, ending his short diplomatic career with the State Department, while Toussaint graciously swept the incident under the rug, but not before pointing out the cunning capabilities of his enemy, André Rigaud, and his top General, Alexandre Pétion.

"Pétion is a skilled and capable leader," Toussaint stated. "He was once part of my officer corps and I unfortunately placed him under the guidance of a not-so-competent leader. He defected to Rigaud. To this day, I do not know whether it was because he is mulatto or felt there was no future with me."

Dr. Stevens departed Ennery. The two planned to meet in early January where Toussaint would be introduced to the new American Commodore, Supreme Commander of the US Naval Mission to Saint Domingue, and Captain of the USS Constitution, Silas Talbot.

On that sunny yet cool day of January 5th, 1800, in the town of Léogâne, nestled on the northern coast of the Southern Peninsula,50 kilometers west of Port-Républicain, the fate of Saint Domingue hung in the balance. Three formidable figures, Toussaint Louverture, General Stevens, and Commodore Talbot, gathered to discuss the ongoing civil war that threatened to tear the island apart.

Rigaud, a formidable rival and a threat not only to Toussaint's authority but also to the fragile trade agreements between the United States and the colony, loomed large in their discussions. Rigaud's fiery rhetoric against the Americans had strained relations, as he accused them of treachery and hostility toward the French Republic.

In these desperate times, the three leaders realized that they had to act swiftly. The tripartite treaty, which had once tied their hands, now required renegotiation. This new agreement would grant Toussaint's navy the authority to rearm and expand its fleet, a significant departure from the original pact.

The British, sensing the growing power of Toussaint and the potential influence of the Americans, had repeatedly seized his armed vessels to undermine his fighting capabilities. British Admiral Parker and Governor Lord Balcarres of Jamaica orchestrated these actions in secret, unbeknownst to British General Maitland, who had initially negotiated the agreement.

Commodore Talbot, recognizing the dire need to assist Toussaint, took unprecedented steps. He placed American naval captains under Toussaint's command, including Captain Christopher Perry of the *USS General Greene.* The stage was set for full cooperation, and the covert involvement of the US Navy in the Civil War had begun.

This was contrary to the current racial position of most persons in the United States, including Talbot himself. A white American Captain taking orders from a person of African descent, especially of a foreign nationality? This could only exist beyond the borders of the United States at the time.

Back home in Newport, Perry attended religious worship in a church that relegated free black congregants to the balcony and out of view of white parishioners. Within the U.S. borders, there was little room for racial equality, let alone a situation where a black man like Toussaint outranked a white man of stature such as Captain Perry.

As for Talbot, he was even more invested in the enslavement of blacks. In the 1770's he owned an African named Sigby and later purchased another named William Roberts while touring Jamaica and had him work onboard the vessels he captained, including the Constitution now servicing Saint-Domingue.

This complex inconsistency in his behavior could be further confused by the fact he shared ownership himself in a slave ship named *Industry* which voyaged from Africa to America's east coast with enslaved black Africans. As part owner, he is culpable for the loss of one hundred Africans thrown off the *Industry* during a voyage.

But Talbot, Perry, and other American officers and sailors marched to a different code in the 18th century when away from American soil. Black and white men routinely worked and slept together on naval and merchant vessels. Here on the ocean, talent mattered more than race. Ship owners and captains sought proficiency and adopted a race-blind hierarchy.

This race-blind system was common wherein white captains handed command of their ships to black pilots to navigate some of the largest Atlantic vessels securely to and from treacherous coastlines.

Before Talbot, Perry, or any other captain, American or otherwise, brought their mighty ships into port at Cap-Français, Port-Républicain, or any other, a Saint Domingue pilot ascended the main deck and instructed white officers and sailors when to tack or wear ship, when to shorten sail, and where to let go the anchor.

In a twist of irony, the Saint-Domingue seafaring workplace permitted black seamen to oversee and command ranking officers and sailors. Here, segregation was impractical and intolerable.

The integrated maritime life had soldiers and sailors working together where black and white Atlantic officers engaged one another and cultivated warm and productive relationships. They strategized together, deferring to the expertise of one another to get the results needed.

This status etiquette could not have been possible in the United States and equipped the American military men to look beyond skin tones and respect each other's ranks – an Officer was an Officer and an order was an order. White American sailors' service in Saint-Domingue followed the orders of a superior black officer because military rank and the respect it commanded trumped civilian racial protocol.

Toussaint never hesitated to give orders to white men of all ranks. After all they had accomplished, he and his deputies neither accepted nor tolerated the argument that Africans were in any way inferior to whites. They had been ordering and killing men of all colors in battle for decades. When they gave an order, they expected obedience without the need to demand it from a lower ranking soldier.

Toussaint wasted no time in leveraging this newfound naval support. He directed Captain Perry to disrupt Rigaud's vital shipping lanes, which the Southern army had ingeniously established for supplies. American merchant vessels, operating in the guise of neutrality, clandestinely imported arms through the port of Les Cayes.

With the naval component in place, Toussaint embarked on a daring campaign in late January, leading his army toward Jacmel.

Rigaud, a thorn in his side and a source of chaos had to be eliminated to restore stability to the island. The fate of Saint Domingue would depend on the outcome of this perilous march and the covert support of the United States.

Four

THE RESCUE OF JACMEL

Jacmel
March 1800

Alexandre Pétion continued to gaze out of the window, his mind heavy with the weight of responsibility and desperation. The picturesque town and harbor that had once been a source of pride now stood as a testament to their grim predicament.

Nearly three months had passed since the ingenious ruse engineered for the young American spy, McCoy, had secured a considerable amount of supplies for the city. It was a brief respite from the encroaching starvation, and now the town was on the brink of running out of food again, even as Dessalines' relentless army continued their assaults.

Dessalines had tested their perimeter defenses repeatedly, at great cost to his men, but they continued to hold. A momentary breach had occurred once, with enemy forces breaking into the city, only to be trapped and slaughtered by its defenders. The fallen horses in the engagement gave them much-needed meat to prolong their survival.

Rigaud sent 500 reinforcements from Les Cayes, about half of what he had remaining, but they never arrived. Reportedly, they had been ambushed by Dessalines' patrols on the road from Côtes-de-Fer, west of Jacmel. Most recently, Christophe's army had now appeared on the scene. Pétion suspected that they were awaiting Toussaint to join them for a full-scale assault.

He knew that defeat was likely inevitable, but he was determined to make the enemy pay dearly for their victory. His force of 5,000 battle-tested, predominantly mulatto troops was ready to fight to their last breath. They understood that dying on the battlefield was a far better fate than falling into enemy hands.

As he considered the meager assets at his disposal, including small arms, ammunition, and a dozen cannons hidden in the hills, Pétion knew that they still had surprises in store for the enemy. He couldn't shake the feeling that this was a last stand, but he was not going down without a fierce fight.

A knock on the door interrupted his thoughts, and he granted permission for the visitor to enter. Rocourt, weary and grim-faced, brought troubling news from the hospital. Medical supplies were exhausted, and they were using shredded uniforms as bandages. The townspeople were demoralized and starving.

However, there was a glimmer of hope. A local woman from Léogâne was rumored to be on her way, bringing medical supplies and food donated from different parts of the south. Pétion questioned how she intended to get past Dessalines and his army, but Rocourt had no answers.

In Dessalines' camp, frustration simmered and tension gripped the leader. His migraine throbbed as he seethed over Christophe's reluctance to advance on Jacmel without explicit orders from Toussaint. His repeated attempts to breach Pétion's formidable defenses had yielded little success, aside from revealing the fierce prowess of the mulatto troops defending the city.

A lieutenant, undeterred by Dessalines' volatile mood, disrupted his thoughts with news of a persistent woman who insisted on entering the city and demanded an audience with the General. Annoyed, Dessalines snapped at the lieutenant, ordering the woman to be sent away for her safety, his head pounding in protest.

"She is very insistent, mon Général."

"Get out of my tent! And get that woman out of the theater of battle!" yelled Dessalines.

As the lieutenant turned to leave the tent, he nearly collided with the determined woman from Léogâne. She had followed him in her unwavering quest to find someone in charge who would grant her permission to enter Jacmel with the crucial supplies she carried.

"I demand to speak with Général Dessalines," she declared firmly.

"I am sorry, Madame. He is not receiving any visitors today," the lieutenant replied.

"I will not leave until either he or someone in authority permits me to enter the city. I have supplies that will spoil if they do not reach their destination," she insisted.

Dessalines, incensed by the ongoing disturbance, stormed out of the tent, his fury evident. He was a formidable figure, tall and imposing, with a powerful, lean physique. His uniform strained against bulging muscles, and his face, though stern, revealed a meticulous grooming of mustache and sideburns, with a hint of reddish tint.

"What is the meaning of this!" he shouted

The woman looked up and saw the mighty Jean-Jacques Dessalines before her. His two fists rested on his waist as he glared down at her, nearly a foot taller than she, first with a frown and quickly softening a bit as he gazed at her face with curiosity.

"Who are you?" he inquired, his voice surprisingly calm compared to his earlier outburst.

"My name is Marie-Claire Heureuse Félicité, Général. I am here to provide food and medicine to the citizens of Jacmel," she replied.

Dessalines contemplated her words, his gaze lingering on her face. Her appearance contrasted his own, with a lighter complexion and a composed demeanor. She hid her hair with a blue turban wrap that highlighted her smooth facial features. Her eyes were a huge dark brown, her lips full, and her skin was void of any imperfections. She wore a bright yellow dress with small breasts that hung high on her chest, pressing on the tight garment that was maybe a size or two too small for her.

"I am sorry Madame, I cannot permit you to enter the city," Dessalines said. "It is much too dangerous."

Marie-Claire's patience wore thin, and she shot him a frustrated glare. "I feel no danger here," she responded.

"Let me give it some thought," Dessalines responded with finality. "Come back here at 6 tonight and I will give you my response."

Marie-Claire gave him a frustrated look. She was running out of patience. However, she decided to acquiesce to his request. The fate of her mission and the citizens of Jacmel hung in the balance with this man, and as she left her determination was unwavering.

Marie-Claire Heureuse Félicité arrived promptly at Dessalines' command tent at 6 pm, as requested, but she was greeted with an unexpected sight. A soldier and a carriage, accompanied by four other soldiers on horseback, awaited her.

"Jeneral la te mande nou pou nou akonpaye ou kote pou dine a," The general has asked us to escort you to a place to dine.

Marie-Claire, intrigued but cautious, examined the carriage with its horsemen stationed strategically around it. The soldier kindly assisted her into the carriage, closing the door behind her, and then took the reins to steer the carriage away from the camp.

They traveled a short distance to a hill where a table had been set, complete with linen, plates, silverware, and a central candle. The Caribbean breeze, cool and gentle, rustled the coconut tree leaves as it carried the scent of the nearby sea.

Escorted by the soldier, Marie-Claire left the carriage and was seated at the table, where she awaited the mysterious host. Four horsemen sped off in the distance, leaving her alone with a server who poured wine into her glass.

Suddenly, from behind a tree, General Dessalines appeared, resplendent in a full-dress uniform but conspicuously unarmed. He approached the table with a polite bow of his head and asked, "May I join you, Marie-Claire Heureuse Félicité?"

"I had my doubts that you would have remembered my name, mon Général".

"It is a unique name, rather distinguished, don't you think?" Dessalines remarked as he took a seat without waiting for her response permitting him to do so.

"It was the name given to me by my parents." She replied.

"Tell me about them, your parents, and where you are from, please," he asked as the soldier poured him a glass of wine.

"I was born in Léogâne. My father is Guillaume Bonheur and my mother Marie-Sainte Lobelot. Both are fine and honorable people; hardworking and decent. They gave me a good upbringing and provided me with what they could, even though we were a poor family, but we were rich because we were a free family."

"Ahh, freedom," Dessalines said as he took a deep breath of fresh air. "It is sweet indeed, isn't it?"

"I can only imagine the sadness of bondage. To be held against your will to labor your life without compensation for another. It must be frustrating?" Marie-Claire empathetically ventured, alluding to Dessalines' past as a slave.

The server arrived with some raw conch cut up into small pieces and mixed with tomato, garlic, and onions, placing the dishes before them. He then bowed and left.

"Slavery is evil, a dark stain on humanity," Dessalines admitted, his voice tinged with sadness. "However, it is imposed on those conquered, and some believe it's a better alternative to death. I am not convinced. Go on, tell me more about yourself."

"I received my education from my aunt, my mother's sister, Élise Lobelot. She was the governess of a religious order and taught me the skills of healing. She was very kind and saw something in me and trained me to be a nurse."

"Ahh, and the reason you are here. To assist in healing those wounded in battle. My enemies?"

"No General. I am here to assist the people, the citizens of Jacmel."

"The people of Jacmel are my enemy. They resist my advancement into the city."

"Those people are not your enemy. They are caught in the middle of this squabble between your Toussaint Louverture and their André Rigaud. They do not want this war. They feel it is a quarrel between those two men jostling for power. Even the previous General Beauvais wanted neutrality and so do his soldiers that you intend to kill."

"Toussaint Louverture has an established mandate to govern the colony. He is the official Governor-General"

"Rigaud has an established mandate to govern the Southern region."

"So, then you agree with Rigaud?" asked Dessalines.

"I despise Rigaud for what he did to the Blancs who were trying to re-establish their farms here in the south. He slaughtered them during the beginning of this uprising thinking they would turn on him and join Toussaint."

"I must admit that the Blancs do prefer Toussaint Louverture over André Rigaud. After all, if it were not for Toussaint, Rigaud would have slaughtered them all earlier in retaliation for siding with the British when they left."

"I am so frustrated with all of you!" Marie-Claire said. "Do you listen to yourself? Someone is always killing someone else. When does it stop?"

They both looked at their conch appetizer in an awkward silence and began to eat, each waiting for the other to re-engage in the conversation.

The server arrived to take their empty plates away and returned with a hot dish of barbecued ramier, a local large pigeon, plantains, rice, and beans.

"I apologize, General. I am your guest and you have been gracious in providing this wonderful meal. I simply want your permission to enter the city and relieve some starvation and misery for its citizens," she stated with a softer tone.

"And why should I let you do that, Madame Heureuse Félicité?"

"Because you are wise and understand that it will serve your purpose," she said with a gamble. "The citizens are not fully supportive of Rigaud. He has brought nothing but death, starvation, and possible destruction of their city. Should you let me in as a humanitarian gesture, it will show them that you have compassion, Jean-Jacques, that you care for their well-being." she reasoned, breaking protocol by using his first name.

Dessalines picked up his glass of wine and guzzled it. The server was there within seconds to refill it. He was confused. This woman intrigued him. She challenged him. Other women he had been with were to breed, to relieve his sexual desires or frustrations. This is the first time a woman challenged him to think, to reason, to question his strategies. He wasn't sure if it was healthy.

"And if I allow you into the city, you will not provide comfort to the enemy army?"

"I will not, Jean-Jacques," again addressing him by his first name as she cut a piece of the ramier and put it in her mouth. It tasted so good she thought.

Dessalines looked at her, elegantly chewing the meat, and was mesmerized by this woman. She was strong, but tender. Combative but forgiving. All she wanted was to help others. Who does that? What sort of person devotes their life to this calling? Even priests have selfish interests, he had learned.

"I will allow you passage to the city in exchange for your promise that none of your kindness will go to the enemy army."

"I will only provide medical treatment to a soldier in need. That I can promise you."

"You will not assist any soldiers," Dessalines firmly stated.

"That, I cannot promise. But I will not seek soldiers out to assist."

"It seems that you are stubborn, Marie-Claire," he said, now too reverting to first name.

"And you are not?"

"And you play with words, Marie-Claire."

"And you do not?" she answered.

"How many days do you need inside Jacmel?" asked Dessalines.

"Two to three weeks. That should give me enough time… Jean-Jacques."

"You have one week. That should be quite sufficient."

"How would you know… Jean-Jacques?"

"Why do you keep calling me by my given name?" asked Dessalines.

"Do you prefer that I call you by your title, Jean-Jacques, or should I say Mon Général?" she formally stated, increasing her volume and dropping the octaves of her voice to mimic a soldier as she gave him an amateur salute.

Dessalines opened his mouth but was momentarily speechless.

"I'll take two weeks." She said with her female voice back and her head cocked to the side.

Dessalines opened his mouth to speak once again and she placed her index finger over his upper lip. "Someone needs to curb your stubbornness for your own good," Marie-Claire stated with a smile on her lips as she looked directly into his eyes, which made him somewhat uncomfortable.

"Plus, your delicious food is getting cold. No more talk of Jacmel," she ordered, the smile still clinging to her face.

Dessalines smiled back and began to eat. "Ten days. That is my final offer," as he sat back and watched a smile come across her beautiful full lips.

From thereon, the conversation turned casual; the foods they enjoyed, stories of childhood, their wants, desires, and dreams. It was the first time in a long while that Dessalines had escaped the stress of war. He was surprisingly enjoying himself.

The evening ended and they both went their separate ways. His soldiers escorted her back to her camp and he rode to his tent to rendezvous with a sleepless night, thinkïng not of the next battle, but of the woman, Marie-Claire Heureuse Félicité.

Marie-Claire couldn't sleep that evening. She had mixed emotions of exactly what it was that she felt. Was it the anticipation of entering Jacmel or a strange attraction to the man with a brutal reputation who acted humanely last evening? But there was no time for those feelings. It was time for action.

She exited her tent in the make-shift compound of the volunteers who had joined her from all parts of the Southern Peninsula. They represented Jeremie, Léogâne, Aquin, Coteaux, Dame Marie, Les Cayes, and many more towns and cities. They had all heard of the plight of Jacmel and were eager to help.

Each brought with them wagons loaded with what they had collected these past couple of months. Marie-Claire had sent word to each town of her humanitarian mission but had never expected the outpouring of this much support. Twenty-two wagon loads of everything from food, medicines, clothes, and even household goods were assembled. Altogether, there were nearly 60 people in the caravan of help.

It was early this Saturday morning, the first of March. She had ten days to get this job done and they would need every minute of every day to do so. The early morning dawn had not yet lit the sky and darkness still blanketed the camp.

She could smell the rich aroma of coffee beans being brewed and anticipated enjoying a cup as she strolled over to the traveling field kitchen and the divine aroma of Bernard pouring a cup of the dark, rich coffee with steam rising from the cup.

Ahh, Marie-Claire, I anticipated you would be the first here," as Bernard greeted her with a cheery smile, handing her the first cup brewed.

It was only yesterday that they had arrived and been blocked from entering Jacmel. Less than 24 hours ago, they did not know if this mission would be allowed to be completed. And here they were now anticipating the moment they would enter the city.

"The Lord has been good. He has blessed our mission and allowed us to proceed, Bernard," she answered.

"The Lord and the persuasive powers of our leader, Marie-Claire. How in the world did you convince that blood-thirsty brute named Dessalines to allow us to continue? he asked. "With his violent and unpredictable reputation, I was afraid you would never return."

"His reputation is far worse than he is in person, Bernard. A misunderstood child maybe?" she laughed.

"Whatever it is, you got what we needed. I have instructed everyone to be prepared to move out before first light, around 6 a.m., less than two hours from now. I am preparing breakfast and we should be on time."

"What in the world would I do without you, Bernard?"

"If not me, you would have found another, my dear."

Bernard Delatour had proved indispensable with this project. He was a family friend who she had known for as long as she could remember. He was 10 years older than she and as resourceful as anyone she had ever met. His organizational skills were second to none and his heart was golden. No one else could have been this valuable.

As others began to wander to the field kitchen for breakfast, Marie-Claire made it a point to converse with all of them, even if it was only a sentence or two. She knew everyone by name since they had joined the caravan.

There were people of every age from 14 and on. They were excited to help and giddy with the idea that their past weeks of preparation and assembling the supplies in each of their cities, towns, and villages were finally cleared to be used. Up until now, they weren't certain they would have been permitted entry into Jacmel.

By 5:30 a.m., everyone was assembled in the field kitchen for a meeting. *"Bonjou Mezanmi!"* Good morning my friends! She yelled at the top of her lungs. "Today begins the final and most important part of our project; the distribution of your hard labor over these past few weeks!" Marie-Claire yelled.

Everyone erupted in a cheer.

"You have truly given me and everyone else the inspiration to help the people of Jacmel. And that, we will!" she yelled as people cheered louder in jubilance.

"In less than half an hour, we will be on the road to enter the city no later than an hour or two later. Are you ready?"

People cheered in affirmation.

"Then the time has come. Man your wagons and let us complete our journey!" she yelled as the crowd once again erupted in cheer, rushing to their wagons to be the first in line for the caravan.

"I am so truly proud of you as are your parents and your aunt," Bernard said as he helped her down from the cargo bay of the wagon. This is your time, Marie-Claire. Shine like the beacon you are. Go to your wagon and lead your people. I will clean up here and join at the rear of the line."

Marie-Claire smiled and gave him a huge hug. "Without you, none of this would be possible, Bernard. I would never have had the strength to continue," she said as she buried her head into his chest like a younger sister finding support and courage from an older brother. She gave him one final look with a huge grin and headed off like a schoolgirl to man the first wagon.

Two days later, Toussaint arrived with 20,000 troops. Together with Dessalines' 10,000 and Christophe's 8,000 troops, they formed an imposing army of nearly 40,000 strong.

On his arrival, Dessalines and Christophe wasted no time and went to meet Toussaint at his camp.

Inside Toussaint's tent, they found the Governor General in good spirits, accompanied by Christopher Perry, the captain of the American warship, the *General Greene*. The ship had been harassing Rigaud's troop barges and blockading the Jacmel harbor.

Captain Perry provided a report on the capture of a Danish merchant vessel named the *William and Mary*. This vessel had attempted to break the blockade and resupply Rigaud's army in an isolated cove near Jacmel. She was intercepted with rifles, shot, and powder. The ship's crew was taken into custody, and the munitions were confiscated. The ship was then repurposed as a warship for Toussaint's use.

Toussaint introduced Dessalines and Christophe to Captain Perry, and they spent the evening dining together. During their meeting, plans were drawn up for the *General Greene* to provide firepower for an invasion of Jacmel scheduled for August 9.

The strategy involved the ship bombarding the town from the harbor with cannons, while Toussaint's forces fired on the town from its outskirts. Captain Perry agreed to this plan, even though he knew it exceeded the mandate given by Commodore Talbot, as American vessels were not supposed to engage in combat. Perry reasoned that their actions were in the protection of American trading vessels, which fell within the scope of the trade agreement between the United States and Saint-Domingue – an arguable technicality.

When Captain Perry departed for his ship at about 9 p.m. under the cover of darkness, Dessalines and Christophe remained. Toussaint began; "Dessalines, I understand that you have been engaging in battles with the enemy contrary to my order to stand down until my arrival."

"I did not consider my probes into their defenses as nothing other than scouting for the best possible areas to infiltrate the enemy during our attack, Mon Général. They were simply reconnaissance missions," Dessalines reasoned, knowing he had taken liberty where he had no authority to do so.

Christophe thought it better to stand back and not get involved, even though he had tried to stop Dessalines from his forays.

"You consider the loss of over 300 men 'probes' Dessalines?" asked Toussaint.

The risk was necessary and warranted. My men know well – *"Pa gen manman pa gen papa, Sa ki mouri zafè ya yo"* - There is no mother and there is no father, those who die, that is their problem.

"You and I have long had a disagreement on that saying concerning casualties, Dessalines. You are way too cavalier with the loss of your troops."

"However, I am very effective," Dessalines countered.

"And what of this woman who has entered Jacmel on a humanitarian mission?" asked Toussaint

Dessalines was caught off guard. Who had informed him of Marie-Claire, he thought? Was it Christophe, that *Nèg Kay* - House Nigger *w*ho desires to be Toussaint's puppy dog?

"This woman from Léogâne appeared with an idea to enter Jacmel and tend to the wounded citizens, and to feed those in danger of starvation. I warned her not to engage with military personnel and stated clearly that this mission was sanctioned and authorized by our army," Dessalines argued.

"You have done well, Jean-Jacques," answered Toussaint, using his first name as he always did to soften Dessalines up for a lesson. "Having the citizens understand that we are not here to harm them, but rather assist them is most desirable."

"Thank you, Mon Général," Dessalines answered, relieved that he had pleased the Governor General as he stole a glance towards Christophe to gauge any reaction from him, but found none.

"But I must say you have surprised me with this, shall I say, change of disposition, Jean-Jacques? It is not like you to show mercy, especially at this level," Toussaint mused.

"The citizens, I am told, are not happy with Rigaud's army. They would prefer that Pétion had never arrived at Jacmel altogether." This show of mercy can serve us well when we invade the town and need their cooperation during the occupation," Dessalines stated, not revealing his initial opposition to the idea when first presented by Marie-Claire.

"Correct, once again. Your newfound strategy is, shall I say, refreshing?" Toussaint chided.

"However, I need us to stall the attack until either the 11th or 12th. I did not want to contradict you in front of the American Captain. I gave my word to the Léogâne woman that she could take a full 10 days beginning March 1 to assist the citizens. She will leave the town on March 10."

"Agreed," stated Toussaint. "I will send word to Captain Perry that the bombardment will begin the morning of March 12th."

What is this woman doing to him, Dessalines thought. Since he met her, it is as if his mind is being changed. He will need to be on the alert for these changes so as not to distract him.

After about a 3-hour slow grind to the mulatto army's outer defenses for the city of Jacmel, they were permitted to pass the outer fortifications built in front of the city. Enormous mahogany, palm, and coconut trees formed a barrier 6 feet high as far as the eye could see with many soldiers manning it. This was in addition to the numerous redoubts – dug in trenches for overnight protection which had proved most effective against Dessalines' evening raids.

A contingent of mulatto troops, who had been advised to be on the lookout for their arrival, led the caravan into the city until they arrived at the main square. Two officers approached – one being General Pétion and the other Captain Rocourt.

"I am Général Alexandre Pétion. This is Captain Rocourt. We welcome you to the city of Jacmel. I understand you are the woman from Léogâne?"

"I am," answered Marie-Claire. I have traveled with these brave people to bring supplies to this beleaguered city, Général."

"My army appreciates the gesture. From whom may I say that it is coming from?" Pétion asked.

"My name is Marie-Claire Heureuse Félicité and my entourage is numerous, about 60 in all. We have all labored to arrive on this day. However, to gain access to the city, I was forced to assure that none of these supplies would be distributed to your army."

"And who made you promise this, Madame?"

"Général Dessalines," she answered.

"But of course. That bloodthirsty brute who has been trying to starve us out for the past several months. I am sorry, but I cannot allow that," Pétion firmly replied.

"What can you not allow, Général?"

"The distribution of supplies without any going to the soldiers who protect the fine citizens of this city, Madame. It would not be good for morale."

"Somehow, we will need to come to an arrangement," Marie-Claire said as she was desperately trying to find an answer."

"Do you have a manifest of the goods on these wagons?" asked Pétion.

"We are not that formal, Général. But what I can tell you is that we have 5,000 pounds of cornmeal, 4,200 pounds of rice, 7,000 pounds of beans, 2,000 pounds of sugar, 4,000 pounds of salted cod fish, 2,000 pounds each of salted beef, 1,000 chickens, cooking charcoal and many medical supplies," Marie-Claire answered. "And of course, coffee."

"Quite significant. And what is your plan for all of these supplies?"

"Distribution to the citizens. What is the current census?"

"Many have left for the countryside or other towns. We only have 3,000, maybe 4,000 citizens at most," Pétion replied.

"So we have a stalemate, Général. You will not allow me to distribute supplies to the citizens and I cannot distribute supplies to your army as it would violate my oath of honor to Général Dessalines," Marie-Claire firmly stated.

"Now hang on Madame. We can come to some sort of compromise that will serve us both." Pétion answered.

Bernard arrived at the front of the wagon train to join Marie-Claire. "What has been decided, Marie Claire?" he asked.

"We are discussing that now, Bernard. This is Général Pétion. Général, this is Bernard Delatour." Marie-Claire introduced.

"Honored to meet you, Général. Why don't we set up camp here in the town square as the city appears empty and begin to prepare a meal for the citizens while you work out the details," Bernard said, not waiting for an answer as he scurried back to the food wagon to set up shop.

Pétion looked at Marie-Claire and admired her courage to stand up to him in public as she was doing. He however was keenly aware that the citizens were now forming a crowd to witness what was transpiring between them.

"You will not provide any supplies to my army. You will distribute them only to the citizens," said Pétion. "However, the army has filled the void of government in this city and is now in fact the defacto government; we are forced to provide government services."

"I am not following your thoughts, Général," answered Marie-Claire

"There is always a tax to be paid. In this case, an importation tax of 20% of total commodities. So, for every 10 bags of goods you unload, the government will take two for taxes. That way, you are not providing any supplies to my army, but taxes to the legitimate government of the city. Agreed?"

"A fair solution that has me not violating my agreement with Général Dessalines. If you advise the soldiers of your army to not approach us except in the collection of taxes, it is acceptable, Général," Marie-Claire smiled as she extended her hand to seal the deal.

Pétion shook her hand and departed the scene, leaving Rocourt to work out the details. He wasted no time and immediately began the inventory of the supplies and orchestrated the acquisition of the government's tax on medical and food supplies.

Within an hour, the aroma of food cooking surrounded the streets with citizens coming out in droves when they heard the news. Within two hours, the first plates of hot rice, beans, and goat were being spooned onto the plates of the grateful population.

It was announced that for the next week, meals would be cooked and served twice a day – 10 am and 5 pm. On March 9th, the day before they would depart, all remaining food stocks would be distributed amongst the people to take home.

A field medical clinic was opened where nearly a thousand people flocked for medical care that had been nearly non-existent. Marie-Claire and her team of medical professionals worked tirelessly from morning to night to tend to the lines of those awaiting treatment.

On the night before their departure, the townspeople came out in droves and instead of being fed, they cooked meals with the supplies given them and hosted a feast for the 60 people who had saved them.

They insisted the volunteer angels do nothing but sit back and enjoy their delicious food. A choir of children serenaded the guests with songs of faith, gratitude, and strength during dinner.

A local old-timer thanked the group with a speech of gratitude on behalf of the town and provided a history of the town as bottles of rum were passed around. Dancers entertained the crowd

MÉDECIN

throughout the night as the fires were kept blazing with traditional folklore dances of *Yanvalou, Kongo, Ibo, Petro, and Dahomey*. By midnight, all were exhausted and weary for a great night's sleep.

The next morning, as Marie-Claire departed the city, a feeling of joy overwhelmed her. This, she thought, had been the best 10 days of her life. The wagons rolled out of the city with the volunteers amidst the cheers of crowds assembled to bid them farewell.

Would these people be alive next year? Marie-Claire thought. She prayed they would be but could do no more.

Five

ESCAPE FROM JACMEL

Jacmel
March 1800

In the dimly lit office, Général Alexandre Pétion, and Captain Serge Rocourt, gathered for a secret meeting. They were enjoying their evening cheroots when Captain Lamerique knocked on the door. Pétion greeted him warmly and offered him a cheroot.

"Ahh, just in time, Captain," Pétion stated with a cheery disposition. "Come enjoy one of these fine cheroots smuggled in as a gift."

Lamerique accepted the cigar and Pétion extended him a lit match as he said, "I wanted you to be involved in the planning of our attack on the enemy. I value your opinion."

Lamerique, who had felt somewhat excluded from the inner circle of trust, questioned himself as to his involvement in the planning of any upcoming attack.

"But I was under the impression that any of Général Beauvais' men, like myself, were somewhat excluded from the circle of trust, Général?" asked Lamerique.

"You have proved yourself valuable in my mission here, Captain. I have grown over time to appreciate the delicate position you are in, a sort of juggling act to be sure, between my army and your army here," Pétion said. "I trust that your men have eaten well over the past few days, henn?"

"Yes, they have. And they are very much appreciative. Thank you for your confidence in me," replied Lamerique. "I have come to respect your leadership, Mon Général."

"Then, let me lay out the battle plan, henn?" Pétion responded as he got up and retrieved a map from a table nearby. He brought the map to his desk and laid it out flat, placing rocks on each corner to keep it from rolling up.

"The bulk of Dessalines' army is here – due North of us and camped along the river," tracing a line with his finger. "Christophe is camped to the northeast there, adjacent to Dessalines and also along the shores of the river to the northeast. Toussaint has arrived and is due east of us. In essence, we are surrounded."

"So, what possible plan could there be?" Lamerique questioned as Rocourt looked curiously at Pétion, not seeing where this was going.

"We do the only thing we can do - a bold surprise attack. We march west and cross the river at this point here," Pétion said while pointing at the map. "I had it recently tested and the water is but three feet high at this location. We then head north and reverse back, recross the river at this point here, behind Dessalines' army, and surprise them from the rear," Pétion said as he snapped his finger to the map.

"Before the attack, we will fire all cannons from the fort to this location, designed to drive them upriver to the north," as he again pointed to the location on the map. "Rocourt, you will take charge of the infantry attack, and Lamerique, you will command the cannon fire from the fort. I want your men to remain in the city to defend it from the enemy, should they launch a two-front attack. Questions?"

Rocourt and Lamerique exchanged glances and by their expression questioned the audacious plan. Rocourt then looked up at Pétion.

"Agreed, Mon Général," replied Rocourt. "When is the attack?"

"We will attack on nightfall of March 11th. It will be a full moon with enough light to see our way through."

"Agreed, Mon Général. An excellent plan." Lamerique enthusiastically added, to the curiosity of Rocourt.

"Then go enjoy another good meal with your officers. Keep this plan of utmost secrecy until the morning of March 11. Once announced, no one, I stress no one, leaves the town.

Rocourt and Lamerique turned and began to walk out the door, but Pétion called out; "Rocourt. Stay a moment. I want to go over the inventory of the medical supplies with you. What we will take and what we will leave behind during the attack."

"Do you need me as well," Lamerique asked.

"No, go enjoy your meal, and give your officers my warm salutations. Rocourt was in charge of the taxation and has the necessary information, and this won't take long."

Lamerique left the room and Pétion turned to gaze out of the window.

"Permission to speak, Mon Général?" asked Rocourt.

"Yes, Serge. Speak your mind," answered Pétion.

"Respectfully, sir. Have you lost your mind?" asked Rocourt. "Forgive the informality, but I have known you for too many years and trust you to accept my counsel on your battle plans. It is suicidal to execute such a plan. It is way too risky for little gain!"

"I know that," responded Pétion.

"Then why are we going to do it, Mon Général?"

"We are not, Serge. We will do nothing of the sort. That plan was designed for Lamerique. He will go running to Dessalines to inform him of it. We will be doing something quite the contrary. However, we want Dessalines, Christophe, and Toussaint to think that this is the plan and to lay out a trap for us at that location."

And, why Mon Général?"

"Because we will be escaping the city on that night, here to the east," Pétion said as he pointed to the appropriate location on the map. "Toussaint is located here to the east, the pathway to our escape. When he hears that I will be taking a final stand to attack him in surprise, what do you think Toussaint will do?"

"He will flank his men to the northwest and southwest to squeeze us between Dessalines and Christophe," Rocourt said.

"Exactly. As Toussaint moves West, we will move East in silence and escape by way of the northeast coastal road towards Marigot. Lamerique will probably not fire any cannon that night as he is a traitor to our cause and in collusion with the enemy."

"What if Toussaint attacks before the full moon on the 11th?" asked Rocourt.

"He won't. His attack plan is for the following day, on the 12th," replied Pétion. He plans a bombardment of Jacmel from their American friends."

"How do you know this?"

"I have an informant. The same one who informed me that Lamerique is a traitor is the same one who has given me Toussaint's battle plan. The Americans will fire on this city on the morning of March 12th. We need to be out of here by then."

Rocourt looked at Pétion and smiled. "How could I ever doubt your strategy, skills, and resources, Mon Général? Forgive me for contradicting you."

"Let us go to dinner with our officers. I have a special meal being prepared for these brave souls from the meats of the woman from Léogâne. Tonight, we drink plenty of rum. But remember, not a word to any of them, even your most trusted."

As the morning of March 11th arrived, dark clouds loomed in the sky, promising rain, though none fell. The air was heavy with humidity and only interrupted by a light salty breeze from the ocean. Pétion's soldiers were busy preparing their equipment and arms for the planned attack on the enemy, and engaging in casual and light conversation amongst each other.

Throughout the morning and early afternoon, Pétion and Rocourt moved amongst the soldiers to assess their morale. All of Bauvais' troops were absent, leaving only Pétion's loyal soldiers around the town.

They paused at various groups of soldiers and engaged them in light conversations as they expressed gratitude for the recently acquired food and supplies they were enjoying. It was clear that the men were both apprehensive and confident about the upcoming battle.

Pétion and Rocourt joined the officers at the field kitchen for a late lunch as Pétion had ordered and found the officers' spirits high despite the impending dangerous mission.

They sat at a table together for a meal of salted fish, plantains, and cornmeal. One of the officers produced a small old bottle to compliment the meal that consisted of a mixture of shredded vegetables aged in vinegar with hot peppers they called '*Pikliz*', much to the men's delight.

After the meal, Pétion stood to address them; "You are the finest officers that I have ever had the honor of fighting with. You are fearless, cunning and when necessary – can be extremely violent. You make me proud.

We have laid out our attack plan these past few days and I want to confide in you that it is not the plan we will execute in a few hours."

The officers looked at each other curiously, as Pétion continued, "This plan was provided to the enemy as a ruse. They will await us by the river for an ambush early this evening, but unfortunately for them, we will not arrive to partake in their hospitality, as we have different plans."

"As planned, we will assemble at the front northwest gates of the city and be ready to move out at exactly 6 p.m. However, at the last minute before our departure, we will turn the army around and those at the rear will lead us through the eastern gates and be at the front instead."

"This is to prevent anyone, especially men loyal to Bauvais, from having a warning early enough to potentially reach our enemy and signal them of our change of plans. Any questions?" Pétion asked.

The men looked around at each other and smiled. One of them, a captain, spoke up and said "Does that mean we will not be engaging in battle, Mon Général?"

"Expect and prepare for a fierce battle and hope for none. However, knowing Toussaint, he will split his army as he usually does and send a third to assist Dessalines and Christophe in the planned ambush for us, a third will guard his camp and the other third will be scattered along the shoreline, just in case."

"And what of them?" asked a lieutenant.

"I have a surprise in store. Remember when we first arrived we took half the cannon out of the city?" Pétion asked.

Most answered in the affirmative.

"Well, it is about time we use them. Cannons are most effective when fired from on high where their projectiles have the most velocity. At 7 p.m., the enemy will have two barrages of cannon to confuse them. The one they will be expecting is the cannon fire from our batteries in the fort to the northwest. The unexpected cannon fire will rain down on Toussaint's forces in the east along the shore from our cannons in the mountains. That will force them to scatter to the north, clearing an open path on the coastal road for us to execute our escape."

"Brilliant!" yelled the first captain who had spoken, as Pétion raised a glass of lemonade for a toast. "No word of this to any of your men, even the most trusted, until tonight when we are ready for the reversal. Maintain complete secrecy. Today, we drink this sugary lemon drink. Tomorrow, we drink rum!"

They all laughed as they lifted their glasses, and he dismissed the officers to their units.

Soldiers began to assemble at the town square at 5 p.m. to ready themselves for the attack outside the city. The soldiers of Jacmel, Beauvais' soldiers, looked on, relieved that they would not take part in this crazy suicidal mission that Pétion had ordered.

As they were preparing the cannons to fire upon Dessalines' army along the river, Pétion and Rocourt galloped into the square. Pétion dismounted and walked up to Lamerique. "Are the cannons ready to fire upon the enemy for our attack?"

"Yes, Mon Général. We are ready to rain terror on the enemy and open a path for your attack," Lamerique said.

"Good. Stay with me until we leave," Pétion answered as the hour of 6 pm grew closer.

"We are ready, Mon Général," Rocourt reported as he walked over to Pétion and Lamerique.

"Then, let the attack begin. Lamerique, fire your cannons," Pétion ordered.

"Artillery, fire at will," Lamerique commanded.

Cannon immediately began to unload their payload towards the enemy at the river. Rocourt gave the order to begin the march to the officers. Pétion asked Lamerique to walk with him.

As the cannons opened fire upon the river, Pétion's army surprisingly reversed their course and marched toward the eastern gates as Lamerique looked on in confusion. "I thought we were attacking from the northwest towards the river, Mon Général?"

"Change of plans, Captain. Come with me."

When they arrived at the eastern gates, Pétion turned and said, "Lamerique, I know that you have informed Dessalines of our attack."

Lamerique, being of honorable character did not contradict him. "When you arrest me, I will not deny this. I have done only what I believe is right for my troops. This fight is between André Rigaud and Toussaint Louverture. I am from the same mindset as General Bauvais." Lamerique removed his sword from his sheath and presented it to Pétion. "My sword, and my command, Mon Général. I surrender to you, honorably."

"I do not fault you for your actions. You were never in this war and your loyalty to General Bauvais was never questioned or hidden from me. I understand this and respect you for it. You are a loyal, honorable, and respectable soldier. I would welcome your loyalty, but I know I do not have it. However, take back your sword as well as your command. Your men will now need you, more than ever, to negotiate their future with Dessalines."

"Mon Général, I do not deserve your understanding or your forgiveness," Lamerique said.

"But you have it," answered Pétion. "My army will attempt to escape to the east. We should be out of the area before 8 pm. Stop your cannon fire towards Dessalines well before that. I would recommend a little after we leave so you have credibility for the story you will tell."

Pétion continued, "When Dessalines realizes that his trap will not materialize and we are not marching towards him, he will march on Jacmel for a frontal attack. Raise the white flag and surrender the city. You will tell Dessalines that you intentionally stopped the cannon fire contrary to my orders to foil my attack. It is then that you realized that you had been deceived at the last moment. State that you and your soldiers were left behind since they were not loyal to me," Pétion ordered.

"Yes, Mon Général," Lamerique answered. "I wish you nothing but the best of luck for your escape. I hope we meet one day in better circumstances."

Pétion extended his hand and Lamerique took it and they bid each other farewell.

Dessalines and Christophe were on their mounts on a hill above the area where they anticipated Pétion's river crossing. "According to Lamerique, the bombardment will begin at six and end around eight to clear the area of our soldiers. Once the bombardment ceases, Pétion will cross the river down there, but unfortunately for them be met by our army," Dessalines laughed.

As reported, cannon balls whistled overhead precisely 6 p.m, exploding where their troops had previously evacuated from in preparation. The ground shook after each burst of the barrage that continued unabated until it suddenly stopped minutes before 7 p.m. Christophe and Dessalines looked at each other after a few moments of silence.

"Why the early cease-fire?" asked Christophe.

"It could be they have run out of cannonballs or powder. Let us wait and see if it begins again or if Pétion crosses the river earlier," advised Dessalines.

Suddenly, in the far distance towards the east, a barrage of cannon fire erupted, apparently from the hills. Both Dessalines and Christophe were surprised and confused by the development, but Toussaint's orders were clear that they should await Pétion at this location.

On the eastern front, cannonballs whistled as they violently struck the ground at speeds far faster than those volleyed from the fort, being launched from the hills above. This downward trajectory took advantage of the natural pull of gravity to develop enormous speed so upon impact, the cannonballs were three times more destructive.

Toussaint's encampment was being decimated rapidly with a ferocity unimaginable to the soldiers. A single cannonball would take out dozens of soldiers, indiscriminately obliterating anything in its path.

Soldiers scattered northward to escape the lethal barrage as Pétion looked on with his spyglass. His army behind him lay in wait until the cannons stopped bellowing their charges. Once he was satisfied that the enemy had vacated the eastern path, he ordered a full-scale charge towards their escape.

But Toussaint was always a brilliant strategist. He had sent Dessalines and Christophe to the known point where Pétion was supposed to be, but understood clearly the cunning of his adversary. He had strategically stayed back to the east to direct his army just in case Pétion would make a run for it on the eastern coastal road, which now proved to be a wise decision.

When he had received the intelligence reports from Dessalines that Lamerique had given him, he couldn't comprehend that Pétion would be a man to attempt such a foolish last stand. It was not that he doubted Pétion's bravery, but clearly understood his military ability. Toussaint reasoned that if Pétion had not gone completely mad by attempting the suicide mission to the northwest as had been told, it was a trick to veil his attempt to escape east. Toussaint's caution proved wise.

Mounted atop his magnificent silver warhorse, Belle Argent, Toussaint looked at the destruction that Pétion's cannon had wreaked on his troops and gave him credit for placing his cannon in the hills. After all, Pétion's specialty is artillery, and he has played his hand well.

The sudden ceasing of fire, however, would be the opportune time for Pétion to make a run.

Toussaint kept scouring the area of destruction with his spyglass until it was there. Pétion and his army were moving rapidly eastward to escape. They would be surprised by Toussaint's army awaiting them to the east in anticipation of this possibility.

Toussaint watched Pétion atop his charger at the front, galloping the horse forward and then retracing his steps to the rear of the line to urge the foot soldiers to hurry forward. Toussaint could not but admire Pétion's dedication to the lives of all of his men. Admiral he thought.

He had taught Pétion well, even though their time together was limited. If he had thought differently back then, he would never have assigned the young man to Commander Laplume at Petit-Goâve and Grand-Goâve, but instead have kept him closer to him.

If he had, he probably would not need to kill him now. Such a waste of a good soldier, Toussaint thought. Pétion had been trained at the best military school in France, the same as Napoleon, yet twisted by his mulatto pride to join Rigaud.

Toussaint was now positioned east of Pétion's position. "Keep coming this way, Alexandre Pétion", Toussaint whispered as he spied him in the monocular.

"Yes, Mon Général?" asked the honor guard captain mounted on the horse next to Toussaint, thinking it was he that Toussaint was speaking softly to.

"Have the men hold their fire until I give the order, Captain," ordered Toussaint.

The captain turned and softly barked an order to the man next to him who sped off to relay the message to the others down the line.

The low-hanging clouds could no longer contain the moisture as sheets of heavy rain began to pour. A good omen Pétion thought, but it would also mean that they would have a slower march as horses and men would need to trudge through the thick mud.

Pétion turned to Rocourt. "Keep moving east. I am going to keep the men motivated from the rear to speed things up in this weather,"

Pétion turned Charger and gave the animal a slight kick as he galloped down the line while his men saluted him, 'Mon Général', as he passed.

Every few yards, he would stop his horse and yell, "*Continuez, mes garçons. Avancez! Je me déplacerai avec vous et serai la cible la plus importante lorsque l'ennemi frappera - comme je devrais l'être! Ne les craignez pas. Courez pour votre survie!*" - Continue, my boys. Move forward! I will move with you and be the largest target when the enemy strikes - as I should be! Do not fear them. Run for your survival!

For the next hour, Pétion kept up the pace, tirelessly motivating the line to move forward as the men labored, slipping, sliding, and falling in the muddy terrain as they slowly made their way down the winding coastal road in the torrential rain. The rain

was thick and visibility almost non-existent as nightfall enveloped the line.

Without warning, rifle fire crackled as Toussaint launched his assault on the mulatto and black soldiers. Dozens were mowed down in the overwhelming ambush during the initial volley. As Toussaint's men began to reload, they were answered by a volley of bullets from Pétion's men as Rocourt gave the order to fire their already loaded weapons – their payload yielding devastating casualties.

Toussaint answered the counter-attack with an order to charge and within seconds the two armies were engaged in a violent confrontation of bayonet, sword, and hand-to-hand combat as men on both sides fell in the fury of the battle.

Pétion yelled from the rear to charge forward, as the army began to sprint down the coastal road, engaging any in their path. Toussaint's men kept coming in dozens after dozens from the east and the northern side of the road, hour after hour until Toussaint had no more men left to send. By midnight, over four thousand brave soldiers from both sides lay dead or in their final agony of clinging to life on the ground.

By dawn, Pétion's army arrived in Marigot, a sleepy village about 20 kilometers east of Jacmel, they paused to assess their situation as the townspeople looked on. Pétion knew that the war was over. Rigaud had been beaten and barely had 500 men left and barricaded in Les Cayes. Petit-Goâve and Grand-Goâve had been captured, their stronghold in Jacmel had probably surrendered by now, and other commanders already defeated by the sheer strength and numbers of Toussaint's army. This mission had now turned into survival of his remaining troops.

He held a meeting with his captains, and it was decided to disband the army with each man shedding their French military uniform and heading to their home. They were all from the Southern Peninsula and those with homes to the east would continue as Toussaint's army was well west.

He then turned the remainder of his men to the northwest, about a thousand in all, with the intent of releasing them to their respective towns along the way as they marched towards Miragoâne, then along the northern coastal road to Jérémie where those volunteering to continue would attempt to gain ocean transport around the peninsula to Les Cayes and rejoin Rigaud.

When the news of the civil war reached Cap-Français in July of 1799, Jean and Marie Bayard were extremely worried about their parents who lived in Jérémie. The town was less than two hundred kilometers West of the outbreak of the war at Petit-Goâve and Grand-Goâve.

Jean told Marie that he needed to go to Jérémie and see for himself that the families had made adequate preparations in the event the war would come marching their way. Marie insisted on going to Jean's protests and they packed their bags for an extended stay.

Henry Christophe had decided to join Toussaint and the French Colonial Army and they were not happy about it. Henry and Marie-Louise had three small children under the age of five, but both Henry and Marie-Louise were insistent on him joining the colonial army.

Hôtel de la Couronne, which Henry had managed, was on solid footing as Henry had trained his staff well and promoted Pierre from Maitre d' to acting General Manager in his absence. Jean Junior, now twenty-four, was left in charge of running the import/export and shipping business in Cap Français during his parent's absence.

By September, when Jean and Marie arrived in Jérémie, they were astonished that the town was not in a frenzy over the battles being fought only 200 kilometers away. They visited Marie's parents first and found Gustav in the bustling store, very happy to see them and reporting that business was booming.

Little had changed in the store except they had expanded product lines, now stocking a large selection of armaments, be it pistols, rifles, ammunition, swords, and sabers. "A sign of the times," her brother Gustav remarked as he gave her and Jean a huge warm bear hug.

They had lunch with Marie's parents, Ralph and Odette, at their home who caught them up on all the happenings in Jérémie. Her parents were nearing seventy-five and were ready for their daily afternoon nap at around two.

Jean and Marie then decided to ride to the Bayard plantation and announce their arrival to Jean's parents. They arrived around four and found Jean-Phillippe and Jeanne casually sitting in the garden enjoying the beautiful day with flowers blooming about. Jean's parents, also nearly seventy-five, enjoyed the finer, more relaxed, and leisurely ways of retired life as well.

After the excitement of the reunion, Jeanne insisted on having them stay for a few days and hurried off with the mission of directing the kitchen staff of the children's arrivals and orders for the evening's meal.

Jean's younger brothers, Julien and René, had taken over management of the plantation and had just completed their day's labor in the fields, entered the home, excited at the arrival of Jean and Marie.

The entire family spent a memorable evening catching up, with Marie and Jean marveling at how Julian and his wife Yannick's young girls had grown. René recounted, and they all laughed, at sordid stories of his bachelor life. Julian reported on business affairs and crop yields and of how well it was going with the free workforce as opposed to the old system of slavery. Even his father agreed it was the right move to have made years earlier before emancipation.

The next day, Jean strolled around the property and ended up resting at the Mahogany tree in the lush field that thirty years ago, as a young man back in 1771, he had engineered and built an irrigation system for. He was enjoying the birds flying from tree to tree and the soft whistling of leaves when he birthed an idea.

By that evening, he had drawn up engineering plans for an underground bunker that could hold the family in case of an emergency, such as a hurricane, or what was most on his mind, an enemy army.

He presented the plans to the family and swore them to secrecy. Jean and Marie agreed to bear all the expenses of the project and expand it to be able to hold a dozen of Jean and Marie's families for extended stays if needed.

During the following week, Jean traveled west about twenty kilometers to the town of Bonbon and picked up four dejour laborers for the project. He purposefully didn't want any people from the local area involved. He rationalized that any conquering army would be traveling west, so he didn't want them to interrogate anyone who would know of the bunker. Using workers from the coastal town of Bonbon was ideal as it is so small and insignificant that no army would want to go there in the first place. Their secret would have a better chance of being kept.

Digging and construction of the wooden walls underground and ceiling reinforcements of the bunker took a little over three months into December, but Jean was proud of the facility when completed. It had enough space to easily sleep twelve in comfort and storage for a week's worth of food.

The bunker had ventilation, water facilities, a common gathering area, underground drainage to expel waste, as well as two hidden entrances. Though it wasn't the most comfortable of accommodations, it was adequate for an emergency.

They were still in Jérémie towards the end of March when General Pétion arrived at Jean's warehouse at the docks where they stored coffee awaiting shipment. Jean had not seen Pétion in about four years since Junior's birthday party at the hotel's casino at

Cap-Français but recognized him immediately as he entered the offices.

"Captain Bayard, it is me, Alexandre Pétion, a friend of your son Junior. I stayed at your house a few years back. Do you remember?" Pétion opened in dialog.

"Of course, Alexandre. Come. May I offer you some coffee? Water? Juice?"

"Thank you, Captain Bayard, but I haven't much time. Junior had always told me that you were from here and I came hoping to find you or Junior," Pétion said.

"Junior is in Cap-Français at the moment, but how can I assist you Alexandre?" asked Jean as he noticed the tattered and bloody uniform and Alexandre's apparent weariness.

"Jacmel has fallen. It was my command. There is an army headed this way. Jean-Jacques Dessalines to be precise. He is a butcher and aims to destroy everything in his path. He is looking for me, or I mean us. I have about thirty men with me camped at the city's edge."

"I see, but I am not certain of what use I can be?" asked Jean.

"We need to escape, and I was hoping we could purchase passage on one of your ships. But I would need to provide you with a government promissory note. I must warn you that it is probably worthless as Rigaud and his administration have been defeated. It will certainly not be honored by Toussaint's government," Pétion said in rapid speech.

"No need Alexandre. Get your men here as soon as you can. The ship *Solange* you see docked taking on cargo is leaving at first light for Port-Républicain. You can sail on her" Jean replied,"

"We cannot go to Port-Républicain. That is occupied by Toussaint's army. I was hoping you had a ship headed for Les Cayes?"

"It is currently prohibited by Toussaint's government to travel there. The waters are patrolled by American warships allied to Toussaint," Jean responded. "However, I can divert the ship to Port

Salut, several kilometers west of Les Cayes. It is a day's walk from there."

Pétion closed his eyes momentarily and sighed as if a mountain had been removed from his shoulders. "This means everything to me, Captain Bayard. I have lost many of my men and I seek to save the remaining officers with me to one day see their families. I will not forget you for this" Pétion said. "I will leave our remaining horses for you to sell as compensation."

"Stay and have something to eat. You look terrible," replied Jean.

Jean sent the office boy to the local restaurant with a lunch order for Pétion of chicken and rice to eat right away and an order for thirty-one plates of food, whatever they had on hand, to be delivered at six that evening, five hours from now, for Pétion's men.

Within minutes, Pétion devoured his food like a savage, mounted his horse, and galloped to get his men. They all arrived back about three hours later. The soldiers looked like scarecrows that were half alive. They were grateful for their meals but even after eating, appeared demoralized and defeated.

They departed the next morning on the Ship *Solange* and Jean took possession of a dozen horses that were barely alive with skeletons visible under their skin. He gave them to the local livery stable knowing that nurturing them back to health would probably equal their marketable value.

Three days later, horsemen from the neighboring town of Roseaux, about 20 kilometers east, entered Jérémie in a fast sprint warning everyone that Dessalines's army was on the march to Jérémie from Roseaux after burning half of the town and killing several residents who refused to denounce their support for the Rigaudin cause.

Everyone in town scattered to the outskirts as Jean hurried to warn the Jasmine family of the encroaching army and invite them to the plantation for safety. The hardware store had already been emptied of merchandise as Gustav had the remaining inventory crated and shipped on the ship *Solange* a few days ago with Pétion's men. Jean's warehouse only had a few bags of coffee which he realized would be seized by the approaching army anyway, no big loss.

It took Dessalines two days to enter Jérémie and interrogate the citizens. If they denounced Rigaud, they were spared. If they did not, they were executed, and their belongings confiscated. The army went from plantation to plantation with the same mission

When forty soldiers entered the Bayard plantation, they could see workers in the fields tending to the crops. Their commander had his men assemble them all in the front of the house. "I am seeking the criminal named Alexandre Pétion and anyone in his association. Has anyone seen this man or any of his soldiers around here? barked the commander."

The laborers looked at each other and shook their heads. Just then, Jean came out of the house and approached the commander who was on horseback surrounded by other soldiers on horses as well.

"Welcome to our property Commander. How may I be of assistance?"

Visibly upset, the commander turned and looked directly at Jean, dismounted from his horse, and walked towards him to intercept Jean at the sanded clearing in front of the house. "Who are you?" he barked.

"My name is Jean-Baptiste Hippolyte Bayard, Captain of the Chasseurs Voluntaires de St. Domingue, retired. And you are sir?"

"My name is Jean-Jacques Dessalines, General and Supreme Commander of the Southern Colonial Army. Where is the rest of the family of this house?"

"They are not here General. They left town a few days ago" replied Jean.

"Are you the Bayard with the ships?" asked Dessalines.

"Yes, I am General"

"Did you provide safe passage to that scum and rebel Alexandre Pétion and his men? Think wisely before you answer that question as it may be your last if it is not the complete truth" Dessalines said.

"I did not provide, General. I sold passage to the man and several men with him. I was paid as any other passenger would pay me. That is my business, to provide transportation of people and cargo" Jean said.

Dessalines's forehead began to contort in a wicked frown and his lower lip tightened until his teeth could be seen clenched behind it. Suddenly and without warning he raised his arm and swiftly threw a punch which struck Jean on the right side of his face with a massive blow prosecuted from the huge fist.

Jean was caught off guard and knocked back in shock. As he was steadying himself, another crushing blow hit Jean on the left side of his face. Jean's first instinct was to lash back out and fight, but he knew he would be killed instantly. He had the comfort of knowing that the families were in the newly constructed bunker a kilometer away and well-hidden, so as not to be found.

"You have robbed me of the satisfaction of killing Pétion and his men myself, you piece of shit," as he dealt another crushing facial blow to Jean's forehead. Then suddenly, as if an animal was unleashed, Dessalines tightened both arms as his hands formed a fist. He looked up at the sky and let out one huge primal yell of frustration which had been building inside of him during this yearlong military campaign.

Now he realized it was all ending and he had lost his prey and this man before him was the reason for it. Jean now became the target of his unleashed anger and his rage.

Jean's body received blow after blow after blow until he could no longer stand and fell to the ground. He then endured the pain of Dessalines' boots kicking him everywhere as he went into a fetal position to try and stay alive through the savage beating which seemed like an eternity.

The plantation workers watched horrified, all crying with nothing they could do as they watched the savageness that their beloved Jean was enduring from Dessalines. Finally, one of Dessalines' officers went to his side, as he continued to kick the now still body of Jean, and said *"Jeneral. Mwen kwè nonm sa a mouri"* General. "I believe this man is dead."

Dessalines suddenly stopped and as if in a trance, looked at the soldier addressing him with such intensity and for what seemed like an eternity, which forced the soldier to back away. Dessalines then looked down at Jean's bloody and battered body, realizing he may have gone too far. After all, he had heard reports that this man was almost like family to General Louverture's new pet commander, that Nèg Kay, Henry Christophe, and had vowed to himself not to kill him because of it.

Jean was semi-conscious but dared not move, barely able to breathe as his air passages were filled with blood and mucus. He was also bleeding from his mouth, but remarkably, still alive.

Suddenly, like a switch, Dessalines's face turned to an ugly hatred as he looked at the crowd and spoke; "Listen to me all of you. I am your new nightmare. Anyone who aids the enemy will suffer a fate far worse than this man has suffered here today."

Jean could hear Dessalines speaking in the distance but could not comprehend the words as he was paralyzed and could not move. He then felt warm liquid being poured on him in a stream until he realized in disgust of what it was. He could smell the stench of thick dark yellow dehydrated urine coming out of Dessaline's body and onto him. Yes, he thought, Dessalines was now urinating on him.

It was the ultimate humiliation. Jean had sunken to the lowest level of existence in his entire life as the acidic urine stung the open bloody wounds on his face and neck. But that was nowhere near to the pain it was prosecuting to his heart, his pride, and his will to live. It was the last thing he remembered as his desire to remain conscience left him and his instinct to give in had overcome him. His eyes went dark and he passed out into unconsciousness.

Six

THE UNIFICATION
OF SAINT-DOMINGUE

Jérémie
March 1800

The crowd was in shock with women whaling and men embarrassingly helpless to assist. Dessalines put his huge penis back into his trousers after shaking the last bit of urine over Jean for the show's finale and a display of his power for the benefit of the crowd. He mounted his horse and led the soldiers down the path in full gallop, creating a dust cloud, to exit the plantation.

The crowd rushed to Jean's body, not knowing if they should move him due to broken bones, but decided it was the best course of action. They carried him into the house and laid him on the couch.

Just then, Marie stormed into the house and saw Jean's bloody face, and tears instantly ran down her face. "Fetch water, bandages, towels, and the medicine bag NOW!" she yelled to the staff as she attempted to compose herself and gain control while slowly dying inside at the sight of her bloody husband before her.

Julien and René ran into the room and yelled "They're gone" and stopped dead in their tracks when they saw the sight of their lifeless brother, bloody on the couch. "Is he alive, Marie?" asked Julian.

"He's still breathing and he has a pulse," Marie responded.

"I'll go get the doctor in town. René, you go take care of the elders. Marie: you got this?" Julian quickly asked.

"Yes, Go. Bring the doctor back as soon as you can" Marie said as both men raced outside to pursue their separate missions.

Marie had four men carry Jean as gently as they could to the bedroom and opened up all of the windows to get air circulating in the room. She dismissed the men and began removing Jean's bloody, smelly clothes, and throwing them out the window.

Women came in with a bucket of water, bandages, and the medicine bag. Marie began to gently bathe Jean in a mixture of distilled alcohol and water from head to toe to expose his wounds and disinfect them. She was worried as she could sense his shallow breathing as he remained unconscious, even when she tried to open his eyes.

Their parents had come to see his condition, but it was almost too much for them to bear. They decided that all they could do was pray and await a miracle, as did the entire staff of plantation workers.

Yanick, Julien's wife, proved a brilliantly capable manager who kept the household in order and masterfully directed the staff to continue their assignments so there was food always available for them all.

Julian arrived with the physician near nightfall, and he spent over an hour assessing Jean's wounds until he was finally able to address the family. "Jean has a broken left arm, broken right wrist, and a broken nose. He is suffering from multiple contusions, lacerations, cracked ribs and I suspect internal bleeding of some sort. He has a head concussion and every muscle in his body is experiencing trauma.

"What are his chances of survival, Doctor? Julien asked"

"It is too early to tell at this time. He is a strong fifty-year-old man, so only his will to live can determine what the future will bring. You must keep him hydrated and begin to feed him liquids with protein as soon as he is able. No hard foods right now. Everything must be soft as we know not what has happened inside of him."

"Yes, doctor. What about medications?" Marie asked.

"Crush two aspirins into the water every four hours and mix with grenadine juice in the morning, carrot juice at noon, and melon juice at night. Hydrate him periodically with *Tisanne*, water soaked in lettuce leaves. Keep the wounds clean. Bathe him every day in the alcohol and water as you have done and keep those people praying."

"Yes, doctor," replied Marie.

"I will spend the night here with you in the room and we shall see how he is in the morning. Now, I am hungry. What's there to eat around here?" the doctor said as he gave a brief smile to lighten the moment for Marie.

Jean regained consciousness for brief moments at a time, enough to feed him soup filled with protein. For the next two weeks, Marie did everything she could to nurse Jean back to health. It wasn't until a month later, in mid-April, was Jean able to finally open his battered eyes for moments at a time,

By May he was able to sit up in bed. June had him walk in the room with help, and by July he was able to descend the steps and sit on the porch.

But, all during this time, he never uttered a word and just followed orders without resistance. His eyes remained blank without life, and it was as if his soul had somehow departed his body. Physically though, he seemed to be healing of his injuries.

Marie called in numerous physicians to examine Jean, but all concluded that his physical state was healthy, but the beatings to his head may have damaged the interior parts of his brain.

Henry Christophe contacted Cécile Fatiman, the powerful mambo voodoo priestess and leader of the maroons to the north, who he had seen work wonders for Jean-Baptiste Chavannes back in 1789. During Chavannes' execution, she had conjured up a potion that freed him from experiencing pain and heightened his courage during his torturous dismemberment that helped launch the slave revolts of the early nineties.

She arrived in Jérémie on a late Thursday morning. The servants brought coffee, and an assortment of flaky pates of meat, salted fish, and guava. Cecile spent over an hour with Marie, who recounted the events from the day of Dessalines' attack on Jean, and the long convalescence during the past several months.

Cecile then met alone with Jean, asking varied questions that he didn't utter a single response to for nearly an hour.

Cecile returned to Marie who awaited him on the veranda of the plantation home and asked, "You're saying that in all this time he has not spoken even one word to you?"

"Not a word," Marie said softly.

"What about to anyone else; his father, mother, siblings, workers?"

"Not a word to anyone."

"What was your relationship with him like before the attack?"

"We were partners, in all aspects; parents to our son, business partners, everything. He is my husband. We were, no, we are in love!" Marie responded with moisture in her eyes.

"Were you lovers?" asked Cecile, as she looked directly into Marie's eyes.

"Very much so," Marie immediately responded.

"Passionate lovers?"

"Yes, very much so."

"And the physicians have confirmed that nothing is wrong with him physically?" asked Cecile.

"As far as they can see, no. They believe something is wrong with his brain. Look, I know I am grasping at straws, but I want, I need my husband back. I don't know if I can go on without him," Marie said, finally shedding the tears she had bottled up for so long.

Marie looked over at Jean who was sitting in a rocking chair underneath the huge mahogany tree in the garden. It pained her that he seemed unable to recognize her in any way. How could that be? "Isn't there a potion, a spell, a voodoo ceremony that you can do to help him?" pleaded Marie to Cecile, out of all options.

"Let us walk," asked Cecile.

The two women walked towards Jean. The breeze was warm and the sun shone bright. It was evident that rain would arrive later in the day, as it always did during the summer, but other than that the weather was lovely.

When they arrived near Jean, Cecile turned to Marie. "Stop here and call out to him."

"Jean," Marie called. "Jean-Baptiste," she called again. No reaction from Jean was evident.

"Louder," said Cecile.

"Jean, Jean, Jean Baptiste!" Marie yelled.

It was as if Jean was not there. He neither looked over nor in any way registered their proximity.

Cecile looked towards the paddock beyond where a mare and a stallion were trotting around in circles. "Let us walk," She told Marie again.

"There is nothing I can do for him spiritually," stated Cecile. "He is not possessed by a demon, which exorcising them is my specialty. There is not a potion I can concoct or a leaf or herb that I can boil to cure his condition."

Marie looked at her, disappointed and desperately wanting an answer but not receiving one. They arrived at the paddock and stood in silence for a moment until Cecile asked; "What are the horses doing, trotting around like that?"

"Horses are seasonal breeders," answered Marie. They engage in their mating activities during the longer days of the year so that their foals, born a little less than a year from now, can take advantage of the season's milder temperatures and lush forages."

"How does this happen?" asked Cecile. "How do they know it is time?"

That mare is secreting estrogen that brings her in heat. It makes the stallion's blood boil, causing an increase in testosterone

that initiates sperm production and stimulates his libido… his sex drive," Marie expertly answered.

"And what is the mare doing now?" asked Cecile, watching the strange behavior of the horses in the paddock.

She is assuming the classic breeding posture in front of the stallion. Watch, she may raise her tail, squat, urinate, and believe it or not, wink her vulva at the stallion."

Cecile opened her mouth with a smile and cupped her mouth as both women giggled like shy school girls. "Tell me more," ordered Cecile.

"See there? The process of courtship begins with rituals of smelling, nuzzling, nipping, and nickering that mares and stallions engage in before breeding," schooled Marie.

"Look at the stallion now. He is sniffing the mare's urine to gauge her readiness to breed. The scent will tell him if she is ready for him. He is now uncontrollable and totally in the grip of Mother Nature.

"He is under her spell?" ventured Cecile.

"Essentially, yes. He cannot resist her secretions as they prepare her to receive him into her for breeding when he comes to full erection." Marie expertly stated.

"Look!" yelled Cecile. He is mounting her!"

"That he is," answered Marie.

"Will they do this often," asked Cecile.

"Two to three times, depending on the stamina of the stallion."

"So, all this is initiated by the power of the woman, I mean the mare?" stated Cecile.

"Absolutely. Without her to stimulate him, they would just be eating hay," Marie laughed.

"Then you have come to your answer, Marie."

"What answer?" asked a confused Marie.

"Tell me, has Jean been a winner or loser in life?" asked Cecile.

"He only lost one battle in his life of military and business. That was back in 1779 at the Battle of Savannah against the British," answered Marie.

"Of what Henry told me, the battle was lost, but he was victorious. He saved the Compte d'Estaing and many soldiers that day when he and Henry sounded the warning, correct?"

"Yes, you can say that," answered Marie.

"Then he has never really lost a battle in his life, has he?" asked Cecile.

"I suppose not," answered Marie.

"But Dessalines beat him so severely, humiliated him so publicly. Shamed him incredibly. He has gone into a shell and has locked all the doors and will not come out. He can't face you. He is ashamed and knows not how to get home. To him, he has lost everything. and unaccustomed to loss, there is no coming back from that," Cecile reasoned.

"So what do I do now? Physicians have given up. You have said there is nothing you can do. What am I to do now?"

"It is as simple as that mare driving that stallion to primitive, unthinking, uncontrollable, natural behavior. Mate with him!"

How am I to possibly do that when he is in the state he is in? He doesn't talk to me or even recognize who I am."

"Deep in his mind, you are still there. Your scent. Your touch. Your essence. Your womanhood. Your body. You must use every piece of woman within you to drive him to unconsciously perform like that stallion over there. Only you can cure him now. You are a woman!" Cecile commanded. "Act like one as it is his and your last hope," concluded Cecile.

Within a week, Marie had arranged a week's lodging at the same cottage they had honeymooned in over 25 years prior at Anse D'asure, about 6 kilometers west of Jérémie.

With her she brought every memory she could; Madame Karine's oils that he once loved to massage her with before lovemaking, special outfits, perfumes, and scents that would tantalize him in happier times.

For the first few days, she worked on Jean with little to show for it. He was uninterested in her as she continued to increase the intensity of her methods.

At first, she tried bathing with him, increasing her scents, touching him, rubbing her breasts on his body and face, and increasing her body contact and proximity to him. She would take his hands and bring them to her lips, to her breasts, to her vagina. Nothing seemed to be working.

Then, on the third day while doing so he sprang an erection during the foreplay. With a suddenness that both surprised and shocked her, he turned Marie over and mounted her like an animal, lunging his penis deep inside of her as she grabbed hold of the sheets to hold herself steady. In and out did his penis enter her with deep intensity and the ferociousness of an animal in heat, much like the stallion whose mare had driven him to lose control in the paddock, she felt herself thinking.

It scared her immensely as she did not recognize this man, this animal, who was dominating her with strength and fury that was not like Jean at all. But she allowed this stranger to continue onward; to conquer her, dominate her, control her, and take all of her as she felt he was desperately fighting his way through the ordeal and she had to help him do it, whatever it took. He then exploded into a vicious, primal orgasm that shook him to the point that she thought the bed would collapse or he would rip her insides out as she screamed and panted in a combination of pain and ecstasy. She felt his hot stream of sperm explode deep inside of her, not sure if it was fear, desire, or sheer desperation that climaxed her into a powerful orgasm herself as they both rocked to the violent rhythm. Then suddenly he collapsed and rolled over on the bed panting for breath.

She was still on her knees with her head buried against the sheets from exhaustion, her buttocks pointed to the air, dripping his secretion from her vagina, unable to move and her muscles aching from the aggressive sex she had just been subjected to. She was drenched with sweat and their combined bodily fluid when she finally collapsed as well on her side, looking away from Jean, not daring to face him and scared for what the next few moments would bring. She could not take another sexual episode like that again.

Then he finally spoke, as if woken up from a dream, and said; "Marie? Marie, is that you?"

At first, she thought she was dreaming. It was Jean's voice, but she lay there unbelieving, not knowing if this was a dream or her sheer fear of the episode that had just happened and fearful that he would attempt it again. Frozen with her back to him, she tried to move but all her will would not allow it.

Suddenly, she shivered as she felt his hand gently touch and caress her shoulder. It was warm and loving. "Marie, where are we?" asked his voice. "I have awakened but know not where we are."

She turned around towards him. She was not sure if he knew what he had just done. The aggressive and violent sex he had just forced upon her. The stranger was gone, and Jean had fought and escaped from the dark side through a bridge of primal passion, an animal passion, that brought him back to her.

"It is me, Jean. It is me," she whispered as she burst into tears of pain and joy.

He looked deep into her eyes and she into his. "Why do you cry, my love?" he asked in a soft, loving voice.

She smiled and wiped her tears as they lay there looking at each other for what seemed an eternity until he sat up and said, totally composed as the normal and joking Jean, "I'm hungry! What's there to eat?"

Marie laughed and stood up as he watched her beautiful naked body stroll to the chair and retrieve a robe. Aware of his caressing eyes, before putting the robe around her, she purposefully turned to expose the fullness of her body for him to take in and enjoy, knowing she was now in command of her man and could control his intimacy as she pleased. The familiarity of her husband had returned, this man she well knew and understood. She then wrapped the robe around her, picked up a brush from the nightstand, cocked her head back, and began to brush her hair while her face looked at the ceiling. Her robe would occasionally open, exposing her breasts to him in this act of female power over the male species.

"Stay," she said as she opened the door and picked up a bottle of wine that was cooling in a wooden bucket filled with water, and came back in. She retrieved two glasses from the nightstand and poured the wine. She handed him a glass, went to the dresser, and brought back a tray of fresh bread and cheese.

Jean looked at her with loving eyes, still unaware of why he was so lucky to have a woman like this. "Always prepared. That's my girl," Jean said as Marie remained in disbelief of what had just happened – what was currently happening. Was this a dream she thought? Or is this real?

"Do you remember anything, Jean? Anything at all?" she asked.

"Not really. Everything is sort of a blur. Sort of fuzzy. I only remember being sick for a while, I think. Was I sick? Did I have something serious like *fièvre jaune* - yellow fever?

Marie smiled and said, "There will be time for that, but now it is time to eat, Jean. You need your strength for the next few days. Don't you remember, it's our second honeymoon!"

"Now I remember. This is the same cottage we stayed at after our wedding! I just don't remember the trip getting here this time."

Marie laughed, shook her head, and looked at her man with gratefulness. They finished the bottle of wine with some delicious bread and cheese. "I don't remember anything tasting so good," said Jean. "I feel like I haven't eaten in weeks".

They locked their eyes as they lounged on the bed and simultaneously approached each other for a gentle kiss. As her tongue sought his, their emotions heightened. His penis bulged and her nipples hardened as the gentle kiss turned to one of passion. He took her nipple in his mouth as she moaned with pleasure and threw her arms back in total submission, spreading her legs to allow him entry into her.

At first, it somewhat stung to have him inside of her, but her body fluids began to flow unrestricted as he made love to her; beautiful, gentle, warm love until they once again climaxed as husband and wife, father and mother, reunited from an eternity of hell.

Afterward, they decided to go for a swim in the warm ocean. Marie took his extended hand and followed him outside. She looked up to the sky; "Thank you, my Lord. Thank you, Cecile" as they quickly went to the shore and into the surf.

During the next few days they played in the warm, clear azure water, ate great food, lounged around, and made constant love. They engaged in deep conversation during which time she told him everything that had happened to him. He was in disbelief at first, until small bits and pieces would surface over time.

She refrained from telling him about his sexual aggression towards her during his transitional escape from the dark side. That she would forever keep secret, for if he knew what he had done and how he had acted towards her, he wouldn't forgive himself.

He absorbed it all, much to his amazement, and was forever grateful to her for taking care of him during this darkest of times. He had returned to his life with her and his family.

After the week had come to an end, they went back to the Bayard plantation and were, of course, in celebrity status with the family and workers until they departed for Cap-Français in mid-August to resume their normal life.

Dessalines had continued his rampage through the Southern Peninsula with brutality towards any that failed to denounce the Rigaudin cause. So brutal was he that Toussaint reprimanded him by saying *"Mwen pa t 'vle sa a! Mwen te di nou taye pye bwa a, pa derasinen l"* I did not want this! I told you to prune the tree, not to uproot it!"

In June, a decree reached Saint-Domingue from First Consul, Napoleon Bonaparte, that General Rigaud's mandate to oversee an autonomous Southern Peninsula was null and void and confirmed that Toussaint Louverture was the supreme commander of the armed forces and Governor-General of the French colony.

This had the effect of crushing the final remnants of the Rigaudin rebellion. By July, Toussaint's army had converged with Dessalines' at Rigaud's stronghold of Les Cayes.

Seeing their cause lost, Rigaud, Pétion, Boyer, and other mulatto officers sailed on a French merchant vessel into exile in France. The remainder of Rigaud's army was allowed to claim clemency and join with Toussaint or be put to death. Most all decided to join the unified French Colonial Army of Saint Domingue with only the most ardent rebels refusing and being executed for their convictions. The civil war ended in July 1800.

By August, Toussaint was now the absolute ruler of Saint Domingue. He had crushed a civil war, and eliminated virtually all French bureaucratic rule, apart from Phillippe Roume and Julian Raimond. He had conquered the Spanish and British armies, signed a trade agreement with the United States, and consolidated his power over all factions of the colonial army.

But a situation which he found highly intolerable was that of Spanish Santo Domingo on the eastern side of Hispaniola. Toussaint felt there was a huge opportunity to unify the territory as one Hispaniola, and this was even being encouraged by his American trading partners.

The territory was larger than the French side and extremely fertile. If he could unify the island, the economic potential would be vast. But he needed to move rapidly before some new French treaty or proclamation prohibited him from doing so.

He was justified in his plans as the Spanish government had ceded the territory to France in 1795 by the *Traité de Bâle Suisse* - Treaty of Basel, Switzerland. Nonetheless, Spain had never turned the colonial administration over to the French government until they signaled that they would be ready to administer and protect their former colony and its citizens

France never pressed the issue because Spain's presence in Santo Domingo was in France's best interest for several reasons, the primary being not to disrupt their relations with their European trading partner and the other to keep an eye on Toussaint, in case he decided to pursue independence.

However, Toussaint's mind was made up. He was going to make the move on Santo Domingo and would seek official authority from French commissioner, Phillippe Roume.

Phillippe Roume was in his office at Government House when Ricardo Desbardes and Reginald Luterne were escorted into the room by his secretary. The French pair had arrived from Philadelphia over a year ago on the same ship that had landed the American Trade Envoy, Dr. Edward Stevens, and Toussaint's trade envoy, Joseph Bunel.

Desbardes was a French spy sent by Philippe de Létombe, the powerful French consul to the United States, to gather information on behalf of the French government and wealthy French landowners as to the intended direction of the Louverture administration. France was still too weak to administer the colony as it was engaged in many skirmishes with European powers, especially their war with the British and undeclared Quasi-War with the United States. While in Saint Domingue, Desbardes had been meeting periodically with Roume about the adventures of Toussaint Louverture.

However, the movement of Desbardes, unbeknown to him, was being carefully watched by a counterspy hired by Toussaint's trade envoy, Joseph Bunel. Bunel had spotted Desbardes lurking in the shadows and spying on him while in Philadelphia. So, Bunel decided to pay back the favor in his hometown.

Bunel's spy had reported that though Desbardes had periodic meetings with Roume, he knew not for what reason and had no evidence that Roume was involved in any intrigue or treacherous activity as a result.

Desbardes walked over to Roume's desk and extended his hand. "Phillippe, I want to introduce you to Reginald Luterne. Mr. Luterne is an excellent secretary with very high credentials and references. He speaks and corresponds in English, Spanish and of course his native language of French,"

"It is my pleasure, Mr. Luterne," greeted Roume. What brings you gentlemen to Government House?" he asked as his secretary arrived with a coffee set,placing cups before them and began to pour.

"It is my understanding that the Governor General needs secretarial assistance," Desbardes said. "I am here to offer Mr. Luterne, who so happens to be in the colony, and can extend his excellent services."

"Thank you, Ricardo. But I would recommend you to see the Governor General's staff directly, as I am not involved in the daily administration of his affairs."

"I would prefer if an introduction would come from you, Phillippe. Routing through the Governor General's staff would be a disservice to him as jealous incompetent staff members may not welcome the expertise of a man like Mr. Luterne."

Roume eyed Desbardes with suspicion, but the request was benign and void of any danger. What could it hurt? "Very well, Ricardo, I have a meeting planned with the Governor General tomorrow. I will hand him Mr. Luterne's dossier to him then."

"Thank you, Commissioner," stated Luterne. "I much desire to remain in the colony and if I may say, this employment opportunity would please me immensely."

Roume looked at Luterne. He appeared to be a straight-up individual who maybe Toussaint could use. After all, Toussaint had lost three very valuable secretaries in an ambush last year when Rigaud had tried to assassinate him. He had been pressed to find decent tri-lingual replacements which he needed for Spanish correspondence with Santo Domingo.

Toussaint's economic strategy for Saint Domingue mirrored the previous one of the plantation economies, large industrial plantations instead of small farms for agricultural sustenance. Toussaint knew that this would create huge exports for the colony to enable it to rebuild after years of wars from both external enemies and those from within, as well as provide funding for territorial defenses.

Slavery had been abolished officially in 1794, but he ordered the army to continue to strictly reinforce the adherence to the cultivation work codes – 11-hour days, six days per week with government-regulated compensation. This was far better than slavery's 12-hour, 7-day workweek, but to the workers, it was nearly as bad. Additionally, they were forced to work at the plantations they were once enslaved under unless the plantation owner would not want them back.

But, with this system, agricultural production was on the rebound and exports continued to rise month-by-month. It was now time to incorporate these systems and strategies in the eastern portion of Hispaniola and free the serves under Spanish rule.

As a savvy politician, Toussaint well knew that approval, or at least the appearance of it, from Phillippe Roume as the French commissioner would be instrumental in his plan. After all, Roume was a French administrator in name only, so his stamp of approval was not required but very much desired to implement the plan.

Toussaint did not wait for an official introduction from the commissioner's secretary but strode down the corridor of Government House which he had long considered 'his' building. He was simply providing office space to the commissioner.

"Ahhh, Commissioner. It is always a pleasure to be in your company," Toussaint stated as he entered the huge office.

Roume stood and walked halfway to the open doorway with his hand extended, "Governor General, welcome back to Cap-Français, and I offer my congratulations on your campaign to defeat the rebel Rigaudins."

"Thank you, Commissioner. Can you report on our fine city here and its activities?" Although Toussaint needed no such reports as his hand-picked General, Henry Christophe, handled all things in his absence.

"All appears peaceful and in good order. I must say that trade revenues and government taxes are rising daily with the trade agreements enacted with the Americans."

"I am very pleased with how things have turned out," Toussaint said as a servant arrived with a tray containing a pitcher of water, glasses, and a set of coffee, cups, and saucers. He began to pour both water and coffee.

"It is now time to unify our colony, Commissioner," Toussaint said, referring to Spanish Santo Domingo.

"I would counsel caution on that idea," Roume answered.

"But why, Phillippe?" asked Toussaint, reverting to the commissioner's first name. "It would be in the best interests of our treasury and also our Spanish friends to unify the colony."

"Paris would not be in favor. For reasons beyond my understanding, they desire that Spain still govern the eastern portion of Hispaniola," Roume said, knowing that one of the major goals was to prevent Toussaint from consolidating more power.

"Nonsense. The western territory is French territory for the past 5-years. Further, they violate French law."

"And, what law would that be, Toussaint?" said Roume, also using the first name.

"Slavery is contrary to French law. Egalite, Phillippe! Our French citizens are in bondage contrary to French law and our principles of the revolution. How is it that you can tolerate that and still stand for upholding French laws? Come on, Phillippe. Let us do the right thing!"

"Let us seek counsel from Paris first, Toussaint. It is dangerous for us to venture alone without approval."

"That will take months, if not years of politicians flapping their jaws and debating the future of our island. This land is ours to govern, albeit forever loyal to our mother country. Let us be bold and they will respect us for it, especially when their treasury has much to gain," reasoned Toussaint.

"Toussaint, I dare not join you in this folly without authorization."

"Then, write a letter of introduction to the Spanish Captain-General, Don Joaquin Garcia y Moreno in Santo Domingo, stating our desire to jointly administer the colony and that I will assume the defenses of the eastern portion as his troop strength is insufficient to maintain such a large swath of land. Should he agree, there is no such need for Parisian approval."

"Speaking of Spanish letter writing, have you found a tri-lingual secretary yet?" asked Roume.

"Finding a secretary with those skills is equivalent to finding rare gems in the sugar fields," replied Toussaint. "No, not yet."

"Well, I may have your answer. A Frenchman is looking for employment. A Mr. Luterne. I met him the other day, but I have no openings on my staff. I can have him compose this letter to Captain Moreno and if you approve of his quality of work, you may want to speak with him."

"I approve. Have him write the letter and in two days hence, I will review it and if it is indeed genuine and good, I will consider employing this gentleman."

Two days later, Toussaint approved the letter and hired Reginald Luterne to his staff as corresponding secretary. There was a multitude of backlog in correspondence and reading which Luterne immediately got to work on, however reporting all items of interest to Ricardo Desbardes, essentially being a chief informant to the French clandestine intelligence apparatus.

Without hesitation, the Spanish Captain Moreno dismissed the request. After all, he was of the Spanish nobility and refused to subordinate himself to the orders of a black French general of Saint Domingue. In a letter to Roume, he wrote, 'The French colonial government has no rights towards the administration of the former Spanish western territories of Hispaniola. Therefore, without any official authorization from the Spanish government, your request is hereby denied.

Roume decided to rescind his previous order for Toussaint to administer the former Spanish colony. This gave Toussaint a pretext to charge Roume with disloyalty to France - after all, France owned Santo Domingo by treaty. Toussaint had General Moyiz arrest Roume, and he was held prisoner for nearly a year, albeit in the relative comfort of house arrest.

Toussaint proceeded to amass his troops for the invasion of Santo Domingo. He sent messengers to the villages with assurances that he wanted no confrontation, but the colony violated French law by refusing to disband slavery.

The average Spanish Dominguen was favorable towards Toussaint as they had seen the stabilization of the French territory, the resumption of lucrative trade, and a plantation economy void of forced enslavement. Even the property owners voiced little objection as they desired increased markets for their crops, especially with the Americans.

Toussaint marched towards the capital and encountered only tentative resistance from the Spanish militia. He entered the capital, Santo Domingo City on January 26, 1801, amongst the cheers of its inhabitants as a hero. He immediately emancipated all slaves as his first official act.

Toussaint was well remembered. At the height of his career with the Spanish Auxiliaries, he had held the title of Brigadier General of the Spanish Colonial Army, had received the War Cross from the King, and had brought them much pride from his expeditions. He was remembered as switching to the side of the French because the Spanish refused to abolish slavery – Toussaint, it was proclaimed, was a man of principle.

The free businesspeople of all colors welcomed that the Spanish East would be included in his trade agreements with the British and the Americans. His administrative, diplomatic, and authoritarian concepts to keep law and order were well known and they looked forward to a new era of peace and prosperity.

The landowners tolerated him as they certainly had no choice. The Spanish government had abandoned the colony by treaty. Although they were upset at the abolishment of slavery, they could look next door to a working example of the new freed-cultivating system. If it could work in the western part of the island, it could work in the east as well.

Toussaint Louverture quickly consolidated his power and emerged as the governor-general of a unified Saint Domingue. In March 1801, Toussaint appointed a constitutional assembly to draft a new constitution for the entire colony of Saint-Domingue.

He appointed the mayor of Port-Républicain, Bernard Borgella, as President, and the Chairmanship to his confidant, Julien Raimond. Other members included Roxas, Munos, and Mancebo from the Spanish side of the island, and Lacour, Viart, and Nogérée who were white French Creoles.

Though the assembly was made up of diversified and highly qualified individuals, none were black, except for Toussaint who would be the person to reject or approve the new document.

The constitution they produced was a pure distillation of Toussaint's thought pattern. Following up on Toussaint's opposition to voodoo, Catholicism was made the official religion, the freed slaves were tied to their workplaces, and Toussaint was named ruler for life.

Curiously, this last element had been recommended to Toussaint by the most conservative of American revolutionary figures, Alexander Hamilton. The Americans had very much endeared themselves to Toussaint who was favorable to the United States and presented the best hope for stability in the colony.

Other notable sections of the constitution included that Saint Domingue was a single colony of the French Empire, regardless of skin color, everyone had equal rights, slavery would never exist, the guarantee of equal opportunity and treatment under the law for all races, and when necessary, the importation of additional cultivators to bolster the workforce would be allowed.

It was a well-written constitution with 77 articles encompassing governance, legislation, cultivation, commerce, property rights, tribunals, municipal administration, armed forces, and even morals, as well as other general dispositions that were well laid out in the document.

The Assembly charged Toussaint with seeking French approval but did not prohibit him from promulgating the laws immediately.

Toussaint, without French authorization, promulgated the Constitution on July 7th, 1801, officially establishing his authority over the entire island of Hispaniola.

Seven

THE UPRISING
AGAINST TOUSSAINT

Cap-Français
June 1801

Silas Talbot, Captain of the *USS Constitution* and Commodore of the U.S. Saint Domingue Naval Station was on the ship's deck, awaiting the arrival of their largest 36' longboat tender in transport of a very special guest.

He ordered the mighty 24-pound cannons to bellow a 16-gun salute in honor of General Moyse Louverture, a top general in Toussaint Louvertures army. In writing his invitation, no one could agree on the spelling of his first name. Diplomatic correspondence had always read Moyse or Moise, the French wrote Moïse with the dots, and the locals used the Creole version of Moyiz. Can't these people keep it simple, he thought?

Anyway, he is the commander of the northern region and had arrived for a meeting on the ship. General Moyiz wore a regal dress uniform complete with epaulets and numerous medals. His physique was firm, strong, well-groomed, and he wore a black patch over the right eye. He was a dashing soldier, fond of women as they were of him, the most popular soldier in the army, and beloved, especially by the black population of the North for his ardent championship of them against white abuses and excesses. He stood high in Toussaint's favor as one of his most trusted, capable, and valuable commanders. He was also Toussaint's adopted nephew.

The two men met in the commodore's spacious quarters. They focused on an agenda that included recapping the end of the civil war, pacification of the southern peninsula, and congratulating Moyiz on his most brilliant campaign to prepare for the successful arrival of Toussaint Louverture to the Spanish side of Hispaniola.

They also discussed the current output of the northern plantations, and it was evident that Moyiz didn't fully endorse his uncle Toussaint's vision of an industrial plantation economy as the only path forward to a prosperous Saint Domingue. He much preferred breaking up large, abandoned plantations in favor of smaller family farms for those who did not desire to work on large plantations. Talbot decided to steer clear of providing his own opinion on the subject.

Towards the end of the meeting, Captain Talbot formerly introduced General Moyiz to marine commander Daniel Carmack and members of the *Constitution's* officer corps. Upon exchanging pleasantries, Moyiz invited Talbot and the group to his home for dinner that evening. He told them he would arrange transportation to pick them up at 4 p.m. at the dock.

When Talbot and the officers arrived on shore, two carriages were awaiting; one 4-seater and the other a large 6-seat carriage. The escorts directed Talbot into the smaller carriage and the officers into the larger one, both speeding off in opposite directions.

Talbot arrived at the palatial home of General Moyiz, was greeted by a uniformed butler with white gloves, and escorted to the well-appointed living room. Moyiz was engaged in conversation with Dr. Edward Stevens, the U.S. trade envoy, whom Talbot knew and had worked with very well over the past two years.

They were brought cocktails made of rum and citrus juices, new to Talbot that he very much enjoyed, as they recapped the earlier meeting between Moyiz and Talbot aboard the U.S. Constitution earlier that day.

Talbot confided in them that he had regrettably received his orders to depart Saint Domingue in July for home, as well as the American fleet, but reassured Moyiz that American support for the Louverture regime would continue.

Stevens cleared his throat and said, "I have also been recalled back to the United States, General, I regret to say."

"Dr. Stevens, what is the new strategy as it applies to Saint Domingue with the election of Thomas Jefferson to the presidency?" asked Moyiz. "We have enjoyed years of mutual prosperity with the Adams administration as well as excellent diplomacy with Secretary of State Pickering and Secretary Marshall. Both these men have been dismissed by your government and now you and our Commodore are leaving our colony as well. It is quite inconsistent."

"We are sorry to leave, General. Everything is in the hands of our new Secretary of State, James Madison. He will be at the helm from now on. In presidential elections, when an administration wins, they shuffle the players."

"Regrettable", responded Moyiz as he thought; a slave master is now president of the United States and so is his Secretary of State. An administration of slaveholders to deal with a colony that had long rejected slavery. "I suppose our Governor-General was correct to point out that America's allegiance or lack thereof is but one presidential election away."

The two Americans remained silent until Talbot asked; "I am curious, general. Where have my officers gone to?"

"Ahh, they are in very good company. I have bestowed upon them a gift this afternoon. They are being transported to Madame Babet's for a brief respite," answered Moyiz.

Dr. Stevens burst a brief laugh as Talbot asked, not comfortable with being out of control of his men "A respite? What sort of respite and who is Madame Babet?"

"She runs a local house of fine women, Commodore. The very finest. They will be well serviced and more importantly, cleaned up for dinner with my guests."

"Cleaned up?" asked Talbot.

"With all due respect, Commodore, you have the opportunity to bathe in fresh water daily. They, on the other hand, how may I say this politely, smell the need for a bath. Madame Babet's girls will not associate with them if they are not clean. They consider you people *'dirty Americans'*. So, knowing they will desire what I have prepared for them, they will willingly concede to a bath. So, without them knowing it, I am cleaning them up to spare them any embarrassment as to their odor this evening with my guests."

Talbot smiled and looked at Moyiz who burst out in laughter, followed by Stevens. "I think I will have another one of these rum juices," Talbot said with exasperation.

"With caution, my commodore," counseled Stevens. "They can hit you hard with a punch if you allow them to."

Dinner that evening was a lavish affair with 34 guests, including the Americans. Stevens had long grown accustomed to lavish dinners and multi-racial receptions hosted by blacks and mulattos, but he could only imagine what these young white lads were thinking as they enjoyed most likely the finest of dinners, maybe the finest in their lifetime?

How ironic that the white Americans were in the racial minority among a group of the highest profile people of color in Cap-Français and far ahead of them in civil, military, and social ranking. Back home, in the United States, these black and colored people would not be allowed a seat at the family dinner table but only allowed to serve it.

General Moyiz, once a slave, owned massive land holdings, commanded thousands of multi-racial soldiers, and exercised tremendous authority over a hundred thousand citizens. Most generals employed by the Louverture government found themselves in nearly similar financial circumstances.

After the slave wars of the early 1790s, many property owners abandoned their plantations or may have been killed. Toussaint, wanting to maintain production levels, had appropriated their properties to the local generals who profited handsomely from their production.

Moyiz was seated next to a stunning black creole as he stood and raised his glass; "My friends, associates, and special guests from the United States of America. I welcome you into my home and wish you a most wonderful evening as we together grow closer in our friendships and diplomacy. To America and France!" he said to the cheer of the crowd.

Toussaint Louverture would have been proud of Moyiz and his officers seated at the table. He had tasked Henry Christophe, who was a fine hotelier, to teach his officers in the North the ways of the whites so that they could better interact with visiting dignitaries. Henry had obviously done a good job with this group.

Talbot, realizing that his officers were out of their league, paid special attention to ensure they were on their best behavior. By their lax and jovial disposition, he could tell that they had a pleasant, albeit possibly exhausting afternoon at Madame Babet's as the wine flowed generously during the multi-course, 3-hour dinner.

One of the officers, Isaac Collins, indulged himself slightly too much with the wine and partly fell out of his seat, and would certainly have fallen to the floor if Moyiz's Adjutant General had not caught him. He looked at Talbot, who was mortified by Collins's behavior, calculating what to do with the young officer.

Talbot nodded to marine commander Carmack, sitting next to Collins, who excused them both from the table, taking Collins outside in an attempt to sober him up.

Apart from that incident, the dinner went well with many more toasts, speeches, laughter, and accolades flowing from both sides in praise of each other. A diplomatic coup thought Dr. Stevens.

The following month in July, Moyiz obtained a copy of the freshly minted constitution the day after its proclamation. He scanned the document and grew increasingly agitated and angry that his uncle had not sought his counsel and was shocked at many of the articles it contained.

He felt that it was a betrayal of the revolutionary cause to which he had devoted ten years of his life. He considered it an act of despotism by Toussaint and cooperation with the French government and whites of the planter class. He was outraged that no blacks were included in the constitutional committee!

He had long been dissatisfied with Toussaint's social and economic conservatism which favored the rich planters at the expense of the underpinnings of the revolution. Sure, Uncle Toussaint could claim that the slaves were technically free, but doesn't freedom allow one to choose who he will work for?

Toussaint's labor policies, albeit better than the old days of legal slavery, were still in the service of the old white slave masters. The colony was returning to the old plantation system. This was a complete subjugation of the black agricultural class which he had vowed to protect and who had followed Toussaint as their true leader – the *'Black Spartacus'* as Laveaux had once labeled him. The population had adored Toussaint, but now had begun to resent him.

Even though his uncle strove to maintain social harmony amongst the multiracial population, his policies favorable to the whites were wearing thin on the blacks. Furthermore, many ill-intentioned whites compounded the issues by verbally harassing their workers and taunting them with words like;

'You think you are free, but you are not. You are forced by your government to remain on my land and work for me. I will treat you like a slave and show you that you are far from having freedom.'

Behavior like this prompted Toussaint to provide punishment for such harassment, but blacks wanted more retribution. To them, they would as soon cut the throats of many whites who acted this way. The seeds of dissent were beginning to blossom.

Dessalines was in Les Cayes with Toussaint towards the end of July, having lunch at a downtown restaurant. It was one of those rare moments in time when both he and Toussaint were relaxed. During mid-sentence, Dessalines dropped his fork as he gazed forward behind Toussaint.

Toussaint looked at him astonished, then instinctively turned to see what was behind him that Dessalines was staring at. He looked back at Dessalines; "Yes, she is beautiful, do you know her, Jean-Jacques?"

Dessalines kept staring, forcing Toussaint to once again turn around and then look back at him. "Are you in a trance, Jean-Jacques? I have never seen you like this before."

Sensing eyes were on her, Marie-Claire Heureuse Félicité, the woman from Léogâne, broke from her party and wandered to the table where Dessalines and Toussaint were seated. Both men rose.

Marie-Claire looked upon Dessalines and considered him very handsome, in a rough sort of way. His military uniform extenuated his physique, his mustache and sideburns were immaculately groomed, and his intensity was apparent as she awaited an introduction.

"Madame Heureuse Félicité, may I present the Governor-General of the Colony, Toussaint Louverture."

"It is a pleasure to meet you, General. May I congratulate you on bringing this unnecessary war to an end and restoring peace to the southern peninsula," she said as she extended her hand.

Toussaint took her hand and instead of shaking it, bowed to gently kiss it. "It is I, Madame, who should be in gratitude to you for taking such good care of the citizens of Jacmel, the way you did," Toussaint replied.

"The man you should thank is General Dessalines, Governor-General. He was instrumental in assisting my passage to Jacmel," Marie-Claire said. "As for me, it is the least I could have done in service to my colony."

"Please sit with us, Madame," invited Toussaint as Dessalines pulled a chair out from the table for her to sit.

"Thank you, General. I would so much like to present my views on the future needs of the South."

"I am always receptive to a good citizen such as you, Madame Heureuse Félicité. However, I have just remembered that I am behind schedule for another engagement. However, I would like you to provide General Dessalines with all of your ideas wherein he will submit those details to me," Toussaint said as he rose from the table. "I bid you good day."

Toussaint was well cognizant of the attraction that Dessalines had for the Heureuse Félicité woman. It was obvious. Dessalines behaved completely out of character, which was not like him at all. Those two need time together, he thought as the reason he had invented the need to depart.

When Toussaint left, they looked at each other and smiled. "May I call you Jean-Jacques now or continue with General Dessalines?"

"You enjoy chiding me, "Madame Heureuse Félicité," Dessalines said.

"I will make you a deal. When no one else is around, you call me Marie-Claire and I will call you Jean-Jacques."

"All right then. What is this list of recommendations that I am to listen to?" asked Dessalines.

Marie-Claire proceeded to give him information and recommendations for all parts of the South. Where a school was needed, hospital services, more security, troublemakers who needed discipline, and a host of very good suggestions, Dessalines thought.

They conversed for a long while until she insisted that she must depart. Her family was having a reunion and that is why she had traveled to Les Cayes.

Over the next few days, they met often and Dessalines was infatuated by the woman from Léogâne. He began courting her in the most gentlemanly manner, behavior totally out of character for the General.

Within a month they began speaking of a future together and by the end of August, Dessalines proposed marriage.

"Before you say yes Marie-Claire, I have a confession; I am father to numerous children," Dessalines blurted out."

"How many children?" she asked.

"I have five that I know of, but there may be… many more."

"Then, you must provide housing for them as they will live with us, no?" Marie-Claire said. "As well as the children you and I will birth."

"Some of my children live with their mothers."

"Then, Jean-Jacques, they will live with us as well. So there, you must now find a way to make this right and provide for them all. No child should grow up without a father. Your children will be the luckiest; a father, their birth mother, and me!"

Dessalines could not believe his ears. He had fretted that this complication would be a stumbling block, perhaps even the issue that would end this relationship, which he could not bear. But Marie-Claire was, as he had known all along, the person he met trying to save all those people back in Jacmel. She was an angel.

The wedding was planned for October with a month's furlough after the ceremony. A true honeymoon and time off that Dessalines had yearned for. After the yearlong civil war, he was exhausted.

He had nearly lost his mind in pursuit of Pétion and he had much blood on his hands from the anger he had allowed to fester.

He had sought out Henry Christophe to confess the brutal punishment he had given to Jean-Baptiste Bayard in pursuit of Pétion. After all, Jean was like a brother to that *Nèg Kay,* Christophe. He knew that he had lost his mind that day, the day he realized that his hunt for Pétion had been thwarted by the man. Could anyone blame him for that?

Well, Christophe wasn't at all pleased by it and in his gentlemanly *Nèg Kay* sort of way, didn't forgive him. He would have much preferred slugging it out with Christophe and letting the *Nèg Kay* win a fighting match to make it up to him, but Toussaint's pet was above all that; to proper, he presumed.

But now he was marrying the woman of his dreams. The wedding ceremony would take place in Saint-Marc. Toussaint would stand up for him as best man. Then, next, they would travel to the northwest so he could show her his birth town, the Grande-Rivière-du-Nord, then travel back to L'Artibonite to scout for their future home in the area he was assigned to and responsible for – a wonderful full month in all. He so looked forward to it.

He closed his eyes and prayed to say thanks to *Papa Ogu* – the Voodoo God of many things, but the worship of war is the one he most identified with. He did not believe in the Gods of Toussaint; those white Christian gods who professed forgiveness while forgiving the sins of slave masters.

Papa Ogu alone had kept him alive through the chains and whippings of slavery. *Ogu* who had kept him alive during the rampages of war. *Ogu* who had brought him close to Papa Toussaint. *Papa Ogu* who had now brought him Marie-Claire.

The workers of the towns of Plaisance, Limbé, and Dondon, considered some of the vanguards of the revolution, were not at all satisfied with Toussaint's labor policies.

Moyiz traveled to Dondon to calm the residents who had complained of harassment from white property owners who at times referred to them as slaves. At first, these incidents were isolated, but over time they grew to be more frequent.

Moyiz called a meeting of the local cultivators and labor leaders to hear their complaints at the town's small government administrative building.

"These whites have gone back in time," said one of the black cultivators. My men are constantly complaining of being forced to work more than the 11-hour workday without any additional compensation. If for the whites, they would return to the 7-day work week!"

"One of my men reported that his brother was whipped for working too slow. When he protested, they denied him food and water," said another.

"We want more regulated land reforms. The cultivation agreement specifies that a plot of land will be made available for growing our own food for our families. But the land the white owners give us is the worst on their properties; arid, sometimes not capable of growing anything at all!" yelled another.

Moyiz listened and thought of how many times he had brought up these issues to his uncle Toussaint. How many times he had warned him that the people were not happy with his policies? How often did I tell him that he had stopped making personal visits and with his absence, they would grow disheartened?

Suddenly, there was a commotion at the entrance outside of the main assembly hall where the meeting was taking place. The door burst open and two dozen men stormed in with one carrying a young woman in his arms.

"What is the meaning of this?" asked Moyiz to the apparent leader of the group.

"We want immediate justice. This woman has been violated by Charles Laurent of the Grandeur Plantation in Dondon. He must be arrested for this crime!"

Moyiz got up and went over to the man holding the girl in a soiled, ripped, and dirty old dress. She was bruised with a bloody lip, swollen eyes, and a gash down her left cheek. "What has taken place?" he asked

"This woman is my fiancée," stated the man who was carrying her. Charles Laurent has raped her and told me he did so since she is still his property and on his land!"

"We will look into this matter and bring due justice to you and your fiancé," Moyiz answered.

"No. Nothing will come of this with Toussaint's government. I once praised and worshiped him as Papa Toussaint. "Now, I spit on his name," answered the large leader of the group.

Soldiers, appalled at the insult, approached from the side of the room towards the man and a dozen men behind him scurried forward to his defense. The lead soldier attempted to grab the group leader, but the man was too strong so another soldier arrived to help.

In the frenzy, the large man knocked one of the soldiers down as other soldiers entered the hall at the sound of the commotion with swords drawn.

Moyiz looked in horror as he realized that the blood of many would soon be shed and yelled "Halt! I command everyone to stand down!"

"You are a representative of Toussaint. You will bring no justice for us or this young couple. You and Toussaint have justice only for the whites!" yelled another from the crowd.

"Whatever my old uncle may do, I cannot bring myself to be the executioner of my color," Moyiz stated. "It is always in the interests of the metropolis that he scolds me, but these interests are those of the whites, and I shall only love them when they have given me back the eye that they made me lose in battle."

With this, the cultivators thought, Moyiz had signaled that he was on their side and would possibly break with his uncle Toussaint that night, even though they were not his exact words.

Moyiz adjourned the meeting, but the most ardent of the crowd remained in the town square to plan the removal of Toussaint Louverture from power.

Over the next several days, the black laborers began to organize an insurrection. They planned to massacre the whites, overthrow Toussaint, and place the popular and much-loved Moyiz in power, proving that the black working-class allegiance to Toussaint and the government was only as strong as Toussaint's allegiance to their emancipation and the true meaning of the revolution.

On October 21st, 1801, the insurrection began. The revolutionary group was comprised primarily of lowly black cultivating farmers who sought justice, more radical land reforms, and a curbing of white suppression.

They at first began marching through the streets of the northern province shouting phrases such as "Death to whites!" and "General Moyiz is on our side!" They continued to the countryside spreading the word as they entered plantations owned by white Europeans to cause mob havoc.

The insurrectionist spirit was growing in the North as word spread from Dondon to the towns of Acul, Limbé, Port Margot, Marmelade, and Plaisance. The marchers soon swelled to over 6,000 in numbers, growing each day with recruits, all assuming that the great Moyiz was now their leader as they targeted white property owners.

At the height of the uprising, there were over 300 European victims killed, many of whom were innocent of any wrongdoing. These were mostly white working-class overseers working for absentee plantation owners who ran the properties.

Achieving anarchic proportions, the group marched towards Cap-Français to make demands of Toussaint and his government. When they were told that Toussaint was out of town and unavailable, they rioted, ransacked, and attempted to burn and pillage the city, but were halted by Henry Christophe and his army.

Christophe was worried that the revolt would expand, hearing of the devastation invoked in the suburbs and the outlying towns, he sent a dispatch to Toussaint to come immediately for consultation, direction, and military support.

They arrived in the Artibonite Valley from all over the colony to witness the marriage of General Jean-Jacques Dessalines and Marie-Claire Heureuse Félicité. The ceremony was being held at the Catholic Church of Saint-Marc.

Within the church were all of Marie-Claire's family that Dessalines had provided escorts for in regal style to Saint-Marc. It was always customary to hold the wedding at the bride's hometown, being Léogâne, but due to Dessalines' military assignment as commander of the Artibonite region, it had to be held in Saint-Marc, near Dessalines' command center.

The Catholic Church, only able to hold a couple of hundred people, was by an invitation list personally approved by the couple. As Marie-Claire was catholic, so would Jean-Jacques be. He even sought counsel from the local priest for guidance a week before the wedding, as requested by Marie-Claire and much to Toussaint's approval.

The remainder of the guests, upwards of 1,000 in all, would celebrate with them at the reception, a huge plantation venue on the outskirts of Saint-Marc, where preparations were currently underway for the wedding of all weddings.

Included for the enjoyment of the wedding couple and their guests was the slaughter of three cattle, a dozen goats, six pigs, 250 chickens, 200 pounds of fish, 50 gallons of soup, and an assortment of fixings; rice and beans, potatoes, corn, roots, plantains, and every possible island vegetable in season, cooked by the best chefs of Saint-Marc.

Dessalines had even sent a carriage to transport Louis Delatour, the very best pastry chef and cake maker of Cap-

Français, to St. Marc a week in advance with a dozen of his staff in tow.

Entertainment would consist of a troupe of folkloric dancers, multiracial Creole and French singers, a string quartet, and a 12-piece orchestra in front of a constructed mahogany dance floor.

The wedding ceremony was celebrated by the Catholic Bishop of the region in a formal ceremony that brought tears to the eyes of Marie-Claire's parents, family, and friends.

Dessalines' entourage included members of the military as well as his Aunt Toya whom he had known since childhood. The guest of honor and chief witness was Toussaint Louverture.

Once the ceremony was complete, the couple and the entourage traveled to the plantation for the reception. The carriage turned onto the long entry road of the estate, lined with coconut trees on both sides with 4-dozen carriages following behind. The weather was perfect.

When the carriages stopped in front of the huge home, an army of valets assisted the passengers to disembark and park the carriages if needed.

Dessalines helped Marie-Claire exit the carriage. They went up the stairs to the front doors, through the central hallway, and out the grand rear entrance where they stood on the veranda equipped with 24-foot high columns and were applauded by a thousand guests before descending the steps.

Marie-Claire was splendid in her wedding dress and her entire being was more than stunning. She looked out towards the crowd and waived with a huge smile as she looked up at Dessalines, so proud of him, resplendent in his regal dress uniform sporting epaulets and medals.

Food stations, bars, and servers scurried about as she could not believe the enormity of the wedding. There were so many people present that Marie-Claire did not know, but grateful that all those smiling faces were there to celebrate with them.

Dessalines looked at his bride with a love he had never known before. This is the woman he would spend his life with. All of the

other women, numerous as they were, put together held no candle to her. She was his life now. This would be the best day ever and the beginning of the rest of their lives.

Dessalines also looked out at the spectacle before him. He had spent his very last centime on this celebration and even borrowed some funds as his extravagance towards his bride had no boundary.

He, himself, was a simple man and this wasn't his style. But for Marie-Claire, he wanted to prove to the world the lengths he would go to honor her and make her happy.

Toussaint arrived with Suzanne at the top veranda and they stood next to Dessalines and Marie-Claire as he began to speak; "Today, my friends and citizens of Saint Domingue. We celebrate the union of the very best that our colony has to offer, two people in service to this great colony and of France. I present to you, for the first time, General and Madame Jean-Jacques Dessalines!"

The crowd roared as an honor guard in full dress uniform hurried up the stairs and drew their swords to form a tunnel for Dessalines and Marie-Claire to descend the stairs through – a dozen on each side. They descended the numerous steps with Toussaint, Suzanne, her parents, family, and friends following to be seated at tables where 200 servers prepared to service the immense crowd.

When they reached the bottom of the stairs to be escorted to their seats, the captain of the guard arrived at Toussaint's side; "Forgive me, Mon Général. An urgent dispatch demands your attention.

Dessalines, Marie-Claire, and Suzanne looked back as the captain of the guard dropped his head as if in shame at what he was required to do on this celebratory occasion. Dessalines' face was both puzzled and worried as Toussaint read the dispatch.

Toussaint looked up from the dispatch with worry in his eyes and said in a stern voice; "The northern plains are in flames. Plantations at Dondon, Acul, Limbé, Port Margot, Marmelade, Plaisance, and the outskirts of Cap-Français are on fire. Hundreds have been killed. Christophe needs our help, rebels are in the Cap.

He prevented them from burning the city but knows not how long he can hold on as the rebels are increasing their numbers and will march towards him at any moment.

Without so much as a hesitation, Dessalines turned and looked at Marie-Claire. "This is the life of a military man," he said. "I warned you of this, but had no idea that it would be tested so quickly."

"You are the man I love and I love you for the man you are," Marie-Claire said as her eyes began to flow with tears. "Go and do your duty, my love. I will explain to our guests and carry on in your absence, as is my duty. I will miss you terribly."

Dessalines could watch and even participate in the slaughter of any enemy in its most gruesome form, but to see his new bride shed tears on this day, this of all days, was unbearable to him. These rebels would pay dearly for robbing him and his bride of these precious memories, of that, they can be assured.

Dessalines brought Marie-Claire into his arms and they passionately hugged in front of the unknowing crowd who did not understand what was happening at that moment. He turned with Toussaint, and they rapidly climbed the steps to the rear doors of the home to exit through its foyer to the front door. However, Dessalines turned as they were about to enter, glimpsed Marie-Claire in the arms of Suzanne, sobbing tears of both joy and disappointment, as a gasp emitted from the crowd that realized something was very wrong.

Suzanne, being the wife of the chief military man in the colony, knew and understood her feelings well. She was no stranger to them.

Outside in front of the residence, hundreds of soldiers were mounted on horseback, awaiting them as many more that were in attendance at the wedding reception were getting their deployment orders and hurrying out the front doors.

Depending on the weather and their horse's abilities, the ride would take them two to three days to reach Cap-Français. Toussaint hoped he would be in time to save the city.

When they arrived, they found that Henry Christophe was able to repel the attack and suppress the rebels. Toussaint's heart sank when he heard that Moyiz was reported to be complicit in the rebellion and had done nothing to stop it. He became enraged when it was reported that the bands of rebels were heard shouting "Long Live our new leader Moyiz!"

How could his nephew be behind such treachery? After all, he had taken him into his home as a young boy when his mother had died, raised him as his own, adopted him as a nephew, fast-tracked his military career, and installed him as commander of the entire northern region! Toussaint was both livid and hurt.

While Henry was able to defeat the groups around Cap-Français, there were still many others to confront. Toussaint and Dessalines marched against the uprising in Marmelade, Dondon, and the other towns. The rebellion lacked sufficient military support and quickly fell to pieces. Dessalines was in a fury that it had disrupted his wedding and gave Marie-Claire a broken heart.

Toussaint ordered Dessalines to arrest Moyiz and bring him to justice. Dessalines wasted no time and rode to Plaisance, where it was reported that Moyiz was, with a thousand men. He couldn't believe that Moyiz had done this. He was the one who had trained him for battle when he was but a kid. Look at how he repays us now.

When Dessalines and his men approached the garrison in Plaisance, there were hundreds, if not thousands, of rebels that could be seen which made Dessalines furious. These were the brigands who had destroyed the special wedding day of he and Marie-Claire, he thought, as he yelled charge to his men who galloped towards the garrison with blades raised on high.

The citizen rebels, armed with machetes and hoes became frightened at the site of Dessalines. They knew of his reputation, but when they saw him in person leading the charge of a thousand-man army, they dropped their weapons and ran for their lives. Soldiers also refused to fight the army of Dessalines.

Dessalines entered the garrison and approached Moyiz; "What in the world do you think you are doing; betraying your honor, your family, your dignity?" Dessalines roared.

"It is Toussaint who has betrayed us, the movement we started and shed our blood for. Me, who lost an eye for. He has abandoned the people and has joined with the whites," Moyiz countered.

"You are a fool and a traitor, Moyiz. He has given you everything. You should be loyal to him. We are military men. We do not question our authority, we follow it," Dessalines said as he was thinking if he should kill him right here on the spot, or at least give him a severe beating. But he dared not lay a hand on Toussaint's kin.

"I hereby place you under arrest, Moyiz Breda-Louverture. You will come with us."

Moyiz put up no resistance and brought up his hands to be chained; not thinking Dessalines would do it. He was wrong. Dessalines gave the order and Moyiz was taken out in chains. As he exited the garrison, there were no rebels present. They had all abandoned the cause as Moyiz realized what he had done.

Toussaint was visibly angry when Dessalines and the guards brought Moyiz before him at Dondon. Toussaint dismissed the guards and Dessalines to be alone with Moyiz.

"Hyacinth, how could you do this to me?" Toussaint said, using Moyiz's name given him by his mother and the one Toussaint would affectionately call him during his upbringing. "How could you do this to our colony? The colony you swore allegiance to build with me?" Toussaint asked.

"We fought this fight for the very people who are now revolting against you, Toussaint! They do not like what they have and what we have become" Moyiz said.

"Are they not free Hyacinth?" asked Toussaint, Isn't that what they wanted?"

"They are free but still not free to do what they want to do, Toussaint. You force them to work on plantations they were once enslaved on whether they agree or not. What has changed? They are given one day of leisure to work their gardens?" replied Moyiz. Some of these people no longer want to work at all. Doesn't their freedom mean they have free will?"

"Everyone must work, Moyiz. There is no room for sloth! They must avoid sloth, the mother of all vices!" Toussaint said in anger.

"But that is what some of them want in freedom," answered Moyiz also raising his voice, "What they believe freedom to be!".

"They and this economy cannot sustain themselves and survive with the way they want things to be. Some want to work only their own piece of land, but that alone cannot sustain them either. You know that!" Toussaint shouted.

"Of course I know that. But they do not. And no matter how much I have told them that in the past, they do not comprehend it to be so. They believe they are still enslaved because they must work on someone else's land, their former owners' land. This is not acceptable to them," voiced Moyiz.

"Are we in agreement that they will starve if they try to sustain themselves from a small piece of land without further income to purchase food other than what they grow? What of their clothing, medical care, and a host of other things they need to live?" asked Toussaint.

"Yes, I agree."

"Do you believe this economy will fail if we let them do that?" asked Toussaint.

"I believe it will, in time" answered Moyiz. "But they must experience this for themselves. It may take years, but eventually, they will come to understand the economics of it all."

"We do not have years, Hyacinth. If we do not prove we can produce and render taxes to the metropole, there is an army that is being assembled right now in France to force them back to slavery.

"We do not need France, Toussaint. We must unite and become independent!" shouted Moyiz.

"If that were the case, all of France would one day converge upon us. This new man Napoleon demands production and exports," Toussaint shouted back.

"All our people want is a small plot of land to farm for their family, maybe have some chickens, goats, or one day a cow. They strive to just live in peace, uncle," Moise answered back in a softer tone.

"That is a fantasy. You and I know it cannot be so!" shouted Toussaint, visibly shaking with a level of anger he never knew he could reach. "Their dream is of a long-ago African land, not the reality of this land!"

"And do you fault them for this? To think and dream this way?" Moyiz shot back.

"No, I fault you for not schooling them on reality. We are in the white man's world now, not in the Africa of long ago. We must play by the new trans-Atlantic rules of the world. Whether they like it or not, they are not African and we cannot create an Africa in the new world. They are Saint Dominguen!"

"The citizens will not back down. If I reject their commitment to what they want, they will discard me and find another champion for their cause. Just as they have already discarded you, Toussaint" Moyiz said.

"Dessalines!" yelled Toussaint as he and two guards immediately appeared. "Take him away".

"May God be with you Moyiz as the damage you have done may be the wrecking of everything we have built. Peace be with you" Toussaint said as his final words. Moyiz was dragged away in chains and as he looked back he saw Toussaint make the sign of the cross.

The next day, Officers Pageot and Martiablès of the northern regiment brought charges against Moyiz and demanded he be held responsible during a special counsel on the matter. Toussaint convened a military tribunal but would not even allow Moyiz a voice in his defense. He was fearful that if this rebellion was not immediately extinguished, such a trial would give Moyiz a grandstand, a podium, to ignite further violence and insurrection.

"The documents presented of the investigation into the incident by the inspectors were enough. I flatter myself that the Commissioners will not delay a judgment so necessary to the tranquility of the colony," Toussaint stated to the tribunal.

Upon this suggestion, the Commission gave judgment and Moyiz was sentenced to death by firing squad at the Grand Fort not far from Port-de-Paix in the north. Dessalines was given the assignment to assemble the squad for the execution of Moyiz.

Dessalines seized the opportunity to have Moyiz pay for the suffering he had given him and Marie-Claire. Towards revenge, he chose to fill the firing squad with Moyiz's own loyal officers.

Suzanne arrived the night before the execution to plead for mercy from Toussaint. She cried, pleaded, and went down on her knees and begged, but Toussaint was resolute.

"I have taken my flight in the region of eagles; when I alight, it must be on a rock, and that rock must be a constitutional government, of which I shall be the head so long as I shall be among men," Toussaint said.

"But Toussaint, he is our nephew, our family!" she pleaded.

"It is the very reason he must pay the highest price over any other. He, of all people, is vested to stay the course. He has betrayed me and his people. He chose the easy way, the coward's way. He will pay the ultimate price. That is all Suzanne."

Moyiz was executed the following day by firing squad He died as he had lived. He stood before the place of execution in the presence of the troops of his garrison,

Dessalines walked to Moyiz; With his mighty hand, he ripped the stripes of a general off his uniform and threw them to the ground. "You have disgraced this uniform and your honor. Do you have any final words?" Dessalines asked as he walked away to give the execution order.

Moyiz looked at his officers. These were the men who had served him well. The men he had saved the lives of and they in turn had saved his life on countless occasions. They were good and loyal. He knew their families, attended their weddings, their children's communion, and their birthdays. He loved them all.

In a firm voice, he yelled "Hear my final command, my brothers. Honor me with my final request. Fire on my command, my friends. I forgive you for it and will not hold you in contempt! Farewell! FIRE NOW I ORDER!."

The men picked up their weapons in unison and fired their rifles with perfect aim at Moyiz's heart, instantly killing him to avoid prolonged pain before Dessalines could give the order.

"I did not order you to fire!" roared Dessalines to the men. "I was to give that order!"

The body of Moyiz slumped to the ground, the men bowed their heads and stood there with their rifles by their side as Dessalines looked upon them, thinking; I hope that if it ends this way for me one day, I will enjoy the loyalty and bravery of men such as these, as Moyiz has enjoyed this day.

He could not bring himself to discipline them. "Dismissed!" yelled Dessalines.

To the black laborers of the North, already angry at Toussaint's policy, the execution of Moyiz was the final disillusionment.

They could not understand it. Moyiz symbolized the true revolution and as a result, he was killed for it.

To them, it was Moyiz who had led the laborers against Hédouville at the request of Toussaint. Moyiz also the one who had arrested Roume for Toussaint. Now Toussaint had shot him for taking their side, the side of the laborers and ex-slaves, against that of the whites.

On October 25th, 1801, Toussaint Louverture issued a proclamation addressing the events in writing.

Instead of Moyiz listening to the advice of a father, and obeying the orders of a leader devoted to the well-being of the colony, he wanted only to be ruled by his passions and follow his fatal inclinations: he has met with a wretched end.

In the proclamation, Toussaint repudiated those who participated in the rebellion for their immorality. He encourages citizens to find holiness and morality within their household, as parents, children, and spouses.

Toussaint ended the letter with a threat:

... those who spread sedition will either be killed or enslaved for six months.

Toussaint placed Dessalines in command of all of Moyiz's regiments and ordered him to purge any within the units who had willingly participated in the events that had transpired.

In doing so, thirteen of his aides-de-camp and his secretaries were shot by firing squad. An additional fifteen officers were sentenced to death with an order to shoot themselves in the head with their own pistols.

Moyiz's death had profound implications. His execution was the final disillusionment of the black working class against Toussaint.

Moyiz became a symbol of black unity and the continuance of the revolution.

Eight

NAPOLEON BONAPARTE & TOUSSAINT LOUVERTURE

Paris
September 1801

In France, the Consulate was the top level of Government after the fall of the Directory in mid-1799. By November of that year Napoleon Bonaparte, together with his brother Lucien, engineered a coup that placed Napoleon as First Consul, the leader of the Consulate. He immediately began establishing a more authoritarian, autocratic, and centralized republican government in France. In reality, it was a full military dictatorship with Napoleon Bonaparte at the head.

He was highly supported and persuaded by French Creoles of the planter class towards a return to pro-slavery principles and the restoration of the pre-Revolutionary status quo of white rule.

The powerful Creole faction from Saint Domingue was well aligned with Napoleon. His wife's family owned vast holdings of sugar plantations in the Caribbean which had been negatively affected by the abolishment of slavery.

The Creole lobby petitioned her and her husband relentlessly to re-establish slavery in the French colonies. They reasoned that colonial slavery would not be considered an abdication of France's general emancipation as it would be exclusive only to French colonial territories.

Bonaparte had sent a new commission to Saint-Domingue to confirm Toussaint Louverture's position as now *'acting governor'* of the colony and institute France's most recent constitution. The new constitution proclaimed that French colonies were to be governed by a set of *'special laws'* specific to them that took into account the particularities of each territory.

It further stated that Saint Domingue is not to be represented in the French legislative body or be governed by laws enacted for French citizens. The constitution did not address the colony's general emancipation but was carefully worded to assure blacks of its inviolability.

The prior day, Colonel Charles Humbert Marie Vincent had arrived from Saint Domingue with an urgent dispatch from Toussaint Louverture. It contained the new constitution for a unified East/West Saint Domingue that had already been promulgated by Toussaint and his Central Assembly. It contained an introductory letter, addressed to the First Consul, which in part read;

From the First of the Blacks to the First of the Whites:

Given the absence of laws, and the Central Assembly having requested to have this constitution provisionally executed, which will more quickly lead it to its future prosperity, I have surrendered to its wishes. This constitution was received by all classes of citizens with transports of joy that will not fail to be reproduced when it will be sent back bearing the sanction of the government.

Though the constitution was not a formal declaration of independence, Bonaparte immediately recognized it as a threat and rejected it.

"Who does this gilded African think he is!" Napoleon shouted to his two most trusted friends, also his officers, sitting with him in his study; the Generals Marshal Jean Lannes and Christophe Duroc.

"Though the constitution essentially usurps our French power in the colony, Saint Domingue still identifies itself as a French colony, First Consul" stated Lannes as he leafed through the document.

"This constitution attempts to establish Saint Domingue as equal to France, asserting the colony's autonomy while still trying to receive benefits from us! How dare he!" Napoleon countered. "It also dares to name Toussaint 'Governor for Life' after I just ratified him as 'acting governor' and sent him MY constitution!"

"I think he attempts to be like you, Napoleon," Christophe Duroc added. "You know they say that imitation is a form of flattery?" he chided.

"Stop it, Christophe. I am not in the mood for your sarcasm" Napoleon shot back.

"He does give himself a 'lifetime position', similar to your own title, non?" Duroc was playing with him and had a license to do so as both these men were not only Napoleon's top advisors but his loyal friends for life, drinking buddies, womanizing accomplices, and near brothers.

Bonaparte chafed at the power Toussaint exercised in the colony. "Do you know that in his letter, he had the obstinacy to have the salutation begin with *'Du premier des Noirs au premier des Blancs?'* - From the first of the Blacks to the first of the Whites?' - How dare he put himself on the same level as me, the First Consul of France!" yelled Napoleon.

"There is little we can do while we are still at war with the British, Napoleon. They control the waters of the Caribbean, especially around Saint Domingue" Jean Lannes pointed out.

"Yes, I know, Jean. But that will soon be put to an end"

"Our informants have reported that these former slaves are riling against Louverture's mandatory labor requirements and are rejecting these measures through various forms of resistance. They may overthrow him yet as they think he is trying to reestablish slavery upon them" Lannes said.

"Table this discussion until I have had a chance to fully read this so-called constitution. Audacious to do so without my input and the nerve to propagate it without my permission! Merde!" screamed Napoleon as he poured himself a brandy.

"Anyone else?" as he dangled the bottle towards Duroc and Lannes who nodded in agreement.

"We have another, rather delicate issue to disclose to you, Napoleon," Lannes said.

"What is it, Jean? I don't think I can take much more tonight."

"Alright, some other time then," Lannes added knowing that Napoleon's curiosity would not allow that.

"Tell me, Jean. What now?"

Lannes and Duroc looked at each other for support as they never enjoyed giving Napoleon bad news about his family. "It's Pauline, sir" Lannes carefully said.

"Oh no. Not again. What is it this time?" replied Napoleon thinking that he knew how to subdue kings and princes but had big difficulties in keeping his own family members in order, especially Pauline.

Pauline Bonaparte was the youngest of Napoleon's three sisters. She was now twenty-one and the most promiscuous one. She possessed the most beauty and charm of any woman in Europe and wherever she went, men could not resist her. But Pauline was a nymphomaniac and as much as men loved her, she loved them back. Much to Napoleon's chagrin, she made it very public.

She had large and expressive eyes that could charm Napoleon's entire war cabinet. She ran wild and took many young officers as lovers. Pauline enjoyed her life of decadence and pleasure to the fullest, breaking hearts with ease as a chef breaks eggs in a kitchen.

Napoleon sought to curb her wild lifestyle. He found a suitable husband in one of his most loyal generals, Charles Victoire

Emmanuel Leclerc, a young brilliant military leader who had become a trusted confidant of Napoleon through successful campaigns while he was a captain.

Napoleon entrusted Leclerc to be his chief of staff against the Spanish at the siege of Toulon, then fought with him during the Italian campaigns at Castiglione della Pescaia and Rivoli. He promoted the young Leclerc to Général de Brigade in 1797 – at his 25th birthday celebration. Napoleon gave him stature and prominence to announce officially to the French Directory the signature of the peace preliminaries at Leoben – a great honor.

Pauline Bonaparte and Charles Leclerc were married in an ornate public ceremony in 1797. Leclerc was deeply in love with her and the couple had a son, Dermide, who was born in 1798. After Leclerc left to serve in Western France, Pauline stayed in Paris and quickly became a star of the Parisian high society and tested her powers of seduction to their limits.

”It's Generals Moreau, Macdonald, and Beurnonville” answered Duroc.

“What did she do? Insult them? Refuse to take their advances? What?” said Napoleon.

“The three are friends and Pauline has taken them all as lovers,” Duroc said.

“You are surely joking Christophe! All three!”

“Yes sir. All three at the same time. I mean, not at the same time but they do not know that each of them is her secret lover during this same period. And, they are the best of friends” Duroc responded. “I fear that it will drive a wedge in their relationships and cause us to lose the synergy they have enjoyed in battle together.”

“That is why she is doing it, don't you see? She is toying with them like little mice. She has irresistible seductive powers and control over men, gentlemen. Enormous power” replied Napoleon. “I've got to get her out of Paris, even out of all of France, maybe out of Europe altogether! I do not believe that any man in the world is less fortunate in his family than I. Let us drink our brandy tonight and reconvene first thing in the morning to sort this whole mess out. I am getting a migraine and need to sleep on it all. Summon my physician as you leave."

Duroc, Lannes, and Napoleon met the following day to strategize on what to do. Also invited was Napoleon's third best friend, Jean-Andoche Junot.

"Gentlemen, we have a serious predicament," Napoleon opened with. "It is called Toussaint Louverture. He has become increasingly powerful and arrogant at a time when Saint Domingue's agricultural production is minimal and causing us financial distress. Saint Domingue once constituted half of our treasury, but that has been reduced to a meager twenty percent.

"I have asked Junot to look into this and prepare a report for us. Junot, the floor is yours."

"Thank you First Consul. There are four distinct goals before us concerning the Saint Domingue colony. One, Louverture must be eliminated at all costs. Two, slavery must be reinstituted. Three, the Exclusif system of trade must be re-established and four, the current black army must be disbanded. or at minimum, be controlled by white officers." Junot said.

Duroc spoke next; "We all recognize that Saint Domingue is the golden goose of our West Indian possessions, but it could not be reliably supplied from France because the British fleet controls the Caribbean waters. New Orleans should be the necessary supply center from which food stocks could be more easily shipped to Saint Domingue than from France. Our strategy needs to be a dual one involving New Orleans."

"If New Orleans is that important to Saint Domingue, why not have an overall long-range strategy to achieve the goals outlined by Junot and then take the United States itself while she is still weak and in her infancy?" stated Lannes.

"That will be taken under advisement, but I want to first get Saint Domingue under control and later look at the United States. That strategy may take years and cannot be a success unless Saint Domingue is in our total control. Let us keep our eye on the prize at hand" replied Napoleon.

"This Louverture is not to be taken lightly. He has emerged as the leading figure in Saint Domingue and with good reason. He has defeated the Spanish and British, maneuvered our French Commissioners out of the colony, defeated the rebel André Rigaud in a Civil War, who by the way has been exiled here in France along with his officers, taken possession of the Spanish eastern portion of the island, where you told him not to, eradicated slavery on the entire island and promulgated a constitution to supplant yours. He also had his local assembly declare him governor-general for life" Junot reported. "It is quite remarkable."

Duroc added; "Both Britain and the United States make treaties with Toussaint as though he were the head of an independent state while at the same time he claims that he is a loyal French citizen who serves the colony for France."

"I do not believe his claims of loyalty to France," Lannes said. "Additionally, Britain and the United States deal openly with Louverture to ensure an end to French privateering from Saint Domingue waters. These privateers are well aligned and take orders from us, Napoleon."

"I think we all agree, then, that Louverture must go and that he threatens our colony by possibly maneuvering to seek independence. I have decided to send Charles Leclerc to settle things there. I have asked him to join us momentarily." Napoleon said.

Just then, General Charles Leclerc entered the room. Duroc, Lannes, and Junot kept quiet as Napoleon mapped out the orders.

"Charles, this mission is a major one. As you and I have discussed, we must succeed in taking back Saint Domingue to total French control and restore agricultural production there."

Napoleon said. "Before I move towards the strategy, do you pledge your full commitment to the campaign?"

"Yes, I do. You have my full commitment, First Consul" replied Leclerc.

"Good. Here is my plan which we can adjust once heard. The first stage, which should take no more than three weeks, is to convince the residents of Saint Domingue of France's goodwill and peaceful intentions. Claim that your army is there to protect the colony against foreign aggression and preserve its peace. This will allow your troops to land and take control of the major port cities."

"The second stage, once you establish your military base camps, is to wage war against the rebel army generals to break the masses' morale and leave them leaderless."

"The third stage is to disarm all the blacks and mulattoes and force them back onto plantations to reinstate slavery. Do not allow any blacks having held a rank above that of a captain to remain on the island no matter what you do."

"The planters are increasingly unhappy with the state of affairs in Saint-Domingue and are relying on me to unseat Louverture, restore slavery, and facilitate the rise of the colony once more. Louverture is no more than a rebel slave who needs to be removed, whatever the cost, Charles. Can you do this?" asked Napoleon.

"How many soldiers do you commit to the campaign, First Consul? asked Leclerc.

"I am prepared to provide over 30,000 and two hundred ships by year's end. After that, another 20,000 within 6 months, and more if required. Again, we must get Saint Domingue under control. We need her revenues to fund our government and our army as well as her strategic position in the Atlantic!" replied Napoleon.

Leclerc knew well what made Napoleon such an outstanding leader. He had a strong rapport with his troops, his organizational talents, and creativity all played significant roles. However, the secret to Napoleon's success was his ability to focus on a single objective and he was obviously focused on Saint Domingue. That reassured Leclerc as he knew that once Napoleon was focused, nothing would stand in his way.

"Which brigades do you plan on committing to the campaign, First Consul?"

"The highly capable Admiral Villaret de Joyeuse will command our mighty warship *L'Océan* as your flagship, along with other vessels carrying 8,000 troops from the regular army will be equipped and leave from Brest. Another squadron under contre-admiral Ganteaume will depart from Toulon with 4,200 troops with another 2,400 troops under contre-admiral Linois from Cádiz.

Additionally, more ships will join you, including Dutch, Irish, German, and Polish Legions, as well as a Spanish fleet of seven ships under Admiral Federico Gravina supported by a great deal of financial and material aid coming from Spanish Cuba. In all, over 30,000 troops will be under your command during the first wave with a preparation of double that, or more, if needed.

"That is impressive. What about local intelligence on the island? I understand that our experienced French Domingue soldiers are limited," said Leclerc.

"Ahh, but I have also your secret weapon, Charles, the mulatto troops."

"The mulatto troops?" inquired Leclerc.

"While you were on European campaigns, Toussaint and a mulatto of the southern region named Rigaud had a falling out. It seems that our French commissioners had put them at odds naming Toussaint the Governor General and his subordinate, André Rigaud, also a general, the ruler of the southern region," Napoleon explained.

"That is rather strange. What came of this?"

"Rigaud, who is rather a quite arrogant and entitled bastard, rebelled against the Governor General who tried to rein him in – a sort of civil war erupted in the south and Rigaud was driven from the island."

"And, exiled here?" asked Leclerc.

"Yes. About 1700 of them in all, mostly the most experienced from the southern command; officers, and the best remaining soldiers, that were the most capable and respected who gained passage here," Napoleon continued.

"And what have they been doing here, while in France?"

"At first, I threw them in the stockade while the senior officers, Rigaud, Pétion, Villatte, Geffrard, and Boyer were interrogated. I decided to give them clemency as it could be argued that they were only obeying the orders of that idiot Hédouville who had created such a mess," Napoleon said.

"These men know the terrain, and the people on the island and could be tremendously valuable to you should Toussaint not concede and resist our plans. They are bored and have been sharpening their fighting skills since their arrival, as well as bedding numerous women, with ease, I might add. It seems the more paisley a lady's skin is, the more they are attracted to these handsome bronze soldiers of good breeding."

"And if Toussaint does accept your order to step down and not resist my Governor General status?"

"Have them all travel on the same ship. I will give you signed orders for them to report to our army in Madagascar to get them out of your, and Toussaint's, way if he submits peacefully."

"You have thought this expedition very well, First Consul."

"There is one more tool at your disposal. Leverage over Toussaint. His two sons, Placide and Issac, are here in France, studying under my guidance at the College de la Marche. I have developed a good relationship with them and will ask them to transport a letter to their father on my behalf.

They both seem to look up to me, as they should, and will be instrumental in convincing Toussaint of our good intentions. They should give him an excellent incentive to retire to his farm, after all, he's a year shy of 60 and should be put out to pasture to enjoy his remaining days with his family," Napoleon concluded.

"With these assets disclosed, you can count on me for a blistering success," answered Leclerc.

"Good." Napoleon turned and said, "Duroc, bring in Vincent!"

Duroc turned, opened the door, and signaled to Colonel Vincent that it was time to enter the room. Toussaint had charged Vincent with the task of personally delivering the new constitution to Napoleon. He had traveled from Saint Domingue to do so.

Vincent saluted Napoleon, who never signaled him to take a seat, leaving him the only man in the room standing. "What is this trash that you have delivered to me Colonel?" asked Napoleon.

"I opposed the drafted constitution, First Consul. I warned Toussaint not to publish it without your input and permission, sir." Vincent said.

"I sent you to keep an eye on this rebel, Colonel. Instead, you allow him to steal my colony?" Napoleon said, slightly raising his voice.

"I told him that several aspects of the constitution were damaging to France, such as the absence of provisions for French government officials, the lack of trade advantages, and his breach of protocol in publishing the constitution before submitting it to you for ratification by the French government," Vincent replied.

"And yet he did it anyway. You were supposed to be the strong arm of my government. However, you turned out to be the weak link" complained Napoleon with obvious disdain. "I am taking back my colony, the one you have lost for me, Vincent!"

"How do you propose we do that, sir?"

"I am sending a great army to execute that task"

"I would advise the First Consul to refrain from making such an expedition to Saint-Domingue. These former slaves can be brutal and cunning if they suspect their freedom is at stake. They have defeated the British, the Spanish, and previously, our colonial army," Vincent pleaded. "They will fight to the death rather than be once again enslaved."

"And there is why you have lost my colony, Colonel. You have no backbone and this Gilded African smelled you as a coward. Pack your bags. You are hereby exiled to the Mediterranean island of Elba for one year. During that time, you and I will contemplate the future of your career. Get out of my site as I don't want to see you again until then. Dismissed," Napoleon ended as Vincent saluted and left the room.

Nothing surprised Lannes, Duroc. and Junot when it came to Napoleon when he lost trust and respect for an officer. He could be extremely harsh, but like a strict and strong-willed parent, he would administer justice with the intent of one day dispensing forgiveness, which they hoped he would do for the loyal soldier that Vincent was, a good soldier.

When their meeting ended, as the men were getting ready to leave, Napoleon asked Leclerc to remain. When the others left the room Napoleon said, "Charles, this will be one of the largest undertakings that France has ever mustered. Do you understand that?"

"I can see that Napoleon. Without a doubt, we will prevail."

"Our French colonies, especially Saint Domingue, play a central economic and military role in our country, Charles.

By the late 1780s, half of Europe's tropical produce came from Saint-Domingue. The colony once produced more than all of the American colonies as well as our colonies in Louisiana, Guadeloupe, and Martinique combined. Saint Domingue was once the highest-producing colony in the world!" explained Napoleon.

"I want her back and you must get her back for me! Her commerce once employed 15,000 sailors and over 1,500 ships. The influx of much-needed revenue to our treasury that once constituted half of all tax revenues has been very much lost to low production and Louverture allowing trade with the Americans and the British" sneered Napoleon.

"Plus, beyond that, these trading vessels employ a ready and able merchant navy from which capable seamen can be recruited in times of war, which is essential to my expansion plans. Saint

Domingue was once capable of fulfilling these tasks so admirably before the revolution. I want it all back" concluded Napoleon.

"I vow to you, I will have her back into the French fold forthwith, First Consul."

"Charles. Do this for me and you will be fabulously rich. You will be the Governor General, once the colony is secured, and then we will lay out our plans for the conquest of America. The new country has an addiction to Saint Domingue which I fear I will not be able to tolerate in the future" predicted Napoleon.

"Yes, the Americans will one day need to be dealt with," Leclerc said.

"That land must be secured for France. It will double our land mass there," Napoleon stated.

"Yes, First Consul."

"Then we understand each other well, Charles. I want you to take Pauline with you on this expedition."

Leclerc was thrown off guard. "Pauline, Napoleon? Why? I do not want her exposed to danger. Plus we have our son to think about."

"Our first phase of the operation is about establishing goodwill and trust with the locals there. By you arriving with your wife and son, how can they possibly think that you would be planning otherwise?" replied Napoleon.

"I will do what you ask, First Consul" replied Leclerc.

"You are my brother-in-law and she is my sister. I love you both and would not send you, her, or my nephew into harm's way if I thought it would be dangerous. You are going with our great army and three-quarters of our navy. You have the military might to curb these savages and get them back to the service of France!" Napoleon concluded.

"You can count on me," Leclerc responded.

In the fall of 1801, one of the largest fleets that France ever assembled gathered in Brest, the most western tip of the country. It included the massive 120-gun flagship *L'Océan*, fourteen French and Spanish vaisseaux or ships of the line, five flûtes which are vaisseaux's stripped of their guns to accommodate more passengers, and three frigates.

Getting past the British blockade was a major impediment, but war-weary Britain soon agreed to a ceasefire on October 7th, 1801. On the following day, after Napoleon approved the London Peace Protocols, Bonaparte gave the order to begin the expedition.

by November 25th, provisions, water, ammunition, and 83 fretful horses were led from the arsenal to the armada anchored in the port to join 8,500 regular French troops, 500 officers, 600 civilians, and 1,200 sailors to board the overcrowded men-o-war.

Similar squadrons were also readied in Cádiz, Lorient, Vlissingen, Le Havre, Rochefort, and Toulon for the lethal fighting force of 36,000 strong boarded onto a total of 192 vessels.

Pauline had been convinced, or rather negotiated, to go on the expedition. Napoleon wanted her out of France and Leclerc wanted to please Napoleon. In the end, Pauline insisted on an entourage of ten confidants, a Parisian opera company of twelve, and a theatre group comprised of eight actors, plus jugglers, clowns, mimes, magicians, and others to play in her court, plus a ship to accommodate them – the *Splendid*.

Cap Français was always the talk of all travelers to the West Indies and was labeled the Paris of the Caribbean because of her culture and nightlife. Pauline planned to reinvigorate the Cap Français society and become the queen of the city, the talk of the Caribbean, and the envy of the world.

After weeks of delays due in part to contrary winds, the Brest squadron departed France on December 14th to rendezvous with the other six squadrons in the Canary Islands for the voyage and surprise entry onto Saint Domingue.

Reinforcements would continue to be assembled to follow this first contingent, comprising another 45,000 troops that would be dispatched during 1802 and 1803 with a total upwards of 80,000 soldiers and sailors for the mission by using the navy to provide shuttle voyages to and from Europe.

The Expedition to retake Saint Domingue had begun.

Meanwhile, in the new Capitol of the United States, the newly erected People's House, now known as the White House, would become the home and office of the president. Its first residents were John Adams and his wife Abigail who were the first presidential couple to occupy the building in November of 1800. Within a month, on December 16th, John Adams received the disappointing news that he had lost the election and his stay there would be brief.

By that time, John Adams and Toussaint Louverture had established the most powerful Atlantic trading system in history. Trade encompassed all parts of the now unified East and West of Saint Domingue, all lands under Toussaint's control.

Enormous trade of goods to and from the colony flourished at numerous ports but in the highest volume at Cap-Français and Port-Républicain. So cooperative were the ties that procedures were put in place wherein all vessels engaged in the trade would be required to register and have passports issued by Toussaint's government and the U.S. consulate.

The presidential campaign of 1800 devastated John Adams's political future and historical legacy. Thomas Jefferson's Democratic-Republican supporters labeled Adams as a tyrant, a monarchist, a womanizer, and a lunatic with political arrogance.

His foreign policy team recognized that the new administration's approach to Saint Domingue which had prevailed in previous years would effectively die with his defeat. John Adams departed Washington on Jefferson's inauguration day to reunite with Abigail at Peacefield, Massachusetts for retirement.

Thomas Jefferson quickly named James Madison to replace the Louverture-friendly John Marshal as Secretary of State. Madison quickly began disassembling the progress and Atlantic trade agreements made with Toussaint and Saint Domingue. The Democratic-Republican party was heavily vested in southern states' agrarian principles, and emphatically pro-slavery. The idea of a black-governed, former slave colony in such proximity to southern shores could not be tolerated.

On a chilly Tuesday in November 1801, Thomas Jefferson was visited by Louis-André Pichon, the French ambassador to the United States. "Welcome, Mr. Ambassador. I trust that your trip from Philadelphia was agreeable?" Jefferson greeted his guest.

"Your countryside is most beautiful this time of year, Mr. President," answered Pichon.

"Let me introduce to you the distinguished James Madison, who served as a member of the U.S. House of Representatives from 1789 to 1797, and is now my Secretary of State," introduced Jefferson.

"It is my pleasure to meet you, Secretary Madison" Pichon said as he extended his hand.

"And you as well, Mr. Ambassador. Welcome to Washington."

"I bring you greetings from our First Consul, Napoleon Bonaparte, Mr. President, and Mr. Secretary. He is very much in favor of continued improvement of our relations and cooperatively working together in the future prosperity of our two countries." Stated Pichon.

Jefferson had known in advance that preparations were being made to retake Saint Domingue from his spies in France. An expedition of this size was too large to conceal. "And how can we improve an already well-established relationship, Mr. Ambassador? We have finally achieved peace with Adams no longer the president. I can now assure you of that for years to come."

France is launching an expedition to reinforce the laws of its colonies, specifically Saint Domingue. They have been somewhat, should I say, unruly?" stated the Ambassador.

"Yes, it is a rather unruly bunch of Negros there," Jefferson said as he was quite worried about having a slave state in such proximity to the United States, which was still a slave-holding nation. "I assure you that I have not engaged in any correspondence with the so-called governor of the colony, this ex-slave, Toussaint Louverture. I have also terminated pro-Louverture diplomats and recalled my navy from its shores."

"He will soon be dealt with, in due course," answered Pichon. "Of that, you can be assured. Napoleon wants colonists to return France's Caribbean territories to their earlier profitability as slave-holding plantation colonies" announced Pichot. He knew that Jefferson was pro-slavery and of the planter class. However, he was anticipating a more urgent admittance that he did not like Saint Domingue slaves being free.

"But you freed your slaves, Mr. Ambassador. It is quite difficult to have profitability without slaves. We know that quite well in the commonwealth of Virginia and throughout the entire Southern United States" Jefferson concluded.

"An unfortunate error of judgment from the French revolutionary days and its then experimental republic, Mr. President. But the First Consul plans to correct all that, shall I say, faux pas?"

The three diplomatically danced around the subject until the name of Toussaint was again on the table and Jefferson said "If you want to crush that African, Toussaint Louverture, America would help the French do so. We cannot have a slave-run colony in this hemisphere. It is not natural, but our merchant ships have become quite happy and successful with trade in the colony."

"Then I have a way that we can achieve both of our objectives, Mr. President" stated the French Ambassador. "There will be upwards of 40,000 French soldiers who will need a source of food. Discontinue trade with the colony and we will purchase food and supplies from America and your American ships can provide the transportation to the colony to replace their losses."

And just like that, The Jefferson administration promptly reversed Adams' de-facto recognition of Toussaint's government and began to work towards a prohibition on American trade with the colony.

Though the French Ambassador obtained Thomas Jefferson's reassurances that U.S. merchants would help supply the expedition, these American merchants had profited greatly under Toussaint, and many would continue to supply Toussaint's army as well.

Napoleon had now eliminated the American threat to the expedition as Jefferson enthusiastically anticipated the elimination of the threat of Toussaint Louverture and his black army.

Daniel J.D. Bayard

Nine

THE EXPEDITION ARRIVES

Northern Coast of Saint Domingue
January 1802

The French fleet rendezvoused at the Bay of Samaná at the north-eastern tip on the Spanish side of Saint Domingue. Aboard the flagship *L'Océan*, Admiral Villaret de Joyeuse and Général Leclerc held a meeting of all captains and générals to finalize the plans of conquest.

It was decided that Général Kerverseau would land at Santo Domingo, the Spanish city on the southern coast, Général Rochambeau Fort Liberté, Général Boudet would take Port-Républicain, and he, Leclerc, Cap-Français.

When Toussaint's scouts spotted the armada, more than 100 ships in all anchored in the huge Bay, riders were dispatched to Dajabon where Toussaint was meeting with regional commanders.

Toussaint thought it wise to ride 35 kilometers to San Fernando de Monte Cristi, about a day's ride from where he was, in the northwest region on the Spanish side. Monte Cristi was the tallest mountain in the area and would offer him a wide vista to spot any passing ships from many miles away. If he saw no ships on the horizon, he would continue east towards the Bay of Samaná until he could assess the strength of the fleet himself. Were his scouts exaggerating? 100 ships? How could that be possible? He

simply couldn't believe the enormity of the reported strength of the fleet.

Looking through the spyglass at the top of the mountain surveying the horizon, Toussaint could spot dots, definitely some ships, very far away. He camped with his men overnight and by daybreak the next morning, ships were dotting the horizon as far as the eye can see.

By afternoon, the ships were passing the mountain, and he became filled with dread. "It seems that the entire land of Europe has converged to take our home of Saint Domingue," he remarked to an honor guard soldier next to him. From the distance he was, he could barely make out uniforms but couldn't recognize them as French, possibly the troops from the foreign countries that had aligned with Napoleon.

He then began to compose letters to be dispatched to the various parts of the island; Henry Christophe, head of the island's northern department, Jean-Jacques Dessalines of the western, and Laplume the south with orders that the French could not land without his explicit permission and if they tried to do so, burn down the cities.

On the afternoon of February 3rd, after a pleasant lunch with his wife Marie-Louise, Henry was in full enjoyment of his elegant home in Cap-Français. He was glad to be stationed there and spent all the time he could with his family while his army was camped on the outskirts of the city. Peace had resumed after the Moyiz incident and was slowly returning to a normal pace.

A knock at the door was followed by a messenger who arrived to announce that there was a war fleet outside the bay with twenty-two ships that could be seen flying the French tricolor at the bow of each, but they did not enter the harbor.

Such an armament could mean but one thing. France had come to claim her colony, by force of arms if necessary. He needed to make preparations immediately to meet them, as just yesterday he had received the dispatch from an exhausted horseman who had ridden for days with a letter from Toussaint that in part read;

'Burn the city to the ground if any army tries to enter our land without my giving you explicit permission first...'

Henry mounted his mare and galloped towards town to make his way toward Fort Picolet. The fort was strategically positioned on a hill overlooking the Bay of Cap-Français, serving as a defensive structure to protect the city and its valuable harbor.

The fort features thick stone walls, 60 cannons, and strategic vantage points. The fort was named after French Général Louis Marie, Marquis de Picolet, who served as the French governor less than 50 years ago, and ironically would now be used to defend the city from the French he served.

Henry's mare darted from right to left to avoid smashing into the enormous amount of people who were taking a position to view the sight of the war vessels plying the waters miles from shore. He arrived at the fort courtyard, dismounted, and handed the reigns to an awaiting soldier.

Captain Rouzier came running out of the barracks, as did other soldiers scurrying about in a multitude of activities. Officers were yelling orders in a frenzy as cannons were being repositioned to take advantage of firing angles toward the wide expanse of the ships.

Rouzier stopped, stood at attention, and saluted Henry as three subordinate soldiers to the captain arrived, saluted both he and Henry and waited for permission to speak to Rouzier. "Carry on," barked Henry.

Rouzier looked at the first soldier and nodded. "All grilles of iron are being loaded into braziers to create boulets rouges" he quickly informed. "We have enough for three rounds each, 180 total heated grape shots, 24 cannon balls for each of the 60 cannons, and 800 men readying their muskets, Captain."

"Good. Keep the coal burning hot for the boulets rouges to be ready at a moment's notice. Carry on."

"What say you, Tardieu?" Rouzier asked the next soldier as he came forward.

"Caldrons of hot tar are being heated and readied should they try to scale the walls, captain," Tardieu answered.

"Carry on," Rouzier barked.

"We have enough rations of dried fish, meats, and other staples for a week at least," stated the third soldier.

"Good. Advise all men that there is no liberty until told. All are to report here to the fort. Send messengers to spread the word to all off-duty soldiers in the city."

"Yes, captain," answered the soldier as he also sped off.

"My apologies, Mon Général".

"I see you have all things being readied. That pleases me greatly, captain," answered Henry.

"It is a precaution awaiting your orders," Rouzier said.

"Fire on any ship that comes through that pass and enters the harbor. You do not need to wait for my order. You now have it," Henry said as he looked through the spyglass.

A boy soldier arrived at their side, saluted, and stood at attention. "Yes, what is it?" asked Rouzier.

The young soldier with a stuttering speech impediment said; I,I,Itttt's th, the p,p,p, pilot… sir.

"Yes?" answered Rouzier, obviously quite familiar with the boy's challenging speech. "What does the pilot of the harbor want?"

The boy soldier decided it was just more efficient to point as he spoke, "H,h,h,e asksss th,tha, that you cu,cu, come."

Rouzier nodded to the boy which was a sign to lead the way as Henry followed behind. As they exited the cliff side of the fort, they began to descend the long narrow staircase to the small dock below. Two men were awaiting, one being the pilot of the harbor, a red-faced Frenchman by the name of Blanchard, and another, impeccably dressed officer in a French uniform next to a small schooner tied to the dock.

As they approached, the pilot neither saluted Henry nor the captain, as he was not military but an employee of the dock. The wind had kicked up several knots and the ocean's waves began to produce whitewash as far as the eye could see. A storm is approaching, Henry thought.

The two men moved slightly toward them as the French naval officer began to talk without a salute or introduction to Henry.

"I am Ensign Lebrun, aide-de-camp of Admiral Villaret de Joyeuse and Captain-Général Charles Leclerc. Your pilot has informed us, Général, that you are refusing to allow our ships entry into the harbor. How is that?"

"I have counted over twenty warships, some with foreign colors, at sea there. How would you expect any competent général to allow foreign vessels with armaments of unknown quantity and troops entry into the harbor of such an important city, Ensign Lebrun?" Henry responded.

"Those vessels are serving under the flag of France, though yes, some are foreign," the ensign replied.

"I have no orders to allow them entry. Only the Governor-Général of the colony can issue that order," Henry replied.

"The Governor-Général has issued the order which I am transpiring to you, Général."

"Where is the Governor-Général, Ensign? I do not see him here, nor do I have any orders to that effect."

"The newmGovernor-Général is on a ship awaiting entry into this harbor," Lebrun responded waving his hand towards the fleet as a gust of wind almost removed the hat off of his head as he caught it launching into flight.

"I have it under the correct understanding that Governor-Général Toussaint Louverture is not on one of those ships. He is in eastern Saint Domingue.

"And I can assure you that I sighted the Governor-Général, whose name is Captain-Général Charles Leclerc, on the flagship *L'Océan* not but two hours prior."

"He is not the Governor-Général, Ensign. I have received no orders to obey him or anyone other than Governor-Général Toussaint Louverture.

Ensign Lebrun opened the leather pouch that hung on his shoulder and produced a sealed scroll that he handed to Henry, who broke the seal, uncurled the parchment, and read it out loud so that the men and boy soldier could hear.

I learn with indignation, Citizen Général, that you refuse to receive the fleet and the French army which I command, on the pretext that you have no order from Général Toussaint Louverture. France has made peace with England, and the government now sends forces to Saint Domingue which are capable to subdue rebels, if one must still find them in Saint Domingue.

As for yourself, Citizen Général, I admit that it would cost me a great deal to count you among the rebels. I warn you that if today you have not turned over to me Forts Picolet and Belair and all the other batteries of the coast, tomorrow, at daybreak, fifteen thousand men will be landed. Four thousand are landing this moment at Fort-Liberté, eight thousand at Port-Républicain.

You will find the proclamation from our first consul, Napoleon Bonaparte; it expresses the intentions of the French government but recall that whatever personal esteem which your conduct in the colony has inspired in me, I hold you responsible for whatever may occur.

Général in chief of the Army of Saint Domingue, and Captain-Général of the Colony. Charles Leclerc

"Let me see the proclamation that this letter refers to, Ensign," asked Henry.

"It is only for the intended recipient, Toussaint Louverture. Your letter is the one that you have just read aloud. What if it contained confidential information intended for you alone?" asked Lebrun with an air of condescension.

"It was very complimentary, the letter from your… captain, is it not?"

"Général Charles Leclerc is the new Captain-Général of this Colony and you now report to him, général!"

"You leave me no choice but to doubt what has been written and what you say is accurate. As for all I know, this could be a trick and those ships are not under the French flag at all. Here, take your letter back as it means nothing to me as there is no proof of who is writing these things, and without inspecting the proclamation to validate its authenticity, this is all rather irregular," Henry said.

Without taking the letter back from Henry, Lebrun said "I beg your pardon. I am an honorable officer of the French army!"

"So you say," answered Henry. "Rouzier, continue preparations. Fire on any ships entering the harbor. Ensign, come with me," Henry commanded.

A couple of large drops of rain could be seen coming down and occasionally hitting the ground and the men. The wind kicked up significantly and the loud swishing of coconuts and palms against each other grew anxious.

A soldier was holding two horses that were getting nervous from the weather, dancing and wanting to vacate the area as the first flashes of lightning began to brighten the now-darkening sky. Henry nodded towards the other horse as he jumped on his mare and the Ensign expertly mounted the other without an explanation but knowing it was to escape the incoming storm.

Lebrun galloped behind Henry closely but kept, with interest, his attention on the city. A beautiful one at that, he thought, even though the weather hid its true magnificence. Henry kept up a fast pace as the horses galloped on the cobblestones of the road until they arrived at what the Ensign thought was the home of an important dignitary.

A uniformed soldier met them as they entered the gates to take their horses as they dismounted. The rain was now pouring down heavily as they entered the palatial home that was fully illuminated by lanterns and candles with a sweet aroma of perfumes, Lebrun thought.

"Papa, papa!" yelled a 6-year-old as he barreled down the steps, followed by a uniformed nanny trying to keep up. The boy ran to his father and jumped into his arms, giving Henry a strong hug around his head, not wanting to let go.

"Ensign, meet my son, François Ferdinand, a future officer of France. François, greet Ensign Lebrun of the mighty army of France," Henry stated to his son.

The boy wiggled out of his father's arms to the floor, stood at attention, and saluted the Ensign. Lebrun looked at the boy, stood to attention, smiled, and saluted back as he grew impatient to conclude his official business while Marie-Louise joined them in the foyer.

Henry kissed Marie-Louise on either cheek and turned to Lebrun, "Ensign Lebrun, meet my wonderful wife, Marie-Louise Christophe. Marie Louise, meet Ensign Lebrun."

"It is my pleasure, Madame," as Lebrun bowed his head in respect.

"The Ensign will be our guest for dinner this evening," informed Henry.

"But Général, I must be getting back to the ship and register my report," said Lebrun.

"That is impossible this evening, Ensign. There is a storm and knowing the capable captains of the French navy, those ships are already heading a few miles north, away from shore as a precaution. You cannot return to them tonight. You will dine with us, and my coachman will then take you to the finest hotel in the colony, Hôtel de la Couronne," Henry stated more as an order than an invitation.

Marie-Louise clapped her hands and smiled; "That sounds wonderful, Henry. A special guest from Paris who can provide me with all the latest news, the latest entertainment... and gossip, about my old school town. Let me have the staff arrange for dinner," she said as she sped off to make the proper preparations.

Dinner was incredible, thought Lebrun, as he dined with the family out of exquisite porcelain dishes, crystal glassware, and golden flatware. The three staff members served helpings of beef, potatoes, and roots, which he was not accustomed to but found were very flavorful, followed by the first and second courses of raw conch in lemon-garlic sauce and pumpkin soup.

Good wine flowed generously throughout the evening and a desert of caramelized egg custard finalized the fine meal with his immense delight. Lebrun rated the dinner as one of the finest on record and was thoroughly happy that the général had coaxed him into staying for it.

At 9 pm, the butler arrived and whispered something into Henry's ear at which Henry turned to Lebrun and said; "Ensign, your carriage is waiting," as he stood to escort Lebrun from the dining room.

Marie-Louise said her goodbyes as she ordered the young François to bed, Lebrun could hear her reasoning with the boy that it was past his bedtime, as he protested his wants to wait for his Papa to return.

When the carriage arrived at the hotel, Lebrun was treated as a very important guest and escorted to a superior room with clean evening clothes, a bottle of port, and a tray of cheese awaiting him.

Lebrun felt very strange. He had arrived earlier that day not looking forward to engaging these negros, a few clicks away from savages he thought, delivering the letter from Leclerc, and getting back to the ship poste-haste, with a successful report.

But, what he had found was a polished, sophisticated, and accommodating général Christophe, not a savage at all. He was all business with an official persona that was to the point, pragmatic, and entrenched, but also displayed soft and pleasant personal traits.

He looked forward to what the following day would bring as he poured himself a glass of Port and sliced a wedge of cheese for an awaiting piece of baguette.

It was 2 am at the docks and you would have thought it midday as dozens of torches lit up the area. Every ship on the dock was a bustle of activity as Jean and Marie walked towards their ship, *Laura.*

Men were scurrying up and down two gangplanks tied to the ship; the one on the right for men climbing up with cargo and the other on the left where the men descended empty-handed. It was an efficient method of loading vessels quickly, a new idea recently implemented by their son Junior.

"Things are moving along well here, it seems," Marie said as she scanned the four other Bayard vessels with the same activity; *the Marcelle, the Lily, the Denise, and the Michaele.*

"I'm going to find Junior to make sure things are on schedule. You are coming?" Jean asked Marie.

"I'm going to wait for Yolande. Go ahead, I'll catch up," she said as she gave him a quick peck on the cheek and walked off towards the warehouses.

As a precaution, they were emptying their warehouses as rumor had it that there may be a confrontation with the French fleet. Everyone knew Toussaint could be stubborn if protocols didn't live up to his expectations.

Henry had told him in confidence that his orders were to burn the city if it came to that, so the Bayard businesses were taking no chances. In seeing the activity around the city and here at the docks by others, Jean ventured to think that more people than he knew of the possible pending peril.

Jean strolled over to the next vessel and heard Junior yelling; *"Ann ale, ann ale"* Let's Go, let's go, in Creole with an accent that would be undecipherable from any other black or mulatto dock worker. *"Kontinye deplase, Nou pa gen anpil tan"* Keep moving! We don't have a lot of time, Junior kept yelling to motivate the men on the line.

He and one of his foremen, a man named Carl, were standing on the side of the *Marcelle* supervising the dock workers busily loading cargo onto the *Marcelle* from the warehouses – sugar, coffee, molasses, indigo, lumber, and hardware. Carl had papers in his hands and recorded the inventory being loaded onto the ship.

Jean came over to Junior. "Give me a quick report as I know you're busy."

"I'm thinking late afternoon by the time we get these five ships loaded," answered Junior.

"How many men were you able to muster?"

"On top of our twenty, I've got 32 more de jour laborers. That's all I could find as everyone in town is hiring, so we've got about 10 on each ship.

"You got enough room for all the inventory?" Jean asked Junior.

"Barely, and that's by cramming every nook and cranny below and loading nonperishable cargo on the top decks. So I…"

Suddenly, one of the dejour laborers fell a few feet away from them with a sack of sugar that broke open and spilled its contents. Junior ran to his side, *"Sak pase, Ou bon?"* What happened, you good?

"Patwon, padone m, patwon, tanpri padone m." Boss, forgive me, boss, please forgive me, said the frightened worker, a man maybe in his fifties who obviously had a life of hard labor evidenced by his thin wryly body, skin of hard leather, and hair nearly bald and graying. He wore the remnants of a tattered shirt and trousers that were cut off at the knees.

"Pa kraze lespri w, granpe, se sik sèlman," Don't break your spirit, Grandpa, it's only sugar, Junior said in a kind voice. *"Pran yon ti repo epi tounen lè ou kapab netwaye li,"* Take a break and come back when you can clean it up, Junior said to the man as he helped him up.

The man limped towards the warehouses as Jean wondered if he always had that limp or had this spill just now caused it. He looked at his son, now going up and down the line of men, touching some with affection to give them motivation to keep working, not afraid of his hands touching the wetness of their shirts or backs, or the stench of their human, unbathed skin laboring through the night.

Only ten years ago, that man who stumbled would have been whipped, or worse beaten by a slave master thinking no wrong of it. This is so much better, after slavery.

He looked over at Junor amid his activity and damn, he was proud of the now 24-year-old man his son had become. Firm, but caring, espousing praise and recognition to lead his men. He had taught him well as he had been taught long ago by the Compte d'Estaing during the American Revolution; '*True leaders know that men don't serve you, you must serve them*' to get the most of their energy, he would say. Jean looked around and could see it was well in action here.

Junior was walking back to Jean to complete his report when Marie arrived driving slowly up on a wagon with Yolande, their trusted house manager, and two men. She jumped out of the wagon, as did the others, and before she said a word, the deep rich aroma of dark roasted southern peninsula coffee enveloped them. She approached them with two cups in her hand and said; "Coffee anyone?"

"Maman, how do you know everything I am thinking before I even think it?" asked Junior as he approached to kiss her on each cheek and retrieve his cup. The other she handed to Jean.

"Your mother works best under the pressure of an emergency, be it a hurricane or a pending war," answered Jean.

"*Pote kafe a epi sèvi mesye yo,*" Bring the coffee and serve the people, Marie shouted to her group, as they were already pouring coffee into metal mugs from the huge 20-gallon barrel they always used for this purpose.

"I hope you have a lot of that Maman,", asked Junior.

"Really Junior," asked Jean. "Didn't I just tell you she works best like this?"

"We will have 50 gallons total. I have a crew at warehouse 'C' brewing that, cooking 100 eggs and cutting up two dozen avocados just picked from our backyard tree. Mr. Gilbert is delivering bread by the time it will be ready. A full break and breakfast for the workers at 4 am, Junior?"

A smile lit up Junior's face. "You're the best Maman. I figure a 20-minute break should do it. I'll spread the word."

"Make it 30-minutes, my son. Workers work best with a little digestion," Marie said, more of an order than a suggestion. "Give them breaks five minutes apart so there isn't a big lineup at the food station and by all means, don't start until I give you the word!"

He woke to the sound of roosters announcing daybreak and found himself excited to get out of the room and observe the early morning activity of the city, the first Caribbean one he had ever been to. He quickly washed in the room, dressed back in his uniform, and descended the stairs to the lobby where a bustle of activity had already begun.

A soldier approached him; "Ensign Lebrun, I presume?"

"Yes, it is I"

"Général Christophe has requested that I make myself available to provide any service you may need, and transportation to the house of the Governor for a meeting at 9 a.m. I am Corporal Theyar," the young soldier announced.

"Thank you, corporal. May we begin with some breakfast?" asked Lebrun.

"The restaurant is there," Theyar pointed. "Order anything you would like; the charges are all being paid for by the army."

"That is most gracious," Lebrun replied as he began to walk towards the already busy restaurant. He looked back, "Theyar, will you not join me?" he asked, suddenly realizing that if he had a meal with this man, it would only be the second of his lifetime with negros, Christophe and his family being the first.

"Invitation accepted," answered Theyar. "I am famished."

The two dined on hard-boiled eggs, smoked herrings smothered with onions, tomatoes, plantains, and a root called yuca that Theyar introduced him to. The coffee was rich, dark, and strong, softened with rich fresh cream. The orange juice was freshly squeezed and somewhat tangy, and Lebrun was delighted with the experience, now counting his blessings for not tolerating another morning meal on board the *L'Océan*.

After purchasing the local newspaper, they departed La Couronne in a carriage for the government house. The morning was clear with a light wind he estimated at 10 knots or so as if the storm had never happened. The city was bustling, shops were open and active and people were scurrying about, many clearing branches that had fallen overnight from the storm. He glanced down and scanned the headlines;

EURO FLEET ARRIVES TO SAINT DOMINGUE
Intentions Unknown – Fleet Denied Entry to Harbor

He scanned the article which contained some truths amongst much confusion that provided the reader very few facts – a problem he would mention to his superiors, even eluding to a possible invasion from not so friendly Europeans.

The carriage whipped through the streets, entered the gates of the government house, and quickly slowed to a walk as many citizens were crowding the front entrance path to the building. "Looks like we have a crowd as your welcoming committee, "Thayer laughed. "Are you famous or something to deserve all of this attention?"

Lebrun smirked back the joke, enjoying the company of the soldier in this strange city since the beginning of breakfast where each spoke of their family, friends, and special events in their lives, and developed a friendship in a short period of time.

They pushed through the crowds of confused citizens who were voicing concerns, some upset that the fleet was not permitted entry into the harbor and others claiming it was a European invasion, that France had been conquered, and this was now a consolidated occupying force.

The soldier, with Lebrun in tow, finally got to the main hall that was overflowing with people shouting questions towards Général Christophe;

"Why isn't the fleet permitted to enter the harbor..."
"Is the expedition here to re-enslave our blacks...?"
"I could use the extra business, let them enter..."
"Why isn't the governor général here yet...?"

Lebrun watched with interest, registering each question that Général Christophe answered, admiring how poised, calm, respectful, and patient he was being to the crowd.

A white well-dressed French woman, a Creole Lebrun suspected, who seemed to have respect and high standing in the community, came forth as everyone hushed when she began to speak.

"Général, we have seen the destruction to our city ten years ago. Our beautiful city was reduced to ashes by war and revolution. Many of our people were killed, and possessions were ransacked or stolen. Can you guarantee that this will not lead to our city being torched again? It has taken ten years to rebuild it to the marvelous splendor it is today, better than the previous one," she stated. "Will you tell us that our city will not once again be put ablaze and destroyed?"

"Madame Clérié, it is not I who can determine that. It is the ships and troops in the fleet on the horizon who threaten our city. When you awoke yesterday, you had no notion that you were in danger. We have lived in peace for many years. You have accepted the blacks and the blacks have accepted you. We live together, black, white, and mulatto, in harmony. The only change that has happened, which makes you now doubt your safety, and that of our wonderful city, is a fleet of unknown occupants and intent. We do not even know if they have been sent by the legitimate French government or if it is a ruse to surrender our city, or our colony. Madame, I must await my orders from Governor Général Toussaint Louverture. This meeting is now adjourned. Please go about your business in peace and the hope that the fleet sails away in peace."

Henry turned and walked down the corridor to the Governor Général's office, followed by many officers. Four soldiers stood guard at the entrance to the corridor and when announced, let Theyar and Lebrun pass through.

Two guards were at the door to the Governor Général's office that Henry had just entered. Theyar announced himself to the guards who let them through.

"Ah, good morning, Ensign," Henry greeted with a pleasant disposition. "I trust that your accommodations were satisfactory and that you have had a comfortable night's rest?"

"More than so. I thank you for your hospitality since I have arrived in your lovely city, Général."

"So, you have concluded that we are not savages who need to be conquered after all, eh?"

"And how is your lovely wife, Madame Christophe, and that wonderful boy of yours?" asked Lebrun without any comment or acknowledgement of Henry's previous statement.

"My wife is hoping that you take a letter that I have prepared to your besieging captain général in hopes that you all sail away and that this has been but a bad dream, Ensign. However, you are welcome to stay in our colony and become a citizen, or better yet an officer in our army, at a ranking superior to your current one, might I add Ensign," Henry said.

"That is quite flattering, Général. But my duty is to Captain Général, Charles Leclerc, as well as France. I must deliver your response to the request for our fleet to enter the harbor," Lebrun said in a firm tone and one that took them back to the business at hand.

"Ah, the request," Henry said as he pulled out the letter from his breast pocket that he received yesterday from Lebrun and had tried to return. He brought it up towards the ceiling as he turned it frontwards and backward. "Your captain-général is quite the flatterer and the intimidator at the same time. On the one hand, he makes perfumed compliments and in the same stroke of the pen, very dark threats. My position remains. I do not have authority to grant him entry into the harbor of Cap Français until my Governor Général authorizes me to do so."

Lebrun realized that his mind was made up and any further discussion on the matter would be fruitless and distasteful. "So, I will report back to my commander with your response."

"No need to voice the disappointing news yourself. I would not want you to be in his disfavor. I have drafted a short note, sealed by my wax, for you to deliver to him. Theyar will accompany you to the dock wherein a schooner will transport you to your mighty warship," Henry stated as he walked over to Lebrun. You are dismissed," Henry stated with finality as an order, not a request, as a superior officer would give to his subordinate.

Twenty-four hours earlier, Lebrun would have taken this as an insult to himself and the French government. However, after what he had experienced in the past day, he grew respect for the général before him. It would be much easier for the général to acquiesce to Leclerc's orders, but his principles would not allow it. Lebrun stood at attention and saluted Henry as a sign of respect and Henry saluted back. Lebrun turned to leave.

"Ensign, it has been a pleasure to know you and introduce you to my family. I bid you au revoir," Henry stated back to him with sincerity.

Lebrun nodded his head and followed Theyar out of the building.

Aboard the deck of *L'Océan*, Captain-Général Leclerc read Henry's letter out loud to Admiral Villaret de Joyeuse with Lebrun present. It was a beautiful sunny day and a light wind brought a fresh crispness to the air as seagulls fought and jostled for any bits of food the sailors would toss.

From the headquarters of Le Cap, Henry Christophe, brigadier général commanding the arrondissement of Le Cap, to Général in Chief Leclerc.

Your aide-de-camp, Général, has delivered to me your letter. I have the honor to let you know that I cannot deliver to you the forts and other places confided to my command until beforehand I have received the orders of Governor Toussaint Louverture, my immediate superior, from whom I hold the powers vested in me…

…I would very much like to believe that I am dealing with the French and that you are the chief of the army called "expeditionary," but I am waiting for the orders of the Governor, to whom I have dispatched one of my aides-de-camp, to announce to him your arrival and that of the French army; and until his response has reached me, I cannot permit you to debark.

Henry Christophe

"Report on your visit and interaction with this Général Christophe, ensign Lebrun," asked Leclerc.

"Polished, firm, and well administered, Captain-Général."

"What are their intentions?"

"He will not allow us to debark without a fight. They are preparing their cannon in the fort there, and am sure all other batteries, as well as Fort Belair, are in preparation as well," Lebrun answered.

"Why do they resist us? We are the government of France," barked Leclerc.

"They think us to be fraudulent. Some other army independent of France, a combined Euro army of some sort."

"Nonsense," Leclerc replied as he surveyed the fort with his spyglass. "Admiral, can you destroy the fort?"

"With our munitions, I would fire from 3 vessels at closer range and destroy it within half a day."

"And what of the city? Can we keep it safe during the bombardment?"

"Yes, Captain Général. Maybe some minor damage may occur, but it is far enough away that we can concentrate on the fort without significant damage to the city."

By now, Leclerc thought, Rochambeau who has little patience would have already pulverized Fort Liberte about 50 kilometers east of here, far enough to not hear his cannon. He would undoubtedly make a landing and destroy anything in his path.

Boudet would be doing the same in Port Républicain and Kerverseau on the Spanish side. But here, he was limited in violence. His orders included conserving Cap Français intact at all costs, not counting that his wife Pauline wanted to use it as her new perch of social activity. Where is Toussaint Louverture, he thought?

He looked over at the J-Jacques, the ship that had on board Toussaint's two sons, Placide and Isaac, the secret weapon that could be leverage for Toussaint to cooperate with his mission's phase one. He had in his possession a letter to Toussaint from Napoleon to offer Toussaint retirement with full honor. To be diplomatic and most effective, he would dispatch the two boys and their tutor to personally deliver the letter to Toussaint.

Leclerc was impressed by the report of his aide about the splendid city but also disappointed at the reply from the Général. Lebrun was ordered to pay another visit to Général Christophe, with a sterner message and an added warning that refusal would be considered an act of rebellion.

The next morning, Lebrun came to announce once more that the fleet was that of the newly appointed governor-général of Saint Domingue, his Excellency Charles Victoire Emmanuel Leclerc. He wished Général Christophe good tidings and requested that the city be put in readiness for his landing with some twenty-two thousand soldiers as more ships would be arriving in the next several weeks. Lebrun spoke as if it was the first time this was being announced.

"You say Charles LeClerc has been appointed governor-général? Your government must know that Toussaint Louverture is the governor-général of the island and was appointed for life. What is this about a new governor-général?" Henry asked Lebrun.

"The First Consul simply wishes to relieve Governor Général Louverture of the cares and responsibilities of office and place them on the shoulders of a younger man, so the current Governor can retire and enjoy life. We come on a peaceful errand," replied Lebrun.

"If you come on this peaceful errand, Ensign, why the need for twenty-two thousand soldiers? We have plenty of soldiers, including me, in the service of France on this island for protection. Additionally, this demand should have been made to Governor Général Louverture prior to your arrival. I serve him and until I hear from him, I once again firmly state, I cannot grant any permission to land, sir. My position has not changed since the first interview and that Général Leclerc should follow protocol and direct his request to Governor Général Louverture. As a courtesy, if Général Leclerc sends his diplomatic pouch with his official request in a letter to Governor Louverture, I would dispatch a messenger to him for delivery."

"Général Leclerc demands a landing immediately, not waiting days, if not weeks, to hear back from Général Louverture," Lebrun said, obviously frustrated.

"As commander of this city, I am sure you understand that I cannot compromise its safety and simply allow an army of unknown origin and intent to disembark on our shores without the governor's permission. I am certain that the Governor would surely order an inspection to ensure that Général Leclerc was not being held captive by a foreign power against his will on those vessels. My friend, I will be forced to repel any endeavor to land, with all my resources, should it come to that. Please convey this to your Général" Henry warned.

"That is preposterous!" Lebrun complained before he was escorted back to the dock and transported to *L'Océan.*

Marie Louise came into the main living room after Lebrun had departed. She needed no second glance to tell her that her husband was troubled. She flew to his arms, "Henry, what is it?"

"We are in trouble," he answered "but you must be brave."

She snuggled into his arms and looked up at him. "Could you leave this beautiful place and live in a thatched hut in the fields, Marie-Louise?" Henry asked.

"As long as you are with me, it doesn't matter where we are. I love you! But why do you ask such a question? What has happened, Henry?"

"Twenty-two French warships will enter the harbor here at Cap-Français, possibly as early as by day's end. This can only mean one thing. I have limited troops at my disposal, and it would be some days before I could get reinforcements; therefore, we shall have to prepare for the worst." Henry said with concern.

"Is it you that must stay and fight those horrid Frenchmen? Why can't we both leave for safety?" pleaded Marie-Louise.

"I can't give up without a fight," said Henry.

"That settles it then. I will stay with you and fight as well!"

"No, Marie-Louise. You must escape with François, Françoise, and our baby girl Athénaïs and I will join you later. I want you to realize that if I fight this fleet of French, I shall no longer be a général of France, but considered a rebel – an outlaw and a traitor to France and be hunted."

"Then I will be hunted too along with you. I am devoted to you, my darling husband, whether slave or général" Marie-Louise answered.

They embraced and kissed. "Get only your most needed things ready for you and the children. Be ready to travel at a moment's notice. I will be back," said Henry.

The next morning, Henry had his men prepare a mule train and detached some soldiers to accompany Marie-Louise and two servants with supplies to a safe camp he had prepared in the mountains.

Henry hugged and kissed Marie-Louise and helped her onto her horse. He then hugged and kissed his children goodbye and watched as the mule train departed for the mountains.

When Lebrun arrived back at Leclerc's flagship and gave him the news, Leclerc was not entirely surprised. "It seems they intend to keep this colony for themselves," he said looking at both the Admiral and the *L'Océan*'s captain. "Ready your men for any attack that they may launch against the fleet."

Just then, Leclerc's wife Pauline came up to the three men "Are we ready to go on shore yet, Charles? I am growing increasingly bored here being stuck on these ships!"

"Soon, my darling, very soon" replied Leclerc

"Today is Wednesday. I want to open this weekend with the opera on Saturday. The troupe has been rehearsing Médée by Luigi Cherubini – the latest craze in Paris. It is a wonderful showcase for our sopranos. I am so excited," Pauline said with a clap and smile on her face. The local bourgeoisie will love it, and love me!

"We are working on a landing plan, as we speak, my dear," Leclerc responded to his wife.

You're the Général. Or should I say, Governor Général? Make it happen and have your very best uniform ready. I want you and I to make a grand and spectacular entrance under a thunder of applause!" Pauline excitedly stated as she mimicked a catwalk down the aisle of the grand theater, rehearsing her wave.

The massive French warship was captained by Louis de Latouche-Tréville who looked on with contempt towards the blonde Napoleon, the nickname he heard his men attach to Leclerc. The captain was born into a noble family of naval officers, Latouche enlisted at the age of thirteen and rose to become a competent frigate captain, battling several British ships during the American War of Independence.

His skills were sought after and he was constantly entrusted with important personalities of the time as passengers, notably Louis XVI and the Marquis de Lafayette. He couldn't believe that he had to bear the insult of this little bitch, Pauline, who treated this campaign like a theater setting. He wanted to personally throw her overboard but as Napoleon's sister and Leclerc's wife, had to bite his tongue.

Leclerc looked at his wife and was so infatuated with her that he forgave the childish and immature whims she so frequently displayed. "But Pauline, you haven't yet even met with any representatives from the theater house in the city."

"You are the Governor Général, Charles. Remember that. They cannot have the nerve or will to say no." She then looked at Treville and said "Do you see any problem with my wishes Captain? I would presume you and your crew have the competence to get this mission completed, Oui?

"Yes Madame, we are quite competent. As for the social events, I will leave that up to the Captain Général as I am but a simple sailor," he said with contempt in his tone.

Leclerc could see that his wife did not belong on the deck of a battleship with a man like Treville. He could not afford Treville to lose respect for him, but Pauline would not help in that department.

"Pauline, let me have you taken back to the *Splendide*. This ship will soon become extremely tense and possibly dangerous with all the activity on board and I want to assure your comfort" stated Leclerc.

"Alright, Charles. Just get this business of taking over the city accomplished as soon as possible. I want to return to the *Splendide* to supervise rehearsal of the opening of the opera anyway" she concluded. "Remember, La Médée this weekend."

Pauline was fuming as plans were not in place and she wanted off these ships and onto dry land. The salt air was making a mess of her hair, requiring constant attention from her two coiffeuse.

Back on board the *Splendide,* she immediately sent for the young cabin steward Maurice, a thoroughly handsome mulatto boy of sixteen with bleached blonde curly hair, who had served as her young lover during the voyage. He at first knew nothing of women or sex as he was a virgin, but Pauline made sure that his education would be wide and his deflowering swift.

He had been sent to fill her bath with warm water on the second night of the voyage and she immediately seduced him. She was wearing a nightgown that allowed her breasts to escape it freely and summoned him over to the bed she sat on.

She untied the belt rope of his pants and the garment fell to the floor. She held his balls with her hand which immediately produced an erection as she put his penis into her mouth. Within ten seconds, he ejaculated, and she sucked, swallowed, and licked the sperm from his penis.

Maurice was as shocked as embarrassed and knew not what had happened to him or what to do. He had never experienced such physical pleasure. Pauline took over, just as a teacher would guide a student, and began to educate him on how to please her, how to suck her breasts and her vagina. She quickly reignited his erection and laid him down as she mounted him from on top as deep as she could get him. She rode him until he once again ejaculated and again she sucked and licked him clean again, Maurice enjoying every moment of it.

During the ocean passage, Pauline took advantage of his youth and vibrance. It did not take too long for him to be aroused again and again, her knowing that his premature ejaculations would soon be calmed. She laid down and took him once again inside her, this time with him on top. Then from the side, then from the rear, and over and over until she exploded with a wet frenzy which at first frightened him, aroused him into a long and solid ejaculation inside of her as their body fluids mixed in a soaking of the sheets.

Night after night he became a willing student as he would provide her indulgence and she would dispense instruction. He did as best he could to perform for her as he knew that the night that he failed her may be the last night of receiving this sweet indulgence which he had become quickly addicted to.

And here he was again, happy to be summoned as he was growing jealous each time she visited with her husband, the big général. Maurice conjured up a fantasy that one day she would leave her husband and forever be with him as his wife.

"Come to me Maurice for I am sad," Pauline said with a frown and puckered lip.

"Why my Princess?" asked Maurice

"We must await on these God-forsaken ships a few more days until we dock in Cap Français, Maurice, that's why," Pauline said. "Tomorrow morning, I must go back to the *L'Océan* and speed up the landing with the Général and that stupid captain. Pour me a bath and plan on joining me. I need you tonight."

The next morning, under the scrutiny of spyglasses on them, Leclerc ordered all ships tenders filled with soldiers. It would take hours before all the tenders were filled as he wanted them to row together for both safety and the visual effect on the city's inhabitants.

Henry was with his troops at camp when a messenger galloped in and announced the pending troop landing in the city. Henry ordered his men to retrieve the torches they had already prepared by dousing them with kerosene and they proceeded to burn the city, house by house. The resident's worst fears had come true, they pleaded with the soldiers to not burn their homes or businesses, and the soldiers respectfully pulling them to the side, and out of the way, as they did so.

It pained Henry immensely to realize that he was charged with the destruction of the city he so came to love, but that it was the only way to save the colony, and it was Toussaint's orders.

By late morning, Leclerc stood in horror on the deck of *L'Océan* as Pauline came running to his side. Smoke was billowing out of all parts of the city simultaneously and flames could be seen from far away.

"They are burning my city, Charles! Don't just stand there, do something!" yelled Pauline to Leclerc.

"There is nothing that can be done. It will be hours before we can enter it, and by then, it will have been destroyed," answered Leclerc.

"Find me another city, Charles! How could you let them destroy my plans!" shouted Pauline.

"These Blacks are ruthless and uncaring for anything but themselves. I will soon teach them a thing or two." Leclerc angrily replied.

Take me to Port-Républicain then!" demanded Pauline. "I want a city! You promised me the great city of Cap Français. Now I must settle for second best! You stupid fool!"

"It is a good thing that no one is within earshot, Pauline. They do not know your temper tantrums as well as I do. They would think you are serious."

"Charles. Leave me alone," she said as she turned her back on him.

"You will sail tomorrow, but not to enter Port-Républicain until it is safe to do so. I will be delayed as I must make land here and then make a stop in the city of St. Marc and a fort named Crête-à-Pierrot to the east. I will rendezvous with you soon" said Leclerc. "Will you share my bed with me tonight my Love?" asked Leclerc.

"No Charles, I am not in the mood for lovemaking. I am distraught until you make this right. Have me escorted to my ship and I will see you in Port-Républicain." Pauline said, as she thought of how much she needed Maurice's penis to calm her nerves.

That night, the sky was lit with the flames of the most beautiful city in the Caribbean. The city was denied to the Governor Général and his wife Pauline. Their plans to enter as royalty had literally gone up in smoke.

Marie-Louise had sleepless nights until finally five days later, Henry arrived at the camp. He was at the head of a contingent of one hundred soldiers on horseback and still in the uniform of a French général.

She met him with outstretched arms and tears streaming down her cheeks. She studied his face which seemed to have grown older in the past days but still, he smiled and hugged her in reunion.

"Is all lost?" she questioned, continuing her study.

"Yes, and I am now an outlaw, a rebel, and a criminal" Henry answered.

"Yes, but you are my outlaw, my rebel, my criminal. But most of all, you are my husband and I love you!" she replied. "Will you be followed by the French here?" she asked.

"No," he answered. "These mountains cannot be entered except through areas where they can be ambushed".

"And what of our city, our home? Will they take our belongings?" she asked.

"I had to burn it. Burn it all. I had to and hated to. Your place of birth, the place where I found you and where we conceived our family. But I could not allow it to be a welcome encampment for Leclerc's army."

"Is our home completely gone, Henry?"

"Gone. I had to put the torch to that one first to set the example for the others. It caused me great pain and I was glad you were not there to see it. It was devastating to me."

"Then this will be our home," exclaimed Marie-Louise, leading him inside. "We can be as happy here as in our mansion if the French don't come. What's going to be done now? Does it mean Leclerc has or will reconquer the island?"

"He has entered the ruined city of Cap-Français, but I do not believe he can reconquer the island. I am waiting to have a conference with Toussaint and Dessalines."

Ten

THE INVASION BEGINS

Fort-Liberté
February 1802

Donatien-Marie-Joseph de Vimeur, Vicomte de Rochambeau stood on the deck of the mighty French warship *Trajan*. The ship, a Téméraire-class 74-gun ship of the line of the French Navy, was personally assigned to him by Admiral Villaret de Joyeuse, who as a captain commissioned the vessel in 1793 at Lorient, as a lethal weapon to pulverize Fort-Liberté, just west of the Spanish side, and take the wretched town.

Rochambeau was a frustrated Général who had thus far achieved a lackluster career, always in the shadow of his father, the great Jean-Baptiste Donatien Rochambeau, the Général who brought great honor to France during the American Revolutionary campaign.

He was nearing 50 years old and desperately needed to propel his reputation and shed the introduction of, *'the son of Général Jean-Baptiste Donatien Rochambeau'* each time he was introduced to someone new. The old man was in his eighties and still of sound mind, reminding his son that this campaign would be his last hope to carve his name in the annals of the great French military Généraux.

His aide, the young 19-year-old Charles Frederick, was the son of his cousin Margaret, and much younger than he was at 25 when serving as the aide to his father in Williamsburg back in 1780. He promised his cousin to watch after the boy and purposefully assigned him as his aide to keep an eye on him.

He looked over at the old fort, now over 70 years old, and by his inventory of French records estimated the cannons at about 40. In the morning he will easily neutralize it with half his cannon, 32 on the port side, and an additional 40 cannon from two other accompanying vessels.

They would then make a landing and take the town in time for lunch as he was assured these slaves, or should I say ex-slaves, would run for the hills and abandon the town during the first torrential downfall of cannonballs.

"Get some rest, Charles. Be ready at daybreak as I want you by my side when we plant our division's flag in the town square," stated an excited Rochambeau.

"Yes sir. Should I prepare your parade uniform for the occasion?" asked Charles.

"No need. There is nobody of distinction in this shoddy town. I want to take it quickly and join the action in Saint-Marc. Let's retire. Be ready to move out at first light. And when I say be ready Charles, I don't mean that is your wake-up time," Rochambeau stated with a smile.

"Yes sir," Charles said as he saluted to leave.

At 5:15 a.m., three ships began to unleash hell on the fort with a continued barrage of deadly cannon fire whistling to their targets in the darkness, as 1,200 French Grenadiers prepared for an invasion.

The fort continued to return fire without causing damage to any of the ships and by 8 a.m. there was silence from the fort, Rochambeau deducing that they were already out of ammunition. He ordered the landing from all ships, their tenders filled with anxious soldiers seeking first blood, after months of boredom on the ships.

Light gunfire peppered the incoming army, occasionally knocking a soldier from their tender into the water. By 9 a.m., the first of the soldiers hit the ground and began the onslaught towards the town, about 3 kilometers from the shore.

The second wave of tenders landed to attack the fort where a fierce battle ensued. Rochambeau smiled as he preferred that these savages put up a resistance rather than acquiesce to the superior power of his army. At least that would give the men some field training and stories to repeat.

Rochambeau decided to accompany the troops to the town with Charles at his side. By the time they arrived, they found the town deserted, but fires were burning on the fringes towards the east. The Général directed his army towards that direction through the center of town.

When they arrived at the town square, they stopped and looked around. 'Where are you, savages?' thought the Général. Before he could finish the thought, a spray of gunfire erupted mowing down two dozen men in one volley. Then, two cannons unleashed a volley of shrapnel that tore holes into another dozen men when the firing ended.

"Take cover!" he yelled as the soldiers crouched behind anything they could find. Suddenly a barrage of several dozen enemy combatants dodged out of buildings, running down the streets.

"Fire!" Rochambeau yelled as nearly two dozen of them were hit as the rest scrambled to another street. A captain ordered "Pursue them!" as over 100 soldiers began running after the group.

"I'm going into the fight, Uncle," Charles said as he sped to join the soldiers.

"Charles, wait!" Rochambeau yelled but the boy was out of hearing distance sprinting towards the rear of the advancing army. They turned a corner onto a smaller street to the right as the captain split the group and sent half to the street on the left.

Charles' heart was pounding, and he was giddy, not able to wipe the smile off his face. This is the moment he had been waiting for all these months during, and after training. He had never fired a shot at a real person before and was itching to do so now. He so wanted to kill some of these black savages that he and his friends onboard the ship had boasted about.

The group stopped as they heard a noise on a second-floor balcony to the right. Charles' adrenalin was racing through his trembling body as the young soldiers pointed their rifles to where the noises had emanated from.

Suddenly on the opposite side of the street, two dozen enemy soldiers appeared from second-floor windows and balconies, opening fire on the group from behind, killing or wounding nearly 20 men on the first volley.

"Form a line and ready your arms!" yelled the lieutenant. But by the time they could aim for the left side of the street where the shots had emanated from, they had disappeared. They were then surprised from the right this time as dozens of enemy soldiers opened fire before they could turn and set their sights towards them.

Another dozen or so men were downed, leaving the young soldiers mortified at what had just happened within seconds as their comrades lay dead on the ground or agonizing in pain. Charles lay under cover behind a barrel waiting for an order when the lieutenant yelled "Retreat!"

As Charles got up to join the group in the center of the street for the trot back to the main square, enemy soldiers exited from first-floor buildings. Charles looked up across the road and spotted a young soldier in an old ragged French uniform with his rifle raised toward him. It was surreal he thought. He could see the whites of the young man's eyes, his age no more than 15 he guessed, as everything went into slow motion where seconds became minutes.

Charles began to lift his rifle but realized it was too late to achieve the firing position. The young soldier boy locked eyes with his, both somewhat shocked at the clarity of it all, sharing a strange moment of intimacy together. He felt a strange thump on his left rib as he saw smoke coming from the end of the boy soldier's rifle, and beyond it, the whites of his eyes framing the deep brown pupils. He felt a shocking pain as he looked down at the dusty ground where a puddle of blood had already begun to form, then realizing that it was from his open wound that the liquid was steadily streaming from. He slumped over and lost consciousness.

A soldier came to his side and picked him up and another came to help as they quickly left the scene to head back to the main square.

As they turned the corner on the main street, gunfire could be heard throughout the town. When Rochambeau sighted the two soldiers running with Charles in the center, unconscious and lifeless, dread engulfed him. He ran towards the three, who collapsed upon his arrival of exhaustion, as the entire town cried of hysteria.

Charles' still body lay in the street as he desperately searched for any sign of life, but it was fruitless. The boy was dead, barely before his 20th birthday. He closed his eyes as he heard his cousin's last wish before his departure; *'Donatien, I am placing my only son in your care. I beg you to bring him home safely.'*

It took hours for French forces to subdue the enemy, however many escaped after they set torches to the town, forcing the French to fight fires as Rochambeau marched to the fort where fighting was still being waged.

Sometime after 4 p.m. that afternoon, Rochambeau had realized he had underestimated the will of the enemy. He had thought this would be a casual battle, no more dangerous than a training exercise, and he and Charles would have been enjoying a field lunch by noon. Instead, he was still in the heat of the action and had lost a beloved relative.

The French army entered the fort where dead men lie everywhere. The last of the resisters, about 40 men in all, were against the fort wall and being guarded by several grenadiers.

"Who is in charge of this fort?" bellowed Rochambeau to the men assembled.

A man with a blood-stained and ripped old French army shirt and trousers stepped forward. "Our captain is dead, I have assumed command."

"Your name?"

"Lieutenant Richard Rousseau."

"Where is the rest of this battalion?"

"I do not know," answered Rousseau.

"I do not accept this as surrender. As far as I am concerned, we are still in the heat of battle," Rochambeau stated with Rousseau not knowing what that meant.

"But I have surrendered the fort, Général."

Rochambeau turned away from Rousseau and walked to his captain. "Line up your men and bayonet them."

"But Général, they have surrendered. I had promised them that they would not be killed if they did so," answered the captain.

Rochambeau's face contorted and turned ugly. "They have brought disgrace on our army. They are nothing but savages. "Give me that," he said as he grabbed the rifle from the captain, turned, and stabbed the bayonet into the belly of Rousseau twisting it as the soldier fell to the floor, began to spasm for several seconds and went still. He was dead.

He turned to the captain. "Order your men captain. If you don't, you will be relieved of duty and court-martialed."

"Grenadiers, ready your bayonets," ordered the captain as Rochambeau grinned a tight smile. The French soldiers looked at one another in confusion but did as they were told. The black enemy soldiers dropped their heads, some began to pray and others protested as they had surrendered the fight with the promise of life.

"Advance, ordered the captain as the soldiers advanced on the unarmed soldiers with their backs against the wall. A few of the blacks dashed to the side and were mowed down by grenadiers as the others advanced on the rest of the men, launching their bayonets into their chests and stomachs in a grizzly sight of mass murder until they were either dead or near death and moaning their last breaths.

"Should I have graves dug, mon Général?" asked the captain.

"Yes, but only bury our men except Charles and any other officers. Take their bodies onboard for burial at sea. As for the Africans, throw them over the side to the sharks – dead or still alive," ordered Rochambeau as he turned and walked away.

With far less brutality but equal efficiency, Générals Jean Boudet and Latouche-Tréville were as effective in taking Port-Républicain, the colony's second-largest city.

Troops landed under cover fire from the frigates and swiftly contained any counterattacks from its defenders and ships attacked Fort Bizoton, capturing the entire city before it could mount a suitable defense or burn the city if that was the plan.

The French army marched into Port-Républicain without dispensing much more violence. The surprise attack had worked brilliantly. Boudet was more of a diplomat in warfare, preferring to conquer his enemy through reasoning and mutual agreement strategizing that slaughtering them would not be in his best interest.

He arranged a meeting with the commander of the south, Général Laplume. Laplume, who was in Les Cayes on the southern peninsula, had not yet received any word from Toussaint and ordered his men to cease fire to attend the meeting.

"You are an officer of France, Brigadier Général Laplume," stated Boudet. "This expedition is one of France. You are still wearing the uniform of France, and I, nor have anyone else, has asked you to relinquish it."

"If you come in peace, then why did you send cannon to our fort and land under the hail of fire?" asked Laplume.

The initial cannon was a precaution. A misunderstanding of your intentions, Général. We were under the impression that you would have burned this magnificent city by orders of Toussaint, as

Général Christophe had done to Cap-Français. Thus, Général, you were guilty by association, then.

Laplume had endured years of guilty pressure by Toussaint and felt he was ungrateful for bringing the maroon army of Dieudonné to his side those many years ago. It is he that had disposed of Dieudonné who had wanted to fight for the British against Toussaint.

His only mistake in all those years was being unprepared for Rigaud's attack during the beginning of the Civil War.

"And where does that leave us, the troops of the Colonial Army of Saint Domingue, Général Boudet?"

"Exactly as you are now. You are French soldiers and officers. You will continue to serve France. "

"And our ranks?" asked Laplume.

"All officers will maintain their current ranks and pay, Général Laplume," Boudet advised. "There has been a rumor that this expedition has come to re-enslave the population, it is not so. We have heard in France that Toussaint has gone too far with his strict conservative laws."

"Yes, many of his laws are unpopular and viewed as stricter than the time of slavery."

"How so, asked Boudet?"

"No man can come to Port Républicain without a passport issued by Toussaint, for example," answered Laplume.

"But slavery is over," Boudet said, now playing diplomatically to the petitions of Laplume whom he trusted knew the will of the people.

"Exactly, said Laplume. Our Général Moyiz argued with Toussaint about it. If a man is working a plantation in Saint-Marc and a family member is sick in Port Républicain, he would require a passport to travel. Or if he wanted to work in another town, he was bound to the plantation he was once enslaved under for employment. This is all ridiculous. Toussaint had Moyiz killed because he resisted in the north and tried to voice for his people," protested Laplume.

"Rescind the passport practice immediately in Port Républicain. Give word that any citizen can travel anywhere in their colony," Boudet said. "As for the work requirements, I will take that up with General Leclerc. What else?..."

Laplume began to register a list of grievances against Toussaint as Boudet sought to please him by rescinding the most basic ones and promising redress to the others.

After dispatching Pauline the following day after the fires began, Leclerc entered Cap Français to assess the damage and confirmed that the city was destroyed. He had the army set about putting out fires and making nice with the town's inhabitants who were demoralized, many having lived through the fires during the 1791 slave uprisings.

The torching of the magnificent city of Cap Français completely upset the rich northern Blancs of the colony. Many had city homes and businesses there as well as plantations in the countryside. The disruption to their plantation operations and revenues would continue for months, if not years to come, until the city could be rebuilt, and trade re-established.

He decided he would unleash his first secret weapon as Toussaint had decided to resist. He had tried to enter in peace, but that had only led to the destruction of this valuable city. As he stood on the dock, he looked out towards the harbor and sighted the ship *La Vertu* as it lazily swung at anchor.

Aboard the ship were the surviving leaders of the mulatto faction from the civil war waged several years ago; Rigaud, Pétion, Villatte, and Boyer, along with hundreds of good officers and fighters who knew the terrain well – a readymade army eager for revenge with their blades and possessing a reputation of violent fighting skills. He would have *La Vertu* immediately sail south to Saint Marc and Les Cayes for their debarkation and active duty assignments.

He then looked over at the sailing ship, the *J-Jacques*, which contained his second secret weapon supplied by his brother-in-law; Toussaint's two sons, Placide and Isaac.

They had been enjoying the finest schooling at the College de la Marche in Paris. They also were privileged to special attention from Napoleon to prepare them for their important mission; to convince their father to retire from his duties.

Napoleon had armed them with a powerful letter that contained flattery, praise, compliments, enticements, and finally a veiled threat should Toussaint think otherwise. There was no time for back-and-forth communications. This was a one-time, lay it all on the line letter, from the First Consul.

Also amongst their assets were the two gifted French officer uniforms, including a saber and pistols, personally handed them by Napoleon with the prospect of bright futures in the French military as officers, an enticement for the boys to work extra hard at persuasion, should his letter fall on deaf ears.

To ensure that they behaved as expected, the boys were to be in the company of Monsieur Coisnon, their devoted tutor, and loyal confident, since their arrival in France several years ago. He was the closest thing to family, like a beloved uncle or godfather.

He would dispatch the trio to Ennery, where he had it under expert authority, that their mother was currently residing, to begin a family reunion. Toussaint, wherever he was would not be able to resist seeing the boys and Suzanne of all people would surely know the means to message to Toussaint that they had arrived home.

With those plans decided, Leclerc began to tour the town as its chief comforter. He would stop to speak with the city's citizens as they began the daunting task of sifting through the ashes of their destroyed homes, businesses, and lives. He would portray the complete opposite of Toussaint; compassionate, caring, and like them, in rage at what Toussaint had allowed to happen to them.

He set up his office in the charred ruins of Government House, or what was left of it. The structure, albeit severely damaged, was still a grand and stately building. As he looked up and around him, he could see that nearly a hundred workers were at work cleaning, repairing, laying a new roof, and hauling out the debris.

For three days, Charles Leclerc would entertain all visitors and work towards consolation and campaigning continuously for their love. He was very successful at it.

And so it went throughout the colony. Leclerc's plan to have the citizens see them as saviors and as a counterbalance to the strict ways of Toussaint was welcomed by many.

Whatever ideas that citizens or soldiers would come up with that were contrary to the ways of Toussaint, agree with them, but however, make no promises. Get them on our side no matter what they say, as they went from town to town with this message and secured support from normal citizens and military soldiers alike.

In the first ten days, the French occupied the island's ports, towns, and a large part of the cultivated land.

Placide, Isaac, and Monsieur Coisnon arrived at Sancey, the Louverture's plantation at Ennery. They were accompanied by four French soldiers under special assignment to transport Toussaint's sons and their tutor to the plantation and instructed to await the response from Toussaint to the letter of Napoleon.

When the boys entered the familiar home, with Coisnon following, they called out "Maman, Maman!" which summoned a shocked Suzanne from the salon to the foyer with open arms and tears streaming down her cheeks.

The boys went to their mother, and they hugged in unison as Coisnon looked on, not daring to interrupt the reunion.

When the excitement had somewhat subsided, Suzanne looked to the boys. "Have you forgotten the manners I have instilled in you, my sons? Where is my introduction to this fine gentleman you have entered our home with?"

"Maman, we present to you Monsieur Coisnon, our Tutor from France. Mr. Coisnon, this is Madame Suzanne Louverture, wife of the Governor Général Toussaint Louverture and she is our mother," Placide stated with pride.

Coisnon bowed with formality. "Your humble servant, Michel Coisnon, at your service, Madame."

Saint Jean, Toussaint and Suzanne's 11-year-old burst into the foyer, saw Placide and Isaac, and ran to them. They immediately embraced in a group hug and the boys dashed up to their rooms as if it was only yesterday they had done so, as Suzanne summoned the staff to show Monsieur Coisnon the guest room and prepare a lavish dinner for the evening. She then immediately sent for Toussaint's guards, who had been left for her safety, and dispatched a message to him to come home as the boys had arrived.

A messenger arrived at Toussaint's headquarters in the Artibonite with the message from Suzanne. Toussaint was home within two days, arriving with a contingent of nearly 1,000 soldiers, two hundred of whom were his honor guards with their shiny helmets. The captain of the guard was left to interview the French soldiers, who had set up a camp in the field, as Toussaint walked towards the home.

Before Toussaint could take the first step up to the front door, Placide and Isaac had already come out to the veranda and yelled 'Papa' towards their father with Saint Jean right behind.

After some ceremonial affectionate hugs, father, and sons ascended the stairs where Toussaint met Suzanne, kissed her on either cheek and they embraced in a hug. They turned and entered the home and as Toussaint looked into the study, he saw Monsieur Coisnon, whom he had never met but had much correspondence with, standing in the room.

"Is this the fine man who has schooled my boys in Latin, Mathematics, and many other things necessary for their development?" Toussaint stated warmly as he walked into the room with his sons behind him.

"It is I who has attempted to educate these fine young men who already had the benefit of an excellent upbringing, Governor Général Toussaint Louverture – the faithful servant of France!" Coisnon returned with equal enthusiasm.

"You have my deepest gratitude for the job you have done and I have so appreciated your continued communication with monthly reports of their progress," Toussaint sincerely stated.

"I will let you be the judge of that, Governor Général. Let them dazzle you with their knowledge of all things themselves," replied Coisnon.

Suzanne interrupted the reunion and said, "Come, all of you. It is time for our supper. Toussaint, you must be tired from the trip," she said as she handed Toussaint a lightly sweetened lemonade. Come enjoy your first meal with your sons, and their distinguished educator. Join us Monsieur Coisnon. Come boys to the table."

The two boys could not be more different, though they were to this day inseparable, even more so by the distance from home they had been subjected to. Placide, at 20, was tall, slim and lanky, with skin the color of café au lait, and he sported hair that was beyond curly, and tied in a pigtail. It was nowhere near the afro that grew on 15-year-old Isaac, who was short, like his father, with much darker skin, almost ebony, and not chunky but big-boned.

They all had a lively and wonderful dinner with Monsieur Coisnon as the guest of honor. The boys shared story after story about their adventures in France and each time the conversation would fade, Mr. Coisnon would reignite it by saying to the boys; 'tell your parents of the time when…

After dinner, they continued their conversation in the living room, seated on the comfortable couches.

After a half hour or so, Isaac disappeared and returned about 20 minutes later. He was dressed in a splendid French officer's uniform gifted to him by Napoleon himself during their last visit to the Tuileries Palace where Napoleon on occasion resided.

Suzanne let out a soft gasp, Saint Jean said "WOW", and Placide reached for his mother's hand. Toussaint contained his shock for the benefit of his son, producing a huge smile.

Accessorizing the formal uniform were two pistols tucked in his belt, which Toussaint hoped were unloaded, and an ornate sword that dragged on the floor as he walked.

Isaac formerly paraded over to his father and saluted, waiting for his father to salute back. Toussaint raised his hand in salute and the boy formerly brought up his left hand which held a scroll bound with the tricolor red, white, and blue ribbon, and sealed in wax with the official seal of the Consulate of France.

"I hereby, Governor Général Toussaint Louverture, husband of Suzanne Louverture, father to Placide, Isaac, and Saint Jean Louverture, benevolent leader of the citizens of Saint Domingue, and citizen of France, present you greetings from the First Consul, and this official correspondence he had instructed me to be hand delivered to you."

Toussaint lifted his hand and accepted the scroll, "Correspondence accepted. Your duty has been well performed," Toussaint stated with formality and in his deep voice, as Isaac smiled and looked at Placide for acknowledgment.

Placide nodded his approval as his mother squeezed his hand. Toussaint looked at the scroll made of the finest of parchment and ran his hand down it to absorb the rich feel, placing it on the table next to him to read later.

Isaac had walked to the couch and due to his swords, could not take a seat but stood behind his mother and Saint Jean. Suzanne took his hand and brought it to her shoulder to hold as he stood behind her.

Coisnon looked at Toussaint and stated, "I am sure the innocence of your son, who has transported this most important document, speaks to the stature that you and your family enjoy with France and with the First Consul, Governor Général."

"Come here, Isaac. I want you to tell me the history behind your ornate uniform," said Toussaint as he admired the fine couture of the garment while noticing the unearned epaulets of gold on his shoulders.

Isaac smiled and slowly walked over to Toussaint, trying as best he could to lift the sword so it wouldn't drag on his parents' wooden floors. Saint Jean looked admiringly at his older brother with a smile on his face.

"Yes, Papa. The First Consul invited Placide and I to dine with him at the Tuileries Palace. There were many fine people there, including his brother-in-law, the captain-Général, his most beautiful wife, Pauline, and their son Dermide, along with many other officers and ladies.

"And what conversations did the First Consul enjoy with you and Placide?"

"The First Consul spoke to everyone of the courage of the blacks of Saint Domingue, and how they bolstered our army. He gave us these uniforms, Placide and I, to wear as a symbol of the army's integrated future," Isaac proudly stated.

"I am so proud of how you properly presented the letter and can see how Monsieur Coisnon has exceeded my expectations in the improvement of your education," Toussaint said as he turned to Coisnon. "Thank you Monsieur Coisnon."

Coisnon smiled and nodded as he glanced at the scroll sitting on the table with such informality and lack of urgency, he thought. This is a correspondence from the First Consul of France, yet Toussaint treats it like a casual letter from a distant acquaintance. Very strange indeed. "Shall you not read your correspondence, Governor Général?"

"I believe we have all had a long and eventful day. It is time to retire and tomorrow revisit the issue. Come, my sons," Toussaint said as he opened his arms wide for his two boys.

The boys walked to him, and they shared a hug and kisses. The boys then went to their mother and bid her goodnight as they marched upstairs, Isaac still holding up his sword to not damage any articles in its way. Monsieur Coisnon also stood and said goodnight as he slowly walked to his room.

Toussaint then asked Suzanne; "Would you join me in the study where we can read this letter from the First Consul, alone?"

"Of course. Would you like another coffee?" she asked.

"That would be nice. I will light the room and meet you there."

Toussaint arrived at the study with two lanterns in his hand and carefully lit three more in the room. The heat of the many lamps would be tempered by the coolness of the January night he thought. He untied the ornate ribbon from the scroll and as he was cutting the wax seal with his nail, Suzanne arrived with her favorite porcelain coffee pot, cups and saucers, and matching sugar container on a silver tray.

"Suzanne, come here and read this correspondence from the First Consul. My eyes are weary from the long trip as the dust on the road today was very dry." Toussaint said as the aroma of their best coffee product engulfed the room. "Is that this year's blend from Sancey?" he asked.

"Yes, a fine crop indeed," she replied, finishing the preparation of two cups as Toussaint opened the small double doors of the study that led to the veranda for some fresh air. He could hear the creatures of the night singing their opera with instruments given to them by God. An orchestra of the wild, he smiled, as his thoughts admired the expanse of God's creations.

Suzanne unrolled the scroll and held it with two hands at arm's length to adjust the distance to obtain the best vision with the spectacles that Toussaint had gifted her for Christmas. It helped her to read, but she was still growing accustomed to the new apparatus. She began to speak.

To Citizen Toussaint Louverture, Général in Chief of the Army of Saint Domingue

Citizen Général,

The peace with England and all the other European powers which has just seated the Republic in the first place of power and grandeur, allows at the same time for the government to occupy itself with the colony of Saint Domingue. We send to you the citizen-Général Leclerc, our brother-in-law, in the capacity of Captain-Général as well as First Magistrate of the colony. He is accompanied by a force suitable to ensure that the sovereignty of the French people is respected. It is in these circumstances that we are pleased to hope that you are going to prove to us, and to all of France, the sincerity of the sentiments that you have constantly expressed in all the letters which you have written to us.

She paused and lifted her coffee cup to her lips for a sip. Toussaint looked at her, unable to contain his love and admiration for her. She had stood by him all these tense years. She had not signed up for this life. Their life was meant to be one of leisurely farming their meager coffee and sugar plantations and living a life much simpler than what it had become. It had been ten years since he received that other letter from his prior master, mentor, and friend, the Bayon de Libertat, requesting him to rush to Cap Français and assist him when the entirety of the northern plains was set on fire by the first violent rebellion.

That was the beginning of a new life for him and Suzanne. He looked at her, daintily sipping her coffee, and wondered, had she made the mistake of not preventing him from joining the rebellion and fighting all these years?

Suzanne put her half-finished cup of coffee down and continued…

We have conceived an esteem for you, and we are pleased to recognize and to proclaim the great services which you have rendered to the French people; if her flag flies over Saint Domingue, it is to you and the brave blacks that it is owed. Summoned by your talent and the force of circumstances to the highest command, you have done away with the civil war, put a brake on the persecution of various ferocious men, and returned honor to religion and the cult of God, from whom everything emanates.

"This is very flattering, Toussaint," she said as she lifted her cup and took another sip. "More coffee?"

"No. Please continue."

She put the cup down again, picked up the letter, adjusted her spectacles, and began to read once more…

The constitution which you have made, while including many good things, also contains some which are contrary to the sovereignty of the French people, of which Saint Domingue forms a portion. The circumstances in which you have found yourself, surrounded by enemies on all sides, without the Metropole being able to help you or supply you, once rendered legitimate the articles of that constitution which otherwise might not have been; but today when circumstances are so happily changed, you will be the first to render homage to the sovereignty of the nation which counts you among the number of its most illustrious citizens, for the services you have rendered it, and for the talents and force of character with which nature has gifted you. Any different conduct would be irreconcilable with the idea we have formed of you.

Suzanne stopped at that sentence and looked at Toussaint who had leaned forward from his previous posture of comfortably leaning back in his chair. The First Consul had struck a nerve.

She squinted her eyes at the next sentence, and before reading it, looked at Toussaint with concern.

"Go ahead, Suzanne. Read the rest."

"It is not good, Toussaint. You should brace yourself for the words that come next," she calmly warned.

"Please, continue," said Toussaint as Suzanne lifted the letter and focused her eyes once more on the document.

It would cause you to lose your numerous rights to the gratitude of the republic and would dig beneath you an abyss which, in swallowing you up, might also contribute to the misfortune of those brave blacks, whose courage we love, and whom it would pain us to be obliged to punish for rebellion. We have made known to your children and to their preceptor the sentiments by which we are animated, and we are sending them back to you. Assist the Captain-Général with your counsel, your influence, and your talents. What is it that you can desire? The liberty of the blacks! You know that in all the countries where we have been, we have given that to those people who did not already have it. Recognition, honor, and fortune! After the services that you have rendered, which you will still render in this circumstance, together with the sentiments that we have for you, you must not be uncertain of your recognition, your fortune, and the honors that await you.

"You can stop there, Suzanne. Just read the final signatory line please, interrupted Toussaint.

"It is signed…

Paris, Brumaire 27, Year Ten, November 18, 1801
The First Consul, signed Napoleon Bonaparte

Suzanne rolled up the scroll, handed it to Toussaint, and studied his reaction. "What are you going to do, my husband? What does all this mean to you and us?"

"It means that Captain-Général Leclerc has been neglectful in not sending me this correspondence earlier. This letter is dated four months prior. Why the delay in my receiving it?"

"There was nearly two months of the voyage from France on the ship, Toussaint. That accounts for some time and another many days where you were not available for delivery?"

"And before the captain-Général assures my receipt of this important correspondence from the First Consul, he destroys our forts, kills our people, and ransacks our cities?" asked Toussaint. "What if it is the Captain-Général who has gone mad and is violating his orders from the First Consul? The letter from our First Consul and the actions of the Captain-Général are quite contrary to one another!"

Suzanne was always his balance at times like this. His North star, his compass, "But Toussaint, he writes that he is committed to the liberty of us blacks, as is all of France," she reasoned.

"Can you be so sure? he asked. "I will send my response back to the captain-Général immediately, so he understands my position.

"What are you going to do?" Toussaint.

"You will assist me in preparing an appropriate response and dispatch it with Isaac, Placide, and Monsieur Coisnon. I want Leclerc to understand the severity of all this."

The following day, Toussaint sent his sons back to Cap Français with the four French soldiers and Coisnon to deliver his response to Leclerc. He had his honor guard escort them to the perimeter he controlled to not have their passage hindered along the way by violent clashes.

The colony was in a state of confusion as to what was happening as they contemplated what side to take. Refugees from Cap Français littered the road as they made their way from the charred city to other towns and cities where lodging or relatives would provide them boarding and comfort. Placide looked at the chaos and was deep in thought as to the direction of the colony from here on in.

They arrived at Cap Français, where they had originally departed from less than a week prior, and headed straight for the government house where the captain-Général Leclerc was housed. It was early, about 5 a.m. when they were announced.

Leclerc just nodded to the boys and Coisnon, as his aide handed him the letter from Toussaint that the boys had been entrusted to deliver. He broke the seal and read the letter, skipping over the beginning salutation, formalities, and niceties of correspondence, instead going to the subject matter which he read out loud.

Those rights impose upon me duties higher than those of nature; I am prepared to sacrifice my children to my color; I send them back to you in order that you will not believe that I am bound by their presence. Should they remain among the French, that will not hinder me from acting in the best interests of the inhabitants of Saint Domingue. It will require some time to decide which course I am to take; meanwhile, I beg you to stop the march of your troops, that we may spare the effusion of blood, of which too much as already been spilled.

Leclerc lost his composure as Placide, Isaac, Coisnon, the aide and one of the soldiers looked on.

"Who does this gilded African think he is!" he yelled. "He is violating the orders of his superior in command; the First Consul and me. I am the supreme leader in this colony and I demand him to submit to my authority!

"Should I prepare a response, captain-Général?" asked the aide.

"Does this man not understand that the entire southern peninsula has yielded to my command, that his old nemesis Rigaud is already beginning to administer the area, that the northwest peninsula will soon yield to our attack? That my Général Boudet has secured Port Républicain and is now on the march towards the Artibonite?" yelled Leclerc.

Placide, weary as he was after the near two-day ride from Ennery was registering every word Leclerc was saying as Isaac burst into tears.

"What, you are crying, little Isaac," Leclerc said in a sarcastic tone. "I sent you on your first military assignment with the simple task of convincing your father to do the right thing for the country of France that he serves. That you both serve? And you bring me this trash. This filth of a letter!" he yelled as he ripped up the document in rage.

Isaac covered his face and his ears with his two hands, not wanting to hear anymore. Placide looked upon Leclerc, who from the very first time meeting him and his wife at the Palace of Tuileries, felt they were imposters of sincerity, all full of pomp but no true substance of faithfulness. He now began to despise them.

Leclerc looked at the soldier. "Fetch some fresh horses and get these brats ready to travel back to Ennery" Leclerc ordered.

"But sir, we have been traveling without sleep for two days," replied the soldier.

"Then good, you can be back there in two days. Get these two brats saddled up and out of my site. My aide Lebron will bring you my response to their father, the deceiver, for delivery, and may God help us all" Leclerc said as he began to stomp from the room with Lebron in tow, and suddenly stopped. "Coisnon, you can go to bed. Their special education is hereby revoked," Leclerc said as he exited the room with Coisnon's mouth still open wide.

Two days later, the boys arrived in Ennery on a Thursday morning, exhausted, hungry, and without their Tutor. The soldier had been instructed to hand them off to the first of Toussaint's honor guard sighted on the road and return to the Cap.

Suzanne looked at her boys, barely able to stand, as Placide handed a letter to Toussaint given him by Leclerc, minus any tricolor ribbon, wax, or seal of any type.

"Come with me, my sons. When was the last time you have eaten? You look famished and God knows you need a bath," Suzanne smiled, knowing there was a seriousness in the air about them.

The boys devoured the eggs, ham, biscuits, and avocado within minutes and were so exhausted after the meal that Isaac fell asleep at the table. Toussaint and Suzanne helped them up the steps to bed, reluctantly allowing them to wait until after some rest to bathe.

It was late afternoon before they awoke, bathed, and ravaged another plate of food and drink to quench their hunger and thirst. "Placide, Isaac, meet me in the study when you have finished," Toussaint said as he passed by the dining room.

The boys did as instructed and found Toussaint with Leclerc's letter in hand behind his ornate desk. He was looking out the window when they sat on the two chairs in front of it.

"My sons, it is time for us to have a serious conversation. Placide, you are nearing the age of 21 and well into manhood. Isaac, you are impressive at the young age of fifteen. You are both of age for us to have an adult conversation. Saint Jean is too young for such talk," Toussaint said with seriousness in his voice, such that they had never heard from him before.

"Leclerc is a despot, left to his ways would be a tyrant if not restrained. He has decided to wage war upon us, attack our installations, kill our people, and demand servitude by handing over our defenses," Toussaint said in a calm voice. "This he dares do while we are strong and united. I can only imagine what he would do when we are not strong. I hereby declare war on Leclerc and his army, not war on France."

Isaac looked at Placide for support and looked at his father and said "Papa, …"

Toussaint put his hand up to silence him and continued, "As for our First Consul, he has ripped up our constitution that was duly debated and written by the best scholars that a united Saint Domingue has to offer. Within that constitution, I am its protector. I took an oath and vowed to protect Saint Domingue against all enemies. Is it not an enemy that dares to rip up our sacred document and throw it in the heap of trash?"

"Yes, Papa," replied Placide. Isaac put his head down and said nothing.

"The time has come, my children. The time to decide. Understand that I will not get in the way of your decision but respect it with all my fiber, whatever that decision will be, and however it pleases me or pains me. You, at your young and tender ages, must decide between France and your home of Saint Domingue."

The boys sat still, looked at each other, and back to Toussaint.

"You must decide as there should be no hesitation. How can you not make an instant decision if your integrity is not solid? You cannot have these as two ways, there is only one way," Toussaint said.

Toussaint then looked at Placide. "And, what say you Placide?"

"Forget France," Placide declared. "I have seen through these imposters. They have groomed me, educated me, fertilized me to go against you as they go against each other. I will not. They speak one way and act another. They would just as easily have me become a slave to a land that finds me inferior. I choose to live and die by your side, mon père. You are my only leader, my only educator now."

Toussaint looked proudly at his son. After years of integration into the French way of things, his roots run deep for Saint Domingue, as an ancient mahogany tree clings to her soil through a hurricane. He smiled at Placide and looked towards Isaac.

"I choose France, Papa," Isaac said as he stood from his chair, somewhat defiant. "I am an officer of France. I serve France, and I will not take up arms against her."

"Will you take arms against me, Isaac? Arms against the people you love? Your home?"

"I will protect and serve France against the enemies that threaten her. Whomever they may be."

"And if that enemy is said to be me? A person who has been loyal and served France. A person who almost gave his life for France on many occasions. Would you strike me down, Isaac?" Toussaint caught himself as his voice was beginning to rise. If this would be his last day with this son, he did not want it to be like this.

"My duty is to France and orders from my superiors shall be obeyed. I am a soldier of France."

"Very well, my son. You will always be in my thoughts and prayers. You will always be my son. I will always love you and wish no harm comes to you."

Toussaint looked up and saw Suzanne with tears rolling down her face. She was standing within earshot. What she must be thinking, thought Toussaint. Isaac, the son of his seed was siding against him, while Placide, the seed of another, was standing with him. He loved them both, but Isaac was and had always been the weaker reed. Perhaps if he hadn't been sent to school in France at such an early age, things might have been different. So be it.

He looked up at his wife. "Suzanne, Isaac has decided to stay with you during the upcoming events and join the army of France. Should he desire to return to France, I leave the choice with him. I will always love him, but he has decided his future is with France and not with Saint Domingue."

He looked back at Isaac. "May God grant you the happiness you deserve. You may go with your mother now." Isaac turned with defiance and exited the room with his mother, without another glance back towards Toussaint.

Toussaint then went to Placide and put his head in his two huge hands and kissed him on his forehead. "Come with me."

Two days later, Toussaint was looking out the window of the two-story building in Dondon that was now his temporary headquarters. Surrounding the town were 2,000 soldiers and more arriving by the day as Toussaint's call to arms spread of the upcoming fight for freedom.

Toussaint had dispatched to every town the message; The whites of France and the colony have joined to take away our freedom. Mistrust the whites – they will betray you if they can. Their manifest desire is the return of slavery.

Caches of hidden arms shot and powder were being unearthed and cultivators everywhere in the northern plains were dropping their hoes, bidding farewell to their families, and traveling to the call of Toussaint.

If his orders had reached their intended destinations, he could now count on Maurepas and the Ninth Demi brigade resisting at Port-de-Paix, and if they could not hold it, burning it to the ground. Dessalines had surely set fire to Saint Marc and be traveling south towards Port Républicain.

Christophe would be fighting the French in the mountains around Marmelade, while Général Sans-Souci fought in Grande-Rivière. He hoped that Clervaux and his brother Paul had overtaken the French or burned the towns to deny them access, especially Santiago and Santo Domingo – the two main hubs. But there was no word or confirmation they had received his orders.

At Jérémie, he had a strong commander in Général Dommage, but Laplume was questionable, still licking his wounds from his demotion during the civil war. Laplume would be the weak link, but he was charged with the big cities of Port Républicain, Jacmel, and Les Cayes.

He called for Placide who arrived at a moment's notice. "I know that the First Consul gifted you a fine uniform, my son. The uniform of France. We are still French and if you must wear it, you may," Toussaint said.

"No Papa, I have this uniform. It was given to me by your honor guards."

"Lè sa a, ann al rankontre mesye brav sa yo" - Then let us go and meet these brave men, Toussaint said in Creole, discarding the proper French language several days ago.

They turned and went downstairs where many officers had gathered for a meeting called by Toussaint. He gestured Placide to go outside into the open courtyard where up to five hundred soldiers were gathered. Toussaint looked at Placide, who he now noticed was of his height, albeit many pounds lighter. They walked onto a mound and his son stood side by side with him as he began to address the crowd of soldiers.

"Captain-Général Leclerc offers us shame by destroying the constitution we have sworn to uphold. He wants us to dispose of our liberty and return us to chains. He wants us to bow to his knees and that of the current government of France. Are you ready to wear the yoke of slavery and to submit as cowards or fight alongside me?"

The crowd shouted so loud that Placide had never heard anything so loud before.

"I give you my son, Placide Louverture, who has vowed to be the first to die for this cause if it so warrants!"

The crowd cheered once again and a chant of *Placide, Placide, Placide,* could be heard.

"Take him and accept him at the grade of Commander," said Toussaint who pushed him slightly forward as one of the Honor Guard captains lifted him, and put him on his shoulders and walked through the crowd as soldiers reached to touch the son of Toussaint.

Placide's very being had now changed. Whatever doubts he had before this moment... *would I be accepted, could I do this, would I die,...* was extinguished. All he felt was a sense of belonging, and being home among his people. He had traveled and lived in a foreign land with foreigners for far too long. He was now home and it was this home that he would die to protect.

Eleven

BATTLE OF
RAVINE-À-COULEUVRES

L'Estère
February 1802

Letters had traveled back and forth between Leclerc and Toussaint, with Toussaint tentatively agreeing to step down and cooperate with the transitional government of Leclerc who named him to be his Lieutenant-Governor.

However, Toussaint was suspicious of Leclerc and considered it a trap to have his army lay down their arms, leaving them in a weakened position and subject to Leclerc's diabolical plans.

Leclerc ordered Toussaint to report to him at Cap Français, which Toussaint refused until Leclerc halted his army's march and his soldiers return to their barracks. Incensed, Leclerc issued a proclamation.

Inhabitants of Saint Domingue: The Général Toussaint Louverture had assured me that he was ready to obey any order I give him. I have ordered him to report to me; I have given him my word to employ him as my Lieutenant-Governor. He has not replied to this order except with empty phrases; his is only seeking to gain time. I am entering into campaign and I am going to teach this rebel what the force of the French government is. From this moment forward, he must be nothing more, in the eyes of good French people who live in Saint Domingue, than an insensate monster!

I have promised liberty to the inhabitants of Saint Domingue, and I will know how to make them enjoy it.

I command the following:

Article One: The Général Toussaint and the Général Christophe are hereby outlawed; all citizens are ordered to pursue them.

Article Two...

Placide walked into Toussaint's makeshift office in the town of L'Estère. They had arrived the day before as they were constantly moving from place to place to avoid capture by the French. The town, thus far, had not been invaded and his soldiers were scattered in groups of 300 or so around L'Artibonite near Ravine-à-Couleuvres.

"Have you seen this yet, Papa?" Placide said as he walked into the room.

"Is it the proclamation by Leclerc?" asked Toussaint. I have heard of it, but have not yet seen it."

"A copy was just delivered for you. Here it is," Placide said. He had already read the document and handed the copy to Toussaint.

"I am sure my son that you know its contents. Give me your overview as you are my aide-de-camp."

"It is penned by Leclerc. It begins by labeling you as an outlaw for not obeying his orders to report to him. Also, names Général Christophe as an outlaw as well."

"That's interesting, go on"

"It says that;

Cultivators who have been led into error and have taken up arms will be treated as disgruntled children and returned to agricultural work.

All soldiers who abandon your, Toussaint's army, will become part of the French army…

"That's enough. I see the direction of it. We have more important items to attend," Toussaint said as he cut Placide off.

Placide continued; "Why does he outlaw only you and Christophe?"

"Think, my son, why would that be?" Toussaint asked.

Why does he not name Dessalines, Maurepas, Sans-Souci, and the others as outlaws? They all follow you and fight for you."

"Charles Leclerc is educated in the best military schools of France, just as Pétion. He conducts warfare with incredible skill and utilizes all resources at his disposal. You tell me, why did he write it this way?"

Placide thought a moment, then replied "To isolate you. To have your Générals enticed by shiny jewels to lure them away."

"Exactly. This is a psychological warfare on the people. He has included in this document the black cultivators, the soldiers, and the officers. Each has a reward should they abandon the cause. He is using the weapon of the pen and words as its bullets."

"But why Christophe?"

"That is but ceremony and a temper tantrum. Christophe stole his royal city that he dreamed that he and his wife would rule. Cap-Français was the Paris of the Antilles and it is no longer. Instead of stately buildings and the opera and theater, he has ashes, charred buildings, and the theater of rebuilding to amuse himself."

"I see Papa. He is very clever indeed."

"Yes, and never forget that. When he speaks, you must know that there is always something left unsaid. Now, let us go to the ravine. I have asked all my officers to meet there."

Toussaint's officers, around fifty of all ranks, were gathered at Ravine-à-Couleuvres awaiting their leader the afternoon of

February 22nd. Toussaint arrived with Placide and two dozen dragoons on horseback. He addressed them all.

"My men. The brave souls and defenders of our motherland. Have you all seen the proclamation by the captain-Général?" began Toussaint.

A series of boos could be heard from the crowd.

"You have every reason to fear it. Leclerc is a deceiver and aims to make us fight one another. I do not want anyone forced to fight for their liberty. If you so choose to join his proclamation of empty promises, you are free to leave now. No harm will come to you. That is my word."

The officers looked at each other and saw no one move to leave.

"I see we have no cowards within our ranks!" Toussaint said to the laughter of the men. "Is there no one here who fears the site of the French?"

More laughter.

"Then it is time for us to begin our stand. Prepare your men. I will lead 100 men and attack Morne Barade tonight. This will force the French to remain there to protect the area. We will then go in the opposite direction and attack the French at Lacroix. I understand that Général Rochambeau is in the area and well-supplied. We will relieve him of some of that weight. Be ready to march tomorrow morning at first light," Toussaint ordered. "I will be back by then from Barade,"

Two hundred horsemen left the ravine and rode to Morne Barade. When they arrived, they found the area calm as Toussaint looked through his spyglass. He could see numerous French soldiers lazily walking around.

"Let us wait until there is no more daylight. We will then move at a slow pace towards the town. If they see us, we will charge like hell," Toussaint ordered.

At sunset, the line began to move forward. Two hundred horsemen spread fifty wide and four deep. They were spotted about 100 yards before the town and the bugler sounded the alarm.

Gunshots rang out, falling several horsemen during the desperate charge.

Toussaint was in the front line; "Charge, charge!" he yelled. Placide was racing on his horse in full step with his father as he raised his sword while his adrenaline pumped at full speed and mowed down the first French grenadier he encountered. He then turned and set off for another who was in the process of reloading his weapon and slashed him across the chest.

Placide surprised himself with his fighting skills. Sure he was an accomplished swordsman back at the university in Paris, one of the best. And, his expert equestrian skills, taught by his father, had been developed when he was but a child long before his trip to Paris. But he never realized that he could use these skills so effectively, that they would combine to create a lethal fighter in him. Toussaint's men noticed him in battle and his stature grew on this day.

The horseman next to Placide went down from a volley of bullets. Placide looked in the direction of where they had come and saw three grenadiers reloading their rifles. He looked over and saw that four horsemen also had them in their sights, and together they and Placide charged the soldiers and mowed them down.

The battle intensified with many lives lost on both sides until Toussaint called for retreat. They had prosecuted significant damage that would be enough to keep them grounded the following day as Toussaint's sites were set on Lacroix.

They reached the camp at the ravine at 2 am and were greeted by many of the soldiers who were awakened or on guard. They already knew their instructions for the morning and preparations had been ongoing all day.

Toussaint and Placide retired to their tent to get a few hours of sleep before the battle the next day. "You did well tonight," Toussaint told Placide.

"Thank you, Papa," he said as he rubbed his sore right shoulder from the work it had done this night.

"Your shoulder, what is wrong with it?" asked Toussaint.

"It is not injured, Papa. It is just sore from the battle. My muscle has not been developed as much yet from prior battles, but it will soon be."

Toussaint got up from his cot and went to a bag, the same bag of medicine that Placide recognized from as far back as a child. "Here, rub this on the sore and keep it in your pocket. Rub it on in a few hours before we depart. It will help."

Placide rubbed the smelly oily paste on his sore shoulder. It had a chilling effect on his arm somewhat. He then fell into a deep sleep.

The aroma of brewing coffee awoke Placide. He felt rested but still groggy from the early morning's return and knew that a cup would shake him of his grogginess. Toussaint entered the tent with two cups of coffee and handed him one. "How is your arm, Placide?"

Since he had awoken, he had not once thought about it. Placide lifted his arm high, then around, twisted it left and right, and smiled at Toussaint. "The pain is gone, Papa. What is that remedy you gave me?"

"Everything you need is right here, Placide. All that healed you is found growing on this earth. Healing herbs, roots, and leaves. It is all here for your use. During the wars years ago, a French doctor and I would exchange healing techniques. He was very surprised by the amount of limbs he had to saw off his patients compared with very few of mine. The secret is to prevent wounds from festering."

"Will you teach me this, Papa?"

"Yes, but not now. We have a war we cannot be late for. Let us go.

"Merde!" Général Rochambeau spat, as he struggled to maintain his footing on the slick vegetation that blanketed the valley floor. With each step, he could feel the weight of the mud clinging to his boots, the fertile soil a testament to the abundant rice crops nourished by the nearby river of Estere.

Rochambeau's eyes darted around through the early dawn darkness, his mind racing with thoughts of the man eluding him, that gilded African, Toussaint Louverture. The recent reports suggested that Toussaint was amassing an army in this very region. It wasn't enough for Rochambeau to merely extinguish the flame of rebellion; he longed to be the one who captured the rebel Toussaint himself.

"Damn these slippery leaves," he muttered under his breath. His pride ached at the thought of his men witnessing his less-than-graceful descent into the muck and grime below. He glanced back at the soldiers trailing him, their faces hidden behind layers of dirt and sweat. They were weary, but they shared his determination to track down Toussaint and his cohorts to bring an end to this insurgency.

"Keep moving!" Rochambeau barked, as he hoisted himself up from yet another fall. "We must find him before he gathers more support."

As the Général trudged through the treacherous terrain, he couldn't help but wonder what drove a man like Toussaint to take up arms against the mighty French Empire. Was it simply a lust for power, or was there something deeper that fueled his insurrection?

He didn't care as he clenched his fist, vowing that he would uncover the truth once he had the gilded African in his grasp.

"Stay focused, men!" he shouted, despite the growing weariness in his limbs. "Our prize is near, I can feel it!"

In the murky shadows of this wet valley, Rochambeau pressed on, his resolve as unwavering as the mud that clung to his boots. By any means necessary, he would bring Toussaint to justice and restore order to this land. For his country, for his men, but most importantly, for himself to claim victory.

The first light of dawn began to pierce the morning, casting beams of pale sunlight onto the damp soil below. Rochambeau's breaths came in ragged puffs, his chest heaving with each weary step. Despite the exhaustion that gnawed at his very bones, he maintained a relentless pace, the promise of victory spurring him ever onward.

"Come on, men!" he growled beneath his breath, urging his men forward. "We are close now."

Over 4,000 French regulars scrambled up the embankment behind him, their boots slipping and sliding in the mud. They were a formidable force, but the unforgiving terrain had taken its toll on both their spirits and their bodies. Still, they pressed on, driven by their Général's unquenchable determination.

"Général?" a voice called out softly. It was Dorman, one of Rochambeau's most trusted officers.

"Speak, Dorman," Rochambeau replied, his voice low and hushed.

"Sir, we must proceed with caution. We still know little about the enemy's movements or their numbers in this area. There may be hundreds or possibly thousands."

Rochambeau considered his officer's words for a moment, his eyes scanning the treacherous landscape before them. He knew that Dorman was right, but the thought of allowing Toussaint even a moment's respite was maddening.

"Very well," he conceded, his voice tinged with impatience. "But we must not tarry. Time is our greatest enemy now."

Dorman nodded, his expression solemn. "Understood, mon Général."

As they continued their arduous climb, Rochambeau's thoughts churned restlessly. What if Toussaint escaped their grasp once more? What if he was leading his men on a wild goose chase through this godforsaken swamp? The uncertainty gnawed at him, feeding the growing unease that nestled in the pit of his stomach and feeding the insects, hungry for nourishment and feasting on their blood, forcing their bodies to sting from their penetrating bites.

"Courage, Rochambeau," he muttered under his breath, trying to shake off the dark thoughts that threatened to overwhelm him.

"You've faced greater foes than this. You will prevail. You will avenge young Charles, my beloved nephew, that these savages have taken from me."

The sun continued its slow ascent, casting a golden light upon the weary soldiers as they trudged through the muck and mire. But still, they pressed on, their eyes fixed on the horizon and the promise of victory that beckoned like a siren's song.

"Take three men and scout there above and see if you spot any enemy," Rochambeau commanded, his gaze focused on the top of a small hill.

"Understood, mon Général." Dorman's voice was barely a whisper, but it carried the same determined resolve that had forged an alliance between them. "Lavent, Tornier, Rachide, with me."

The four men moved with practiced stealth, their boots leaving shallow impressions in the mud while they traversed the slippery terrain. Beads of sweat trickled down Dorman's brow as he led the way, his heart hammering against his ribcage like a caged animal seeking escape.

"Stay low, keep quiet," Dorman ordered, pausing at the halfway point on the ascent. He crouched down, signaling for the others to do the same. Lavent, Tornier, and Rachide followed suit without question, their eyes locked on their leader.

The moment Dorman's scarred hand clasped the spyglass, his pulse quickened. Fog hung heavy in the air, a damp shroud that enfolded man and land alike impeded his vision.

He extended the spyglass to its full length, the brass cylinders gliding smoothly despite the dampness. Bringing it to his eye, he scanned the valley below with a practiced ease that belied his tense nerves.

"Anything?" Lavent whispered, the words barely audible above the rustle of leaves underfoot.

"Patience." Dorman's voice was low and steady, but his thoughts were far from calm. What would they find here? It was rumored that the rebels had a cache of arms, a hidden treasure of guns and ammunition that were issued years ago by some dumb commissioner named Sonthonax. What an idiot to arm these savages, he thought.

As he swept the spyglass across the landscape, the fog began to dissipate, revealing the lush foliage and terrain beneath. He caught glimpses of a meandering river, its waters swollen from recent rains, and the scattered huts of a village nestled amidst the greenery. But where were the men whose presence had sent them on this treacherous journey?

"There!" Rachide's sudden exclamation jolted Dorman from his thoughts. "By the river – movement!"

"Quiet, damn it!" Tornier hissed, casting a wary glance back toward their comrades below. "These savages can hear well and can slit a throat even better!"

"Where?" Dorman demanded, his heart pounding as adrenaline surged through his veins.

"Over there, by the cluster of trees near the bend," Rachide replied, his voice barely above a whisper now. "I saw something – someone."

"Let me see," Dorman said, training his spyglass in the direction Rachide indicated. As he focused on the spot, he held his breath, fearing that any noise would betray their position. Slowly, shapes began to emerge from the fog – shadows at first, and then men. Men with rifles.

"Merde," he breathed, the word slipping past his lips before he could stop it. A young enemy combatant suddenly looked his way but soon determined it must have been an animal or bird and turned away. He lowered the spyglass, his eyes meeting those of his comrades. They understood the gravity of the situation; they had found the enemy.

"Stay here," he commanded in a hushed tone, his gaze fixed on Lavent, Tornier, and Rachide. "Keep an eye on them. I must report this to the Général."

"Be careful," Lavent warned, his voice strained with concern. "We don't know how many more are out there."

Dorman nodded, acknowledging the warning as he turned and began his descent back down the hill. His mind raced, thoughts of what lay ahead for them all spiraling through his consciousness like leaves caught in a whirlwind. The weight of responsibility settled heavily on his shoulders, a burden he had no choice but to bear.

The sun was just beginning to rise, casting an ethereal glow upon the verdant valley that stretched out before them. Toussaint and his son Placide, both astride their powerful steeds, rode side by side with determination etched upon their faces. The rhythmic beating of hooves echoed through the morning air as they approached the forward front.

Captain Déjean, a man of impressive stature and unwavering loyalty, stood at attention with his honor guard, awaiting the arrival of his commanding officer and friend. As Toussaint and Placide drew near, Déjean's chest swelled with pride for the men who had come to symbolize hope in this desperate fight for freedom.

"Any sign of the enemy?" asked Toussaint, his voice steady and commanding, even in the face of potential danger.

Déjean hesitated for a moment, his eyes narrowing as he scanned the horizon. He knew that the answer he provided would weigh heavily on the decisions made in the coming hours. "Not yet, mon Général," he replied cautiously.

Toussaint nodded, his dark eyes revealing a hint of concern beneath his stoic exterior. He knew well the treachery of their enemies, how they could appear without warning like ghosts in the night. And while he trusted in the abilities of his men, he could not shake the gnawing feeling that the coming battle would test them all. His spies had reported that Rochambeau was on the march for him and would stop at nothing until he brought him back to justice, dead or alive in shackles.

Glancing over at Placide, he saw the same fire within his son's eyes that burned within his own heart. It was a fire fueled by the desire for the freedom of their people - a dream worth fighting for, no matter the cost. And as they stood together on the precipice of war, facing an uncertain future, Toussaint found solace in the knowledge that they were united in purpose.

"Stay close, my son," he murmured to Placide, his voice barely audible above the cacophony of men preparing for battle. "We will face this enemy together, and we shall emerge victorious."

Placide nodded, his jaw set with determination as he gripped the reins of his horse tightly. He knew that the path before them would not be an easy one, but he also knew that their cause was just. And as he looked upon his father - a man who had risen from humble beginnings to become a beacon of hope in their struggle for freedom - he felt a surge of courage ripple through him.

Toussaint pulled out a mouchwa tèt, a head scarf, from his vest pocket, mauve in color, and tied it tight around his head, covering his graying hair. In three months, he would be 60 years old. He never imagined himself in battle at this age. He then folded his tricorn, and placed it neatly in his saddle bag, making it more difficult for the enemy to spot him as the highest officer in command.

Toussaint reached into his other pocket and pulled out another mouchwa tèt. "Tie this to your head, my son, if you can fit all of that hair into it. You young seem allergic to the cutting of the hair, I see," he smiled as he somewhat admired the license of the youth to wear his hair like that; long and almost down to his shoulders, tied in a ponytail. Placide was considered a Grimo by the locals; a tropical blond mulatto with skin the color of café au lait, light-colored tan eyes, and tan-blondish coarse hair. A good-looking boy, Toussaint thought.

Placide accepted it and tied it on his head, pushing as much of his curly and kinky long hair beneath it, leaving the tail to stick out behind the mouchwa tèt. Toussaint looked on and smiled, wanting to burst out in a rare laugh.

And suddenly there it was, cawing high in the air, and a familiar friend of Toussaint. The *malfini* hawk had followed him as a good omen to every successful military encounter he had fought in for years. It was a good sign this day, that majestic bird cawing loudly from high above, warning him of the enemy and sending him the message of victory. He looked at Placide and then pointed to the bird. "She claims we will be victorious this day, my son".

The warmth of the sun's first rays caressed Toussaint's weathered face, casting a golden hue across his dark skin as if nature itself were anointing him for the battle ahead. He observed the men around him - their faces etched with determination and hope - knowing that on this day, they would fight not just for themselves but for generations yet unborn.

"Captain Déjean," he said, his voice strong and resolute, "our time is now."

"Indeed, mon Général," Déjean replied, his eyes sweeping across the valley as if seeking out any sign of the enemy. "But give us a little more time. I have sent two of my scouts, Titon and Mason - one north and the other south there to climb the hill and report back. They should be here shortly as the morning light is beginning to get bright."

Toussaint nodded, his gaze following the path Déjean had described. His heart pounded in his chest, a steady drumbeat echoing the urgency of the moment. He knew that each passing second brought them closer to confrontation, and he could not help but wonder how many of these men - these brave souls who had joined him in defiance of tyranny - would live to see another sunrise.

"What strength are we this morning?" he asked, steeling himself for the answer.

Déjean hesitated, his eyes betraying a flicker of concern. Toussaint could sense that something was amiss, but he needed to hear it - to know the full measure of what lay before them.

"Speak, Captain," he urged, his voice a whisper as gentle as the breeze that stirred the tall grasses beneath their horses' hooves.

"Général," Déjean began, his voice heavy with the weight of responsibility, "we have assembled a formidable force, but there are never enough when facing an enemy such as ours."

As Toussaint listened, he felt a knot of unease tighten in his stomach. But he also knew that fear was a luxury he could ill afford. They had come too far and risked too much to turn back now.

"Captain," he said, his voice steady and resolute, "we may be few, but our cause is just. And when we fight for freedom - for the very essence of our humanity - there is no foe who can stand against us."

Déjean met his gaze, and for a moment, the two men shared an unspoken understanding - a bond forged in the crucible of war. Fear and doubt were ever-present companions in the dance of death, but on this day, they would face them together, united by their conviction that there could be no victory without sacrifice.

"Indeed, Général," Déjean replied, his words echoing the resolve that burned within Toussaint's heart. "We shall stand as one, and we will not yield."

Captain Déjean's voice rang out, steady and clear, as he began to recount the strength of their forces. "We have 250 dragoons, all with fresh horses, 1500 elite grenadiers, and an infantry of cultivators, 1,200 strong, who have unearthed their weapons and joined our revolt these past several days, even more last night which I had not time to count."

"Untrained, but with heart we can be sure," Toussaint mused aloud, his gaze lingering on the newly minted soldiers. They were raw and untested, bore no uniforms, and wore mostly rags if they had any, to cover their bodies. But there was a fierce light in their eyes that spoke of their desperation for freedom. "They fight for their freedom and to escape bondage. That will somewhat make up for their lack of training."

As he surveyed the ranks, Toussaint felt a swell of pride mingled with concern. Each man stood ready to lay down his life in the pursuit of liberty, but would it be enough? The French were a formidable adversary and large in numbers that had filled those many ships he had seen sailing at Monte Cristi, and he knew all too well the price of failure.

A sudden commotion at the edge of the encampment drew Déjean's attention. He strained his eyes, trying to discern the cause of the disturbance. As the figures came into focus, he recognized one of the scouts, Titon, returning from his mission.

"Captain!" Titon called breathlessly, *"Mwen pote nouvèl!* I bring news!"

The anxiety that had been gnawing at Toussaint's gut flared into something more acute, and he braced himself for whatever tidings the scout had to share.

Titon's chest heaved as he struggled to catch his breath, the urgency of his message evident in every labored gasp. *" Kapitèn,... Mason... se franse yo ki touye l"* Captain,... Mason... he's been killed by the French."

The words hit Déjean, Toussaint, and Placide like a physical blow, and for a moment, all he could do was stare blankly at the scout before him, his mind struggling to process the loss – the first even before contact with the enemy. Mason had been one of their best, a man who had fought alongside Déjean since the earliest days of the revolt and whose skill and determination had saved countless lives.

"Tell me what happened," Toussaint demanded finally, his voice raw with grief and anger.

"I found his body near the edge of the rice fields," Titon explained, his face a mask of sorrow.

"Voye Madichon sou yo!," Curse them! Toussaint spat, his fists clenching tightly to the reins of Belle Argent.

As the silence stretched on, Titon was uncomfortable with the weight of the news he bore. At length, he cleared his throat and added, "There's more, Général. After discovering Mason, I continued my reconnaissance as ordered. Over the hill, there are thousands of French soldiers, just waiting in the rice fields. It seems they have been gathering their forces in secret, preparing to strike us when we least expect it."

Toussaint closed his eyes and took a deep, steadying breath. This was worse than he had feared. Thousands of French soldiers, poised like a viper ready to strike at the heart of their rebellion. But they would not go down without a fight.

"Thank you for the report, Titon," he said quietly, his jaw set with grim determination. "Now, gather your strength and rest. We will need every able-bodied man when we face the French."

As Titon nodded and walked away, Toussaint's mind raced with plans and calculations. "Déjean, assemble the men."

"Officers?" asked Déjean.

"No, everyone," replied Toussaint.

The soldiers, most men and some women who had arrived with the cultivators assembled across a small stream and made a crowd for as far as Toussaint could see. He remained mounted on Belle Argent with Placide and Déjean also mounted at his side.

His heart swelled with pride and a fierce love for these men and women who had chosen to stand beside him in their fight for freedom, anxiously awaiting their leader to speak to them and provide them with hope.

"Brothers and sisters," he began as loud as he could, his voice carrying across the still air. "We are gathered here today to face an enemy that seeks to shackle us once more in chains. The French do not belong in this land - it rejects them, as we reject their tyranny!"

A murmur of agreement rippled through the crowd as Toussaint walked Belle Argent to the left and right so all could get a portion of what he was saying. Placide and Déjean remained in place.

Toussaint continued, passion evident in every word, "Know this: the French will die here in droves, for our cause is just and our hearts are strong! We will be victorious, and if any of you should fall, your sacrifice shall be avenged, and this land will remember you, but deny them the satisfaction of remembrance for this land rejects them. Their bones will rot after their blood has filtered into our soil to irrigate our crops, like dead fish. Be ready to fight," he finished as he cantered Belle Argent to his hind legs to the pleasure of the crowd.

A roar of approval erupted from the throng, and Toussaint knew that even against such overwhelming odds, their spirit was unbreakable.

"Captain Déjean," he said, turning to the honor guard commander at his side. "I will lead our forces into battle. I must stand with them, shoulder to shoulder, as we fight for our freedom."

"Général, I must advise against it," Déjean replied, concern etched into his features. "Your leadership is invaluable, but so is your life. If you were to fall..."

Toussaint shook his head, cutting him off. "No, I cannot ask these brave souls to risk their lives for the cause if I am not willing to do the same. My place is with them, on the front lines leading them, facing the enemy together."

Déjean hesitated, clearly torn between his duty to protect his Général and his understanding of Toussaint's resolve. Finally, he nodded, giving a solemn salute.

"Very well, Général. I shall follow your lead."

Toussaint's eyes scanned the hill before them as the sun had now fully risen, casting a golden hue over the scene and glinting off the polished armor of his honor guard.

"Papa," Placide said, drawing Toussaint's gaze to his son, who sat confidently astride his own steed. "I am ready."

Toussaint studied his son's face, struck by how much he resembled his mother – the same fierce determination, the same unyielding spirit. It was a rare gift to witness such bravery, and he knew he could not have asked for a better ally in this fight.

"Good," he replied, his voice full of warmth and reassurance. "Remember, my son, we do not fight for ourselves. We fight for those who cannot, for the generations yet to come. We must be their champions, their protectors."

Placide nodded solemnly, understanding the weight of their cause. "I will make you proud, Papa."

"As you always have, Placide," Toussaint affirmed, touched by the quiet strength of his son's words.

With a deep breath, Toussaint tightened his grip on the magnificent warhorse, Belle Argent, her powerful muscles rippling beneath him as she responded to his touch. Her silvery coat gleamed in the sunlight, embodying the promise of hope and freedom that drove them forward as she grunted and danced, eager to engage in the familiarity of a run into battle.

"Soldiers, one and all!" he shouted, raising his sword high above his head. "The time has come to take back what is ours! To reclaim our land and our liberty from those who would seek to claim it and have us chained once again! Today, we fight as one!"

A deafening roar erupted from the assembled troops as Toussaint began to walk Belle Argent up the hill with Placide and 200 horsemen alongside and the infantry behind, many in uniforms and many not, who were barefoot.

When he reached the top of the hill and looked down, he realized that the enemy knew they were coming. They had formed their battle line – the classic French position. For Toussaint, this was not his favored form of warfare, out in the open like this, but fate had brought him to this place and this battle.

"Charge!" he cried, spurring Belle Argent into a gallop, with Placide and the honor guards thundering alongside them and the infantry on the run down the hill. The earth shook beneath the pounding hooves of their steeds as they surged forward, a tide of steel and resolve sweeping towards the French lines.

Placide looked back to see that the horsemen were running farther and farther ahead of the trailing infantry. As he looked forward, the French line was getting ready to fire. They were within firing range. Toussaint kicked Belle Argent one last time, the sign the steed understood as the final spurt before impact.

The sound of rifle fire erupted as a barrage of bullets rained down on them, one whizzing by Placide so near that he heard the wind part to allow its path. Easily two dozen men were hit and fell to the ground, but that did not deter the charge, 30 yards, the French front line was reloading, and another fresh line was aiming, 20 yards as the new line fired and more of the honor guard were fallen, 10 yards and the surreal feeling of slow motion gripped Placide as he could see the faces of the enemy as if they were across from him at a dinner table. The young boy with freckles, the older man with a beard, and the soldier with a pigtail had all arrived on this day to test their fate for either French honor or our freedom.

Placide braced for impact as the clash of steel on steel rang out like a cacophony of death as the horsemen barreled into the front line of soldiers – some falling to the fate of hacking bayonets. The air was thick with the acrid scent of sweat and gunpowder.

Toussaint's breath came in ragged gasps, his sword arm growing heavy as he cut down yet another French soldier. The enemy swarmed around them, an overwhelming tide that seemed to have no end as hours of fighting took their toll on both sides.

"Papa!" Placide shouted, his eyes wide with fear as more French soldiers appeared in droves from the fields. "They just keep coming!"

"Stay focused, my son!" Toussaint replied, his voice strained but steady. "We cannot falter now; not when so much is at stake!"

As Belle Argent reared beneath him, her hooves lashing out at the encroaching soldiers in a fighting dance of her own, Toussaint couldn't help but feel a creeping sense of dread. The French force was relentless, pouring onto the battlefield like ants drawn to sweet honey. For every enemy he struck down, it seemed two more took their place.

"We must hold our ground!" he bellowed, as the troops of the infantry engaged in hand-to-hand combat. "Our victory depends on it!"

"Behind you!" Placide yelled, lunging forward to intercept a bayonet aimed squarely at his father's back.

"Thank you, my son," Toussaint whispered, his chest tightening with gratitude and fear. If not for Placide's quick reflexes, he would have met his end on the blade of a French soldier. Toussaint's heart clenched as he surveyed the carnage before him, the product of hours of the gruesome fight. The ground was slick with blood and littered with the broken bodies of friends and foes alike.

His forces had fought valiantly, but they were being pushed back inch by agonizing inch. The enemy's numbers seemed endless, a tidal wave threatening to engulf them all.

"Retreat!" he finally screamed, his voice hoarse from shouting orders and cries of defiance. "Fall back to the valley! We will regroup there and plan our next move!"

"Are you sure, sir?" Captain Déjean asked, disbelief coloring his features even as he parried an incoming attack. "If we give up ground now—"

"Captain, I know what I am doing," Toussaint replied tersely. "Our survival is paramount. We have already lost too many brave souls today. We must live to fight another day."

He locked eyes with Placide, who nodded in agreement. "You heard my father! Retreat!" Placide said with an authority in his voice that Déjean found unable to resist, forcing him to admire and respect the young man even though the order was directed to him.

"Fall back!" Captain Déjean echoed to the infantry, his expression grim but resolved. "Protect the wounded as best you can!"

As the order spread through the ranks, the retreat began. Toussaint's men staggered back, their retreat slow and methodical – a testament to their discipline and unity even in the face of overwhelming odds.

Rochambeau had been directing the attack from where the French soldiers were emanating from. As they arrived, he would expertly point and direct them to the pockets of resistance where more strength was needed. He was momentarily taken aback by the sudden shift in tactics with Toussaint's retreat. He surveyed the battleground. It had been a long, tiring battle for their men and many lay dead on the ground amongst the enemy.

He looked at the troops and their faces were ashen, tired, disillusioned, and some scared. Many were soldiers who had not seen real battles outside of training. They boasted that they would best the savages during their long sea voyage and now, they see many of their comrades, their friends lying lifeless before them. The fact that these 'savages' could fight this hard, so valiantly, and inflict such casualty forced them to doubt their prior convictions.

The sound of cries and moans, from both his men and the enemy, was deafening as he neared the battlefield where over a thousand lay still. He came across the first lifeless body of an enemy soldier and kicked him over with his boot. The man had a gash from a French sword across his chest that exposed his ribcage, the whites of bone visible through the red of muscle tissue.

He kicked another over. This one was still alive, but barely, letting out a painful groan. He unsheathed his sword, put it to the man's neck, and pushed on it hard as the sword created a fountain of blood and the crunching sound of the neck bone, killing the man.

As he cleaned his sword on the man's trousers, he called over Damond, then sheathed his weapon.

"Yes, mon Général?"

"No quarter. Take men and inspect to make sure all enemies are dead and those who are not, kill them. Get our men who are still alive to the medic station and line up the dead for burial," ordered Rochambeau.

"And the dead enemy soldiers?"

"Damn them… Damn them all…" Rochambeau muttered under his breath, his fury and frustration threatening to consume him. Damond hesitated and left to do what was ordered.

How could they have come so far to not have captured or killed Toussaint, thought Rochambeau? He had appeared in open site, brazen enough to be so near their blades. Yet, he lived to fight again and continue to assemble his rebellion. I will find you Toussaint, and kill you,' he promised.

"Papa," Placide said gently, "did we win or lose this battle?"

"There are no winners and losers in war, Placide. All of us are losers who have lost someone, or many, dear to us," Toussaint replied, forcing himself to meet Placide's gaze. "We inflicted severe casualties upon them and showed that we are resolved to win. That will wear well on their thoughts and that is a win, if we can call it that. Now go and help your men."

As the last echoes of gunfire faded into silence, Toussaint and Placide stood on the muddy banks of the Petite-Rivière. The battle had been long and arduous, but at last, they could breathe a sigh of relief, and wash the blood off of them in the lazy river.

"Placide," Toussaint called out, wiping sweat from his brow, "help the wounded men cross the river. We must make haste."

"Of course, Papa," Placide replied, his voice hoarse from hours of shouting. He set to work, helping or guiding the soldiers across the slippery stones beneath the water's surface, his exhaustion momentarily forgotten in the face of duty.

"Once we've crossed, we'll head to the fort at Crête-à-Pierrot," he announced, his eyes narrowing as he scanned the horizon. "We'll be safe there, and can plan our next move."

"Crête-à-Pierrot?" Placide asked, pausing momentarily as another soldier made it safely to the other side. "Isn't that where Dessalines is stationed?"

"Oui, I believe so. I had sent a message for him to get there. I am in hopes he has arrived to reinforce commander Lamartinière, one of the best and most loyal of the Mulatto troops," Toussaint said.

As they reached the opposite bank, Toussaint allowed himself a moment to reflect on the sacrifices that had led them to this point. "Let us not forget those who fell today,"

"I will never forget," Placide agreed, his voice heavy with emotion.

"What about Dessalines? Shall we send word now, Papa?"

"Oui. Marcel!" Toussaint called, beckoning to a young soldier who stood nearby. "You have proven yourself swift and reliable. Ride to Crête-à-Pierrot. Seek out Général Dessalines and inform him that we will be there by morning."

"Of course, Général," Marcel replied, his chest swelling with pride despite his fatigue. "I won't let you down."

"See that you don't," Toussaint warned as he ordered the march to the fort without stopping, without rest.

Twelve

THE BATTLE OF CRÊTE-À-PIERROT

Artibonite Valley
March 1802

The sun hung low in the sky, casting long shadows across the dusty streets of the old village. Général Jean-Jacques Dessalines, mounted on top of his mighty black horse Galipòt surveyed the scene with a steely gaze, his dark eyes fixated on the crowd of 800 white French civilian prisoners huddled together before him. Men and women, young, old, and even children, their faces etched with fear. They shared one thing in common when they spoke in their hushed whispers: their unwavering allegiance to his enemy, the French.

"Général," one of his officers approached, his voice edged with desperation. "We don't have enough provisions to maintain both our troops and these prisoners and as for this town, there is not much here. Most have left with anticipation that French forces will soon arrive."

Dessalines clenched his jaw, already aware of the dire situation. He couldn't afford to weaken his forces by dividing their meager rations. Yet, he also couldn't risk letting these prisoners go free only to aid or join the enemy ranks. A solution formed in his mind, brutal but necessary.

"Advise the remaining townspeople that all supplies must be given to the cause and to leave the area as I intend to burn the town. The French cannot inherit a comfortable base in which to launch their attack on the fort. As for the prisoners, round them up," he ordered, his voice steady and cold. "Have the men slit their throats. We can ill afford to feed them, but we can make use of their deaths."

"Général!" The officer's eyes widened in horror. "You cannot be serious!"

Dessalines didn't take his eyes off the crowd as he responded, his voice firm and measured. "Their loyalty to France makes them our enemies. They would have us all dead or enslaved if given the chance."

"Général," whispered one of his lieutenants, shifting nervously at his side. "These are innocent civilians."

As he spoke, the whispers of the prisoners reached his ears, a cacophony of prayers and pleas for mercy. The sound stirred something deep within him, but he pushed it down, reminding himself of his duty to his people.

"Mon Général," came another hesitant voice from his ranks, "Is there truly no other way?"

"Silence!" Dessalines snapped, his steely gaze piercing through the officers. "Listen well - we do what we must to win this war. If you value our people's freedom, you will obey my orders without question, or you can join the ones who enjoy your mercy."

The officer swallowed hard, his Adam's apple bobbing nervously. "Yes, Général," he murmured, before turning to relay the command to the soldiers.

His orders were given, and the soldiers moved in amongst the prisoners who began to panic, screams and tears filling the air as they realized what was unfolding by the looks of the soldiers with cutlasses in their hands. Dessalines watched it all unfold; this is necessary he told himself.

The cries of the prisoners tore through him like a cold wind, chilling him to the bone as he thought of his wife Marie-Claire. What would she think of him now? A monster for sure. He closed his eyes for a moment, steeling himself against the emotions that threatened to overwhelm him. He once could accomplish this task without trepidation, but since meeting the graciousness and kindness of her soul, he wondered how a woman like that could love a man like him.

As prisoners were led forward to face their execution, Dessalines watched his men's hands tremble at the task. "Stay strong, my brothers," Dessalines whispered under his breath as one after another, lifeblood spilled onto the parched earth. "Our people's freedom depends on your unwavering resolve."

One by one, the prisoners met their fate as most sobbed and pleaded, while others bravely accepted their fate. Their deaths were punctuated by the sickening sound of steel slicing through flesh and the pitiful gasps of their final breaths after their throats were slit. The stench of death filled the air, but Dessalines remained steadfast on Galipo, an immovable pillar of determination.

On this brutal day before continuing to Crête-à-Pierrot, he had made a choice that would forever define his legacy and bolster his reputation as a butcher.

"Général," a voice broke through his thoughts. Lieutenant Bouchard had arrived by his side and stood at attention. Bouchard had been charged with executing the prisoners by the ravine, his face pale but composed. "The deed has been carried out."

Dessalines studied his lieutenant's eyes, searching for any sign of judgment or doubt. To his relief, Bouchard held steady under his gaze, his unwavering loyalty clear. "Very well," Dessalines replied, his voice barely above a whisper.

"Sir," Bouchard hesitated, and then continued cautiously, "the men are concerned about our lack of provisions. We're running out of food."

"Tell them not to worry." Dessalines clenched his fists, the enormity of the situation sinking in further. "I have made arrangements," though he knew not if that was true. He hoped that the commander of the fort, Louis Daure Lamartinière, a mulatto in their army, would not hold it against him for how he had persecuted mulattos after the civil war in the south. Would he deny him food for his men at the fort? If he did, he would find it necessary to kill him. Lamartinière was a mulatto and he hated mulattos.

Lamartinière had served under Toussaint's nemesis André Rigaud to effectively fight the British, and later in the civil war. Toussaint had given him clemency for his betrayal, or what he reasoned, a loyal soldier taking orders. He now served Toussaint after Rigaud and that traitor Pétion left for France.

"Arrangements?" Bouchard asked, curiosity mingling with trepidation.

Dessalines averted Bouchard's question and said, "Those slaughtered overnight will serve a dual purpose; relieve our need to feed them and act as a powerful psychological weapon against our enemy." Dessalines swallowed the bile rising in his throat, forcing himself to confront the gruesome reality. "Leave their corpses to rot in the street and the ravine."

"Sir... I understand we must do what's necessary, but..." Bouchard trailed off, struggling to put his thoughts into words while maintaining his loyalty and respect.

"Speak your mind, Lieutenant," Dessalines urged him, aware of the internal battle waging within each of his soldiers.

"Isn't it a bit... extreme, sir? To use their deaths this way?"

"Extreme times call for extreme measures," Dessalines responded coolly, his heart pounding like a drum in his chest. "We must show our enemies we're not to be trifled with. We must make them fear us."

"Understood, Général." Bouchard's voice held a hint of resignation, though he saluted and turned to leave.

"Wait," Dessalines called after him, suddenly struck by the weight of their actions. "Tell the men... I know what I've asked of them today is not easy. But I promise them this: we will emerge victorious. The French will understand our resolve."

"Of course, sir." Bouchard bowed his head briefly before disappearing into the darkness, confused by the unfamiliar glow of humanity in the Général's heart.

The sun had barely begun to rise after the night of slaughter, of death, casting an eerie orange glow over the old village. The streets ran red with blood, the air heavy with the coppery scent. The bodies were left where they fell, their glassy eyes staring up at the sky, as if questioning their fate. Flies began to gather, drawn to the stench, as the sun rose higher, and the day's heat began to arrive.

The village had been transformed into a macabre tableau, a testament to their desperation and willingness to do whatever it took to claim victory.

"Let us hope that history will remember our cause," Dessalines whispered, his eyes lingering on the lifeless faces of the men, women, and children who had paid the ultimate price. "And not just judge this day upon us."

"Burn the town!" Dessalines shouted.

Amongst the heat of the flames, the army retreated from the village, leaving behind a gruesome message for their enemies.

The moon, a pale specter in the indigo sky, cast its ghostly light upon the soldiers as they trudged through the muck of yet another rice field. Toussaint led his weary men with Placide and Captain Déjean at his side. Their destination was Crête-à-Pierrot, a fort promising refuge from their relentless foe. Shadows writhed like serpents under the soldiers' boots as they pushed through the night.

"Papa," Placide spoke, his voice barely audible over the sound of rustling water and vegetation caused by the many on their march. "The men... They're exhausted," he said, not wanting to confess his own exhaustion, lest his father think less of him.

Toussaint glanced back, his eyes scanning the haggard faces of his soldiers. Each step bore the weight of over 600 comrades lost in the battle of Ravine-à-Couleuvres. Their spirits haunted the darkness, whispered in the wind that ruffled the trees above.

"Placide," he said, his voice steady despite the ache in his heart. "We cannot afford to stop. Not now."

"Général, the men understand the importance of reaching Crête-à-Pierrot, but their bodies are weak," Captain Déjean interjected, concern etched on his face.

"Captain Déjean," Toussaint replied, keeping his gaze forward. "I know it is difficult, but we must go on. If we falter, then their sacrifice will have been for nothing and possibly after their rest, they could be dead if the French arrive with reinforcements."

As they marched, many of the injured required assistance and in some cases to be carried, slowing their pace. Now and then, an injured soldier would succumb to their wounds, requiring others to stay back to bury the dead. The men muttered prayers under their breath, seeking solace from the anguish that gnawed at their souls.

"Papa," Placide ventured again, his voice wavering. "How do we honor those we've lost? How do we carry their memory when our hearts are burdened with grief?"

Toussaint paused, his eyes searching the moonlit path ahead. He could feel the weight of their loss pressing upon him like a crushing tide. But in that darkness, there was a flicker of resolve.

"Placide," he began, his voice somber yet resolute. "We honor them by continuing to fight for what they believed in. We honor them by remembering their names and their faces, by telling their stories now and to future generations."

"Remember," he continued, turning to look at the weary soldiers who marched alongside them, "that our fallen comrades were our brothers and sisters in arms. They fought for freedom and justice. And so, we must carry on their legacy until our last breath."

Silence fell upon the ranks, broken only by the steady rhythm of their footsteps and the clanging of their armaments. Though their bodies were weak and their spirits heavy, the men found strength in Toussaint's resilience. As they marched through the night, they carried not only the burden of their exhaustion but also the memories of those they had lost.

And so, under the watchful eye of the moon, the army pressed onward towards Crête-à-Pierrot, the voices of their fallen comrades urging them forward into the darkness and through the night.

The first light of dawn painted the sky with shades of pink and gold as Toussaint surveyed their meager supplies. The soldiers had been rationing their food, but now even that was running low. He clenched his fist, feeling the grit of determination stir within his chest.

"Captain Déjean," he called out, his voice steady despite his hunger gnawing at his insides. "Take stock of our remaining supplies. We need to make them last in case they run low at Crête-à-Pierrot."

"Oui, mon Général," Captain Déjean replied, already moving to inspect the army's provisions.

As the men continued their march, the sun rose higher in the sky, its heat doing little to alleviate their exhaustion after 24 hours of marching. Their empty stomachs groaned in protest, but they pressed on, driven by the knowledge that every step took them closer to their goal.

"Stay vigilant," Toussaint instructed his troops. "The French could be right behind us. We can't afford to slow down."

"Mon Général," a newly returning scout said in excitement. "I spotted a stream not far from here with good water, free of mud. Perhaps we could fill our canteens?"

"Good thinking," Toussaint nodded, grateful for any small reprieve. "Lead the way."

After the soldiers filled their containers and refreshed their skin with the cool, clear water from the stream, the army resumed their march, each soldier fixed their eyes on the horizon, fueled by the fierce conviction that burned within them.

By late afternoon, the sun hung low in the sky, casting long shadows as Toussaint neared the village below the fort. Smoke still rose from the charred remains of buildings, a grim testament to the massacre that had taken place under Dessalines' command. The stench of death lingered in the air, the bodies of French citizens lying where they had fallen, their faces frozen in expressions of terror and agony.

"Stop," Toussaint ordered, his voice hoarse from exhaustion. The soldiers obeyed, their eyes darting around the desolate scene before them, seeking solace but finding none.

"Général?" Captain Déjean queried; concern etched on his face as he approached Toussaint.

"Get the men to search for any remaining supplies, but do it quickly," Toussaint instructed, his gaze fixed on the devastation surrounding him. "We can't afford to stay here long."

Captain Déjean nodded and began barking orders, sending small groups of soldiers off to rummage through the wreckage as Toussaint spotted an old woman seated on a rickety straw chair in the village center and approached her. She was at least 85 or 90 Toussaint thought, with raggy white hair, a face full of lines, hunched over, and toothless.

"Kisa ki te pase isit la?" Toussaint asked of the woman. What happened here?

"Desalin, se sa ki pase" she said with a high-pitched, nasally voice. Dessalines, that is what happened.

Desalin te fè sa? Toussaint asked, not needing further confirmation. Dessalines did this?

"Lè ou voye yon mons touye yon mons, kisa ou panse ki pral rive? The old woman responded. When you send a monster to slay a monster, what do you think will happen?

Even in this remote village in the heart of Artibonite, Dessalines' reputation had preceded him. He could be equally cruel to both friend and foe, black or especially whites and mulatto, ex-slave or not. Rumors of his strict enforcement of Toussaint's cultivator labor laws even placed him behind a whip on occasion to coax cultivators who refused to work, skills learned from earlier practices as a slave driver back at the Cormier plantation years ago.

A while later, Placide called out, jogging towards Toussaint with a small sack slung over his shoulder. "We found some food and supplies in one of the charred buildings that was overlooked. It's not much, but it should help."

"Good work, son," Toussaint replied, forcing a smile onto his face. "Distribute what you can among the men and let's move out. There's no time to waste."

As the soldiers prepared to leave the ravaged village, Toussaint took one last look at the destruction wrought by Dessalines' merciless hand. His stomach churned, bile rising in his throat as they passed the ravine and discovered even more corpses being feasted on by wild pigs, a rare find of plentiful meat for them.

Toussaint took out his pistol and nodded towards Déjean and Placide, who understood him and pulled out their rifles as well. Three other honor guards present also pulled out their rifles. With his pistol, Toussaint pointed to them, one-by-one to identify which pig each of them was to shoot. He then held up 3 fingers, and quietly counted down with his nods as they looked at him. At the end of the countdown, in unison, they each expertly shot 6 of the pigs dead.

Placide studied the situation as soldiers hurried to extract the pigs while maneuvering over the dead cadavers. The vile realities of war forever etched in his mind.

Dessalines led his men up the steep, rocky path that wound its way to the fort atop the steep hill overlooking the village. The weight of their recent actions hung heavy upon them all, but they trudged onward, their duty unwavering. A gust of wind carried the faint, sickening odor of death from far below, he thought, and Dessalines clenched his jaw, pushing away the memories of those lifeless faces.

"Général," a soldier beside him called out, gesturing at the imposing stone walls looming above them. "This fort will be our fortress in the days to come. The French won't dare challenge us with such a vantage point."

"Indeed, it holds great strategic value," Dessalines acknowledged, his eyes surveying the bastion of hope. "We must hold onto this fort as from here, we control access to the Cahos Mountains, and thus, the heart of the island."

From one of the fort's many embrasures, where cannon barrels jutted out like the fingers of a giant steel hand, Louis Daure Lamartinière watched Dessalines' army labor up the mountain. The wind carried the scent of sweat and determination to his high perch, and he knew that these were men who would not be easily turned away.

"Friends or foes," he muttered under his breath as he raised a spyglass to his eye. He had a wide vantage point in which to survey any who may want to arrive at the fort, but it was only through the magnifying lens that he could discern their true nature. As the division flag of Jean-Jacques Dessalines came into focus, Lamartinière's heart sank like a stone in water.

The last time he had been in proximity of that brute, they had been on opposite sides of a war. Lamartinière was a mulatto, one of Dessalines' forever arch enemies. He was the illegitimate son of a white farmer and a mixed-race woman. Lamartinière's father owned a sugar plantation and refinery near Léogâne. He had recognized his mulatto son but, on his deathbed, left his entire estate as an inheritance to his white legitimate son who wanted no relationship with Lamartinière.

Without property or money, Lamartinière had enlisted as a soldier in the French army and was assigned to André Rigaud as a junior officer. From 1793 to 1798 he fought alongside Rigaud against the British invasion of the island and after they defeated the British saw an opportunity to take possession of the family's lands after his brother ran into financial ruin.

Though he didn't play a significant role in the Civil War and was glad that he didn't, he was nevertheless called up for service by Rigaud for a short period.

He turned and looked admiringly at his wife, Marie-Jeanne, walking into the courtyard of the fort and making sure everyone was on point. Her dark hair cascaded like a waterfall down her back, he thought, and her face a study of both beauty and determination. She served as Lamartinière's second in command – a woman whose presence seemed at odds with the brutal reality of their struggle, yet whose fierce gaze revealed the iron will that had earned her a respected role among the fighters.

When Dessalines finally arrived at the outer gates, in front of his massive army, Lamartinière went to greet him. He hoped that their previous encounters would not hinder the synergy they required as a fighting force.

"Welcome to Crête-à-Pierrot, Général," said Lamartinière, his gaze steady and his voice filled with the confidence born of experience. "I had received word last week from one of Toussaint's messengers that you might arrive. We have prepared accommodations for you and your men."

"Commander Lamartinière," Dessalines said without pausing for any cordial exchanges, "We must ensure that Crête-à-Pierrot is fully prepared for the onslaught that awaits us. We cannot afford any lapses in our defenses."

"Agreed, Général," Lamartinière said, nodding firmly. "We will be ready."

Dessalines scanned the fortified walls and well-trained soldiers busy at work that surrounded him. This place, this fort, could be the key to victory or defeat. But there would be no easy path ahead, and he knew it.

While surveying his surroundings he spotted Marie-Jeanne, taking in her fierce determination as she barked orders to the soldiers around her. As a Général, he was no stranger to commanding respect and loyalty from his troops but witnessing that same authority coming from a woman – made him somewhat uneasy.

"Commander," Dessalines began, hesitating momentarily as he weighed the situation. "I gather that is your wife I have heard of that serves on your staff?"

"She is my second in command and one of the best soldiers in the army, Général," Lamartinière replied, his voice holding a note of pride. "Do not underestimate her," as Lamartinière's gaze met Dessalines', unwavering in its intensity. "My wife has chosen this path, just as I have. She knows the risks, and we accept them together."

"Very well," Dessalines said, his mind wrestling with the idea of placing a woman in harm's way. But there was no time for doubt or hesitation now. Victory would be hard won, so every soldier willing to stand and fight would be needed, regardless of who they were.

Dessalines then looked to his right and addressed his lieutenant, "Gather the men, I want a word with them," an order that was immediately obeyed.

"Brothers," Dessalines began, his voice strong and steady despite the tremor that quaked through his body. "I know we are tired, hungry, and thirsty. But we must not let this break our spirits."

He strode purposefully toward an open powder keg, the eager flame of the torch reflecting in his eyes. As he held the fire near the blackened container, the soldiers watched in silent anticipation, their eyes wide with fear of whatever unknown came next.

"Should the French breach these walls," he declared, his gaze sweeping over every one of his troops, "I will ignite this powder keg and bring them down with us. We will not be taken prisoner, nor will we surrender this fort. We will either emerge victorious or perish in a blaze of glory, but we will never yield to our enemy."

The air within the fort grew thick and heavy as Dessalines' words settled over the men. "Do you understand me?" he said, more of a statement than a question. He could feel their fear, taste their uncertainty.

Lamartinière with Marie-Jeanne by his side looked at Dessalines standing high on the ramparts. They looked at each other, not needing any explanation of their thoughts. "Has he gone mad?" asked Lamartinière.

"He wouldn't be the first here to do so, my husband."

As the sun dipped below the horizon, casting an ominous glow over the fort of Crête-à-Pierrot, more troops began to appear on the horizon. As the column marched nearer to the fort, they could make out the division flags of Toussaint's army marching out of the village.

A few hours later, after ending a grueling 30-hour march, they arrived at the fort, now bursting with men and women. This time, Lamartinière and Dessalines together went to the outer gates to meet Toussaint.

They saluted Toussaint, Déjean, and Placide, on horseback, who returned the salute and dismounted. "Welcome to Crête-à-Pierrot, Général. We received word yesterday from your messenger that you would be arriving," Lamartinière said.

"Thank you, Commander, Dessalines" Toussaint said as he nodded to them each. "This is my son, Placide. He fights in our ranks, and this is Captain Déjean. It took us a while longer than expected as we have many injured."

Lamartinière and Dessalines both nodded to Placide and Déjean. How many injured do you have?" Lamartinière asked.

"We have a little over 100 who need immediate medical attention, and another 200 or so with mild injuries."

I will send for Marie-Jeanne and have her team attend to them immediately. What of provisions, do your men have sufficient supply?

"No, not much. What is the situation here?"

"We are well provisioned, but of course for a head count of 300. Général Dessalines has just arrived with nearly 1,200 soldiers and a similar lack of supply. How many are you?"

"About the same – a little less at 1,100," replied Toussaint.

"Then our 45-day supply of food has been reduced to maybe 7 days, 10 days if we severely ration."

"What sort of supplies?"

"Cornmeal, rice, beans, a stock of 40 goats, 200 chickens, and 25 pigs," replied Lamartinière.

"Then yes, we will need to ration wisely and devise a long-range plan. Please have Marie-Jeanne tend to my wounded. I will be pleased to see her once again. Placide, show him where they are, and assist in getting them settled. Déjean, have Lamartinière show you where to strike camp and advise the troops," Toussaint ordered.

To Lamartinière he said, "We killed 6 large pigs on the way a few hours ago that we want to share in the spirit of good comradery. Have your butcher cut them up and pass them to all, albeit small portions."

"Yes, mon Général," Lamartinière said as he departed with Placide and Déjean.

When they left, Toussaint addressed Dessalines.

"Dessalines," his voice firm despite the turmoil roiling within. "Explain yourself."

"Général?" Dessalines replied turning back to face Toussaint as he was looking at the group walk away.

"The carnage you left back in that village?"

"I did what was necessary for our cause," Dessalines replied nonchalantly.

"By slaughtering innocent civilians?" Toussaint demanded, anger flaring in his chest. "What purpose does that serve?"

"They were far from innocent," Dessalines countered, his tone unyielding. "They were French, our enemy. We must show them that we are not to be trifled with, that we will fight to the last man."

"By committing atrocities?" Toussaint asked, his voice strained. "This is not the way, Dessalines. We are fighting for freedom, for justice. We cannot become the very monsters we seek to vanquish."

"Sometimes, Général, one must be a monster to defeat a monster," Dessalines replied, his gaze unwavering.

Toussaint clenched his fists, his thoughts remembering what the old woman had said; *'Lè ou voye yon mons touye yon mons, kisa ou panse ki pral rive?'* When you send a monster to slay a monster, what do you think will happen?

Toussaint struggled to contain the fury that threatened to consume him. He searched Dessalines' face for any hint of remorse, any sign that he understood the weight of his actions but found none. With a heavy heart, he turned away, knowing that this was a battle he could not win – not now, at least.

Toussaint spent the evening visiting with various troops huddled around fires as they cooked their meager meals with the supplies given them. The cooked meat of the pigs was being delivered from camp to camp for their enjoyment. He visited the camps of not only his army but Dessalines' and Lamartinière's as well. He would rub the shoulders of one, hear a story by another, learn of their families, and bond with them as much as he could with Placide at his side.

On completion, he and Placide sought out Dessalines and Lamartinière and sat with them for a late meal. As they began Marie-Jeanne Lamartinière also arrived. She was dressed in a man's military uniform with a steel belt from which hung a Sabre and a rifle slung over her shoulder. A silver serving spoon on a fine chain hung from her sash she used to ration sips of water to the injured when it was in short supply. She placed the rifle in a corner, walked to the table, and saluted.

"Welcome, Marie-Jeanne. It is so good to see you once again, albeit not in the most casual of circumstances. Please report on the condition of my casualties," asked Toussaint.

Sixty are serious with amputations of a leg or arm that will be required for half, thirty are critical with half a chance of survival and a dozen will be dead by morning. Two hundred will need some form of medical attention to prevent the festering of their wounds and a couple of hundred have minor sword slashes, sprains, and the like, mon Général."

"Will you join us?" asked Toussaint as Marie-Jeanne felt more informal and went to her husband and landed a kiss on his neck.

"No, Général. I must tend to the wounded. I will get something later. May I be excused?"

"Before you go, Madame Lamartinière, I am somewhat uneasy with your presence here with such a dangerous confrontation on the horizon," Dessalines said as he put a piece of bread in his mouth and looked at her rather annoyed husband, thinking they had already settled this matter previously.

Marie-Jeanne turned to face him, her dark eyes burning with defiance. "Général Dessalines, with all due respect, my title is Captain while serving this army, not Madame. In any event, I can assure you that my gender does not define my abilities. I have trained alongside these men, fought with them, and bled with them." She lifted her rifle, running her fingers along its polished length before meeting his eyes once more. "Do not underestimate me because I am a woman. I will fight to my last breath to protect this land and our people."

For a moment, Dessalines said nothing, his gaze locked onto hers.

She then continued. "Instead of asking about my skills, Général, should you not inquire as to your injured?"

"Captain Mercier is tasked with that duty" he replied as he gave a curt nod and placed another hunk of bread in his mouth. "Very well… Captain. I hope your courage and skill are as formidable as they say it to be."

"Count on it," she said as she left the room.

Dessalines turned to Lamartinière and said, "I don't know how you do it, having your wife in the presence of all of this."

"She would have it no other way," Lamartinière said. "Have you seen her shoot her long rifle yet?"

"No, but I've heard rumors," Toussaint chimed in to break the obvious tension between the two men, noting that Dessalines was using Lamartinière's wife as his psychological prod.

"She can down a duck in flight up to 100 meters on a windy day, Lamartinière said with pride.

"Not a chance," challenged Dessalines under his breath.

"If a battle should come here, I will ask her to give you an exhibition," Lamartinière said, somewhat bragging.

"Let's get to the business at hand," interrupted Toussaint. "There is not enough food here for our combined armies, we are low on munitions, need more cannon and we have no idea how far the French forces have advanced or where they are," Toussaint replied.

"So, here's what we will do," he continued. "Dessalines; take your men to Hinche, 60 kilometers east, and destroy any forces you sight on the way. Round up as many supplies as possible and use your horses to transport them back here. Pay the local suppliers with government vouchers. It should take you no more than four days."

"I will head northeast and get the munitions that we had stored in the mountains several years ago for an occasion just such as this. I will give my men a day to rest and leave the following day, so I have plenty of hands to return with the ammunition.

Lamartinière, you will have your men dig numerous moats around the fort. Not for water, but for men. Our enemy Pétion had effectively used them at Jacmel, as Dessalines can attest to."

Dessalines puckered his lips and thought how Toussaint could not leave his losses of Jacmel to rest. He had sacrificed many men to test the defenses that Pétion had erected in those stupid trenches of his in front of the city. Now Toussaint brings it up as a reminder? he thought.

"Dessalines, leave 250 men to assist and I will do the same. We must dig them quickly. Any questions?"

"We will be ready, mon Général," Lamartinière responded without hesitation as Dessalines nodded in affirmation.

As dawn's first light broke over the horizon, Commander Lamartinière stood atop the eastern wall of the fort surveying the landscape with steely eyes and watching the army of Dessalines march out of the area. Toussaint would depart the following day.

"Commander!" shouted Sergeant Dubois, breathless from his ascent up the wall's steps. "The men are assembled and ready for your orders."

"Very well," Lamartinière replied, his voice tinged with grim determination. "Begin laying out the trenches. I want two rows, each wide enough to accommodate many men behind the protective earth. That should be sufficient to make any Frenchman think twice before attempting to scale the mountain and breach these walls."

"Understood, sir." Dubois saluted and hurried off to relay the commander's orders.

As the soldiers began their work, Lamartinière couldn't help but feel a twinge of admiration for the resolve of the French. To attempt an assault on a fort in such difficult terrain would be a hard task, yet there was no doubt in his mind that they would try. It was this very tenacity that had fueled their conquests around the world, and he knew it would take more than trenches to stop them.

"Commander," came a voice from behind him. It was Lieutenant Charpentier, a young soldier who had risen quickly through the ranks due to his keen strategic mind. "If I may, I have a suggestion regarding the trenches."

"Go ahead," Lamartinière permitted, intrigued by the prospect of new tactics.

"Perhaps we could dig a series of smaller trenches between the two main rows," Charpentier proposed. "These could be used as platforms for riflemen, providing additional cover and crossfire opportunities as well as re-supply corridors back and forth. This would increase the effectiveness and lethality of our defenses and make it much more difficult for the enemy to advance."

"An excellent idea, Lieutenant," Lamartinière agreed, impressed by the younger man's ingenuity. "See to it that your plan is implemented."

"Yes, Commander," Charpentier saluted before hurrying off to join the soldiers.

As the fort's defenses began to take shape, including the repair of several walls, Lamartinière allowed himself a moment of silent contemplation. He knew that victory was far from assured, but with each trench dug and every cannon positioned, he felt a small measure of hope grow within him. If Toussaint returned with more cannon and firepower, perhaps, against all odds, they could hold their ground.

"God help us," he whispered, his gaze never leaving the mist-shrouded valley, knowing that the French would soon emerge from that veil, ready for battle in numbers that would be overwhelming. "For we'll need all the help we can get."

The scent of iron and decay hung heavy in the air as Marie-Jeanne moved among the wounded soldiers, her delicate fingers tending to their broken bodies with a motherly touch. Her husband was out digging trenches, preparing for what they all knew would come - an onslaught of French forces bearing down upon them. But here, within the makeshift infirmary, it was her turn to fight a battle of her own.

"Madame," a young soldier whispered through gritted teeth as she carefully applied a poultice to his mangled leg. "I fear I will not survive the night."

"Non, Cherie," Marie-Jeanne murmured, her eyes scanning the swelling and pus that threatened to overtake him. "You'll see more days yet." She hoped her words held more truth than she felt as she filled her silver spoon on the chain with water from a gourde she carried and fed it through his clenched teeth.

A sudden commotion at the entrance caught her attention. A tall man, clad in tattered French attire, was being roughly shoved into the room by two of Dessalines' men. His hands were bound, but he held his head high, a look of defiance in his eyes despite his captivity.

"Captain," one of Dessalines' men announced. "This man is a doctor," shoving the captive forward towards her. "He's French. The Général wants him to heal our soldiers - or else."

"Or else?" Marie-Jeanne repeated, her voice softening. She understood the gravity of the situation, but it pained her to think of threatening another healer with death. "Untie him," she ordered the soldier, who did what he was told.

She approached the man cautiously, studying his features - the sharp angles of his face, the intensity of his gaze. He did not seem like a man who deserved such a fate.

"*Je suis désolé,* Monsieur," she said gently. I am sorry. "We are all fighting our own battles here. Will you help us?"

"*Je n'ai pas le choix, Madame,*" he replied with a wry smile. "I don't have a choice. Allow me to introduce myself. My name is Michel Étienne Descourtilz, and yes, I am from France, yes, I am a doctor, but more so I am a botanist, a scientist who studies plants.

"I am well aware of the discipline, Dr. Descourtilz."

"I was in this land searching for new remedies when I was captured," protested Descourtilz. I have no quarrels against anyone here and have many friends among you who have assisted in my research.

"To study plants? You have certainly come to the right colony, doctor," replied Marie-Jeanne.

"However, it appears fate has other plans for me." His eyes scanned the room, taking in the suffering that surrounded him. "How can I help?"

"Seems like we can help each other. Tania over there is an expert in *Fèy Bòkò*," plant medicine, Marie-Jeanne offered. "You will learn much in the next several days… or weeks. My name is Captain Marie-Jeanne Lamartinière. My husband is the commander of this fort. If you join me in healing, you will no longer report to the men of Dessalines."

"That would be so wonderful, captain," he said, a smile finally arriving on his lips after so many days of sadness and apprehension towards his future plight.

"Kite l avè m. Li anba lòd mwen kounye a," Marie-Jeanne ordered the soldiers of Dessalines, taking license where she had none. Leave him with me. He is under my command now.

"Nou resevwa enstriksyon pou nou pa retire je sou li, madame... Mwen vle di Kapitèn," the young soldier responded. We are instructed to not remove eyes from him, madame… I mean Captain.

"If you stay, then you will do as I say. Now take a bucket each and begin to transport water to fill those gourds from the cistern downstairs. When done, go to the kitchen and bring the soup broth I ordered for the patients. After that, report back to me for further orders, understood?" Marie-Jeanne said in a firm tone.

The two soldiers politely saluted and went about their business, deducing her to be a woman not to be reckoned with.

Marie-Jeanne watched as Descourtilz worked alongside her and the local healers, his hands deftly stitching wounds and setting bones. He seemed to have a natural affinity for her team's methods of administering healing with leaves, herbs, and cooked-up ointments, absorbing their knowledge like a parched sponge. They in turn learned new techniques from his European art of medicine. An equal exchange she thought.

Despite the grim circumstances, she couldn't deny a flicker of hope kindling within her chest - hope that perhaps, together, they could save more of these soldiers and hold back the encroaching tide of more death.

Sometime later, Marie-Jeanne whispered to him as they worked side by side, her voice barely audible above the groans and murmurs of their patients. "Your skills are impressive, Docteur Descourtilz,"

"Merci, Capitaine," he replied, his eyes never leaving the task at hand. "But I cannot let my captors' threats sway me from my purpose. I will save these men if I can, not out of fear, but because it is the right thing to do, and a respect for my oath."

"Oui," she agreed quietly, her heart swelling with admiration. "We will save them together, and perhaps find a way to bridge the divide between our people. For now, we must put aside our differences and tend to those who need us most."

On February 12, 1802, suspecting the French expedition was about to land at Port-de-Paix, Général Jacques Maurepas burned the city down by order of Toussaint and retreated to a nearby mountain named Les Trois Pavillons. When French Général Humbert arrived, he saw the city in flames and marched against Maurepas the following day. He was completely defeated.

When Charles Leclerc heard this terrible news, he sent Général Debelle against Maurepas, who also suffered defeat. However, in his report to Leclerc, Debelle had placed all responsibility for the costly defeat on the French Général Humbert, as opposed to the superior fighting skills of Maurepas' army which would have been an insult to the French campaign. Leclerc ordered

Humbert placed under arrest and aboard the French fleet for return to France.

Nearly a month after his defeat by Maurepas, Debelle, known to his friends as the "Apollo" of the army, was ordered by Leclerc to pursue Dessalines to L'Artibonite. The pressing weight of responsibility pressed down upon Debelle's shoulders like an invisible yoke, driving him to push his troops further, and faster, to prove to Leclerc his worth. He would find Dessalines, whatever the cost, and defeat him. He greatly sought redemption.

"Général," panted a lieutenant, his face flushed from exertion. "We've sighted the Fort de la Crête-à-Pierrot!"

"Good," Debelle replied curtly, wiping rivulets of sweat from his brow. His heart raced as he envisioned confronting Dessalines, finally proving himself after the debacle at Port-de-Paix. He would not allow another failure to tarnish his reputation or his career.

As they neared the village in the shadows of the fort, the unmistakable sound of native drums reached Debelle's ears, sending shivers down his spine. A voice inside him whispered that perhaps he was being too hasty, too eager for redemption, but he silenced it with a defiant snarl. No, he would crush these rebels and restore his honor.

"Forward, men!" he shouted. "Stay alert for signs of the enemy."

The stench of death hung heavy in the air as Debelle and his men entered the village at the bottom of the mountain. The gruesome sight that greeted them was enough to make even the most hardened soldier's stomach churn, as many spilled their contents from both the stench and the sight of it all; bodies of French men, women, and children lay strewn about, all with their throats slit and blood staining the dusty ground beneath them. He registered the sound of yet another soldier vomiting.

"Mon Dieu," whispered one of Debelle's lieutenants, his face pale with horror. "If this is Dessalines' work, he has truly outdone himself this time."

Debelle clenched his fists, rage boiling within him like molten lava. "This is unforgivable," he spat, his voice trembling with barely contained fury as he held a kerchief to his nose. "We must put an end to this madman's butchery. Gather the men – we march immediately!"

"Sir, we have only half our forces with us," cautioned another officer, concern etched on his face. "The rest are still en route. Should we not wait for them to be at full strength, and have these men rest from their long march?"

"No! Every moment we waste, more innocent lives can be lost," Debelle replied, determination burning in his eyes like twin torches. "I will not stand idly by while Dessalines continues his reign of terror. We attack now!"

With that, Général Debelle led his men towards the imposing walls of Crête-à-Pierrot, driven by righteous anger and a thirst for vengeance. As they approached the fortification, his mind raced with thoughts of the atrocities perpetrated by Dessalines and his men, fueling his already fiery temperament, even though it was not known if Dessalines had left the area or remained at the fort.

Debelle's thoughts turned inwards, his mind a whirlwind of emotions. Would his impulsive decision to strike at Crête-à-Pierrot without the full force of his army prove disastrous? Or would his rage-fueled determination lead to victory against the seemingly unstoppable Dessalines?

"Focus!" he admonished himself, shaking off any lingering doubt. "The men need me at my best. We can – we must – defeat this monster and bring justice to those who have suffered at his hands."

They arrived within striking distance of the fort. With his troops gathered on the front line, he turned to them and said; "Remember those poor souls at the village. We will fight for our fallen countrymen and show no mercy, for they have shown none. Are you with me!"

A roar by the crazed French soldiers, still reeling from the sight of the village, surprised even Debelle. They were anxious for

battle and the dead bodies only served as fuel for their hatred of the enemy. "Charge! he ordered.

"Vive la France!" cried the soldiers, their voices united in a chorus of determination and defiance.

Commander Lamartinière was ready and grateful that Toussaint had given the order to build the trenches. His men dropped into them in swarms with their rifles at the ready. Cannons began to spit their fiery destruction on the advancing French, shaking the ground and rocking even the fort on high.

With the thunderous sound of cannons echoing in his ears, Général Debelle stood at the forefront of his 1000-man strong battalion, his eyes narrowed with steely determination. His nostrils flared as the acrid scent of gunpowder filled the air, and he could almost taste the iron tang of blood on his tongue.

"Fire!" Lamartinière roared, his voice a clarion call amidst the chaos and clamor of battle. Obediently his men unleashed another volley of artillery fire upon the French, the deafening blasts tearing through the ranks like a sharp scythe through wheat.

"Damn it!" Debelle muttered under his breath, his hands clenched into fists as he watched his soldiers fall. "We cannot falter now. Not when we are so close."

As Toussaint rounded a corner on the road, he sighted the French army laying siege to the fort – hundreds upon hundreds of enemy soldiers, their flags waving in the breeze. Their tricolor uniforms gleamed in the harsh light of day, Toussaint knew Lamartinière would be greatly outnumbered if Dessalines had not returned ahead of him, but he could see they were giving the French a fierce welcome.

He pulled Belle Argent to a stop and took a deep breath, preparing himself for the worst. Placide's eyes met his, full of determination and courage. Toussaint could feel his resolve strengthening as he took in the sight before them, the fort valiantly defending and the French valiantly attacking.

He turned to Placide and the rest of the guard, "We must help them. Follow me to victory!" he yelled as Belle Argent cantered on his hind legs.

"Générale!" the voice of the French soldier called from behind. Debelle turned to see his officer, face streaked with sweat and grime, panting heavily from exertion. "The horsemen – it is Toussaint Louverture's famed honor guard – they're preparing to charge a counterattack!"

"Then let them come," Debelle growled, his eyes flashing dangerously. "We will cut them down where they stand." The officer nodded, fear and admiration warring within him, before hurrying back to rally their men.

"Steady yourselves!" Debelle bellowed to his troops, drawing his sword and raising it high above his head. "Hold your ground and fight like you've never fought before! We will not be driven back!"

"Charge!" yelled Toussaint, and without another word the honor guards kicked their horses into a gallop, the mighty hooves pounding against the ground as they rushed towards the chaos ahead. Toussaint could hear the shouts and screams of war, muffled by the roar of the cannons and bullets. His heart raced like a drum as they drew closer, urging him on.

And then they were amongst it - troops running left and right, cannonballs flying overhead, smoke clouding the air as Toussaint and his men charged into the rear of Debelle's forces.

Toussaint spotted Lamartinière at the front of the fort, his face etched with determination. "Now!" he cried, pointing towards the enemy's weakest point.

The honor guard split up, surrounding the besieging army. They fought with a fury that surprised even the most seasoned warriors. Swords flashed in the sunlight, cannons boomed, and blood spilled.

As the tide turned in their favor, Toussaint looked up to see Lamartinière waving his sword in victory as French soldiers abandoned their march and ran in retreat. Relief washed over him, and he let out a fierce war cry, once again understanding that he had cheated death.

Belle Argent whinnied beneath Toussaint, spittle flying from her mouth as it shook its head, nostrils flaring. The taste of fear and blood hung heavily in the air. The smell of smoke and gunpowder lingered, mixing with the sounds of cheering and the clattering of weapons being put away – the sounds that excited Belle Argent the most.

Général Debelle had called the retreat after seeing the overwhelming might of Toussaint's horsemen and the destruction they from the fort. Had he been too impulsive he thought? Should he have waited for the remainder of his troops before yelling charge? Just as doubt threatened to overtake him, a searing pain lanced through his side, stealing his breath and nearly toppling him from his feet. Gritting his teeth against the agony, he glanced down to see blood staining his uniform, his vision swimming dangerously. As a result of the adrenalin pumping in his veins, he had not realized that he had been shot.

"Général Debelle!" a nearby soldier cried out, rushing to his side. "You're injured, sir!"

"Never mind me," he hissed through clenched teeth, struggling to remain upright. But as he tried to gain command, his legs buckled beneath him, and darkness began to creep into the edges of his vision. The last thing he heard before slipping into unconsciousness was the desperate cries of his soldiers and the thunderous sound of hooves retreating into the distance.

Toussaint looked around at the carnage that lay before them. Men lay dead or wounded from both sides, some soldiers were crying for their mothers while others cursed their luck. The air was thick with dust and sweat, making it hard to breathe. He dismounted from Belle Argent, feeling sick to his stomach from the sight of so much violence.

Placide stood beside him, eyes wide with horror but also admiration. "We did it," he said softly, placing a hand on Toussaint's shoulder. Toussaint nodded, his heart heavy. They had saved the fort, but at what price? The taste of victory was bitter on his tongue.

He turned to Placide, his voice hoarse from shouting orders throughout the day. "We must bury our fallen comrades with honor," he ordered. Placide nodded, understanding the importance of respect for those who had given their lives. "As for the French, find one that is injured but still mobile. Tell him to give his commander a message to come retrieve their dead and wounded. We would cease fire for 24 hours to allow them time. He has my word on this."

As their men began to dig graves in the hard, rocky soil, Toussaint couldn't help but think of the families who would be left behind. Marie-Jeanne arrived with the familiar face of Dr. Descourtilz to tend to the injured, hoping against hope that they would recover. The wounds were vicious, some too deep to be mended by anyone but time itself.

"Dr. Descourtilz, what a surprise, a pleasant one at that, to see you here. How is it you come to be?" Toussaint asked.

"Transportation courtesy of Général Dessalines," the doctor replied. "I am happy to contribute my services, but whether I was here or not, you have quite an expert medical team headed by that lovely and capable woman Marie-Jean, wife of the commander."

"She is a lot of woman, she is. We are blessed that she is on our side," Toussaint replied.

"You'll be happy to note that your Général did spare the lives of your wonderful orchestra, or at least what is left of them," said the doctor.

"They are here! That is just wonderful. We can all use a little musical distraction. If you arrive at the fort before I, instruct Gabriel to tune his instruments. Our victory today calls for some distraction, don't you think?" asked Toussaint.

"Fine music is a form of medication, would you not agree?" smiled the doctor.

"It's music to my ears!" Toussaint said, laughing at himself for the amusing play on words as the doctor began to laugh also, both stealing a rare sense of comedy at the expense of their current predicament.

Toussaint had met the doctor, really a botanist, at government house during a reception at Cap-Français. He much enjoyed talking with the botanist on one of his favorite subjects, the talk of healing plants of all sorts and how this land had an abundance of them. What a small world to find him here now, at a time when we need him most. He looked up to the sky; "it is your doing my Lord, isn't it", he said out loud as he made the sign of the cross.

The sun rose on the 12th of March, casting a blood-red hue upon the smoke-streaked sky. The uneasy silence hung heavily in the air as if holding its breath before the storm. Captain-Général Leclerc stood at the edge of the battlefield with Général Boudet, his brow furrowed with determination and his eyes burning with an unquenchable fire.

So incensed and focused was Leclerrc to apprehend his prey, Toussaint Louverture, that he had vowed to never take off his boots until Louverture was in his custody weeks ago, joining the campaign himself. This was now personal. 400 of Debelle's men had been either killed or wounded in the first launch.

"Men!" he bellowed to the soldiers assembled behind him. "Today, we take the fort of Crete at Pierrot! This is our chance for redemption for the army that came before you, for glory! Do not let fear or doubt cloud your mind. Follow your Général Boudet to victory!"

A chorus of battle cries erupted from the ranks of the most experienced and qualified of the French army. Their voices joined together in a symphony of courage and loyalty. As one, they charged toward the looming fortress, their hearts pounding with adrenaline and their weapons gleaming in the crimson light.

"Stay close to me," Boudet commanded to his aide-de-camp, Lieutenant Moreau. The young man nodded, a mixture of fear and admiration dancing in his eyes as he followed his commanding officer into the fray.

The air crackled with tension as they approached the fort, every soldier ready to face their destiny head-on. But fate had different plans. A hailstorm of bullets rained down upon them from the newly constructed defensive trenches, cutting through their ranks and creating shouts of pain and anguish that filled the air.

"Push forward!" Boudet roared, undeterred by the carnage around him. His unwavering resolve inspired those who remained, and they redoubled their efforts, closing the gap between themselves and the enemy fort.

But as they neared the fort's towering walls, another devastating volley of lethal cannon and gunfire tore through their numbers and would be repeated hour after hour in the bloody fight. Boudet gritted his teeth and cursed under his breath until finally, he yelled "Retreat!" to his men, his voice hoarse and cracking with the unaccustomed weight of defeat. "Fall back!"

As they fell back, Boudet could feel the eyes of his enemies watching them from the fort, their silent judgment weighing heavily upon his soul.

"Général," Lieutenant Moreau spoke hesitantly, his youthful face stained with soot and blood. "What do we do now?"

"We regroup," he said, his voice soft but resolute. "We learn from our mistakes, and we carry on."

Boudet surveyed the battlefield, his heart sinking. The air was thick with smoke and the acrid stench of gunpowder. His brigade, once a formidable force, now lay scattered across the blood-soaked ground, their lifeless eyes staring up at him in silent accusation; he had lost 480 men who had fought alongside him.

"Général," a voice called out weakly, drawing his attention to a grievously wounded soldier. "What... what do I do?"

"Stay strong, son," Boudet replied, trying to hide the despair creeping into his voice from the pain emanating from his right heal. He surveyed his boot which was soaked in blood, the blood he could feel by the slushing of his socks within. "We'll get you help."

His gaze shifted to Général Dugua's brigade, fighting on the other side of the fort, where a similar scene of devastation also occurred with the loss of 300 men in the assault. The cries of the injured mingled with the distant sounds of battle, creating a cacophony of suffering.

"Damn it all!" Boudet muttered under his breath, clenching his fists. "How did we come to this?"

As the remnants of the two brigades limped away from the battlefield, Boudet couldn't help but reflect on the cost of their failed assault. The weight of his decisions bore down on him, threatening to crush what little resolve remained.

The sun dipped low in the sky, casting long shadows·over the battlefield as the groans of injured men filled the air. With each step, Boudet clenched his jaw against the searing pain radiating from his wounded heel. He looked at his fellow Générals; their injuries apparent in the grimaces etched on their faces.

"Merde!" Leclerc hissed through gritted teeth, one hand clutching at the injury near his crotch. "We can't keep going like this."

"Agreed," Dugua wheezed his voice barely audible as blood bubbled between his lips. The two bullets lodged in his chest made each breath a laborious struggle.

"Lacroix, you must take command," ordered Leclerc. "It is unfathomable that these savages have felled 3 great French Générals in one battle!" he angrily yelled. "And before us, Debelle, who is still in the infirmary. They must pay for this!"

Boudet's gaze shifted to Général Lacroix, whose keen eyes surveyed the carnage around them. At that moment, Boudet envied Lacroix's unscathed condition but knew that the burden of leadership was no small weight to bear. As Lacroix turned to face the others, determination shone in his eyes.

"Very well," Lacroix said, steeling himself for the task ahead. "We'll regroup and strategize our next move.

"Gentlemen, tend to your wounds. We'll need every ounce of strength we can muster," Leclerc said.

"Are you certain you're up for this without us, Lacroix?" Boudet asked, concern lacing his voice. "It's not an easy path to tread."

Lacroix met Boudet's gaze with unwavering conviction. "I am, my friend. I only hope I can lead our men to victory and end this senseless bloodshed."

"Then Godspeed, Général," Dugua murmured, his breath coming in ragged gasps, not realizing that they would soon be his last, as death was but hours away.

Thirteen

THE SIEGE OF CRÊTE-À-PIERRO

Artibonite Valley
March 1802

Under a blood-red sun, the haunted village lay silent, its air still heavy with the stench of death. The French had retreated far to the west, unable to bear the grisly sights and stench of death left behind by Dessalines' ruthless hands. Toussaint surveyed the desolate landscape from the fort's ramparts, his keen eyes scanning the horizon for any hint of movement.

"Captain," he called out, gesturing to one of his trusted officers, "send scouts to gather information on the French movements – I need to know which cities and towns have fallen or are still resisting." His voice carried the weight of urgency, betraying his growing concern about the whereabouts of Maurepas, one of his most effective Générals. Unbeknownst to him, however, Maurepas had already surrendered to the French along with many other Générals. Toussaint had been unable to communicate with them as many of his messengers had been intercepted by the French with dispatches meant for them.

"Right away, Général," the captain replied, saluting before hastily gathering a group of scouts and dispatching them into the surrounding countryside.

Despite the grim scene outside, the mood within the fort was as good as it could be under the circumstances. They had defied all odds, repelled multiple attacks, and inflicted severe casualties upon the French army. Toussaint allowed himself a moment of satisfaction as he recalled the sight of at least 1,000 to 1,500 French dead, their bodies strewn across the battlefield like broken puppets. He whispered a silent prayer of gratitude that losses on his side amounted to no more than a couple of hundred.

"Général, we should celebrate our victory," suggested one of his lieutenants, "The men need something to lift their spirits."

Toussaint nodded thoughtfully, considering the proposition. "That's a fine idea. Very well," he agreed, "let us have music tonight after dinner and church services. But remember, our enemy remains close – we must not become complacent."

As the evening drew in, the white French musicians who had initially been captured by Dessalines were more than happy to play for the occupants of the fort. Their mission in life was to perform, and perform they did.

The fort was transformed into a temporary haven of warmth and camaraderie. Soldiers and officers alike gathered in the courtyard, their faces lit by flickering torchlight as they listened to the musicians play soothing melodies. For a few precious hours, it was as if the horrors of war had been banished beyond the fort's walls. Though most soldiers would have preferred the deep inspirational drums of Africa, they knew Toussaint frowned on the practice of voodoo and that would have reminded him of that.

Toussaint stood at the edge of the gathering, his thoughts drifting back to Maurepas and the uncertainty that lay ahead. 'If only I could reach him,' he mused, his brow furrowed with worry.

As the sweet melody of violins and flutes floated through the air like therapeutic medicine, Toussaint stepped into the makeshift infirmary. The gentle music was a stark contrast to the pungent smell of antiseptics and sweat, which hung heavy in the room. Rows of injured men and women lay on the floor, their bandaged limbs a testament to their bravery.

Toussaint's eyes met those of Marie-Jeanne, who stood by Docteur Descourtilz, the botanist turned physician. Together with their team, they kept a watchful eye on the patients, moving from one to another, tending to wounds, and offering words of encouragement.

"Docteur Descourtilz," Toussaint called out gently, careful not to disturb the resting soldiers. "How goes the healing?"

"Slowly but surely, Toussaint," the Docteur replied, wiping his brow with a soiled handkerchief. "These people are fighters, inside and out."

Beside him, Marie-Jeanne nodded solemnly. "They've been through so much, yet they hold onto hope."

"Hope is a powerful weapon, indeed," Toussaint murmured, his gaze drifting over the faces of the wounded. His heart swelled with pride and compassion for these brave souls.

"Is there anything I can do to help?" he asked, turning back to the medical team. "I do have a grasp for the art of healing, you know."

"Your presence alone means more than you know," Marie-Jeanne answered, her voice filled with gratitude. "It gives them strength."

"Then let me offer what comfort I can," said Toussaint, determination etching his features.

As the sweet music continued to play, Toussaint made his way slowly through the infirmary, pausing at each to speak softly to the injured. He clasped hands, listened to stories, offered quiet reassurances, and said prayers with them. Each soldier seemed to draw strength from his touch and gentle words, their eyes shining with renewed determination.

"Thank you for your sacrifice," he whispered to a young woman whose arm had been amputated. "Your courage will not be forgotten."

"Your leadership keeps us strong, Papa Toussaint," she replied, her voice barely audible but filled with fervor.

"Then we shall continue to fight, side by side, so our people can remain free," he vowed, and the woman's eyes glistened with unshed tears as her thoughts drifted to her family far away.

As the orchestra played on, the wounded drew solace from the music and the presence of their leader, their spirits buoyed by his unwavering faith in their cause. And though the road ahead was long and treacherous, they knew that together, they would prevail.

Toussaint's gaze swept across the room, taking in the sea of wounded soldiers. Of the two hundred present, most were on the mend, and the twenty or so whose lives hung in the balance, their futures remained uncertain.

"Docteur Descourtilz, your efforts will not be forgotten," Toussaint assured him, clasping the Docteur's hand firmly.

"Thank you, sir," responded Descourtilz, his eyes weary but resolute. "We do what we can."

He could see the gratitude in Descourtilz's eyes as he nodded, acknowledging the recognition. Toussaint turned to Marie-Jeanne and the other medical staff, offering his heartfelt thanks as well. "Your team has done a remarkable job in caring for these brave souls. Your dedication and skill give hope to those who fight for our cause," he said, his voice carrying conviction. "Please know that your sacrifices are deeply appreciated."

Marie-Jeanne smiled, her eyes shining with pride, and the others murmured their gratitude in response.

With a determined stride, Toussaint approached the bedside of an older soldier, his body battered and bruised. The man's eyes fluttered open at his approach, and he attempted to sit up, wincing in pain.

"Easy now," Toussaint cautioned, resting a gentle hand on the man's shoulder. "You need to rest."

"Sir, I…" the soldier began, but Toussaint cut him off with a wave of his hand.

"Your actions have spoken louder than words ever could," he comforted the injured man. "You have fought valiantly, and we are all grateful for your service."

The soldier's eyes glistened, and he nodded his head in acknowledgment, visibly moved by Toussaint's words.

For those whose time was running out, his presence alone seemed to bring them a measure of solace. The knowledge that their leader recognized their sacrifices appeared to lighten the burden of their impending fate.

Lacroix had assumed command when Générals Boudet, Debelle, and Leclerc left to receive more advanced medical treatment in Saint-Marc for their wounds. Général Dugua had perished and would never leave this place. He was now in charge and vowed that what had happened to this date here would not be repeated.

"Captain Dupont," Lacroix called out, summoning a weathered officer to his side. "Gather a group of scouts. We need information, more reconnaissance on enemy movements and positions before we mount another assault."

"Right away, Général," Dupont replied.

As Lacroix watched Dupont depart, his thoughts drifted to the ex-slave agricultural cultivators hiding amongst the thickets that lined the roadways. Their constant harassment of his troops and attacks on the supply wagons had been a thorn in his side. The locals were emboldened by the victories of those within the fort and fueled by their fear of losing the freedom they had so recently gained.

"Damn these ambushes," Lacroix muttered under his breath, frustration mounting within him. "How are we to make any progress when we're constantly under siege from all sides?"

The sweet strains of music from the fort wafted down into the valley below, reaching the ears of the French soldiers encamped there. It was a subtle reminder, courtesy of Toussaint, that their enemy remained defiant, unbroken – and ready for whatever challenges awaited them in the days to come.

"Mon Dieu," Lacroix said, his eyes narrowing as he tried to discern the familiar tune being played from the fort.

"Sir?" the lieutenant asked, his brow furrowed in confusion.

"Listen," Lacroix ordered, raising a hand to silence the young officer, captivated by the beautiful strains of the folkloric tune of the small string orchestra emanating from within the fort's walls.

"Remarkable, isn't it, Général?" the lieutenant said, a note of awe creeping into his voice. "Such beauty amidst the horrors of war."

"Indeed," Lacroix agreed, his steely demeanor softening ever so slightly. For a moment, he allowed himself to be swept away by the music, transported to a time when life had been simpler, when his days had been filled with laughter and love, rather than blood and battle.

"Général," the lieutenant spoke up again, pulling Lacroix from his reverie. "What do you suppose the purpose of this music is? A taunt, or an invitation to lay down our arms?"

Lacroix considered the question, his gaze never leaving the fort. "I cannot say for certain," he admitted, his mind racing with possibilities. "But whatever their intent, we must not allow ourselves to be swayed by sentimentality. Our mission remains clear - we are here to capture that fort and secure this land for France."

"Oui, mon Général," the lieutenant nodded, solemnly. "We will follow you to victory."

"See that you do," Lacroix replied.

The wind carried the melodies like whispers through the grass, seeping into the hearts of the weary French soldiers.

"Is it a trick?" one soldier murmured, his eyes glazed over from pain and exhaustion.

"Or is it meant to mock us?" another chimed in, clenching and unclenching his fists.

Général Lacroix stood amongst them, his gaze fixed on the distant fort from which the music emanated. He listened intently, the notes tugging at his very soul. It was a strange sensation – a mixture of pride, longing, and sorrow that stirred within him.

"Général," a young officer whispered, his voice barely audible above the lilting tune. "What does this mean?"

Lacroix turned to face the officer, his eyes searching for an answer he did not possess. "I believe... I believe they are trying to remind us of what we fight for, and who we fight against," he finally said, the words heavy on his tongue.

"Then... are they truly our enemies?" the officer asked, his confusion evident.

"Sometimes, the line between friend and foe is blurred by circumstance," Lacroix mused, his mind drifting back to battles long past. "But we must never lose sight of our duty – to serve our country and protect her interests."

"Even if that means fighting those who share our love for France?" the officer pressed, his brow furrowed in thought, confused by the patriotic and folkloric French tunes that serenaded them.

"Especially then," Lacroix replied, his voice firm. "For it is in times of turmoil that our loyalty is truly tested."

"Général Lacroix," a young officer approached, his voice wavering with uncertainty. "Those tunes... They stir something within us that we cannot ignore."

"Speak your mind, Sargeant," Lacroix urged, his eyes meeting those of the conflicted soldier.

"Sir," he hesitated before continuing, "those French patriotic melodies have the men questioning – are these so-called savages truly our adversaries, or are they simply fighting for what they believe is right?"

The Général sighed, his gaze drifting toward the distant fort which stood proudly against the darkening sky. He had seen many battles in his time, but none quite like this – where the lines between friend and foe were blurred by shared patriotism and a love for their homeland.

"War has a way of twisting our perceptions," Lacroix began, his voice heavy with the burden of his experiences. "We are here to serve our country, and sometimes that means facing difficult questions about who we fight and why."

He paused, allowing his words to sink in, before adding, "But remember, it is not our place to question the orders we have been given. We must follow them, even if it brings us face to face with our brethren."

"Général," "I cannot help but wonder… are we merely pawns in this game of politics? Are we truly here to better this land or simply to subjugate those who fight to retain freedom?"

Lacroix's gaze remained fixed in the distance, his jaw tight. He took a deep breath before turning to face the soldier, his weathered face lined with the weight of his command.

"It is not our place to question the reasons behind our orders," Lacroix said firmly, his voice betraying a hint of the turmoil within. "We must serve our country, whether we understand the full scope of its intentions or not."

"But Général," the soldier persisted, his eyes glazed with a mix of fear and defiance. "How can we fight against those who share our love for France, who play our anthems and patriotic folklore so well, even as they prepare to battle the very country they seek to honor?"

"Enough!" Lacroix barked, silencing the soldier. He took a moment to compose himself before continuing, his tone softer but no less resolute. "We are here because we were ordered to be. You are a soldier of France. Your task is to follow those orders, regardless of our personal feelings."

Rain whipped across the landscape while Général Dessalines led the march resolutely towards Plassac, his eyes fixed on the darkening horizon's storm clouds up ahead. He could feel the weight of responsibility pressing down upon him to secure the ammunition they so desperately needed.

"Général," one of his lieutenants called, his horse struggling to keep pace with the mighty Galipòt, Dessalines' dark warhorse. The young man's breaths came in short gasps, betraying his exhaustion and fear. "What do we intend to do when we reach Plassac?"

"Find whatever supplies are left and bring them back to the fort," Dessalines replied tersely, his jaw clenched as his eyes scanned the horizon for any sign of danger. "With the constant onslaught of the French, we've depleted nearly all stocks there. Every minute counts."

"Keep your wits about you, lieutenant," Dessalines warned, his voice low and urgent. "We don't know what awaits us in Plassac.

The lieutenant nodded, his eyes wide but resolute, "Yes, Général."

The sun finally chased away the rain clouds just in time to dip below the horizon, casting long, eerie shadows across the earth. Dessalines' mind raced with plans and contingencies. What if the powder was wet, or the munitions stolen? He needed alternatives.

"Stay focused, men," he called out, his voice steady and commanding. "We know not what we will find and if enemy awaits."

The oppressive weight of the darkening sky bore down upon Dessalines and his men as they neared Plassac, their boots sinking into newly produced mud with each determined step from the recent storm. There was an orange glow in the distance that grew stronger as they approached, casting an eerie light over the landscape, and Dessalines felt fear coiling in his chest like a vice.

"Damn it all," he muttered under his breath, quickening his pace. He could hear his heart pounding in his ears, a relentless drumbeat urging him forward.

"Sweet Mother of God," the lieutenant whispered, his voice tremulous with awe and terror. They had crested a hill, and there below them lay the ammunition depot – a blazing inferno that lit up the night like a hellish beacon.

"Dragoons, with me!" Dessalines shouted as the horsemen galloped with him toward the still-smoldering ruins of the buildings in the distance, leaving the infantry to follow.

"Général...what's happened?" asked the horsemen next to him, his eyes wide, reflecting the flickering flames that danced across the ruined structures.

"An attack, most likely," Dessalines replied, his voice taut with barely suppressed rage. "Stay close, keep your eyes open." His mind raced, calculating the risks and consequences of this unforeseen disaster. "We can't afford to lose any more time or resources."

As they carefully approached the burning buildings, the heat from the fire intensified, sweat beading on their brows as the air around them crackled with searing energy. Yet, Dessalines couldn't help but feel a cold, gnawing dread deep within him, knowing that without the supplies they desperately needed, the fort was vulnerable.

"Général, what do we do now?" The lieutenant's voice wavered, his fear palpable.

Dessalines clenched his fists, resolve hardening within him like tempered steel. "We'll find another way, Lieutenant. Failure is not an option." As soldiers, they'd faced countless setbacks and losses – but they had also learned to adapt, to persevere.

As they toured the inferno, the fire would ignite pockets of hidden gunpowder creating small explosions. As they ventured deeper into the inferno, they came across several bodies of men who gave their lives in an obvious fight to protect the inventory.

"Stay alert," Dessalines ordered, his voice cracking with suppressed fury. "There could still be enemy soldiers nearby." His eyes darted from one burnt-out husk of a building to another, searching for any signs of movement.

The men gripped their weapons tighter as they moved cautiously around the flames. Sweat trickled down their brows, smoke stinging their eyes as the intense heat drew nearer. Heavy boots crunched over charred debris, while the acrid smell of smoke filled their nostrils.

"Général, do you...do you think anyone survived this?" the lieutenant asked, his voice barely audible over the roar of the fire.

Dessalines frowned, his gaze fixed on the flames. "I don't know," he admitted, his chest tightening at the thought of not knowing. "But our priority is securing whatever supplies we can find."

As they approached the heart of the destruction, Dessalines surveyed the scene with despair welling up within him. Twisted metal and shattered crates littered the ground, their contents reduced to ashes. The once-sturdy walls of the depot were now little more than blackened skeletons, offering no protection from the relentless blaze.

"Damn it," he muttered under his breath, clenching his fists as frustration coursed through him. He knew that every minute they spent here brought the fort - and the soldiers waiting there - closer to disaster. But what was left to salvage?

"Général, look!" the lieutenant called out suddenly, pointing to a partially burned building not yet destroyed. "Maybe there's something in there!"

"Let's hope so," Dessalines replied grimly, feeling a flicker of determination rise within him. If they couldn't find ammunition, they would need to come up with another plan - and fast.

As they entered the building, their hopes were immediately dashed. It was empty, probably the reason they left it standing. They had seized whatever ammunition they could carry and burned the rest.

"Général," the lieutenant ventured, his voice barely audible above the crackling flames, "what do we do now?

Dessalines looked at the young lieutenant and said; *"Nou pwal jwenn yon solisyon. Nou toujou jwenn yon solisyon!"* We will find a way. We always find a way, as Dessalines mounted Galipòt for the ride back to the fort. Remaining here was no option.

The relentless sun scorched the fort as Docteur Descourtilz wiped the sweat from his brow. Soldiers, their suffering bodies sprawled across the floor of the makeshift infirmary, moaned in the stifling heat.

Men lacking water and food, in the oppressive heat, chewed lead bullets in the hope of quenching an unbearable thirst. By this crushing they produced a muddy saliva which they strangely found delicious to swallow. Must be mass hysteria, the doctor deduced.

Marie-Jeanne, her ebony hair plastered against her forehead, moved among the injured men with a weary but determined grace. Clutching her silver spoon, she administered precious drops of water to those who needed it most. The lives of these soldiers depended on her rationing decisions as the main cistern was empty and all that remained of the water was the emergency barrels in storage.

"Marie-Jeanne, we can't go on like this," Dr. Descourtilz implored, gripping her arm. "We need to find more water or –" he hesitated, unable to complete the grim thought.

"Docteur, I know," she interrupted, her gaze steady. "But for now, we must do our best with what little we have." She turned back to the injured, her spoon dipping into the pool of liquid that remained in the earthenware bowl.

"What are you thinking, Marie-Jeanne?" Descourtilz asked, studying her face for any sign of a plan forming. "Please, tell me there's something we haven't considered yet."

Marie-Jeanne paused, her spoon hovering above a soldier's parched lips. She sighed, her eyes distant. "I wish I had an answer, Docteur. But for now, all I can offer is this small comfort of water and my steadfast care for the injured."

As Marie-Jeanne moved from one soldier to another, her thoughts raced with frantic urgency. There must be a solution, something they hadn't tried yet. These men were relying on her, and she refused to let them down.

Marie-Jeanne's spoon hovered above the cracked lips of a young soldier, his wide eyes pleading for relief. She could see the weariness in his face, the lines carved by fear and exhaustion. As she tilted the spoon, allowing a few precious droplets to fall into his mouth, she could feel the weight of everyone's desperation bearing down on her, waiting for their turn to savor the spoon of water, albeit but a measly few drops.

"Water! Please, give me more!" he cried, the tortured plea of an injured soldier driven mad by the merciless heat and overwhelming thirst. With surprising strength, he lunged towards Marie-Jeanne, his fingers clawing at the gourde she held.

"Stay back!" she commanded, her voice firm but tinged with panic. The suddenness of the attack caught her off guard, and the gourde slipped from her grasp, crashing to the ground. Water spilled across the parched earth, seeping into the dirt like blood from a fresh wound.

Many of the injured nearby crawled to scoop up the moist mud with their hands, putting it in their mouths to squeeze whatever moisture they could from the muck to relieve the dryness in their mouths.

"Damn you!" another soldier bellowed, enraged by the reckless act that had cost them probably 500 spoons of Marie-Jeanne's water rations. The remaining injured soldiers, fueled by their desperation, began to rise, their bodies weak but their intentions clear. They wanted to tear apart the man who had robbed them of their most vital resource.

"Stop!" Marie-Jeanne shouted, interjecting herself between the mob and the crazed soldier. "I know you're angry, but this isn't the answer!"

"Step aside, Madame," one of the soldiers growled, gritting his teeth. "He deserves what's coming to him."

She shook her head, her eyes blazing with determination. "No one here is to blame. Our situation is dire, but we must remember who we are. We are soldiers, and we stand together."

"Stand together?" spat another man, his voice hoarse. "He's taken our water, and now we'll die because of him!"

"Enough!" Marie-Jeanne snapped. "We won't survive by turning on each other."

The tension in the air was palpable as the injured soldiers hesitated, torn between their anger and the truth in her words. But as they looked into her eyes, they saw the fierce determination that had carried them this far.

"Fine," one grumbled reluctantly, lowering himself back onto the ground, but the other vengeful men stood firm, the group now moving to corner the reckless, selfish man. Their eyes were filled with murderous intent, their hands clenched into fists, ready to deliver justice.

"I said leave him!" she commanded, stepping forward with a newfound sense of urgency. "This won't bring back the water!"

"Damn you, woman!" one of the men snarled. "He deserves to die for what he's done!"

"Death would be too kind," another added, his voice cold and unyielding.

Marie-Jeanne knew they were right - the man had been reckless and selfish - but she also knew that if they got a hold of him, he would face a punishment far greater than he ever would have imagined. It was then that she made a decision, one that would haunt her for the rest of her days.

"Stand back," she ordered, her voice steady as she approached the doomed man. He looked up at her, his eyes wide with fear and pleading for mercy. She hesitated for a moment, the weight of her decision heavy on her shoulders. Then, with a swift, decisive motion, she drew her knife and slit his throat.

"Let this be a mercy killing," she said to all within her range, her voice laced with sadness. "May his death serve as a reminder that we must stand together if we are to survive."

As life drained from the man's eyes, and blood scurried to the ground like a serpent through the grass, Marie-Jeanne felt a wave of sickening guilt course through her veins. She had taken the life of an injured man who sought her help, all in the name of unity, but at what cost she thought? Would they truly be able to band together, or was this just another step towards their inevitable downfall?

Dr. Descourtilz came back from a stroll he had taken in the courtyard of the fort to clear his head and get some relief from the blistering heat inside. He had re-entered the room in time to witness the execution and hurried to the scene.

Marie-Jeanne looked up at him, her tears unable to fall from her eyes due to lack of hydration to fuel them. "Why?" he gently asked.

"To save him from a horrible death? To save him the agony of his plight? To save him from being torn limb from limb? To save him from going mad? To save him from our dire situation, To…"

"Enough," Descourtilz interrupted as her voice was now racing and getting louder.

"Pick one, Docteur. Any of those reasons and another dozen more," she said, composure retaking her as she gained back her control.

Descourtilz looked at the three men who were going to attack the man and said firmly, "Pick him up and take him to the burial detail."

The men looked at the Frenchman and immediately did as they were told. After all, they had gained enormous respect for him, his ability to heal them, in the past few weeks.

Marie-Jeanne looked up, now fully composed and back to her normal self. "Come," she said, her voice barely audible above the sound of her racing heartbeats, "we have work to do."

The sun hung low and blood-red in the sky as Dessalines and his men approached Morne Nolo, their hearts heavy with the knowledge that they had failed to secure much-needed supplies for the besieged fort. The road ahead, once a symbol of freedom and progress, now lay choked with the detritus of war: shattered carts, discarded weapons, and the mangled remains of soldiers from both sides of the conflict in various stages of decay. The stench of death clung to the air like an oppressive fog.

"Général, look!" one of his men exclaimed, pointing toward a barricade erected by Général Hardy's troops further up the road. A chill ran down Dessalines' spine as he beheld the sea of tricolor French soldiers, their bayonets glinting menacingly in the dying light. His jaw set, determination coursing through him like fire.

"Men," he bellowed, his voice carrying over the desolate landscape, "we have fought long and hard to dare to be free. Let us now fight to keep it." Dessalines then repeated the battle cry they had heard him say so many times before; *"Pa gen manman, pa gen papa"* - There is no mother and there is no father, *"Sa ki mouri zafè yo,"* those who die is their problem.

"Ahhhhhhhhh" the men loudly yelled with their familiar battle cry in response to his words. It was a bond of loyalty and courage, each man ready to lay down his life, for Dessalines first, second for the cause he pursued.

Dessalines felt a swell of pride and responsibility expand his chest, knowing that these brave souls would follow him into the very jaws of death if asked, or if ordered.

"Attack!" he roared as he spurred Galipòt, the animal's huge muscles surging man and beast forward as Dessalines drew his sword and pointed it to the sky, the gleaming blade slicing through the air like a harbinger of doom. His men raised their swords as well and their ponies surged around him, a wave of unstoppable force racing towards the blockade of Général Hardy.

As they crashed into the blockade, the sound of metal on metal filled the air, accompanied by the guttural screams of men locked in mortal combat. Dessalines fought with the ferocity of a cornered tiger, his every move calculated to bring death to the French who stood in his way and fueled by the rage of what he had found, or more, not found at the munition's depot.

"Press forward!" he yelled over the sounds of battle, his eyes locked on the other barricades in the road that separated them from their destination. He could see the fear in the eyes of the French soldiers as they realized that these were not mere rebels they faced, but men who would expertly fight to their dying breath for their survival.

"Général," one of his captains called out, "we're breaking through!"

Dessalines allowed himself a grim smile, knowing that this was only the first step in what would surely be a long and arduous journey. Still, it was a victory, however small, and it bolstered his spirits as he continued to cut a swathe through the enemy ranks.

"Keep pushing!" he shouted, his voice strained but determined.

The scent of blood and sweat joined and the cries of the wounded tore through the air like the crashing of waves on a rocky shore. Dessalines stood amidst the carnage, his chest heaving as he surveyed the devastation around him, nearly a hundred of his men and an equal number of French lay lifeless on the unforgiving ground, their eyes forever frozen in expressions of pain and fear.

"Mon Général!" called out one of his remaining lieutenants, panting as he stumbled through the scattered corpses. "We have broken the French line, but at a great cost."

Dessalines' jaw clenched, anger contorting his features into a thunderous scowl. "Gather the survivors," he commanded, his voice hoarse with exhaustion. "We press on to the fort."

As they moved forward, the sounds of battle fading behind them, Dessalines' mind churned with a mixture of relief and anguish. He had lost nearly 100 brave souls, yet he could not afford to dwell on the cost.

"Général," the captain said, struggling to keep pace with Dessalines' determined stride. "How do we proceed? Our forces are weakened, our resources strained."

"By any means necessary," Dessalines replied, his gaze fixed unwaveringly on the distant horizon. "We will reach the fort, and we will hold it against the French until our last breath. We cannot afford its loss as that fort is the door to the Cahos mountains."

The words echoed through the ranks of the ragged soldiers, spurring them onward despite their weariness. They would continue, driven by the indomitable spirit of their leader, and the hope that their sacrifices would not be in vain.

The sun hung low in the sky, casting a fiery glow over the besieged fort as Dessalines and his remaining men stumbled upon the desperate scene. The French had encircled the stronghold, their red and blue uniforms a dark stain against the lush green of the landscape as they observed, hidden within a grouping of thick brush.

"Général," the captain quietly said, "there is no opening in the enemy's defenses".

Dessalines squinted at the enormity of the French army before him. If he could count them all, he would have calculated the number to be 12,000, far too many for him and his band of men to bring any help of significance. The only survival plan had to be the abandonment of the fort. But how could Lamartinière accomplish that? They are surrounded by multiple divisions of the French army. How could he even get a message to Lamartinière with an order to evacuate? The fort is now unreachable. its occupants doomed to death or surrender.

A burst of the March wind whipped across Rochambeau's graying hair as he surveyed the imposing fort from a distance. The sun cast long shadows on the terrain, but he could not obscure the figure of Dessalines in his mind, the prize that eluded him for so long.

"Général Rochambeau," a subordinate called out, breaking his concentration. "We have confirmation from General Hardy that Dessalines was heading this way. He is likely inside the fort."

"Very well," Rochambeau replied, his voice cold and calculated. "Prepare the troops. We attack at dawn to finish with this business." The siege had gone on too long he thought. They had been here for weeks. He turned away, his thoughts consumed by the inevitable victory ahead.

As the first light of day approached, the French forces readied themselves for battle. Rochambeau's eyes were steely and unflinching as he watched the enemy fortifications. Inside its walls, it was estimated there to be no more than 1,200, which included men, women, children, and the wounded. This was reported by a spy from within who had snuck out of the fort a few nights back.

"Remember our purpose here, men," Rochambeau bellowed as his soldiers fell into formation. "These savages must not disgrace the great Empire of France!" His words echoed like thunder across the battlefield as the men strained to hear him and the wind whipped at his hair, unprotected by the tricorn hat on his hand. "Have you not followed me as we fought and triumphed together in Italy and Egypt?

The soldiers let out a cheer. "Are we not the elite of the French empire?" Rochambeau continued.

Another loud cheer came from the soldiers, this time louder than before. "Remember our victories," Rochambeau yelled, his eyes blazing with passion.

Another loud cheer.

"Remember the glory we together achieved in those far-off lands! We cannot allow ourselves to be disgraced by mere slaves, rebels, barefoot savages who dare defy the might of France!"

Yet another unified cheer, louder than before.

"À l'attaque!" he cried, and with that, the battle commenced.

The French forces surged forward, their boots pounding the earth beneath them as they charged toward the fortified redoubts. "Push through! Do not let them hold you back!" Rochambeau roared, spurring his men onward.

Within the fort, Lamartinière commanded his forces with unwavering determination. He knew that this battle would shape the course of history, but they had little ammunition left to fight it. Dessalines had not yet returned with stocks from the munition's depot and by the numbers of the army down below, doubted that he ever could.

"Stand firm, my brothers!" Lamartinière bellowed. "Hold your fire as we need to make each bullet count, we cannot falter! Steady your aim" he coaxed the soldiers of the fort.

Lamartinière could see the impatience on the faces of his men in the trenches below, nervously staring at the lethal enemy marching towards them. "Steady now," he calmly added to them, then turned towards the ramparts; "Point the cannons downward, we will strike them at close range," he ordered to make them most lethal since they only had a few cannonballs left.

The French kept getting closer as they began to fire their weapons at the men in the redoubt trenches. 100 meters, Lamartinière thought, "Steady men, hold your fire," 90 meters, 80, "Ready, cannon only … Aim… FIRE!" Lamartinière yelled.

Cannon balls ripped into the French attack with devastating results. Rochambeau looked behind him to see his troops being decimated, body parts flying in the air as barrages of cannons lashed through the crowd of charging men. He had assumed that they would be out of ammunition by now.

"Riffles on the ready in the front line!" ordered Lamartinière to the men in the trenches. "Aim for the man directly in front of you," he said as the French front line drew closer. "FIRE!" he yelled as the men in the trenches unleashed a fiery round of bullets at the attackers all at once.

Rochambeau watched with growing frustration. His forces were strong, but the defenders held their ground. The French

Général gritted his teeth, his breaths coming in ragged gasps as he willed his men onward, but instead, they were getting chopped down, falling with devastating fury.

"Fight, damn you, fight!" he screamed, his words barely audible over the din of battle. "Do not let these savages stand in your way!"

But despite his fervent exhortations, the French attack faltered. The fort's defenses held, and the brutal onslaught was pushed back.

"Retreat! Fall back!" Rochambeau ordered, his voice strained with frustration. He could not accept defeat, not when victory was so close at hand. As his men retreated, he vowed to himself that he would not rest until Dessalines and Lamartinière were brought to heel.

"By God," he whispered, "this is far from over."

The sun glared down upon the battlefield, casting harsh shadows over the blood-soaked ground. Rochambeau stood before his troops, nostrils flaring as sweat trickled down his brow. Though they had been pushed back for now, he knew defeat was not an option. He could feel it within him, a fire that refused to be quenched until victory was his.

"Soldiers!" he bellowed, his voice strong and commanding despite the heat. "Look around you! Look at what these savages have done!

His men, weary from the battle, looked to see their friends, their comrades, strewn amid the rocky terrain of the hillside. They needed hope, a reason to believe they could overcome the seemingly insurmountable odds.

"We must continue, my mighty men. We must take this fort today. Now!" Will you follow me to victory?"

"Oui, général!" one soldier shouted, raising his rifle into the air. Others quickly joined in, their voices growing louder, more determined.

"Nous sommes les fils de la France!" another cried. We are the sons of France! "We will not be defeated!"

"Oui!" the chorus of voices rose like a wave, sweeping across the battlefield. "Pour la France!"

Rochambeau's heart swelled with pride as he watched his soldiers rally before him. Their spirit, unbroken by the morning's fighting, only served to strengthen his resolve.

"Then let us show these savages the true might of France! Let us show them what happens when they dare to stand against us!" He raised his sword high above his head, the sunlight gleaming off its razor-sharp edge. "En avant, mes frères! Pour la gloire et la victoire!" Charge my brothers, for the glory and the victory!

"Pour la France!" the soldiers roared, their voices echoing across the battlefield. They surged forward, once more throwing themselves against the fort's defenses with renewed vigor.

As the battle raged around him, Rochambeau's thoughts were a whirlwind of strategy and determination. He would not be denied this victory. He would see Dessalines and Lamartinière pay for their defiance, even if it meant tearing down the fort, stone by stone.

"By God," he murmured, his eyes narrowing as he watched his men fight, "they will rue the day they crossed the French empire."

The air was thick with the smell of gunpowder and sweat, punctuated by the cacophony of gunfire, the clash of steel, and the cries of the wounded.

"Allez! Allez!" Rochambeau shouted, urging his men on. He watched, his jaw set in grim determination, as they hurled themselves against the fort's defenses for what seemed like the hundredth time. The rebel soldiers fought with a ferocity that belied their small numbers, but Rochambeau refused to let doubt creep in. These were slaves, some once savages, he reminded himself; they could not stand against the might of the French empire.

"Push forward!" he bellowed, raising his sword to rally the troops. "For France, for glory!"

"Pour la France!" chorused the soldiers, their voices hoarse from hours of battle. They surged once more, this time closer toward the walls of the fort, desperation lending strength to their weary limbs.

As the chaos swirled around him, Rochambeau found his thoughts turning inward. How had it come to this? Had he underestimated the enemy, or had his arrogance blinded him to the possibility of defeat?

But each time they got nearer the walls, devastating musket fire rained down on them from the trenches and the ramparts of the fort, and the thunder of cannons had become a deafening cacophony on the battlefield, the acrid smell of gunpowder filling the air. Amidst the chaos and destruction, a figure emerged on the ramparts that gave the French soldiers pause. A woman, her voice strong and defiant, urging her brothers in arms to continue the fight.

"Kouraj, frè m yo" she cried, Courage, my brothers!" her words cutting through the tumult like a knife. " *Pa lage! Nou pral siviv ak genyen!"* the woman would yell. Don't give in! We will survive and win. Marie-Jeanne Lamartinière stood tall, a beacon of hope for the weary defenders of the fort.

"Who is that woman?" one of the French soldiers asked, his eyes wide with disbelief as he glanced over at his comrades, seeking confirmation that he wasn't imagining things.

"Wife of the commander himself, I've heard."

"Impossible!" a third soldier scoffed, unwilling to accept that a woman could hold such power over her fellow fighters. "She's just a commoner, a woman, a mere distraction."

Yet even as he spoke, it was clear that Marie-Jeanne's presence was anything but a distraction. Her words stirred something deep within the hearts of her compatriots, giving them the strength to push back against their attackers.

"Look at her!" one of the defenders shouted, raising his rifle high above his head as he gestured towards Marie-Jeanne. "If she can stand tall in the face of our enemy, so too can we!"

"Oui, mon frère!" agreed another, his face streaked with sweat and grime.

Marie-Jeanne could feel the weight of the rifle on her shoulder as she moved nimbly along the ramparts, the scent of gunpowder and sweat filling her nostrils. Her Mamluk-style costume clung to her body, offering both protection and a sense of pride. The cutlass at her side gleamed in the sunlight, a glint of defiance against the relentless onslaught.

"Here, take these!" she called out, thrusting a handful of musket balls into the hands of a young soldier whose eyes were filled with a mix of fear and determination. He nodded his thanks, quickly loading his weapon before returning fire as she observed the men in the trenches relentlessly fighting to keep the approaching army at bay.

Her heart pounded in her chest as she continued to dart back and forth along the ramparts, distributing ammunition and lending her strength wherever it was needed most. The air hummed with the cries of the wounded, the roar of cannons, and the crackle of gunfire.

The ground trembled beneath Marie-Jeanne's feet as the French launched another relentless assault. They just keep coming, she thought as she raised her rifle, her hands surprisingly steady despite the adrenaline coursing through her veins, pulling the trigger with frenzied enthusiasm. The bullet found its mark, and a French soldier crumpled to the ground.

Another enemy soldier took the fallen man's place, his gun aimed squarely at Marie-Jeanne. "Damn you," she spat under her breath, reloading her rifle as quickly as her shaking fingers would allow. Time seemed to slow as she raised her weapon once more, her world narrowing down to the singular focus of taking down this foe.

With a crack, the shot rang out, and the second soldier fell. Marie-Jeanne's chest heaved as she tried to catch her breath, the taste of gunpowder and sweat heavy in her mouth. A third, a fourth, and another invader shot, as she kept herself moving, reloading, aiming, and firing to unleash her deadly skills of marksmanship on the approaching invaders.

"Retreat!" a French officer screamed, his face contorted with rage and humiliation. "Fall back!"

From his position, Rochambeau glared up at the retreating soldiers, his eyes burning with fury. "Imbeciles!" he bellowed, veins bulging in his neck. "You disgrace the French Empire! You let mere slaves best you!" They had once again retreated and would not celebrate this day, but only wallow in the agony of defeat.

When they had descended the hill, Rochambeau's gaze swept across the camp behind, settling on a figure standing apart from his French soldiers, imposing even from this distance. "Alexandre Pétion!" he cursed, his voice cracking with desperation as he observed Pétion and his buddy Jean-Pierre Boyer casually enjoying one of those sweet-smelling cheroots, the smoke encircling them as if they were at a Paris Café on a leisurely Sunday afternoon.

They were the half-breeds. The sons of white men fathers who couldn't resist the primal scent of black women. They were the spawn of lust, that feeble weakness amongst men with no honor, the byproduct of the devil himself.

A horde of them had arrived in France, after their defeat by Toussaint and Dessalines, wearing their French military uniforms with such glamour. They were the newest hit of the Paris social circles, invited to numerous parties as if to add pepper to a soup. They were toys to rich women and scandal surrounded them. Detestable, he thought.

Napoleon had insisted they come on this expedition, just in case. Just in case of what? That his own Générals could not best these savages, these half-nèg mongrels designated as mulatto. They're simply mules. But here they are, and a thorn in my ass.

Sent by Leclerc with written instructions that if I didn't take the fort with this last assault, to spring them into action. Merde!

Lacroix came over to him and spoke. "Another devastating day, Général." delivered more as a statement, not a question.

Yes, Lacroix. "We have again failed in our attempt to breach that God-forsaken fort!" Rochambeau said as he realized that once again his opportunity for victory had been washed away.

"I'm calling on Pétion, and of what I understand his lethal skills, to bring us victory over these so-called 'warriors' who have repelled our attacks, Général."

"You can't be serious. Just give me another day."

"Our orders are clear. Today was your last chance. Pétion is in charge effective immediately," Lacroix said as he turned and walked towards Pétion.

"Merde," Rochambeau cursed under his breath and kicked a rock with his boot, similar to a spoiled child throwing a temper tantrum.

Général Alexandre Pétion walked the battlefield and surveyed the carnage, his dark eyes narrowed in determination. Bodies littered the ground, young faces contorted in pain or frozen in their last moments of defiance. The French had lost nearly 2,000 men. They had no choice but to change tactics, he mused. They knew that another direct assault on the fort would only lead to more bloodshed and death of these young soldiers.

"We must starve them and pound them into submission. They may have repelled our assaults thus far, but they can't hold out forever," he said out loud to Jean-Pierre Boyer, his young captain standing at his side.

Pétion looked back at the French soldiers who emitted an air of dizziness, somewhat caught in a sort of alternate reality. What had they been thinking, trying to conduct frontal assaults on a fort commanded by the likes of Lamartinière and Dessalines, Pétion thought, not knowing Dessalines had left the area. Most of these men, except the most experienced that campaigned across Europe and Egypt, were kids, fresh out of training and the officers new to their command from military school. Could I have performed well back when I was a mere rookie?

He looked up at the fort above and could just imagine his nemesis Dessalines and smiled, almost letting out a laugh that didn't escape his captain, his friend and sidekick for many years standing next to him.

"What's so funny? asked Boyer.

"I would love to be a fly on the wall of that fort," answered Pétion. "Can you imagine Dessalines up there? Pacing like a caged animal, an incarcerated prisoner? He's a field commander, not a fort commander. He must be driving a calm and steady man like Lamartinière crazy. I wonder if he's claustrophobic?"

"Wouldn't that be something? I've never met the man, but have heard rumors of his ferocity, Boyer interjected. "Look at what he left behind in that village down there."

"You have no idea of what this man is capable of, Jean-Pierre. Everything he does is to advance his mission to win a war. That's why he left those dead in the village. To stir up emotions in these young French soldiers; anger, fear, hatred, all negative emotions designed to give him the fighting edge," Pétion explained.

Boyer just shook his head.

Pétion continued, "He's the type of man that would throw his soldiers into our defenses back in Jacmel just as a test, not caring who lives or dies, as long as he gets his results. He has this saying, '*Pa gen manman, pa gen papa - Sa ki mouri zafè yo.*"

"And that inspires his soldier?" asked Boyer.

"Like you have no idea. They go into battle not caring about death. He's convinced them that if they die, they will go under the sea to the paradise named Africa after their death. They follow him without question. Quite brilliant really, henn?"

"I guess you can call it that, if you're into that sort of thing," Boyer said, still trying to grasp the concept.

"It must be killing him right now if he knows that I, who he had besieged back in Jacmel, is the one that will now besiege him, henn?

Boyer chuckled.

He hates the fact that I escaped Jacmel without the opportunity of killing me," Pétion added. "They say he searched the entire southern peninsula for me, an obsession many said nearly drove him mad," he continued, unable to resist a little laugh.

Boyer joined in laughter at the irony of fate, happy to be once again on the battlefield alongside not only his superior but most of all, his friend.

They had left on the same ship for France together after being chased from the island after their Civil War defeat a couple of years back. On their arrival in France, they were all arrested and thrown into jail for several weeks.

Luckily, Napoleon forgave Rigaud. After all, it was that crazy French commissioner, Houdeville, who had forged a wedge between Rigaud and Toussaint by carving out the southern command and ordering Rigaud to take charge. Napoleon deduced that Rigaud, as a loyal soldier, was only following orders. It wasn't Rigaud's fault for starting the war, the blame went to Houdeville whom he summarily dispatched to Saint Petersburg, Russia so he would have little reason to deal with him.

They were finally released from that miserable Bastille prison, then languished at the fort awaiting their next deployment, which never came. Rigaud became relentless in his insistence to maintain their battle readiness through intense training. He wanted revenge and knew that one day he would return here to face Toussaint.

Lucky for them, the training was only on weekdays. Rigaud permitted the officers weekend leave, and they would immediately head straight for the night spots and bordellos, with an account financed courtesy of the Southern Command treasury. Rigaud had confiscated government funds when he escaped and sailed to France, unbeknown to the French government. *'We are the legitimate administration of the south of Saint Domingue, however in exile,'* Rigaud would claim. *'Governments in exile need financing to maintain their government,'* he would say.

"You happy to be back, Jean-Pierre?" asked Pétion.

"Like you have no idea," Boyer responded. "Paris is nice and all, and so is the countryside, and the women. But there's nothing like this place, this beautiful land. Look at it; the mountains, the ocean, the sky, and damn the warm weather! I hate France in the winter, humid and damn cold, did I ever tell you that?"

Pétion laughed and slapped his back. "Yes, we're home thank God. For years I'd craved a decent cup of coffee and finally got one when we docked in Saint Marc. Let's go make plans and preparations. I've got a Général Dessalines to catch, and taking that fort is the key."

They looked at each other and laughed once more as the French officers standing in the distance wondered what was so cheery in this miserable Godforsaken place that made those half-breeds so happy. "Savages," one French soldier declared.

Soldiers at the fort caught wind of Général Alexandre Pétion's arrival, and a palpable sense of dread permeated the air. Whispers spread like wildfire through their ranks, each man knowing all too well the famed artillery specialist's reputation for turning the tide in even the most desperate battles. Those mulattos could be extremely violent, they knew.

"O bondye, Pétion la. Nou mouri mwen asire w," they whispered. Oh my god, Pétion is here. We're dead, I assure you.

"Is it true?" a soldier stammered, his voice barely audible above the din of nervous chatter. "Pétion is here? He's arrived with his cannon?"

"Oui," Sergeant Laurent confirmed grimly, his spyglass scanning the horizon as if he could divine the enemy's intentions by sheer force of will. "We should prepare ourselves for the worst."

Sweat trickled down the young boy's brow as he tightened his grip on his musket, his heart pounding in his chest. He had heard tales of Pétion's innovative tactics, the way he decimated entire battalions with his lethal precision of the cannon.

As the sun dipped below the mountains, casting the fort in an eerie twilight, Pétion assembled his officers and unveiled his strategy that would make even the staunchest defenders tremble. His men worked tirelessly to haul heavy cannons up the steep mountain overlooking the fort, their muscles straining under the weight of the deadly payload.

"Are you sure this will work, Général?" Boyer panted, wiping the sweat from his brow as he directed the men to maneuver the cannon into position.

"Trust me, Captain," Pétion replied, "From this vantage point, we can rain hell upon them from above and over their walls to strike directly at their heart. No amount of preparation can save them from this."

The first thunderous boom of the cannon shook the very ground beneath Lamartinière's feet, causing him to stumble. He glanced around at his men, each man wearing the same expression of grim determination.

"Keep your heads down!" Lamartinière shouted, his voice barely audible above the deafening roar of cannon fire. "It's Pétion," he cursed. "He has begun."

For three days and nights, Pétion bombarded the fort mercilessly, nonstop, and in brutal succession, each explosion leaving a cloud of smoke and debris in its wake as the blasts chipped away at the fort's walls. The once-strong structure began to crumble under the relentless assault, their defenses weakening by the hour.

"Mon Dieu, when will it end?" Marie-Jeanne muttered, her voice soft as she tended to a wounded soldier. "Stay focused," she whispered, trying to sound more confident than she felt.

The relentless three days of pounding had persecuted enormous damage to the fort, but even more so were the psychological effects on the starving men.

On the fourth day, Pétion changed tactics. Expertly, he began to lob cannonballs, timed to explode seconds after landing in the interior courtyard of the fort. The explosions were sudden and devastating, leaving little time for the defenders to react and escape their fury.

"Get down!" they would yell, throwing themselves onto the ground as another cannonball whistled through the air, followed by a tense few seconds of silence, then an ear-splitting explosion. You could feel the heat from the blast that would singe a soldier's skin, the smell of burning flesh filling their nostrils.

The acrid stench of gunpowder and charred flesh hung heavy in the air as Commander Lamartinière surveyed the ruins around him. The once-proud fort had been reduced to a smoldering heap of rubble, its defenders battered and bloodied by Pétion's relentless assault. The commander's face was etched with grim determination, his eyes haunted by the knowledge that he would have to ask even more from men who had already given so much.

"Brothers," he called out, his voice ragged but resolute as he addressed his men assembled in the fort's courtyard. "We are facing the darkest hours of our cause. I ask now for volunteers who are willing to give their lives to save their comrades and our fort from further destruction."

There was a hushed silence, broken only by the intermittent whistling of cannonballs overhead as Lamartinière explained what he was asking: "I need volunteers willing to counter the cannon balls devastation by using your bodies as a shield to protect your comrades. Let me be clear, you are sure to be killed, but you will not have died in vain on their terms. You will die by your choice and be remembered as a hero."

Several gasps could be heard, followed by silence as the men looked at each other, wondering if even one of them would volunteer for this outrageous plan.

A soldier, with one of his arms amputated, evidenced by a bulge emanating from his shoulder and a cloth tightly wound with a small rope around it, came forward. "I will do this. I will die to save others."

"I'd rather die doing something than die cowering in a corner," said another who came forward and joined the one-armed man. Surprising Lamartinière, one by one, soldiers stepped forward to volunteer, their faces a mixture of determination and despair.

Suddenly, a cannonball dropped into the fort nearby counting down its deadly explosion. The one-armed man, without waiting for an order, sprinted towards it, hurling his body onto the still-smoking projectile in the courtyard as all others ducked for cover.

The explosion sent shockwaves, body parts, and blood through the air, and the one-armed man's world dissolved into a blur of searing pain and deafening noise, but Lamartinière no other soldier was killed or injured by the explosion.

Lamartinière looked at the others and proclaimed, "He bravely saved men, maybe you, and his pain is now over. We honor his sacrifice. He will forever be remembered"

"Pou libète!" yelled a volunteer. For liberty! And that became the chant of the volunteers. First, the one, then the dozen, then the hundred, who were now in the volunteer patrol, chanting *"Pou libète!" "Pou libète!" "Pou libète!" "Pou libète!"*

In the following days, one by one, they gave the ultimate sacrifice, lunging themselves, hour after hour, into a death by explosion while crying liberty as their final word on earth to save their comrades.

And after each suicidal sacrifice, everyone within the entire fort who had heard the blast knew that one of their own had given the ultimate sacrifice to save others. In unison they would cry *"Pou libète!"*

Fourteen

ESCAPE FROM CRÊTE-À-PIERROT

Artibonite Valley
March 1802

Roaring laughter could be heard from a corner of the enormous camp that held nearly 12,000 French army troops. Lacroix had ordered a pause in fighting to allow that half-breed Pétion, as he called him and his horde of mulattos, time to pound the fort into submission on their own. It was a welcomed reprieve from the risk of being called into action, thought Captain Croissant. Charging up that hill was like pulling the trigger of a pistol to your head, without knowing if it was loaded or not.

Croissant approached a large group, numbering nearly 100 men, as they formed a semicircle to create a makeshift theater, with some sitting and others standing. Another burst of laughter roared as Croissant arrived at the front.

There he saw the most peculiar spectacle of anything he had ever seen. A black man, apparently some cultivator from a nearby village he presumed, acting out the old Medieval European form of comedy as a Mime, that theatrical art adapted from ancient Greek and Roman theatre.

Another roar of laughter came from the crowd as the captain looked around and was astounded by this. It was the first time in weeks he had seen anything more than a frown on the faces of the troops. But this was altogether bizarre, they were laughing their guts out in an uncontrollable fit of frenzy.

He looked at the weird-looking black man who was acting sort of crazy, deranged even. His skin was black as coal with only his face covered in white lime, ugly as sin, and dressed in rags using Mime to act out a funny story through body motions without the use of speech, and remarkably to an almost theatrical perfection compared to those he had witnessed in Paris.

The man's final act of the absurd during the ending of his skit when he turned around, pulled down his dirty ragged trousers and exposed his buttocks, also covered with white lime, to the roar of the crowd.

Général Rochambeau suddenly entered the area as the man was still exposing himself with his butt pointing towards the crowd. As the général looked at the men, and they looked back, the laughter stopped, and an eerie hush came over the crowd.

The black man was in a performance of rolling his ass in some form of primitive dance in a way that no white man could ever do. He sensed that something had changed, stopped, stood up, and turned around, naked except for his trousers wrapped around his feet on the floor.

A gasp from the crowd erupted, some of the men with their mouths open and all in awe at the size of the man's huge penis, dangling like that of a stallion stud towards the floor. He had an awkward smile on his face and then jumped in the air in an attempt to reignite the laughter of the crowd, but the men dared not utter a laugh, though Croissant thought it quite hilarious.

Croissant went over to the Général and said, "A distraction for the men, sir. They seem to enjoy it."

Rochambeau looked at him, then to the silent men, then to the crazy black man, and then back at Croissant with a look of puzzlement. "We do not have time for crazy funny monkeys, captain."

"But sir, after all of this time out here, we thought that."

"Shut up and shoot that savage," barked Rochambeau.

The soldiers gasped as they had grown a liking to whom they called *Le nègre fou,* the crazy Nigger. The man had arrived just yesterday and had already performed multiple times around the camp. After each performance, the men would take him to friends in different areas of the camp to perform his routine for their pleasure as well. They would even give the man a centime for a good performance.

The black man pulled up his trousers and stood there as the captain said, "Please Général. This man has done nothing wrong to deserve that."

"He has trespassed onto my camp, captain"

"But sir, please?"

"Very well, I spare him. Get him out of my camp and send him up the hill to the fort so he causes no more distraction here amongst my men. With luck, a sniper will shoot him on the way."

"But Général, surely"

Rochambeau interrupted Croissant and barked, "I gave you an order, captain. Obey it and get that man out of here and make sure he travels up the hill. Shoot him if he resists!"

"Oui, mon Général."

So, the man was led out of the camp in silence. Croissant wasn't even sure if the man could utter a word or not. Maybe he was mute?

When they got to the bottom of the hill of the fort, the black man saw the morbid battlefield where soldiers were removing the dead and turned to leave.

"Non mon ami, you go there," Croissant said with a sad face, not knowing if the man would get killed on the way. "There," he said as he pointed towards the fort.

The black man frantically shook his head no, got down on his knees, and began to act again, this time not a comedy but a man begging as if sentenced to death, his two hands cupped in prayer, still not uttering a sound.

"I am sorry, mon ami, but the Général does not seem to like you as much as the rest of us. He is in charge, oui? Now go!" again pointing to the fort.

The five soldiers with Croissant felt bad for the man. One approached and gave him some water and the other some bread, patted him on the shoulder, and pointed to the fort.

The man got up, nodded to the soldiers, and turned to leave, his face contorted as if given a death sentence. He wearily began to labor up the hill as if he were walking to the gallows for his execution under the watchful eye of the soldiers.

An hour later, the Mime got nearer to the fort, fearful of Pétion's cannon balls whistling overhead that would land within its walls, followed by the sound of a muted blast. They seemed to be timed precisely every hour or so and coming from a hill in the distance.

By the time he reached closer to the entrance, the sun had begun to set. "Who goes there?" called out a sentry from the trenches.

For the first time, the Mime spoke, with a voice deep, loud, confident, and resolute "I have a message for your Commander Lamartinière from Général Dessalines. Open the gates and take me to him at once," he commanded.

On the morning of March 24th, 1802, Lamartinière, was ready to abandon the fort and fight their way through enemy lines. He knew the risks and understood the potential casualties that would ensue. However, if they stayed here, they would surely perish as Rochambeau had called 'no quarter', the order for no prisoners to be left alive, a certain death. With his officers, they developed the plan and instructed the troops on what would transpire.

The Mime came with a message two days ago. He was a military officer and spy, a lieutenant in the army of Dessalines, carrying an order from the général to abandon the fort as he would not be arriving with either reinforcements or munitions.

Lamartinière had been torn for days; stay and fight to the end, or attempt a possible suicide mission and escape through the heart of the French army? But he was a soldier, and a soldier does not question the orders of his superior in command. He took as Dessalines' order as a license to forfeit the strategic position and abandon it. The sortie would be dangerous indeed, but he had no choice, somewhat happy that the decision was made for him.

It was a moonless night that swallowed the fort as if it were a ghostly maw. The air was heavy with the metallic tang of blood and the stench of gunpowder that clung to every surface of the walls. Lamartinière, his face etched with exhaustion and streaked with sweat, surveyed the crumbling fortifications. They were all starving and had little ammunition left to defend their perch.

"Commander," whispered a captain, barely visible in the darkness, "the men are ready."

Lamartinière nodded. His heart clenched at the thought of abandoning the place they had fought so fiercely for, but he knew there was no other choice. With a deep breath, he barked the order, "Evacuate the fort!"

As the evacuation commenced, the agonized wails of the wounded echoed through the fort. Lamartinière gritted his teeth, suppressing a surge of guilt. He was leaving behind those who couldn't be moved, their lives forfeit to the enemy that surrounded them, and hoping and praying that the French would be merciful upon them. There wasn't any other choice. Survival demanded sacrifice.

"Commander!" A grizzled veteran approached with a weathered grim face, out of breath from just having returned from a reconnaissance mission. "We've secured the eastern route through enemy lines. You were right, the eastern path is lightly guarded as most of the enemy is concentrated west. We quietly ambushed and killed the guards blocking the path and hid their bodies in the brush."

"Good," Lamartinière replied, nodding. "Gather the troops and move quickly. We cannot afford to be discovered."

"Right away, sir." The veteran saluted and hastened to carry out his orders.

As the last of the able-bodied soldiers filed out of the fort, Lamartinière allowed himself a final glance at the battered stronghold as another of Pétion's cannonballs crashed into the courtyard. However, there was no need for any of the volunteers to throw themselves on it. The occupants had already left. The walls, once unyielding, now crumbled beneath the oppressive weight of Pétion's artillery.

In a tribute to the fallen souls, he whispered, "May we meet again, brave souls," his heart heavy with grief. He knew it was inevitable that some of them would join the ranks of the dead before the night was through.

Taking one last look at the fort, Lamartinière turned on his heel and vanished into the darkness, leading his weary troops away from the fortress that had been their home and their prison.

Under the veil of night, Lamartinière led his remaining troops through the treacherous terrain that separated them from freedom. The darkness was both their ally and their enemy, providing cover but also hiding unseen dangers beneath its cloak. He strained his ears, listening for any sound that might betray their presence to the French soldiers who stood between them and freedom.

"Stay close," he whispered to his men as they crept forward. "And keep your wits about you."

Lamartinière had spent countless hours studying the enemy's movements, searching for any weakness that could be exploited. His mind raced with potential scenarios, analyzing the risks and benefits of each. He knew that the smallest misstep could spell doom for them all, but failure was not an option. As the weight of responsibility bore down on him, Lamartinière steeled himself for the challenges ahead.

As they approached the French lines, Lamartinière signaled for his men to halt. A well-timed distraction would be their key to success. With deft fingers, he carefully lit a makeshift torch doused with kerosene and tossed it into a nearby brush. Flames erupted moments later, lighting the night and casting eerie shadows across the landscape, drawing the attention of the French sentries.

"Here is our escape route, down that eastern path," Lamartinière whispered with a sense of urgency. "Louis, let's go, one by one, and in a line, take your people down it. Quickly and quietly, right now, go!"

French soldiers who were awake at this hour were running quickly to extinguish the flames from the fire that Lamartinière had ignited. They were still out of sight in the pitch darkness and far from their main encampment. Lamartinière thanked the lord that there was no moon. Making matters worse for the French was that the fire had dilated their pupils to bright light. It would take many seconds for their eyes to adjust to the darkness where they hid.

Lamartinière could sense Marie-Jeanne even before she arrived by his side. "I'm here, husband," she whispered, panting in her familiar voice from the recent run. She was accompanied by a couple of dozen women and children.

"How many wounded were able to attain mobility?" asked Lamartinière.

All, except for 32 that we were forced to leave behind. Dr. Descourtilz elected to stay and care for them. He is French and will claim he was a prisoner forced to help heal them, which is not far from the truth. After all, he was originally captured by Dessalines and taken prisoner. The doctor will plead for their mercy and to allow him to continue to treat them for as long as it takes. He gave me his word," Marie-Jeanne said.

"Take the women and children down that path now. I will meet you on the other side," Lamartinière said.

"No, I stay with you," Marie-Jeanne answered firmly.

Lamartinière brought his lips to hers in a strong embrace, each of their tongues seeking the strength of the others, passion to its peak fueled by the impending danger. He then whispered, "I need you on the other side. That is an order, soldier! Now go."

She looked into his eyes with no further words needed. She turned and left, but not before looking back, hoping and praying she would see him again.

"Sir," a soldier whispered urgently, pointing to something in the distance. Lamartinière squinted, trying to make out what the man saw. It was a small group of French soldiers, likely stragglers from the camp, coming their way.

"Steady," Lamartinière commanded, raising a hand for his men to halt. "Let them pass."

The French soldiers seemed oblivious to their presence as they lit their tobacco, passed around a bottle of rum, and cursed a young soldier who they claimed had clumsily lit the wildfire. They soon disappeared into the night from whence they came to go harass him.

"We're not out of danger yet. Stay vigilant," said Lamartinière.

"Maintenant!" Lamartinière hissed, urging his men into action. They darted for the path, slipping past bewildered French soldiers who were too preoccupied with the fire to notice their presence.

It took an entire hour, but he had seen them all enter the path. The damp, earthy scent of the surrounding field filled Lamartinière's nostrils as he led his remaining men through the darkness. He could feel the weight of their gazes on him, relying on his unyielding spirit to guide them out of this desperate situation and the last to leave for safety.

As they cleared the end of the French lines, Lamartinière allowed himself a moment of relief. They had done it. Against all odds, they had broken through the enemy's defenses and lived to fight another day. He knew that the road ahead would be long and arduous, but for now, they had claimed a small victory in the face of overwhelming adversity.

"Commander, how many do you think we lost?" a soldier whispered, his voice quivering with emotion, barely audible above the rustling of leaves beneath their feet.

"Enough," Lamartinière muttered, his jaw clenched. "But we will honor their sacrifice by living to fight another day."

They continued their trek, the silence broken only by the occasional snap of a twig underfoot or the labored breathing of the fatigued men.

Twelve thousand men, Lamartinière thought, shaking his head in disbelief. And yet we managed to escape. The thought ignited a spark of pride within him, but it was short-lived, quickly replaced by the gut-wrenching reality of how many lives were lost or left behind.

In his final report, Général Lacroix wrote;

"The retreat, which the commander of Crête-à-Pierrot dared to conceive and execute, is a remarkable feat of arms. We surrounded his post to the number of twelve thousand men; he fled, did not lose half his garrison, and left us only his dead and wounded. This man, brigade leader Lamartinière, is a mulatto to whom nature gave a soul of the strongest caliber. Our losses had been so considerable that they greatly distressed the captain Général Leclerc.

François Joseph Pamphile, Viscount of Lacroix
Général de l'armée Française

Clouds had arrived in time to bolster the worsening mood of Captain général Leclerc as he surveyed the battlefield left behind by the enemy, his face betraying a hint of distress. The wind whipped around him, carrying with it the humid stench of death.

"Général," a lieutenant approached hesitantly, "we have nearly completed the count. Our losses are greater than we initially estimated."

Leclerc clenched his jaw, dreading the numbers he knew would follow. "Report," he ordered.

"Nearly two thousand men, sir," the lieutenant said, his voice wavering slightly. "Many more injured."

"Damn that Lamartinière," Leclerc muttered under his breath. Out loud, he asked, "And what of their forces?"

"Hard to say, sir. But it seems they lost half their garrison… 600 maybe?"

"Impossible!" Leclerc roared, his eyes blazing with fury. "How could they have escaped our siege with so little loss, by God? I had twelve thousand men surrounding them!"

"Commander Lamartinière led a night sortie, sir," the lieutenant replied. "He managed to break through our lines. They couldn't react fast enough."

Leclerc's hands trembled as he considered the implications of the enemy's cunning maneuver. He took a deep breath, trying to regain control of his emotions, thinking how he had underestimated the rebels.

"Sir, what do we do now?" the lieutenant asked anxiously, sensing the weight of the situation.

The sun had overpowered the clouds and now cast an eerie shadow over the scenes of carnage that lay strewn before him. Rochambeau had entered the fort. "Mon Dieu," he whispered beneath his breath.

He stepped callously over the fallen bodies of rebels, their lifeless eyes staring accusingly up at him. But it was not the dead or the dying that occupied Rochambeau's thoughts as he strode deeper into the fort; it was the one man who had eluded him.

"Général," called out a young officer, hurrying to catch up with him. "We've searched the entire fort. There's no sign of Dessalines."

"Damn him!" Rochambeau spat, slamming his fist hard against a crumbling wall, his thick glove somewhat shielding his knuckles from pain and injury. Dust and debris rained down upon them, but he paid no heed. "How can one man be such a thorn in my side?

"Perhaps he fled when he realized the battle was lost, sir," the officer suggested tentatively.

"Or perhaps he never intended to stay and fight in the first place," Rochambeau growled, his mind racing with thoughts of what devious strategy the rebel leader might have planned next.

As they continued their search, Rochambeau's fury only grew. Each empty room, each shattered barricade, served as a mocking reminder of the rebel's escape.

"Général," the officer said, suddenly hesitant. "This man claims to be a doctor who was reported captured and forced to tend to their wounded. He wants to speak with you."

"If he is a doctor, send him to our camp. I am sure they can utilize his services there," barked Rochambeau.

"He says he is the doctor for the injured rebels, sir.

Just then, Dr. Descourtilz arrived by their side. "Dr. Descourtilz, at your service," as he extended his hand to Rochambeau who neglected to reciprocate,

"What is this nonsense that you are taking care of the rebel wounded, doctor?" asked Rochambeau.

"That is correct, Général."

"Captain," Rochambeau barked, turning to the man beside him. "Have your men finish these wretches off. They are of no use to us."

"Sir?" The doctor exclaimed, shocked at what he just heard.

"This is a battlefield, not a hospital, doctor. These are enemies, not patients. Now, if you so please, vacate the fort and lend your services to French patriots who await your healing hands."

"But Général," his gaze flicking from the Général, to the officer, to the wounded rebels, some of whom had begun to weep at the implications of the order that Rochambeau had loudly given for them to hear.

"Enough!" Rochambeau snapped, his patience finally wearing thin. "I have no time to concern myself with the fate of those too weak to flee. They are enemies of France. My enemies and certainly yours." He then turned to the captain, "Did I stutter, Captain?" his voice cold and hard, like iron. "These men are pathetic. Dispose of them."

"Y-yes, sir." The captain swallowed nervously and then turned to his soldiers. "You heard the Général. Make it quick."

As the sound of gunfire, coming from soldiers pistols blowing holes through the skulls of the damned echoed through the courtyard, Rochambeau turned away, his thoughts already focused on his next move. Dessalines had escaped him once more, but he would not allow that to happen again.

The doctor's knees buckled at the sight of the killings as he broke down and spilled tears for the men, for the past month of despair, and for himself. A vacation in paradise that had turned into hell. An avalanche of grief overwhelmed him as he dropped to his knees, unable to stop his cries.

Rochambeau stormed from the fort, leaving the cries of the wounded, and of the doctor, to fade into the distance behind him.

Général Lacroix stood atop a small hill, surveying the scene before him with an iron gaze. The sun hung low in the sky, casting long shadows across the battlefield below the fort at Crête-à-Pierro, and painting the world in hues of gold and crimson. He could still smell the acrid scent of gunpowder lingering in the air, a bitter reminder of the violence that had taken place only days earlier. He would leave a battalion of a thousand men to secure the fort, bury the dead, and re-establish law and order in the area. The village would be burned, forever scorching it off the earth, as a tomb to those poor souls executed by Dessalines and still lying in the streets.

"Sir," Captain Beaumont approached, his voice laced with concern, "the troops will be ready to march by first light."

Lacroix nodded, his mind already working on how best to conceal the extent of their losses from the locals. His pride stung at the thought of having to resort to such tactics, but he knew it was necessary if they were to maintain any semblance of control over the island. They could not show the devastation that the rebels had extracted from them, the mighty French army.

"Have the men form up in a square formation, with a hollow center," he ordered, his voice firm and unwavering. "We must keep our casualties hidden from prying eyes who may have counted our numbers when we first arrived."

Captain Beaumont hesitated for a moment, then nodded in understanding. "Yes, Général. I will assure you it will be done."

As the captain hurried off to relay the orders, Lacroix's thoughts turned inward; how did we underestimate them so gravely? he wondered, his grip tightening around the hilt of his sword.

At precisely 6 am the following morning, Lacroix's forces were ready to move out. Rochambeau would march tomorrow and Hardy the following day, leaving the roughly 1,000 soldiers to mop up the operations.

"Général Lacroix, the men are ready," Captain Beaumont announced, snapping Lacroix out of his reverie.

"Very well," Lacroix replied, squaring his shoulders and setting his jaw. "Let us be on our way."

With measured steps, Lacroix led the column of soldiers down the winding road that would take them back to Port Républicain.

As they marched, the hollow center of their formation skillfully concealed the wounded and the dead, hiding the true extent of their losses from any curious onlookers.

In his heart, Lacroix knew that this battle was but a taste of what was to come. The rebels were growing bolder, more cunning – and in their eyes burned the unquenchable fire of revolution. Who had won the month-long battle at Crête-à-Pierro was questionable. Sure, they had taken the fort, but at a cost significantly higher than any of them had expected. The rebels had escaped to fight another day and there were no significant assets or intelligence recovered within the fort.

As the sun rose in the east, he couldn't help but feel a shiver of foreboding run down his spine.

"Stay vigilant, Captain," he murmured to Beaumont as they marched side by side. "I fear this is only the beginning."

"Indeed, Général," Beaumont agreed, his eyes scanning the sugar fields nervously as drums could be heard in the distance, "We must prepare ourselves for whatever lies ahead."

Toussaint had made plans to retreat to the Chassériau plantation, near Grands Fonds. In the distance, shadows of the Petit Cahos mountains loomed like ancient guardians, their peaks wreathed in a creeping mist as they neared the property. Toussaint had stopped under a tree to accept a dispatch from Lamartinière's messenger who stood before him.

He stared down at Lamartinière's report of the besieged fort, his heart heavy with regret. He had arrived too late to help, and now all that remained were the smoldering remnants of a lost battle. He fought back the urge to curse himself for his tardiness, knowing that doing so would serve no purpose.

"Général Toussaint," a voice called out, and he glanced to his side to see Dessalines approaching on his horse Galipot with a lieutenant riding at his side, his face a mask of grim determination.

"I am glad to see you unharmed, but I wish it could have been under better circumstances."

There would be time for mourning later, Toussaint thought, but for now they needed to focus on their survival and the continued fight.

The once-thriving fields of the Chassériau plantation stood in eerie silence, sugar cane fields ravaged by fire of recent battles as they rode onto the property.

"Have we come to this place to forge a new path forward?" Dessalines asked.

"Yes, it will be our temporary headquarters, for now," replied Toussaint. As they entered the dilapidated plantation house, they found a room with a large table that had miraculously survived the mayhem. Maps and documents lay strewn across the surface, remnants of past hopes and dreams. Toussaint picked up a map of the island, tracing his fingers along the contours of the mountains and rivers that defined their homeland.

"Rochambeau will expect us to regroup and retaliate quickly," Toussaint mused, his brow furrowed in thought. "Perhaps we should take advantage of that expectation – feign weakness and draw him into a trap."

"An interesting proposal," Dessalines agreed, leaning closer to study the map. "But how do we ensure he takes the bait?"

"By striking at his pride," Toussaint replied, a spark igniting in his dark eyes. "We know that the French returned to Port Républicain after they conquered the fort. If we spread the word of a planned retaliatory attack on the city, Rochambeau may feel compelled to meet us head-on, hoping to crush our rebellion in the field once and for all."

"Then, when he marches out of the city to meet our forces, we can strike from the shadows, catching them in the rear, unawares and off-guard," Dessalines added, a grim smile creeping across his face. "It is a risky maneuver, but it may be our best chance to turn the tide in our favor."

Toussaint nodded, his resolve hardened by their shared determination. Deep within him, a fire burned – a fire fueled by the memories of those who had fallen at the fort, the lives taken by Rochambeau's ruthless command.

"But, what about the danger of Desrances? asked Dessalines.

Toussaint contemplated what Dessalines had just said. Lamour Desrances, born in Africa, was brought to Saint-Domingue as a slave and ran away to become a maroon. He fought with the maroon bands in the slave revolt of 1791 and ended up gaining power and control over the mountains surrounding Port Républicain and Saint-Marc, he was, however, a sworn enemy of Toussaint.

"He's a rebel against our cause as far as I am concerned. An arch enemy. He will align with the French and fight against us, just as he fought against us with Rigaud in the Civil War."

"Then certainly the French will attempt to sway him and use his forces again, against us, as Rigaud had done in the past. Rigaud has returned and can persuade him again to do so."

"Let us make our plans, then," he said, his voice steady and unwavering. "For the sake of our people, for the freedom we have fought so hard to achieve, we must ensure that this gamble pays off."

As they continued to strategize into the night, stars pierced the darkness above like silent witnesses to the unfolding drama below. The future remained uncertain, the path ahead fraught with danger and sacrifice. But in that moment, as Toussaint and Dessalines plotted their next move, hope flickered like a fragile flame, refusing to be snuffed out.

And as the French settled back into the uneasy calm of Port Républicain, they remained blissfully unaware of the storm that was brewing in the mountains, poised to descend upon them with all the fury of a people long oppressed.

The drums of the night would continue.

Fifteen

PAULINE ENTERS PORT RÉPUBLICAIN

Port Républicain
April 1802

The sun dipped towards the horizon, casting a golden glow over the turquoise waters that lapped at the white sands of the many beaches scattered along the coastline. Pauline stood on the deck of the *Splendide*, her eyes drinking in the stunning beauty surrounding her. A warm gentle breeze played with her dark curls as she leaned against the railing, fingertips tracing the worn wood with an absent-minded grace.

"Bring the opera company to the deck!" she commanded suddenly, her voice ringing out clear and authoritative. "I want music as we sail past the gorgeous island of La Gonâve."

A flurry of activity ensued as her entourage hastened to obey. The performers, resplendent in their colorful costumes, filed onto the deck, their voices harmonizing in a hauntingly beautiful melody that seemed to dance upon the wind. Pauline closed her eyes, allowing herself to be swept away by the transcendent power of the music, and of her ability to command such a performance.

"Ah, La Gonâve," she murmured, opening her eyes to gaze upon the lush green island as it drew nearer. "How I long to explore your secrets, to bask in your natural splendor."

She sighed wistfully, her thoughts turning to the city of Cap Français, the jewel that had been stolen from her grasp by those savages. "No matter," she thought fiercely, clenching her fists. "Port Républicain will be mine, and I shall make it into the new Paris of the Caribbean!"

As the ship sailed on, Pauline's vision for her future home took root in her mind, blossoming into grand designs and ambitious schemes. "This city shall be my masterpiece," she vowed silently, her eyes alight with determination. "A testament to my power, my authority… and my indomitable spirit."

The sound of applause brought her back to the present, and she turned to see the opera company taking a bow before her. She clapped her hands, a small, triumphant smile gracing her lips.

"Bravo!" she called out, her voice filled with genuine admiration. "Your talents never cease to astound me. I look forward to the day when all of Port Républicain will be able to witness your genius."

The *Splendide* forged its path through the glittering waters of the Caribbean, with Pauline thinking that nothing would stand in her way.

As the ship glided into port at Port Républicain, she admired the majestic palms lining the harbor, and beyond them, she could see the gleaming white facades of grand mansions and elegant public buildings, all testament to the city's rapid recovery from the chaos of years past. As the ship drew closer to the dock, she noticed how meticulously organized the streets were, laid out in clean, straight lines like the veins of a carefully planned masterpiece.

"Captain, you have done well," she murmured, her eyes devouring the sight before her. "Port Républicain is more beautiful than I had dared to imagine."

"Thank you, Madame Leclerc," the captain replied, his tone reverent. "I have only followed the course set for me. The true beauty lies within the city itself."

Pauline smiled, barely able to contain her excitement as she prepared for her triumphant entrance. She envisioned herself at the helm of this thriving metropolis, guiding it to even greater heights under her benevolent rule as the wife of the new Governor Général.

As the ship docked, Maurice, the young cabin boy with whom she had shared many passionate nights during their voyage, called out, duffle bag in hand, "Pauline, wait for me, I am coming!"

As he began to descend the plank to go on shore. She called him back, her voice cold and imperious. "Where do you think you are going, Maurice, and haven't I told you that in public, my name is Madame Leclerc?" Pauline scolded, her tone icy and authoritative. She could feel the eyes of the other passengers and sailors upon them, their curiosity piqued by the exchange.

Maurice shifted uncomfortably under her unwavering stare, swallowing hard. "Yes, Madame Leclerc. My apologies," he stammered, his hands fidgeting at his sides, beads of sweat forming on his brow. It pained her for the inevitability of what would come next for him.

Maurice hesitated, looking up at her with uncertainty in his eyes. "I... I thought I was coming with you," he whispered, "but you are already leaving…Madame, without me?"

"Did you now?" Pauline replied, as she raised a perfectly groomed eyebrow, her gaze unwavering. "Well, you thought wrong. You have served your purpose on this voyage, but your place is not by my side in Port Républicain."

"But, Madame—" he stammered, his face flushing with disappointment and hurt.

"Enough!" she snapped, cutting him off. "Your time with me is over. Now, return to your duties and forget about what transpired between us. That was a mere interlude, an amusement during our journey. You are a cabin boy, Maurice; know your place you silly boy. The voyage is over and so are you and I. Be thankful. Now you must return to do what cabin boys do, whatever that is."

"I cannot go back. I won't go back. I belong with you. I'll do anything" pleaded Maurice.

"Maurice, I do not mean to disappoint you but what you have had with me these past weeks is the best you will ever achieve in your lifetime. The food, the leisure, the comfort… the sex. It was a young man's fantasy for you and one you will remember your entire life. Call it my gift to you. But now you must go back to reality. Goodbye Maurice" she said as she turned to go on shore knowing she would never set eyes on him again.

Maurice loved her. She was his first love. He began to shed tears as he saw her disembark and dreaded returning to the hard life of shipwork. She was right, though, things would never be as good as they had been these past two months. For that, he was devastated, his life virtually over. Maurice's face crumpled at her harsh words, and he retreated up the plank without another word, his shoulders slumped in defeat, duffle bag dragging on the floor behind him.

Pauline watched him go, feeling a twinge of regret for her cruelty. But she knew that she could not afford to let sentimentality cloud her judgment now, not when she was on the brink of claiming her new realm.

"Power demands sacrifices," she reminded herself as she adjusted the elegant hat atop her head. "And this is just one of many I will have to make."

With her eyes set firmly on the bustling docks ahead, Pauline began her descent onto the soil of Port Républicain, ready to take her rightful place as its queen and reshape it into the Paris of the Caribbean.

The air was filled with the mingling scents of saltwater, tropical flowers, and the tantalizing aroma of premium roasting coffee beans – an intoxicating cocktail that invigorated her senses. She took a deep breath, drawing in the energy of the city as she watched the people of Port Républicain going about their daily routines, with a sense of exhilaration.

She stepped off the plank and was approached by the city's mayor, "Welcome Madame Leclerc, wife of our new Captain Général and sister of the great First Consul, Napoleon Bonaparte. Allow me to introduce myself. I am Paul Jean, the mayor of this wonderful city."

"Ah, the pleasure is all mine, Mr. Mayor.

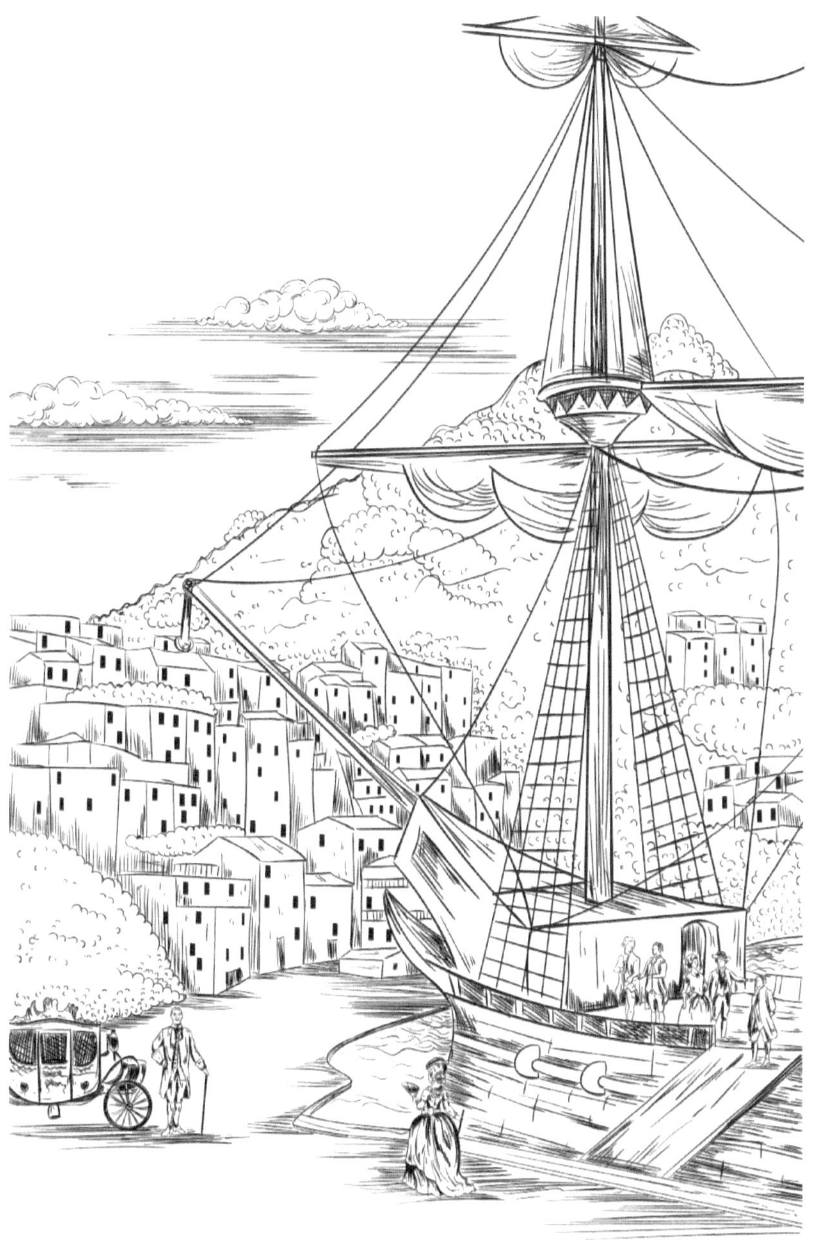

"Général Leclerc has purchased a lovely home, a mansion really, albeit unseen, that we are sure you will be pleased with," offered the mayor.

Pauline smiled. She did not expect that Charles would have had time to make such arrangements, "Take me to it, please," Pauline responded, her voice a melody that seemed to captivate those around her. As she spoke, her eyes sparkled with anticipation, eager to explore the new life that awaited her.

"Very well, Madame Leclerc," said the mayor, gesturing towards a waiting carriage. Pauline graciously accepted his offered hand and stepped inside, settling into the plush couch as the carriage began its journey through the city.

The April sun was warm but not hot, casting a golden glow over the city's bustling streets. She breathed deeply, relishing the crisp freshness that was so different from the stifling heat of the ship's interior.

"Isn't it lovely here, Madame?" murmured the mayor, clearly pleased by her visible delight.

"Indeed, Mr. Mayor," she replied, her gaze drifting to the vibrant colors of the buildings, the laughter of children playing in the streets, café's filled with patrons, bustling shops, and residents strolling the sidewalks, obviously enjoying the fine weather. "It's quite charming, a refreshing change from what I've grown accustomed to."

The carriage wound its way through the city, destined for the suburb of Martissant, right outside the city. Within a short ride, the driver turned into a driveway bordered by tall palms and manicured gardens.

The carriage rolled to a stop, and Pauline felt her heart race as the huge metal gate before them creaked open. A servant, dressed in crisp white and black attire, bowed deeply as he granted them entrance to the estate. As the carriage proceeded along the cobblestone drive, she marveled at the perfectly trimmed hedges that lined the path, their green leaves glistening in the sunlight.

"Is this really mine?" she whispered under her breath, unable to hide her excitement. She leaned out of the window, taking in the sprawling gardens that seemed to stretch on forever. Her eyes were drawn to the vibrant flower beds filled with lush and colorful crotons, bougainvillea, and hibiscus, their colors blending harmoniously with the lush greenery that surrounded them.

"Indeed, Madame Leclerc," replied the mayor, a proud smile on his face as he watched her reaction. "This estate belonged to a fabulously wealthy French planter before the unfortunate events of the civil war forced him to flee. It has since been waiting for a new owner to restore it to its former glory."

"Then I shall do my best to exceed your expectations," Pauline vowed, her determination stoked by the potential she saw in the estate. The scent of jasmine wafted through the air, mingling with the aroma of roasted coffee, and fires burning charcoal, that lingered everywhere. She could already envision herself strolling through the gardens each morning, breathing in the fragrance of her new home.

As they approached the main building, the carriage slowed, allowing Pauline a moment to appreciate the grandeur of the mansion that stood before her. Its elegant architecture spoke of a time when opulence and luxury were the norm, and she knew instantly that this was where she was meant to be.

"Welcome home, Madame Leclerc," the mayor said warmly as a servant opened her carriage door, and another uniformed servant the front door.

Stepping over the threshold of her new home, Pauline's eyes widened as she took in the grandeur before her. The massive tan stones that made up the walls seemed to hold within them the whispers of a past long gone, and the high ceiling beckoned her to reach for the sky itself. She ran her hand along the smooth plaster, feeling the weight of colonial history beneath her fingertips.

"Madame Leclerc," the mayor addressed her, his voice echoing in the expansive entryway. "Shall I give you a tour of the house?"

"Please do," she replied, her voice filled with a mixture of excitement and awe.

They strolled through the opulent main parlor, where elegant chandeliers dangled from the ceiling like crystalline raindrops. The fine furnishings adorning the room spoke of countless soirees spent in the company of high society, and Pauline could almost hear the laughter and music that must have filled these halls.

But it was when she wandered out onto the veranda that she truly felt her heart soar. The view below revealed a stunning oasis just steps away from the mansion. A circular staircase spiraled gracefully down, straight into the pool of crystal-clear water shimmering in the sunlight like a mirror reflecting the heavens above, as another staircase led to the patio and gardens surrounding the pool.

"Mr. Mayor, this is simply breathtaking," she exclaimed, leaning against the balustrade as she gazed upon the tranquil scene below and bathed in the serene sounds of the waterfall.

"Indeed," he agreed, joining her at the railing. "The pool is constantly replenished by that natural waterfall, fed by a mountain stream," as he pointed up to the cascading water descending from the mountain. "I believe the previous owner had it constructed as a special personal retreat for himself when he was in town from his plantation."

Pauline closed her eyes, allowing herself a moment to imagine the sensation of the cool water on her naked skin, washing away the weariness of her journey and the weight of expectation that came with her position. The sound of the waterfall whispered promises of peace and renewal, and she knew that she would spend countless hours in this haven.

"Thank you for showing me this," she whispered, her voice barely audible over the gentle cascade of water. "I can already feel the healing power of this place."

"Madame Leclerc, it is our hope that your time here in Port Républicain will bring you the happiness and fulfillment you so richly deserve."

"Thank you, Mr. Mayor" she whispered as she stood there on the veranda, the sunlight playing upon her face like a caress from the heavens, Pauline knew she had found a home where her spirit could truly soar. "I love it!" she exclaimed to the Mayor, unable to contain her excitement. "How many rooms does the home have?"

"It has twelve plus a huge master bedroom," the mayor replied, his voice brimming with pride as he gestured towards the grand house.

"Twelve?" Pauline echoed, her mind already racing with thoughts of how she could transform each space into a sanctuary for art, music, and luxurious comfort. She imagined evenings filled with candlelight and laughter, with friends and lovers gathered around tables laden with sumptuous feasts and fine wines.

"Indeed," the mayor confirmed, watching as Pauline's face lit up with enthusiasm. "This home was designed for those who appreciate the finer things in life, Madame Leclerc."

"Please, call me Pauline," she insisted, her tone warm and inviting. As they walked together along the cobblestone paths, she couldn't help but feel a sense of camaraderie with the man who had welcomed her so graciously to his city. "I am eager to make Port Républicain my own, and your guidance is invaluable to me."

"Of course, Pauline," the mayor responded, clearly pleased by her request. "I am at your service."

"Port Républicain is fortunate to have you as its mayor," complimented Pauline.

"And Port Républicain is also fortunate to have you, Pauline, wife of the new Governor General, to reside in our lovely city," the mayor replied, his voice filled with genuine warmth. "I do not doubt that your presence here will bring beauty and vitality to our city."

"Is it manned with a staff?" she asked the mayor, unable to suppress the thrill that coursed through her veins at the thought of commanding such a grand estate.

"Indeed, Madame," the mayor answered, his voice filled with pride. "I have taken the liberty of supplying your initial staff for the first month out of the government treasury. If they please you, you may keep them, or if not, replace them with your own staff. The staff is of twenty persons including groundskeepers, cooks and helpers, servers, housekeepers, pool staff, a butler and property manager."

A vision of bustling activity filled Pauline's head - the elegant soirees she would host, the exquisite meals prepared by skilled chefs, and the impeccable service that would attend to her every whim. Her heart raced as she imagined the power and influence, she would wield over her new domain.

"Thank you, Mr. Mayor, I believe I shall name this palace Habitation Leclerc," she said, barely able to contain her glee. "How is it that the city is so orderly, calm, and serene during a period of apparent agitation by the population on the island?"

"Général Boudet," was the immediate answer. "Général Boudet has been truly invaluable to our city," Mayor Paul continued, his voice swelling with pride. "His presence here has fostered a sense of unity and trust among our diverse population in your husbands, the new Governor Général's mission here."

Pauline nodded thoughtfully, her mind already racing with plans for how she might use this to her advantage. If she could win the favor of such a beloved figure, her influence would surely grow exponentially.

"Arrange a meeting at your earliest convenience with the illustrious Général Boudet please, Mr. Mayor," she instructed her tone both gracious and firm. "I believe that the Général and I have much to discuss."

"Of course, Madame Leclerc," he responded, inclining his head in assent. "I shall send word to the Général immediately. Will that be all, Madame, I mean Pauline?"

"You have been most gracious and generous with your time, Mr. Mayor, "and I seek not to abuse it. Your warm welcome here shall not go unnoticed."

"Au revoir et à bientôt, Pauline," the mayor said as he turned and left.

Power is only as valuable as one's ability to wield it, she thought to herself as she watched her new pawn, the mayor, depart. I will make certain to harness every ounce of it. "Général Boudet," she whispered, a slow smile spreading across her face. "I look forward to our meeting."

The sun dipped low in the sky, casting a warm golden glow over the bustling city of Port Républicain. Général Boudet stood at the edge of the city, gazing out over the sprawling metropolis he had conquered. His brow furrowed as he recalled the recent battles, the brutal chase of Dessalines and his forces through Leogane and Saint-Marc, and the bloody assault on the fort at Crête-à-Pierrot, a memory that still haunted him, and an injury that still inflicted occasional pain.

"Général Boudet?" called a messenger several days later, breathless from his haste. "I have been sent by Mayor Paul with an invitation from Madame Leclerc. She requests your presence tonight at Habitation Leclerc for dinner."

Boudet's eyes narrowed slightly, considering the implications of this invitation. He was well aware of Madame Leclerc's position as wife of the Captain Général and her sibling connection to the First Consul. As the golden light danced across the city, Boudet realized that this could be an opportunity, a chance to further solidify his position and influence within the colony.

"Very well," he replied, offering a curt nod to the messenger. "Tell Mayor Paul and Madame Leclerc that I accept their gracious invitation."

That evening, resplendent in his finest ceremonial uniform, Général Boudet arrived at Habitation Leclerc. The mansion was a vision of elegance and opulence, and he couldn't help but marvel at the gardens and breathtaking architecture. As he stepped inside, he was greeted by the melodious sound of the opera company, their voices floating gracefully through the air, and the murmur of conversation among the guests.

"Ah, Général Boudet!" exclaimed Mayor Paul, approaching him with a warm smile. "I am so glad you could join us. Madame Leclerc is eager to meet you."

"Thank you for the invitation, Mayor Paul," Boudet replied, his eyes scanning the room as he considered what might unfold during the evening. What did she want from him, he wondered?

"Come," urged the mayor, leading Boudet through the gathering. "Let me introduce you to our esteemed hostess."

As they approached Pauline, he was taken aback by her beauty. She was dressed in an elegantly simple crème gown of a light fabric that broadcasted the sublime features of her body. Boudet's thoughts raced, weighing the potential consequences and rewards of this meeting. He knew the power she held in her hands, and he was determined to use it to his advantage.

"Madame Leclerc," said Mayor Paul, gesturing toward Boudet, "may I present Général Jean Boudet?"

"Général," Pauline purred, extending a delicate hand for him to kiss. "I have heard so much about your heroic efforts. I am delighted you could join us tonight."

"Thank you, Madame," Boudet replied, brushing his lips lightly against her hand. "It is an honor to be here."

"Please, call me Pauline," she insisted with a coy smile, her eyes sparkling with intrigue.

"Very well... Pauline," Boudet conceded, feeling the weight of the evening's possibilities bearing down on him. "Now, I must circulate with my guests," she said as she abruptly left the two men.

The game had begun with her first move, Boudet thought, and he intended to play it to the very end.

A servant arrived with wine for Boudet and the mayor. Boudet allowed himself a small sip and scanned the lively crowd, taking note of the opera singers performing by the pool and the theater troupe entertaining guests with scenes from their upcoming play.

"Quite the gathering, is it not?" Mayor Paul remarked, following Boudet's gaze. "Madame Leclerc certainly knows how to make an entrance, even arriving with her personal entertainment."

"Indeed," Boudet murmured, his eyes finally settling on Pauline as she held court among a circle of admirers. She looked radiant, her smile bright and her eyes alive with mischief as she regaled her audience with tales of Parisian society.

As if sensing his gaze upon her, Pauline turned and locked eyes with Boudet. Her expression shifted subtly - still smiling, but now tinged with a hint of intrigue. Excusing herself from her admirers, she approached Boudet with a sway in her step that drew appreciative glances from several onlookers.

"Général Boudet, I've been hoping to speak with you," Pauline said, her voice low and inviting. "I need your opinion on a somewhat delicate and private issue. Would you mind, Mr. Mayor, if I stole your hero away for a few minutes?"

"Of course not, Madame Leclerc," the mayor replied amiably, raising his glass in a gesture of acquiescence. "I trust you will take good care of our esteemed guest."

"Have no fear, Mr. Mayor," Pauline assured him, her smile enigmatic. She turned to Boudet and extended her hand in a silent invitation.

Boudet hesitated for a brief moment, acutely aware of the undercurrents at play. His thoughts raced as he weighed the potential consequences and benefits of whatever private matter Pauline wished to discuss, but ultimately, his curiosity won out. Gently taking her offered hand, he allowed her to lead him away from the lively throng, their laughter and music fading into the background as they ventured deeper into the heart of Habitation Leclerc.

As they walked, Boudet couldn't help but steal glances at Pauline, whose beauty was only enhanced by the warm glow of lanterns illuminating their path. At thirty-one, he had seen many beautiful women in his life, but there was something about her that captivated him - the way she moved, the sultry curve of her lips when she smiled, the wicked gleam in her eyes that hinted at hidden depths.

"Beautiful evening, isn't it?" Pauline remarked, pausing at a huge open window, looking up at the inky sky studded with stars. "I find the night air so refreshing after a long day."

"Indeed, it is quite pleasant," Boudet agreed, his gaze lingering on her face before reluctantly tearing away to scan their surroundings. Despite the serene setting, he couldn't shake the feeling that he was being drawn into a situation fraught with danger and intrigue.

"Général," Pauline began, her voice low and serious. "Your reputation precedes you, and I am most impressed by your accomplishments. Yet, there is something that concerns me."

"What is it, Madame?" Boudet asked, his brow furrowing with concern as curiosity gnawed at him.

"Your allegiance, Général," she replied, meeting his gaze squarely. "To whom do you truly owe your loyalty? To my brother, the First Consul? Or to my husband, Général Leclerc? I need to know where you stand."

Boudet's heart raced as he considered her question, his mind a whirlwind of conflicting thoughts. He had always been dedicated to serving France and upholding its values, but circumstances and politics often complicated matters.

"Madame," he began cautiously, "my loyalty is to France, and to those who lead it with honor and integrity. I serve your brother and your husband because they represent the ideals that I hold dear - *liberté, égalité et fraternité.*"

"Ah, a man of principles," Pauline mused, her eyes narrowing slightly as she studied his face. "But tell me, Général, what if those you follow begin to stray from those very ideals? Would you still stand by their side, or would you seek to right their course?"

"Madame," Boudet replied, carefully choosing his words, "if ever such a situation were to arise, I would do everything in my power to ensure that the ideals we all hold dear are upheld. My loyalty is unwavering, but not blind."

"Very well," she said, her expression unreadable. "I appreciate your candor, Général. It is a rare and valuable trait." With that, she turned on her heel, leaving him standing alone under the watchful gaze of the stars.

As Boudet watched her go, he felt both relieved and uneasy, knowing that he had passed some sort of test, but uncertain of what lay ahead. The night air, once refreshing, now seemed heavy with portent and unanswered questions.

Then, without warning, she suddenly turned and returned. "Come with me, Général," she said, more of a command than a request. Interesting he thought, she commands a Général of the French army in such a cavalier manner.

Pauline led him to what was the master bedroom, bathed in the soft warm glow of flickering candlelight, casting shadows that danced across the walls and ceiling. The scent of jasmine filled the air, and bright red strands of bougainvillea decorated the room, mingling with the subtle undertones of sandalwood. Boudet hesitated at the threshold, all too aware of the potential consequences of entering such an intimate space with the wife of his commanding officer.

"Please, Général," Pauline said, her voice low and inviting as she closed the door behind them. The sound of the lock latch clicking into place sent a shiver down Boudet's spine, the finality of it echoing through his thoughts. She turned to face him, her dark eyes shining like polished onyx in the dim light.

"Général, I want to thank you for capturing this city for me. I am in love with it already," she stated, her fingers absently brushing against the heavy brocade curtains that framed the large windows.

"Madame, it is my duty to serve France and its interests," Boudet replied cautiously, struggling to maintain his composure in the presence of such beauty and power. He could feel his heart pounding in his chest, the rhythm was erratic and unfamiliar.

"Of course," Pauline murmured, a knowing smile playing at the corners of her lips. She crossed the room, her silken gown whispering softly against the polished floorboards. As she moved closer, Boudet's breath caught in his throat, the scent of her perfume intoxicating and heady. "But I would be remiss if I did not show my gratitude for your efforts."

"Your words are more than enough, Madame," he managed to say, his voice barely audible above the pulse that roared in his ears.

"Are they?" she asked, tilting her head to one side as she studied him. Her gaze seemed to pierce through him, laying bare his most secret desires and fears. Boudet felt as if he stood at the edge of an abyss, teetering between duty and temptation.

"Madame," he began, swallowing hard against the knot that had formed in his throat, "your happiness is paramount to all those who serve under your husband's command. I am gratified to know that my actions have brought you joy."

"Indeed, they have," Pauline replied, her smile enigmatic as she glanced around the room, her eyes lingering on the ornate canopy bed that dominated the space. "And yet, Général, I cannot help but wonder what else might be achieved if we were to join forces in a more... personal capacity?"

Boudet's mind raced, torn between the allure of such an alliance and the knowledge that to pursue it would be to risk everything he held dear. In the silence that stretched between them, the whisper of the flames seemed to grow louder, their shadows twisting and writhing like restless spirits. He took a deep breath, the scent of jasmine and sandalwood filling his senses, his heart racing within his chest, the pounding sound echoing loudly in his ears as if to drown out Pauline's seductive words. He tried to focus on the flickering light of the candles, their flames casting an ethereal glow upon her porcelain skin, only serving to heighten her allure.

"My men are the ones to thank. I simply command them," he replied, struggling to maintain a distance between them, both in body and mind.

"I understand you were injured chasing that butcher Dessalines in battle, Jean," she said, causing him to flinch at the use of his first name that was, as calculated caution, never offered to her.

Her voice was like velvet, soothing and yet dangerous all at once, wrapping around him with an invisible force that threatened to pull him under. Boudet clenched his fists tightly by his side, nails digging into his palms in an attempt to anchor himself to reality. He swallowed hard, feeling the weight of the decision that lay before him.

"Indeed, Madame," he responded, forcing a tight smile. "But it is merely a flesh wound, nothing that should concern you."

Pauline's eyes glinted with mischief, her gaze wandering over his form as if assessing the extent of his injuries. She took a step closer, the rustle of her gown barely audible above the whispers of temptation that seemed to fill the room.

"Your bravery is commendable, Jean," she murmured, her breath hot against his cheek. "But surely you must understand the importance of taking care of oneself. No one can afford to be reckless in these times, not even a valiant Général such as yourself."

Boudet's resolve wavered, the boundaries between duty and desire blurring more with each passing moment. The heat emanating from her body was intoxicating, tendrils of longing snaking through him as he fought to keep his thoughts from wandering down a path from which there would be no return.

"Madame," he whispered, his voice barely audible above the pounding of his heart. "I assure you, I am well taken care of."

"Are you, Jean?" she questioned softly, her eyes locked onto his as if daring him to look away. "Or is there perhaps some part of you that remains... unfulfilled?"

Her words hung heavy in the air, a tantalizing invitation that beckoned him with a power he could not deny. Boudet's mind raced, torn between the path of duty and honor, and the seductive call of forbidden passion.

The candles continued to cast flickering shadows in the room, their soft glow illuminating Pauline's face as she studied Général Boudet with a mixture of curiosity and desire. He stood before her, his normally imposing figure seeming somehow diminished under her intense gaze. The air was heavy with tension, each breath he took feeling more labored than the last.

"The physicians have taken good care of me, Madame," he answered, swallowing past the knot in his throat.

"Call me Pauline," she insisted, her voice a sultry whisper that sent shivers down his spine. "Let me see your injury, Jean."

Boudet hesitated, acutely aware of the impropriety of such an act. Yet something in her eyes, a smoldering hunger he could not ignore, compelled him to comply. Slowly, he unbuttoned his jacket and removed it, revealing the bandages wrapped tightly around his torso under a well-developed chest and arms of muscle.

Pauline's eyes widened slightly, a hint of concern flitting across her features before being replaced by determination as he now regretted not showing her his foot injury instead. Why was he not thinking straight?

"Sit," she commanded, gesturing to a nearby chair. As she moved to stand behind him, Boudet couldn't help but notice the delicate sway of her hips, the way her gown seemed to caress her every curve in a slow dance of seduction.

"Does it pain you much?" she asked, her fingers gently tracing the edge of the bandage as if testing its limits.

"It is bearable," he replied, gritting his teeth against the sudden surge of sensation her touch elicited. Her presence was like a flame, drawing him closer despite the threat of being severely burned.

"Such stoicism," she murmured, the warmth of her breath washing over his neck. "But is it truly necessary, Jean? Are you not deserving of some reprieve from your burdens?"

Her words struck a chord deep within him, stirring a longing he had long kept dormant beneath the weight of his responsibilities. He wanted to give in, to allow himself this fleeting taste of solace. And yet...

"Madame... Pauline," he clumsily corrected himself, forcing the words past the ache in his chest. "I am honored by your concern, but I must uphold my duties above all else."

"Even at the cost of your happiness?" she challenged, her fingers gently brushing against his cheek. The intimacy of her touch threatened to break the last remnants of his resolve.

"Especially then," he answered, his voice barely more than a whisper. In that moment, as the battle between duty and desire waged within him, Général Boudet knew that regardless of the outcome, he would emerge forever changed.

The steady rhythm of his heartbeat seemed to echo and amplify in the silence that followed Pauline's words. Général Boudet could feel the blood rushing to his face, a stinging heat that threatened to betray his inner turmoil.

Without warning, she reached behind her and undid the clasp that was holding her loose-fitting gown. It fell to the floor with a soft rustle, leaving her completely exposed. Her twenty-one-year-old figure was seductive as her breasts pointed in his direction, hard nipples pale pink and contrasting with her long flowing black hair.

"Consider this a thank you for capturing this city, Jean," she murmured, her eyes never leaving his. "I also want to soothe your wounds. I am yours for the taking, soldier. Consider me a gift from the First Consul Napoleon, and I am equally as grateful for you delivering the city."

Boudet's mind raced, torn between desire and duty. How could he accept such an offer without betraying everything he stood for? His thoughts turned to his men, who had fought so valiantly by his side; to Charles Leclerc, whose trust he had earned through years of loyal service.

"Pauline, you must understand..." He hesitated, his throat suddenly dry. "I... I have sworn myself to the cause, to my comrades, and my commander. How can I justify accepting this... indulgence?"

"Because you are human, Jean," she replied softly, her fingers trailing down his chest. "You have sacrificed so much, risked your life for your country. Do you not deserve even a moment of pleasure and peace? No one will be the wiser."

His breath hitched as her touch sent shivers down his spine. The intensity of his longing for her was almost unbearable, but so too was the weight of his conscience. He clenched his fists at his sides, willing himself to resist the temptation before him.

"Pauline, I cannot," he whispered, his voice desperate. "I am honored by your offer, but this... it isn't right."

"Very well," she said quietly, her face unreadable. "I understand, Jean."

As she stepped away from him, Boudet felt both relief and regret wash over him in equal measure. He had made his choice, but he knew that he would never forget this moment – the moment when desire and duty clashed within him, leaving him with nothing but the bittersweet memory of what could have been.

Although he had tried to steel himself against temptation, Boudet found his resolve crumbling in the face of such intoxicating beauty. While she was turned away from him, he couldn't help but stare and be captured by her curved hips and the shape of the cheeks of her buttocks.

Pauline seemed to sense his weakening, and turned, her eyes smoldering with unspoken promises as she stepped closer to him. He knew he shouldn't allow this to happen, but every fiber of his being ached with desire.

"Jean," she whispered, her breath warm on his skin as she took his hands, placed them on her breasts, and guided his thumbs to her erect nipples, "do not deny yourself this moment of happiness."

As if a dam had burst within him, all thoughts of duty and loyalty were washed away by a tidal wave of passion. With a low groan, he pulled her against him, their bodies melding together as if they had been created for one another. He lifted her effortlessly into his arms and carried her to the bed, where they surrendered themselves to the ecstasy that awaited them.

From that night on, Pauline's life became a hedonistic whirlwind. As her husband waged war across the island to chase rebels and restore order and security, she reveled in the pleasures available to her in Port Républicain. Lavish parties filled with laughter, indulgence, and entertainment became her daily fare, while her nights were consumed by passionate nightly encounters with Jean Boudet.

"Madame Leclerc, you have outdone yourself once again!" exclaimed one of her many admirers, taking her hand and twirling her around the dance floor. The music swirled around them like a heady perfume, and she laughed with pure abandon.

Amidst the revelry, however, there was always a whisper at the back of her mind – a nagging voice that reminded her of her duty as wife to Charles. But each time it surfaced, she pushed it down, choosing instead to lose herself in the ever-changing sea of faces that populated her world, each one offering a new opportunity for pleasure and excitement.

"Madame," cooed another admirer as he offered her a glass of wine, "you are truly the queen of this city. Your beauty, your charm – they have bewitched us all."

"Indeed," she replied with a flirtatious smile as she sipped from her goblet, allowing herself to be swept away by the intoxicating allure of this new life. As long as Charles remained preoccupied with his military endeavors, she would continue to dance on the edge of scandal and oblivion, reveling in the freedoms that Port Républicain offered her, and her secret lover Jean Boudet.

But deep within her heart, she knew that this hedonistic existence could not last forever. Sooner or later, reality would come crashing down upon her like a tidal wave, threatening to drown her beneath its merciless weight. And when that time came, she would be forced to confront the consequences of her actions – the tangled web of passion and betrayal that she had so willingly woven around herself.

For now, however, she allowed herself to be carried away by the swirling tide of desire, ever mindful of the storm that brewed on the horizon.

As the light of the full moon cast a festive air over the city of Port Républicain, Charles Leclerc hobbled through the grand entrance of Habitation Leclerc, pain radiating with each step. Was it from his wounded crotch, or from boots he had refused to remove until Toussaint Louverture was caught, which for weeks, he had not been. He had no clue where the pain emanated, all he knew was that it was just painful.

His uniform was stained and tattered, bearing witness to the ferocity of the battles he had fought to secure the island for France. As he made his way into the opulent living room, the sound of laughter and music assaulted his ears, and he gritted his teeth against the unwelcome cacophony.

"Ah, my dear husband," Pauline cooed, her voice dripping with saccharine sweetness as she approached him. Her eyes traveled down to his injury, and a cruel smile curled her lips. "It seems that the war has taken quite a toll on you – most notably where it hurts the most."

"Pauline, do not mock me," Charles growled, his face reddening in shame and anger. He leaned heavily on his cane, feeling the weight of his wife's callous words like a physical blow. "You know nothing of the sacrifices I've made for this country."

"Indeed," she replied flippantly, twirling a strand of her raven hair around her finger. "And yet, here you are, home at last, while your brave soldiers continue to fight and die for your cause."

Charles clenched his fists, his knuckles turning white with the effort of restraining himself. He could feel the simmering rage within him, threatening to boil over at any moment. And then, as if fate were conspiring to push him over the edge, he caught snippets of whispered gossip floating through the air.

"Did you hear about Madame Leclerc and Général Boudet?" one guest murmured to another, their voices barely audible above the din of the party. "I hear they've been carrying on quite the scandalous affair."

"Indeed," the other replied, nodding conspiratorially. "One can only imagine what her poor husband must think."

Charles's heart thundered in his chest as the realization struck him like a bolt of lightning: Pauline had betrayed him once again and with one of his trusted men, again no less. The humiliation was more than he could bear, and his fury threatened to consume him.

"Is it true?" he demanded, his voice low and dangerous as he turned to face his wife. "Have you been sleeping with Boudet behind my back?"

Pauline arched a perfectly sculpted eyebrow, her expression a mixture of feigned innocence and defiance. "And if I have? What right do you have to judge me, Charles? You've been gone for weeks, leaving me alone to fend for myself in this godforsaken place."

"Enough!" Charles roared, his patience finally snapping. He slammed his cane against the floor, the sound echoing through the room like a gunshot. "I will not tolerate your insolence any longer, Pauline! You are my wife, and you will behave accordingly."

"Or what?" she challenged, her eyes flashing with anger. "You'll cast me aside like some common harlot? I am Madame Leclerc, sister of the First Consul himself! And I will not be treated like a mere possession!"

"Then remember your place, woman! And get these people out of my house!" Charles spat, his voice shaking with barely contained rage. "For as long as I am alive, you belong to me – and I will not suffer such betrayal in silence!"

As Charles stormed out of the room, Pauline watched him go, her pulse racing with a mixture of fear and exhilaration. She knew that the storm brewing between them would soon come to a head, and when it did, there would be no turning back. But for now, she would continue to ride the wave of pleasure and intrigue that had become her life in Port Républicain, even as the gathering clouds loomed ominously overhead.

The echo of laughter and the clink of glasses filled the opulent ballroom during a victory reception for the officers in honor of the taking of the city, but Général Leclerc found it impossible to focus on the festivities. His heart thudded against his ribcage, a kettle drum sounding off the cadence of war as he scanned the room for his quarry. The gossip surrounding his wife Pauline's scandalous affair with Jean Boudet burned in his ears, and fury coursed through him like white-hot lava.

He spotted Boudet near a window, laughing with another officer. The man's casual demeanor felt like an affront to Leclerc's honor. With each step, the Général's anger intensified, his boots striking the marble floor in a staccato rhythm that betrayed his resolve.

"Général Boudet," Leclerc growled as he drew closer, causing the laughter to die down. "A word, if you please."

"Of course, Captain Général." Boudet's smile disappeared as quickly as the sun sank below the horizon, replaced by a wary expression. He excused himself from his companion and followed Leclerc out onto a moonlit balcony as the men looked on, knowing what the conversation's subject matter would be.

"Is it true?" Leclerc demanded, his voice barely above a whisper but sharp enough to cut glass. "Have you dared to lay hands on my wife?"

Boudet hesitated but knew he couldn't deny the accusation. It was as though he could feel the weight of his secret love for Pauline bearing down upon him, crushing him beneath its relentless force. "Yes, Captain Général. But I must tell you, it was not just lust or idle curiosity. I fell in love with her."

"Love?" Leclerc spat the word as if it were poison. How dare this man speak of love when he had so carelessly torn apart the delicate fabric of trust and loyalty that held them all together?

"Please understand—" Boudet began, but Leclerc cut him off.

"Understand?" Rage bubbled beneath the surface of his carefully controlled exterior. "You have betrayed me, your fellow officer, and sullied my wife's name. Do you truly expect me to understand?"

Boudet lowered his gaze in shame, unable to meet Leclerc's wrathful stare. The truth was, he couldn't even understand himself –

how he had allowed his feelings for Pauline to consume him so completely that he had forgotten his duty to his comrade-in-arms.

"Forgive me," Boudet whispered, the words tasting like ashes on his tongue. "I never meant to cause harm."

"Your apologies mean nothing to me now," Leclerc replied icily. "This is a matter that cannot be simply swept under the rug or pardoned with just a few words."

Leclerc stood taller than his small stature, his jaw clenched as he regarded the man who had once been his friend and confidant. Though the betrayal stung like a fresh wound, he knew he must set aside his personal feelings for the sake of their mutual duty.

"Effective immediately, you are to leave Saint Domingue for Guadeloupe," Leclerc commanded, his voice steely and cold. "You will find that your belongings have already been packed and sent to the docks. Your ship leaves at dawn."

Boudet's heart clenched painfully in his chest, the reality of his punishment finally sinking in. He would be leaving behind everything he had come to know and cherish, the stature of being labeled the hero of the city, and of course, even Pauline, the woman who now haunted his dreams.

"Understood, Général," Boudet replied, his voice barely audible above the howl of the wind and the noise from the party inside. He averted his gaze from Leclerc's wrathful eyes, finding solace in the flickering shadows cast by the dimly lit lantern.

"God help you if our paths ever cross again," Leclerc warned darkly, his voice laced with venom. "Now get out of my sight."

Boudet swallowed the lump in his throat, and the pride in his chest, forcing himself to stand up straight and salute before turning to leave, however, his salute never received an acknowledgement.

The walk to the docks was a blur, every step weighed down by the crushing weight of his guilt. The salty tang of the sea air filled his nostrils as he approached the ship that would take him away from his new celebratory life as conqueror and savior of this city, such a loss he thought. He couldn't shake the image of Pauline's face from his mind, her once-warm smile now replaced by a look of utter disappointment and anguish.

He had to see her again, right now, tonight, he thought as he spotted a stallion, already saddled and ready to ride him quickly to Habitation Leclerc. The Général had drills in the morning and would spend the night at the barracks he was sure. He would go quickly and come back to the docks in the early morning hours to fulfill his duty. He had to be with her one last time.

In the early morning twilight, Pauline stood on the veranda of Habitation Leclerc, her gaze locked on the dim horizon.

"Pauline," Boudet murmured, coming up behind her and wrapping his arms around her waist. "I don't want to leave you."

"Shh," she whispered, laying a hand over his where it rested against her stomach. "You mustn't speak of such things. Not now."

"Forgive me," he said softly, pressing a kiss to her shoulder. "But I cannot bear the thought of being away from you."

"Nor I you," she admitted, her voice choked with emotion. "But we both knew this day was inevitable. You have your duty, and I... I have my husband."

"Curse that wretched man!" Boudet spat, his grip tightening on her. "If not for him—"

"Enough," Pauline interrupted, turning within his embrace to face him. "We cannot change what is, Jean. All we can do is cherish the memories we've made together and hope that, someday, fate will bring us back to each other's arms."

"Promise me," he implored, his eyes searching hers. "Promise me you'll wait for me, Pauline. That you'll hold onto this love we share, no matter what may come."

"Would you have me defy my own brother, The First Consul himself? He is the one who forced me to marry Charles, you know," she asked, a sad smile tugging at her lips.

"Your loyalty should be to your heart," Boudet insisted. "Not to some title or name."

"Then I promise," she whispered, her eyes shining with unshed tears. "I will wait for you, Jean Boudet. Until the end of time, if that is what it takes."

Relieved, he breathed, pressing his lips to hers in a desperate, searing kiss that spoke volumes of the passion they shared.

"Go," she urged him as they finally broke apart, her chest heaving with emotion. "Before it's too late, and we can't bear to part."

"Goodbye, my love," Boudet murmured, his hand lingering on her cheek for one last, lingering moment before he turned to leave.

As Pauline watched him disappear into the shadows of the early morning, she couldn't help but wonder if this was truly the end of their story or merely the beginning of something new and dangerous. She had made a promise to Jean, but now she had to face the consequences of that choice – and the wrath of a husband who would stop at nothing to protect his honor and reputation.

As the first light of dawn began to break over the horizon, Boudet stood on the deck of the ship bound for Guadeloupe, his heart heavy with remorse. The sound of the creaking ropes and groaning wood mingled with the cries of the gulls overhead, a cacophony that seemed to echo the turmoil within him.

"Is this truly what I deserve?" he wondered, his eyes scanning the receding shoreline of Saint Domingue. "Could I have done anything differently, or was I always destined to betray those closest to me?"

He could still feel the lingering warmth of Pauline's touch on his skin and the memory of her laughter in his ears. But now, as the ship began its journey across the vast expanse of the ocean, Boudet knew that he must leave it all behind – for the sake of those he had betrayed, and for his path towards redemption.

Daniel J.D. Bayard

Sixteen

ONE BY ONE
THEY SURRENDER

Plaine du Nord
May 1802

The air hung heavy with the scent of early April blossoms, a gift of the frequent rains, but a deceptive sweetness that belied the tension in the makeshift camp where Toussaint and Dessalines stood, poring over a map spread across a rough-hewn table. The first light of dawn filtered through the trees, casting dappled shadows on their faces as they plotted their next move.

"Rochambeau and Leclerc will not expect us to divide our forces," Toussaint said, his voice low and measured. "They believe we fear the might of their armies. We shall use their arrogance against them."

Dessalines nodded, his eyes fixed on the map, his mind racing with strategies and calculations. "Indeed. While they hunt for us in the open, we'll draw them into the fields and forests where our knowledge of the terrain will be our greatest advantage."

"Then it is settled." Toussaint punctuated his words with a decisive tap on the map. "You will lead our men westward, and I shall head north to gather the remainder of General Christophe's troops."

"Agreed." Dessalines' heart swelled with determination as he looked up from the map and met Toussaint's gaze.

"Remember, Jean-Jacques, we must remain united in purpose. Our people depend upon us," said Toussaint.

For a moment, the weight of their responsibility silenced both men. Then Toussaint broke the stillness, his voice tinged with equal parts resolve and emotion. "We have come too far to surrender now. I would sooner die than see our people shackled once more."

"Then let us make our stand," agreed Dessalines.

As they prepared to part ways, Toussaint couldn't help but reflect on the path that had led them here. The stakes were higher than ever before, and the road ahead was fraught with danger. But he had faith in Dessalines, in Christophe, and the tenacity of their fighters.

"Keep your wits about you, Jean-Jacques," he said, offering a tight smile. "We shall meet again soon, and then we will show Rochambeau and Leclerc what it means to fight for freedom."

"Until then." Dessalines returned the smile, his eyes alight with fierce purpose as they clasped hands.

With that, they set off – Toussaint to the north, and Dessalines to the west – each man driven by the same unyielding fire that burned within them both.

As Dessalines led his men westward, the sun began its descent towards the horizon, casting afternoon shadows over the landscape. The dense foliage whispered secrets carried on the breeze, and the earth seemed to throb beneath their feet, as though it too sensed the impending clash. Dessalines' eyes scanned the terrain, his instincts sharpened by long years of combat.

"Stay alert," he cautioned his troops, his voice low and steady. "The French may be waiting for us at any moment."

In the distance, the mountains towered like ancient sentinels – silent witnesses to the struggle unfolding below. Dessalines knew that General Rigaud had been busy forging alliances prior to his deportation back to France. Rigaud had been caught scheming behind the scenes to exact revenge on Toussaint Louverture for his defeat in the civil war. Leclerc, not taking kindly to violating orders, quickly had him arrested, sailed back to France, and thrown in prison.

But nothing could have prepared him for the sight that awaited them as they neared Port Républicain.

"Bondye mwen," My God whispered one of his officers, his face ashen. "What have we stumbled upon?"

Before them, instead of the French Army they had anticipated, stood an overwhelming army of 5,000 menacing, shirtless, maroon warriors, armed with machetes, axes, hoes, and other makeshift weapons, assembled like a formidable wall of defiance. Their leader, the powerful Lamour Desrances, stood at their head, his piercing gaze locked onto Dessalines.

Desrances shouted out, slowly and loudly pronouncing each syllable of his name, "Jean… Jacques… Dessalines…, you were expecting French regulars, no?" He then let out a harsh, deep-throated laugh that echoed through the valley. "Instead, you find yourself face-to-face with the true spirit of Africa, and now of this land, embodied in the warriors of the maroon!"

A loud and rehearsed low-pitched primitive chant of *"whooo, whooo, whooo,"* permeated from the warriors as they jumped up and down itching for the fight and directed to intimidate Dessalines' men.

Dessalines clenched his jaw, forcing down the surge of panic that threatened to overwhelm him. Turning to his men, he spoke with determination, "We have fought against greater odds before, my brothers. These warriors may be cunning, but so are we. Stand your ground and fight with me, with all the fury that burns within you. *"Pa gen manman,"* Dessalines yelled.

"pa gen papa," the loud chorus of followers yelled

"Sa ki mouri?" yelled Dessalines

"zafè ya yo," laughed the chorus. *"Ahhhhhhhhh!"*

Dessalines yelled the battle cry, *"A Laso! A Laso!"*

"Ahhhhhhhhhh" followed the troops as they charged toward the enemy.

The sun blazed down mercilessly, casting a fiery hue on the battlefield outside of Port Républicain. Sweat and blood mixed in the dirt beneath their feet as Dessalines and his men fought with every ounce of strength they possessed. They were better trained and equipped but heavily outnumbered and despite their fierce determination, it became increasingly evident that the maroon warriors were not to be bested easily.

After nearly two hours of bloody, grueling fighting, Dessalines cried, "fall back, fall back!" his voice hoarse from exertion. "Regroup and prepare to strike again!"

His men obeyed, but there was a haunted look in their eyes, a realization that the odds were not in their favor. As they retreated, Dessalines surveyed the chaos before him, his chest heaving with each ragged breath. He was a man unaccustomed to loss, but conceded, that this time there was no more need to fight.

As darkness fell over the battlefield, littered with bloody dead bodies from both sides, word spread of the defeat that had befallen Dessalines and his men.

In the quiet confines of Ennery, Toussaint received the news of the devastating defeat of Dessalines with a heavy heart, his brow furrowed in thought.

Henry," Toussaint said, pacing the room as his trusted general watched silently. "Our situation is dire. We cannot afford another such loss. Jean-Jacques, I am sure, fought valiantly,"

"Perhaps we should focus on disrupting their supply lines," suggested Christophe. "Or we could send scouts into the mountains to gather intelligence on their movements."

"Both good suggestions," Toussaint replied, his eyes taking on a steely glint. "We must also consider forming new alliances..."

"New alliances?" Christophe raised an eyebrow. "With whom?"

"Where is that letter you received from Leclerc you showed me yesterday?" asked Toussaint.

Henry produced the letter from his pocket and handed it to him. Toussaint scanned the letter once again. The letter was an open invitation for General Henry Christophe to come to Gonaïves with a guarantee of safe passage, as there was an arrest warrant for both he and Toussaint. "You will go to Leclerc," Toussaint said forcefully.

"To Leclerc, Général? What forever for?"

"To see what he has to say. We are heavily outnumbered. If we can stall and bide the time, our other Général will soon be here,"

"But Dessalines is defeated. Deserances assured us of that," replied a confused Henry.

"Not Dessalines. General Lafyèv jòn," Toussaint said. "General Yellow fever will be here within six weeks, maybe less, as the rains have been heavy and constant this year. General Yellow Fever helped us defeat the British, so can he help us do the same to Leclerc's army."

"So, you want me to stall?"

"Precisely, Henry. Find out what he has to say and report back to me."

Henry arrived in Gonaïves, his heart pounding as he approached the two-story storefront that had been converted into a military installation. The building loomed before him, with flags of France and the standard of the colony flapping in the wind, its facade a stark reminder of the French presence on the island. As he dismounted his horse, sweat trickled down his brow, both from the oppressive heat of the day and the weight of his mission.

"General Christophe," a voice called out, breaking his reverie. A young soldier stood at attention, clearly awaiting Henry's arrival. "I am to escort you to General Leclerc."

"Lead the way," Henry replied, masking his apprehension with the stoicism of a seasoned general. He followed the soldier inside the building, where the air was thick and heavy, filled with the scent of ink and gunpowder.

The door to Leclerc's office creaked open, revealing a room adorned with maps and battle plans. Leclerc sat behind a massive wooden desk, his eyes cold and calculating. As Henry stepped forward, their gazes locked, and for a brief moment, the gravity of their meeting seemed to hang between them like a specter.

"General Christophe," Leclerc said, rising from his chair and surprisingly extending a hand. Their palms met in a firm handshake, and Henry could feel the subtle tremors of his nerves betraying his confident exterior. He had not expected such a warm reception, albeit possibly a fake one, especially after the burning of Cap Français.

"Captain General Leclerc," Henry replied, his voice steady despite the tension coiling in his chest.

"Please, have a seat." Leclerc gestured toward a nearby chair, and Henry obliged, his gaze never leaving the other man's face.

"Your family," Leclerc began, eyes locked on Henry's stoic face, "I've been told they are quite lovely. My aide spoke highly of you and your wife's hospitality and the love of your children upon his return." A brief flicker of concern crossed Henry's expression from Leclerc's familiarity with his family, but he remained silent, waiting for him to continue. "May I call you Henry?"

"As it pleases you, General," Henry replied, his voice steady despite the unease churning within him. It was unsettling, this sudden shift in Leclerc's demeanor – as if they were old friends, rather than adversaries bound by political necessity.

"General Toussaint Louverture has sent me to discuss the current situation in Saint Domingue," Henry began, his words measured and deliberate. His mind raced, contemplating the possible outcomes of this meeting and how best to navigate the treacherous waters of diplomacy.

"Excellent," Leclerc replied, his lips curling into a satisfied smile. "Let's get right down to the business at hand, shall we?"

"Though General Louverture has earned much well-deserved respect and praise for what he had accomplished in the past, the citizens are not happy in the present. The planters feel he has erred in judgment. The ex-slaves feel he has put them back in bondage. The mulattos hate the free blacks and vice versa, and the petit Blancs hate everyone. This is no way to progress into the future, Henry. Would you agree?"

Henry's jaw tightened as he considered Leclerc's words, the truth of them an unwelcome weight upon his shoulders. He thought back to the desperate faces of the men and women who had turned to him for guidance, trusting him to lead them toward a brighter tomorrow.

"General Louverture has done his best to keep things in order," Henry replied carefully, his voice tinged with frustration. "It is not his fault that the white planters don't want to pay what the laborers deserve, that many ex-slaves must be forced to work, and that our French agent Hédouville fueled the flames for a civil war that need not have been. This helped further the wedge through mulatto and black relations. I do not fault Toussaint Louverture for this."

Leclerc's expression remained impassive, but Henry could see a flicker of something – perhaps understanding, or even sympathy – in the depths of his eyes. He wondered what thoughts lay behind that inscrutable facade and whether Leclerc could truly comprehend the complexities of the challenges that Toussaint had to contend with.

"General Christophe," Leclerc began, his voice cool and measured. "Your loyalty to Louverture is admirable but let us not forget that even great men make mistakes." He paused for emphasis, letting his words hang in the air between them. "He had his nephew Moyiz put to death without the benefit of a defense at trial, Henry. A loyal soldier who had served France well was not permitted to plead his innocence whether guilty or not! Did you agree with the General on this?"

"Orders are one thing," Leclerc said, interrupting Henry's thoughts. "But blind obedience can be dangerous, especially when lives are at stake. Remember that, General Christophe."

Henry nodded hesitantly, his mind a whirlwind of conflicting emotions. He knew Leclerc was right; he had always questioned, even protested, the decision to execute Moyiz without a trial. But loyalty to Toussaint Louverture had been ingrained in him for so long that it was difficult to shake, even now.

"Read this proclamation by the First Consul, Henry. Then provide me with your answer." Leclerc held out a crisp sheet of parchment, his gaze unwavering. The paper crackled in protest as it passed between them, the bold black ink stark against the ivory background. It bore Napoleon's signature, a flowing scrawl that seemed to hold an air of authority all its own, and the seal of the First Consul, its intricately carved insignia gleaming beneath a layer of red wax.

Henry accepted the document, his fingers brushing against Leclerc's for a brief moment. His heart beat rapidly in his chest, the sound of it thudding in his ears, drowning out the distant cries of the gulls outside. He unfolded the parchment, eyes scanning the words that would determine the fate of this meeting.

As he read, he could feel Leclerc's gaze upon him, studying his every reaction. It was unnerving, like being dissected by a skilled surgeon, each layer of skin peeled back to reveal the vulnerability beneath. But Henry knew he must remain steadfast, his expression betraying nothing of the turmoil within.

When he finished reading, he looked up at Leclerc, his dark eyes meeting the other man's icy blue ones. "I am a loyal soldier of France," he stated, his voice steady despite the storm raging inside him, "and according to this, I hereby report to you, Sir."

Leclerc's lips twitched into a brief smile as he regarded Henry with newfound respect. For a moment, it seemed as though they were no longer adversaries, but allies united by a common goal – peace and stability for this troubled land. And perhaps, just perhaps, that was enough.

Candlelight flickered across the room, painting the walls with a warm golden hue and casting an eerie glow on the faces of both men.

The atmosphere was thick with tension, the air heavy with the scent of wax.

Henry stood before Leclerc, his hands clasped behind his back, his thoughts racing. He had come to this meeting as a representative of Toussaint Louverture, but now he found himself questioning everything he had ever known – his loyalty, his allegiances, even his very identity as a soldier. And yet, despite the turmoil within him, there was something undeniably compelling about the man who now claimed to be his leader.

Leclerc leaned forward, his eyes piercing into Henry's soul as if searching for the truth that lay buried deep within. "So as your leader," he asked slowly, deliberately, "I can count on your loyalty, is that correct, Henry?"

Henry hesitated for a moment, his heart pounding in his chest He knew what was at stake – not just his own life, but the lives of countless others who depended on him for guidance and protection. But could he truly abandon Toussaint, the man who had led them through so much hardship, the man who had taught him so much about honor and duty?

"And what of the other Generals, Henry?" Leclerc asked, his voice cutting through the silence like a knife. "I have offered you and all officers their same rank and position in the same army you claim loyalty to, the Army of France. This colony does not belong to General Louverture, nor does it belong to me. It belongs to the people of France and the First Consul is the current head of the government of France. Would you agree to that?"

Finally, after what felt like an eternity, he lifted his chin and met Leclerc's gaze squarely. "Yes, Captain General," he said, his voice firm and resolute.

"Then, as a soldier of France, do we not take orders without question. We, the soldiers, are the instruments of the people. And the people are represented by the political leadership of the government. The First Consul is that designated leader, and he has given the army orders. Orders that we must follow. What is your decision, Henry?"

"I service the army of France. I see now that you are the leader of that army in Saint Domingue, and you are acting under the direction of the First Consul. "I am at your service, Governor General," the first time he replaced the title Captain for General.

"Good, then that settles that," Leclerc replied, his eyes never leaving Henry's face. He seemed to be studying him, weighing his sincerity against some hidden measure known only to himself. Then, with a curt nod, he continued, "We have a long and difficult road ahead of us, General Christophe. There will be challenges, setbacks, and perhaps even betrayals. But if we are to succeed in our mission, we must stand united – not just as soldiers, but as brothers."

Henry swallowed hard, his mind racing with the implications of Leclerc's words. Could he truly put aside his past loyalties and embrace this new vision for Saint Domingue? And what would it mean for him and the men under his command?

As if sensing his inner struggle, Leclerc reached out and placed a reassuring hand on Henry's shoulder. "I know this is not an easy decision for you, Henry," he said softly. "But I believe that together, we can make a difference. We can bring peace and prosperity back to this troubled land and ensure a brighter future for the people here."

With those words, something inside Henry seemed to shift and settle into place. A new resolve took root within him, planting the seeds of a fresh loyalty that Henry presumed would grow and flourish in the days and weeks to come. And as he looked into Leclerc's eyes, he knew that he was making the right choice – not just for himself, but for his family, for all of Saint Domingue, and yes, for Toussaint as well.

"Thank you, Governor General," he whispered, his voice thick with emotion. "I will do everything in my power to honor your faith in me, and to serve the people of this colony with all my heart."

"Very well, then," Leclerc said, releasing his grip on Henry's shoulder and stepping back. "Let us begin."

The sun was setting as General Henry Christophe rode back to Ennery, the weight of Leclerc's correspondence pressing against his chest. As he approached the plantation, he noticed the air was thick with tension and a sense of unease. He dismounted and walked toward the main house, where he found Toussaint pacing back and forth on the veranda, deep in thought.

"General," Henry called out, his voice wavering slightly. He knew that this meeting would change everything – for better or worse.

Toussaint looked up sharply, his eyes piercing through Henry like daggers. "What news do you bring, Henry? What does Leclerc want now?"

Henry handed over the letter from Governor General Charles Leclerc, watching as Toussaint's eyes scanned the page, growing darker with every word. He could see the anger simmering beneath the surface, ready to explode at any moment.

"General Leclerc should feel *'highly satisfied if he could induce me to concert with him and submit to the orders of the Republic'*. I have always been submissive to the French Government, as I have invariably borne arms for it," Toussaint spat the words, his knuckles white as he gripped the paper.

"Governor General Leclerc has offered you peace," Henry replied cautiously. "He is willing to lift the arrest warrant and allow you to retire with honor, surrounded by loyal men of your choosing."

"Peace?" Toussaint scoffed bitterly, staring out into the gathering darkness. "Is that what you call it, Henry? Submitting to the whims of a man who has shown nothing but contempt for us and our people?"

Henry hesitated, struggling to find the right words. He knew that Toussaint's pride and love for his people were at odds with the new reality of their situation. But how could he make him see that sometimes, surrender was the only path to true victory?

"General, I understand your reservations," Henry began, choosing his words carefully. "But we cannot continue to fight against our government. If we accept this offer, we can work from within to ensure a better future for Saint Domingue."

Toussaint's fists clenched at his sides, the muscles in his jaw jumping with barely contained rage. "If that man had treated me with the respect I deserved from the start, we would not be in this position," he spat, his voice like the crack of a whip. "And now he expects me to simply bow to his whims?"

"Leclerc has made mistakes," Henry admitted, choosing his words carefully, "and so have you. But this offer represents a path forward for all of us. You would retire with , with the benefit of a pension, be assigned your honor guard, who would also receive a stipend from the government, and be able to continue to provide for your family."

Toussaint's jaw clenched, and for a moment, it seemed as though he might tear the letter to shreds. But then, with a heavy sigh, he looked back at Henry, his eyes filled with weariness and resignation. "Retire?" Toussaint scoffed, his eyes flashing with indignation. "What kind of leader retires while his people still suffer under the yoke of colonial oppression?"

"With all due respect, Toussaint. Next year you make 60 years old, your two sons are now technically enemies, you are estranged from Issac, Placide is in constant danger of being killed in battle, and Suzanne is broken-hearted," Henry pleaded, his voice tinged with desperation, "you have given so much to this cause, but you must also think of your future. If we continue down this path, there may not be an island left to save or a future for you and your family."

Toussaint closed his eyes, his chest heaving with each labored breath as he grappled with the weight of this decision. In the silence, the distant cries of tropical birds seemed to mock his inner turmoil.

"Your loyalty does you credit, Henry," he finally whispered, his voice heavy with resignation, "But I realize that your loyalty is now for the benefit of Leclerc, and not me."

Henry winced at the comment that felt like a hard slap across his cheek.

"Tell General Leclerc," Toussaint said firmly, "that I accept his offer." The finality in his own words sent a shiver down his spine, but he held his head high, determined not to show any sign of weakness. But if I sense that his intentions are anything less than honorable, then I will not hesitate to take up arms once more."

"Thank you, General," Henry said, his voice quivering with relief. "I know this is not an easy decision, but it may be our best chance at securing a brighter future for Saint Domingue." Henry chose to leave at once and travel to Cap Français, as Leclerc had left Gonaïves for the main city, with an affirmative response from Toussaint. He chose not to spend the night, lest Toussaint back down from his decision to retire by the time morning arrived.

The sun was beginning to set, its fiery hues staining the sky like the blood that had been shed in their fight for freedom. As the shadows lengthened around him, Toussaint couldn't help but wonder if this was the beginning of a new dawn or the descent into an unknown darkness.

The morning sun cast long, golden fingers of light through the palm trees as Toussaint Louverture stood at the edge of the cliff overlooking Cap-Français. The ocean below glittered like a sea of diamonds, its serene beauty belying the turmoil that raged within him.

His heart ached with the weight of his decision, but he knew there was no other choice. He had to end this nightmare for his people, and if trusting the French was the only way, then so be it.

"General," a voice called from behind him, and turned to see one of his men approaching him, "Are you ready? Your horse is prepared."

"Thank you," Toussaint replied, his voice tight. As he walked towards Belle Argent, his mind raced with thoughts of all that had led them to this moment. He could feel the heavy gazes of his remaining generals, and other officers assembled upon him, their faces a mix of hope and uncertainty.

Toussaint swung into the saddle of his faithful companion who he thought also felt the weight of the day. Belle Argent had been with him through the glory of victory and now, the agony of… defeat? Is it defeat he wondered? He did not know.

Once saddled, he looked back at the long line of honor guards awaiting, already mounted, gleaming in their shiny metal helmets, the flags ceremoniously flapping in the wind and the horses anxious to stretch their legs for the journey to Le Cap. He was so proud of these men. They had sworn and upheld their allegiance, many with the forfeiture of their lives, to his cause. He must make it right for them on this day.

This day will make history, May 6th, 1802. A good date he thought as they rode towards Cap-Français. It was a beautiful and sunny day as the wind tugged at his hair, carrying with it the scent of salt and promise. Toussaint knew that this decision would shape the future of Saint Domingue and its people, but he also knew that he must be steadfast in his convictions. For they were all he had left to cling to.

As they neared the city, they sighted a dust cloud manufactured by a contingent of 500 French Dragoons with General Hardy at the lead, their horses' hooves rumbling the earth as they drew nearer to them. When the two armies finally halted, they stared at each other on the road, the first time not engaged in a battle. General Hardy gave his mare a slight kick and approached Toussaint with two officers at his side and Toussaint and two of his officers did the same.

The silence gave an eerie and ceremonial air to the event as flags of each contingent flapped gloriously in the wind as the two powerful men greeted each other.

"I am General Hardy, commander of the 3rd Battalion of the Army of France. I bring you greetings and a welcome from the Governor General to meet with him.

"Toussaint Louverture, Governor General of Saint Domingue and Commander in Chief of the Colonial Army, newly retired. I accept the Governor General's Invitation to parlay."

Hardy nodded to the officer on his left who turned his horse and rode back towards the French column. He barked and ordered the 500 horsemen to split ranks standing half on the left and half on the right sides of the road facing each other, providing a ceremonial passageway in the middle large enough for three horses wide.

Hardy and the remaining officer turned their horses and joined the third officer who led them down the road toward Cap Français. Toussaint, accompanied by his two senior officers, led the honor guard towards the city.

Upon passing through the city gates, throngs of people lined the streets to see the spectacle playing out before them. The honor guards of Toussaint were resplendent in their uniforms and shiny helmets as they expertly rode with disciplined precision into the city behind Toussaint who waved right and left to the crowd as if he were a conquering Ceasar coming home from a successful campaign in a foreign land.

When they reached the front of Government House, Toussaint dismounted and strode purposefully towards the stairs as Leclerc waited at the front doors with a contingent of six officers.

Toussaint's heart pounded in his chest as he climbed the stairs with six of his officers and when he reached the top he spoke in a commanding voice; "Governor General Leclerc," he announced, his voice steady despite the turmoil within him. "I have come to negotiate the terms of my retirement and the integration of my army under your command."

Leclerc regarded him coolly, his eyes betraying a hint of surprise but also a flicker of satisfaction. "Very well, General Louverture," he replied. "Let us discuss the terms of your surrender."

Toussaint's jaw tightened at the word 'surrender,' but he pushed aside his pride and focused on the task at hand. Leclerc gestured him inside as the officers on both sides created a path for them to enter; Toussaint's men on the right and Leclerc's on the left.

He and Leclerc spoke in the familiar surroundings of what was Toussaint's old office, still being rebuilt after the fires. As they spoke, he agreed to acknowledge Leclerc's authority in exchange for amnesty for himself and his remaining officers and soldiers. It was a bitter pill to swallow, but one that he knew must be taken if Saint Domingue was ever to know peace again.

"May this be the beginning of a new dawn for our island," Toussaint said solemnly as they shook hands, sealing their agreement.

As he left the office, his heart heavy with both relief and trepidation, Toussaint couldn't help but wonder what the future held for him and his people. But deep down, he knew that whatever challenges lay ahead, he would face them head-on, just as he had always done, for the sake of the land he called home.

The sun blazed in a cloudless sky, mercilessly bearing down on the parched earth. General Jean-Jacques Dessalines stood at the edge of a cliff, overlooking the vast expanse of Saint Domingue's coastline. His eyes were drawn to the dark, lingering plumes of smoke from his recent ongoing battles, a constant reminder of the devastation that had befallen his people.

"General Dessalines," a low voice called from behind him. He turned to find one of Toussaint's messengers, a young man named Paul, standing before him with a solemn expression and a sealed letter in hand.

"Tell me the news," Dessalines demanded, his voice tinged with impatience and dread.

"General Louverture has negotiated an end to hostilities with Leclerc," Paul reported hesitantly, his gaze shifting away from Dessalines' piercing stare. "He has agreed to acknowledge Leclerc's authority in exchange for amnesty for himself and all remaining generals, officers and soldiers. He orders you to cease fire."

Dessalines snatched the letter from Paul's hand, ripping it open with trembling fingers. Anger flared within him like a roaring inferno. He had fought tirelessly alongside Toussaint for the freedom of their people, and now, it seemed that dream was slipping through their fingers like so much sand.

"Damn him!" Dessalines spat, hurling the letter to the ground. "Toussaint should have declared full independence when we first learned of Leclerc's expedition!"

"General, please understand," Paul implored, his voice trembling. "Leclerc's forces were overwhelming. General Louverture did what he believed was best for our people."

"Best for our people?" Dessalines scoffed, casting a scathing glance toward the smoldering horizon. "Look around you, boy. Does this look like what's best for our people?"

Paul opened his mouth to reply, but Dessalines cut him off with a furious wave of his hand. "No more words," he growled. "Go back and tell Toussaint that I will submit to the French – but only because I have no choice."

"General Dessalines--" Paul began hesitantly, but Dessalines' glare silenced him.

"Go!" Dessalines ordered, his voice laden with fury and despair. As he watched Paul retreat, he couldn't help but feel a sense of betrayal gnawing at his heart.

In relenting to the French, they were sacrificing everything they had fought for, and in the process, severing the bond of brotherhood that had united him and Toussaint for so many years. But as Dessalines stared out at the charred landscape before him, he knew that he, too, must swallow his pride for the sake of Saint Domingue and those who called it home.

The following day, Galipòt ran at full speed through the field towards 2,000 of Dessalines' troops assembled there, letting out the final tantrums of fury that his owner required. The two were synchronized in a familiar rhythm and at each stride Galipòt would let out a familiar grunt in a staccato beat.

When they reached the front line of the horsemen, standing at attention, their division flags flapping defiantly in the wind, Dessalines brought Galipòt to a halt and forced him to canter long and high with his front legs dancing in the air, and he then addressed his troops in a loud and commanding voice.

"Koute Byen! Si Desalin rann tèt li a la Frans san fwa, li pwal trayi la Frans san fwa!," Listen well! If Dessalines surrenders to France a hundred times, he will betray them a hundred times. he began, his men fully knowing what would be happening today. A surrender, a full surrender by their leader.

He forced Galipòt to run left and right as he spoke as if in protest of the task at hand. "Take courage, I tell you, take courage. The whites from France cannot hold out against us here in Saint Domingue. They have fought well at first, but soon they will fall sick and die like flies. I repeat it, take courage and you will see that when the French are reduced to small, small numbers, we will harass them and beat them; we will burn the harvests and then take to the hills. They will be forced to leave. Then I will make you independent. There will be no more whites among us."

The men were initially confused but now they fully understood what their commander was saying, had always said from the beginning; *'Live to fight another day,'* They were now no longer confused but solid in purpose. They would acquiesce to the French and await their commander to rise once again against the French and call upon them to fight.

In a slow and familiar battle cry, Dessalines yelled *"PA GEN MANMAN!"*

"PA GEN PAPA!," yelled the men in a loud resilient response

"SA KI MOURI?" Responded Dessalines in a defiant loud yell.

"ZAFE YO" they cheered followed by the familiar battle cry of *"Ahhhhhhhhh"*

This was the army of Dessalines. Men loyal to him first, and his cause second. They would die for him with pleasure as they went into battle knowing, as he had told them countless times before, that if they died it would secure their place in the sea beneath them. The paradise that is Africa, where their honorable death would be celebrated alongside their ancestors who went before them.

That is what made his fighting force the most feared and the most lethal of any. Feared more than Maurepas, Christophe, and all other generals, even Toussaint's shiny honor guard. These men, Dessalines knew, would follow him into death with their eyes wide open, wherever he took them.

He turned Galipòt around and they began their march to the city of Cap Français.

Crowds came out in droves, as many as had come out to see Toussaint march in, for a firsthand look at the man feared with the reputation of a ruthless butcher. And Dessalines did not disappoint them. He rode in the streets with an air of defiance as everyone could see that his submission was a forced show of loyalty.

He entered Government House, filled with white, black, and mulatto officers, and cringed at their presence, and as expected there, standing next to Leclerc, was the Nég Kay, Christophe. They locked eyes as Dessalines approached. Leclerc turned, without so much as a handshake, and walked to his office as Dessalines followed. As Christophe watched the door close, he felt a strange air of doom circulating around him. Is this all too simple, he wondered. What am I not fully grasping?

The sun dipped low on the horizon, casting a warm orange glow across the secluded retreat of Ennery. Toussaint Louverture stood on his balcony; hands clasped behind his back as he gazed out over the lush landscape. The sweet scent of tropical flowers wafted through the air, mixed with the familiar aroma of beans cooling from the recent roast. But Toussaint's thoughts were far from peaceful.

He sighted Jean-Paul and Maurice, two of his trusted honor guards, strolling the dirt path adjacent to the coffee crop, but instead of their customary rifles or swords, one sported a pick and the other a hoe slung over their shoulders. He and them wore uniforms no more.

So, this is what retirement looks like, Toussaint thought. He had provided each of his honor guards with a large swath of land to plant and grow crops, teaching them the art of farming. They would work the land and split the profits from the yield.

With few exceptions, the men seemed to enjoy their newfound purpose, albeit their armaments tucked away, oiled and maintained, for any eventual turn of events.

His mind turned to Leclerc, "Damn him," he muttered under his breath, the bitterness in his voice a stark contrast to the serene surroundings. He was a prisoner in his own home - a proud man brought low by treacherous former allies. He was retired, but his movement was restricted as they feared he was not yet fully submissive to French authority. His heart burned with the desire for vengeance, and yet the knowledge that he was powerless to act only served to stoke the fires of his rage.

"Sir?" A gentle voice interrupted his dark reverie. It was Mars Plaisir, Toussaint's trusted valet, normally direct with Toussaint, now standing timidly in the doorway. "Dinner is ready."

Louverture nodded curtly, turning away from the view to follow Plasir inside. As they walked, he glanced at the newspaper clutched in his servant's hand. The headline screamed of the latest horrors befalling the French invaders: yellow fever, their unwitting ally, tearing through their ranks like a vengeful phantom.

"Another 15,000 dead," Louverture mused aloud, seating himself at the dining table as he addressed Suzanne. "Nature itself seems to be conspiring against them."

"Indeed, Toussaint," Suzanne replied hesitantly as a servant set plates of food before them. "But what will become of us if the French continue to struggle against the forces of the maroons?"

"Bonaparte underestimated the resolve of our people," Toussaint reasoned, eyes narrowing. "He thought he could conquer Saint-Domingue with ease, but he has met with more resistance than he ever imagined. Eradicating maroons from the mountains will not be easy."

"General Leclerc must be feeling the pressure," Suzanne ventured cautiously as Plasir refilled Toussaint's wine glass. "Do you think he might reconsider your position?"

"Leclerc is a desperate man," he replied, cutting into his meat with uncharacteristic savagery. "And desperation can lead men to make foolish decisions."

As he chewed his food, the gears in Toussaint's mind continued to turn. He knew that Leclerc was struggling to maintain control over the island and that his forces were being decimated by both disease and insurrection. The French general had underestimated the difficulties of subjugating Saint-Domingue, and his campaign was crumbling around him.

"Perhaps," Toussaint mused, swirling the wine in his glass as he considered his options, "there may yet be an opportunity for me to strike back at those who have betrayed me."

"Toussaint, what are you thinking, plotting?" Suzanne asked, sensing the change in her husband's demeanor.

"Never mind," was his reply, forcing a smile onto his face. "It is but a fleeting thought. For now, we must bide our time and watch as our enemies tear themselves apart."

For even in his confinement, Toussaint Louverture remained a force to be reckoned with. And as the sun set on another day in Ennery, the seeds of his revenge began to take root.

Deep within the heart of the Massif du Nord, between Le Cap & Gonaïves, a fire scorched the night sky, casting eerie shadows on the faces of the maroon rebels who huddled around it. San Souci and the powerful voodoo Manbo priestess Cecile Fatiman, their leaders, stood apart from the group, their eyes intent upon the flickering flames.

"Word has reached us," San Souci said, his voice barely audible above the crackling fire. "Toussaint Louverture, Dessalines, and Christophe have surrendered to the French."

"Traitors!" spat Cecile, her eyes flashing with anger. "They've sold out our people to those slave masters."

"Indeed," San Souci agreed quietly, his gaze never leaving the fire. "But we will continue to fight, Cecile. We will not let their betrayal be the end of our struggle to remain free."

"Of course not," she replied fiercely. "We refused to submit before, and we refuse now. We will show them what true loyalty to our cause looks like."

"Then we must strike soon," San Souci decided, finally turning to face her. "The French are weakened by the yellow fever and the collapse of their campaign. It is time for us to take advantage of their vulnerability."

"Agreed," Cecile nodded. "Our people need hope, and they need it now. We must rally our maroon fighters, assemble our great army, and prepare for battle."

In the days that followed, the maroon bands led by San Souci and Cecile grew bolder in their defiance, striking out against the French forces with renewed vigor. They knew that, although the main generals of the colonial army had given up, their fight was far from over.

During the day they relentlessly struck French targets with guerilla-style warfare and then retreated to hide in the mountain camps where no French would venture. At night they gathered around their fires to feast on their bounties, and participate in and enjoy the traditional dances of Ibo, Congo, and Petro.

Tonight, dancers were honoring the fierceness and determination of Cecile. She sat in the semicircle with many others watching the dancers with their knees bent, their hands on their knees, their backs constantly undulating, and their shoulders rhythmically rising and rolling away from their bodies. They moved to the beat of the drums, which started slowly and burst into a feverish pitch.

Cecile was pleased with the celebration, particularly the dancers. It renewed a sense of belonging within her, between them all, and one with the Gods. The men and women were dancing with thighs together in a rhythm, with pelvic thrusts and hip gyrations. They then would separate with a pirouette, spinning on one foot with the other raised foot touching the knee of the supporting leg, over again, doing the same movements with lascivious gestures until they would collapse in exhaustion, only to be replaced by another set of dancers. Cecile clapped her hands together with joy.

Later, they would pray to the Gods together, they even whispered prayers for the souls of those they had once considered allies. For Toussaint Louverture, Dessalines, and Christophe had become symbols of betrayal in the eyes of the maroons.

"Who would have thought," Cecile mused one evening, as she and San Souci watched their comrades preparing for the next day's battle, "that we would come to view our former leaders with such contempt?"

"Heroes can fall, Cecile," San Souci replied solemnly. "But it is up to us to carry on their legacy – the true legacy of freedom and independence for our people."

"Yes," she agreed, her voice filled with determination. "And we will do whatever it takes to make that dream a reality."

San Souci nodded, his gaze fixed on the flickering flames. In the firelight, the resolve etched upon his face was unmistakable. As the maroons prepared to continue their fight against the French, it was clear that their spirit remained unbroken, even as the foundations of their world threatened to crumble around them.

The mountain air was damp and heavy, weighing down on another maroon camp far away to the south, nestled in the Massif de la Hotte, between Jérémie & Les Cayes. Makaya stood at the edge of a cliff, overlooking the valley where the French forces struggled to survive. His heart swelled with pride as he saw their once-mighty army reduced to mere shadows of their former selves.

"Commander Makaya!" called out one of his lieutenants, approaching him with urgency. "We have reports of more European soldiers succumbing to the fever. Our scouts say that they are dying in droves - 30 to 50 men each day."

"Good," Makaya replied, his voice cold and unyielding. "Nature is, and will always be, on our side, my friend. The rains have brought forth the yellow fever, and it's working its way through the French ranks."

"Indeed, Commander," the lieutenant agreed, though his face bore a hint of unease. "But we must be cautious. Not all of our men are immune."

Makaya studied his lieutenant for a moment before responding. "True, but we were born here and have lived with this threat all our lives. We have developed resistance, and we understand how to protect ourselves and our families. The French, however, are ill-prepared for such a foe. They came here expecting an easy victory, disrespecting nature, and now they're paying the price."

He gazed down at the remains of the town below that had been burned to the ground, leaving the Europeans without medical supplies, clothes, or shoes. The destruction they had wrought upon themselves left them weakened and vulnerable, and Makaya knew that it was the perfect moment to strike.

"Tell the others to ready themselves for battle," he ordered, turning away from the valley below. "We will show the French that Saint Domingue cannot be conquered so easily. We strike tonight at midnight."

As they prepared for the impending fight, Makaya's thoughts drifted momentarily to the other maroon leaders far away in the Massif du Nord. He wondered if San Souci and Manbo Cecile Fatiman shared his determination, his unwavering desire to see their homeland freed from the shackles of tyranny, not knowing they were already actively engaging the French army.

"Very well," Makaya said, steeling himself for the battle ahead. "Let us remind the French that they cannot break our spirit. Today, we make another stand and remind them of that."

With grim determination etched upon their faces, the Maroons launched themselves into the fray, a force to be reckoned with, born from the very heart of Saint-Domingue itself.

General Charles Leclerc's eyes darted around the makeshift hospital, taking in the horrifying tableau before him. Sweat-soaked bandages-stained crimson littered the ground, while the moans and cries of fever-stricken soldiers filled the air. The stench of disease hung heavy, a suffocating presence that seemed to claw its way into his lungs with every breath he took.

"General," Captain Duval said, stepping up to Leclerc's side. "This is... this is a disaster."

"Indeed," Leclerc whispered. He could feel despair gnawing at the edges of his soul, threatening to swallow him whole. With each passing day, the situation grew dire.

"Report, Captain," he ordered, jaw clenched as he willed himself to focus on the task at hand.

"Sir," Duval began, his voice shaking slightly. "We've lost nearly a third of our original forces. The hospitals are overflowing, and the European troops are dying at an alarming rate. We have no resources left – the cities we needed for supplies were burned to the ground during the initial push."

"Merde!" Leclerc cursed, slamming his fist against a nearby table. It did little to quell the anger boiling within him. "How many additional troops do you estimate we need?"

"Based on the current state of the rebellion and our losses, at least 25,000, sir," Duval replied, his voice heavy with defeat.

"Twenty-five thousand..." Leclerc repeated, letting the number sink in. He knew that even if he requested reinforcements from Napoleon, it would take months for them to be assembled, transported, and arrive. And by then, who knew how many more of his men would be lost to disease or battle?

"Captain," Leclerc said, desperation creeping into his voice. "We must find a way to turn the tide of this war, and quickly."

"Sir, with all due respect," Duval hesitated, choosing his words carefully. "Perhaps it is time we considered negotiating with the Maroons, like we did with the colonial generals.

Leclerc's eyes flashed with anger at the suggestion. "No," he snapped. "We will not negotiate with them. We are here to bring Saint-Domingue back under French control, and that is what we shall do."

"Understood, General," Duval replied, bowing his head.

"Dismissed," Leclerc said, turning away from the gruesome scene before him. As he walked away, he couldn't help but feel the weight of his failures crushing down upon him. He had been sent to pacify this island, to restore order and prosperity. And yet, all around him, he saw only chaos and death.

"Damn you, Toussaint," he muttered under his breath, a bitter rage swirling within him. He knew in his soul that it was Toussaint who was fueling the fire of insurrection, even from his home prison.

But as he looked back at the makeshift hospital one last time, he knew that it was more than just Louverture who stood in his way, but the land itself. It was an entire people, fighting to keep their freedom with a ferocity he had never encountered. "This land rejects you," as Toussaint would say.

And as he was beginning to fear, it was a fight that might well be impossible to win.

The sun dipped below the horizon, casting an eerie crimson glow over the sprawling plantation that served as Leclerc's field headquarters. In his dimly lit makeshift office, he hunched over a rickety table, pen in hand, sweat streaming down his brow as he drafted a letter to the First Consul, his brother-in-law, Napoleon. The words came slowly, painfully, like pulling teeth.

"Every day, the blacks become more audacious," he wrote, his hand trembling with frustration and exhaustion. "I am not strong enough to order a general disarmament or to implement the necessary measures you had ordered."

His thoughts were interrupted by the heavy footsteps of General Brunet entering the room. Leclerc didn't look up but continued writing, his voice barely audible as he spoke. "Brunet, I have a task for you. One that requires your utmost discretion."

"Of course, General," Brunet replied, his curiosity piqued.

"First, we must discuss Louverture." Leclerc's jaw clenched as he forced out the name, bile rising in his throat. "I fear he has become a liability. It is time...to remove him from the equation, as a necessary precaution."

"Remove him, sir?" Brunet asked cautiously, his eyes narrowing in suspicion.

"Indeed," Leclerc said, finally looking up from his letter. "I want you to lure him into a conference under the pretense of discussing future cooperation. Once he has arrived, arrest him as a common criminal and ship him to France with his family and manservant."

"Betray him, sir?" Brunet's voice wavered with uncertainty and uneasiness. He knew the implications of such an act, and the potential repercussions weighed heavily on his conscience.

"Betrayal is a strong word, General," Leclerc countered, his dark eyes boring into Brunet's soul. "I prefer to think of it as...securing our future. And the future of Saint-Domingue."

"Understood, sir," Brunet replied, swallowing hard and steeling himself for the dastardly task ahead.

"Good," Leclerc said, returning his attention to the letter. "Now leave me. I must finish this missive to the First Consul."

As Brunet strode from the room, Leclerc's pen scratched against the parchment, each word a confession of his inadequacy. "The government must begin to think about sending out my successor," he wrote, the words feeling like a betrayal of his pride, his ambition.

But as the last rays of sunlight disappeared, swallowed by the encroaching darkness, Leclerc knew he had no choice. He could not win this fight alone. And as much as it galled him, he had to admit that perhaps Louverture had been right all along: this land and the people of Saint-Domingue would never surrender their hard-won freedom without a struggle.

A struggle that, despite Leclerc's best efforts, might yet prove insurmountable.

Seventeen

THE ARREST OF
TOUSSAINT LOUVERTURE

Ennery
June 1802

The sun dipped low on the horizon, casting long shadows across the hills of Ennery as Toussaint Louverture read the enticing invitation. A parley with French Divisional Général Jean-Baptiste Brunet to discuss the future of Saint Domingue, a chance to create something new and lasting, and Toussaint's input was most desired. The parchment crackled softly in his hands, and he considered the possibilities.

"Father, you cannot trust them." Placide's voice broke through his thoughts, his son standing firm, his tan eyes filled with worry. "This could be a trap."

Toussaint looked up at his son, noting the familiar stubbornness that mirrored his own. He glanced around the room at the faces of his retired honor guard, all sharing Placide's concern. They had been through countless battles together, standing against the forces that sought to enslave their people. Their loyalty was unwavering.

"Général Brunet offers an opportunity for peace, and a way forward" Toussaint said, aware of the weight of his decision. "We cannot ignore the chance to improve the lives of our people."

"Father, please reconsider." Placide stepped closer, his voice pleading. "Your presence here in Ennery is essential. We need you."

He felt the pressure of those words and the responsibility that came with leadership. But he also knew the cost of doubting every gesture of goodwill. How could they ever move forward if they remained mired in suspicion?

"Placide, my son, I understand your fear. But sometimes we must take risks for the greater good," he said softly, placing a reassuring hand on his son's shoulder.

"Sir," one of the officers interjected, his grizzled face etched with concern, "we have fought too hard and lost too much to fall for their tricks. Let us send someone else in your stead."

Toussaint contemplated the officer's words, his mind racing with the potential dangers and rewards of attending the parley. He knew that every decision he made had far-reaching consequences for those who looked to him for guidance.

"Your concerns are not lost on me," he said finally, addressing the room. "But I must go. The future of Saint Domingue depends on our ability to find common ground with the French, and that is final."

Silence settled over the room, heavy with the weight of unspoken fears. Toussaint could see the worry in their eyes, but also the trust they placed in him. He would carry that responsibility with him as he walked into the lion's den, for the sake of their people and the generations to come.

Toussaint and Placide set out for Brunet's home, a half-day ride away. Toussaint could feel the tension radiating from his son, but his thoughts were occupied by the potential positive outcomes of the meeting.

As they approached Brunet's sprawling estate, Toussaint noticed an unusual number of French soldiers patrolling the grounds. He felt a chill creep up his spine but forced himself to maintain an air of confidence. They dismounted their horses, handing the reins to a waiting servant.

"Welcome, Toussaint Louverture," called out a smooth voice, dripping with false warmth. A tall, impeccably dressed man emerged from the shadows, flanked by armed guards. "I trust your journey was uneventful. My name is Captain Rolande. Général Brunet sends his regrets as a prior engagement precluded his attendance."

"That is most regrettable, Captain. My son and I have ridden half a day from Ennery to accept his invitation," Toussaint replied, studying the man before him. His instincts screamed at him to turn back, but he pushed the feeling down, reminding himself of the importance of diplomacy. "Shall you be representing him in our discussions?"

"Of course. But first..." the captain gestured to his guards, who swiftly closed in around Toussaint and Placide. The betrayal cut deep, and Toussaint's mind raced, searching for a way out of the trap he'd so willingly walked into.

"Captain, what is the meaning of this?" he demanded, trying to keep his voice steady.

"Forgive me, but I have my orders," the captain replied, the earlier warmth vanishing from his face. "You and your son are under arrest."

Toussaint's heart pounded in his chest as the reality of the situation washed over him. He thought of the concerned faces of Placide and his officers. "On what charge are we to be arrested, may I ask?"

"Conspiracy to commit insurrection," the captain stated.

"Very well," he said, raising his chin defiantly as the guards shackled his wrists. "We are innocent and have done nothing to warrant any charges of the sort," Toussaint protested.

The captain was unable to meet Toussaint's eyes, turned away, and excused himself from the room. The sound of his footsteps echoed against the high ceilings, leaving the two prisoners alone with their captors.

"Papa," Placide whispered, fear lacing his voice as the guards tightened the shackles on him. "What do we do now?"

"Stay strong, my son," Toussaint replied, glancing at the retreating back of the captain. "We must face our fate with courage and dignity. Let us not give them the satisfaction of seeing us broken."

As they were led through the opulent corridors of Brunet's home, Toussaint took in every detail: the plush carpets beneath his feet, the gilded frames adorning oil paintings of French aristocrats. It was a world he'd fought to break free from, and yet here he was, once again a prisoner within its confines.

"Where are you taking us?" he demanded as the guards ushered them into the courtyard where a carriage awaited. He sighted his six honor guards being detained by at least twenty French soldiers, but he was unable to do anything about it.

"Cap Français," one of the guards replied gruffly, shoving him forward. "You'll be deported to France to face your charges."

"France?" Placide's eyes widened in alarm, and Toussaint could see the unspoken question in his gaze: would they ever return to their homeland?

"Have faith, Placide," Toussaint murmured, trying to calm his own racing heart.

The journey to Cap Français was a blur of rumbling wheels and relentless jostling, the scenery outside the carriage window a cruel reminder of the paradise they were being torn away from. Toussaint's thoughts swirled with anger and frustration, but through it all, he clung to the belief that this would not be the end.

"Papa," Placide spoke up, his voice hoarse from hours of silence. "Do you truly believe you can still make a difference, even from across the ocean?"

"Of course, my son," Toussaint replied, squeezing Placide's hand as the carriage neared its destination. "If there is one thing I have learned in my years of struggle, it is that the human spirit cannot be contained by chains or distance. We will rise again, and our captors will come to regret their actions today."

As the carriage came to a halt in Cap Français, the looming threat of deportation weighed heavily on them both. Toussaint's thoughts went to Suzanne, Isaac, and his youngest son, Saint Jean. He must get word to her somehow to go into hiding before they come for her.

The sun bore down on Lamet's dark skin, sweat trickling along the ridges of his brow as he worked in the fields of the Sansey plantation. The air was thick with the musky scent of damp earth and sisal, an almost suffocating aroma that clung to everything within its reach. As Lamet pulled at the long fibers, something caught his senses – a faint vibration, a whisper of movement carried far on the hot breeze.

"Renald," he called out, his voice hoarse from the heat. "Look there, in the distance towards the Général's house. I think it is a column of soldiers entering the property."

Renald squinted through the haze, his throat tightening as he too observed the cloud of dust rising like a specter over the land. It stretched at least a meter long, an ominous sign of the presence they both feared. Without another word, Renald dropped his rake, and Lamet released his grip on the scythe. They exchanged a knowing glance, adrenaline surging through their veins as they raced toward their huts to retrieve their hidden weapons.

As they ran, others in the field noticed the commotion and the distant threat on the horizon. With a shared sense of urgency, men and women alike began to abandon their posts, charging towards their dwellings to arm themselves against the potential enemy. It was no secret that Toussaint had been lured away from the haven of Sansey, leaving those who remained behind on edge, ever watchful for signs of trouble.

The earth trembled beneath the thunderous gallop of four hundred hooves, kicking up a suffocating cloud of dust in their wake.

One hundred French dragoons charged towards the Sancey plantation with a ferocity that left no doubt as to their intentions.

Auguste and Lovelie stood at the guard gate, their eyes wide with shock as they beheld the overwhelming force bearing down upon them. For a brief moment, time seemed to slow as they exchanged a desperate glance, both understanding the gravity of what was unfolding before them.

"Ready your weapon," Auguste whispered to Lovelie, his voice barely audible over the deafening roar of the approaching horses. "We must hold them off for as long as possible."

"Are we to die here, Auguste?" Lovelie's voice trembled, betraying her fear. Her heart pounded in her chest like a drum, threatening to drown out all rational thought.

As the first wave of horsemen drew near, Auguste and Lovelie raised their weapons, aiming at the foremost riders. They knew their chances were slim, but they would not go down without a fight. Each breath felt heavier than the last, choked with the dust kicked up by the charging horses.

"Fire on my mark," Auguste commanded, his voice steady despite the terror clawing at his mind. He hesitated for a split second, waiting for the opportune moment. "Now!"

But they never had the chance to pull the triggers. Bullets tore through the air, cutting them down before they could even get off a single shot. Auguste and Lovelie collapsed to the ground, their lifeless bodies crumpled on the unforgiving dirt.

The sound of gunfire cut through the air like a whip, followed closely by the ground-shaking thunder of hooves. Suzanne's eyes widened, her heart leaping in her chest as she rushed to the veranda, Isaac close on her heels. The wooden floorboards creaked beneath their hurried footsteps, echoing the frantic beat of her pulse.

She sighted her 11-year-old, Saint Jean, in the yard throwing rocks at a makeshift target he had set up on top of the fence; 'Are those my masonry jars for sealing my guava?' she thought. That will come later. "Saint Jean! Saint Jean! Come here quickly!"

The boy stopped what he was doing, running to his mothers side as she was not one to be taken lightly, especially when she used that voice.

"What is it Maman?" he said as he arrived by her side, looking at Isaac staring in the distance.

"Saint Jean, stay behind me," she whispered urgently, her hands trembling ever so slightly despite the stoic facade she maintained. But Isaac, ever the impetuous youth, brushed past her and stood at her side, his gaze fixed on the approaching storm of dust with Saint Jean behind them both peeking through the crack between them.

"Do not worry, Maman," he said confidently, though the quaver in his voice betrayed his fear. "It is probably only a troop of soldiers passing by to pay their respects to Papa."

"Let us pray that you are right, my son," she whispered, squeezing his hand as the first of the French soldiers drew near. And deep within her trembling heart, she prepared for the storm that was about to engulf them all.

Mars Plaisir, Toussant's manservant arrived at the veranda and said, "Soldiers coming, what do they want here?"

"I am not sure Mars, we shall know soon enough," replied Suzanne.

The dust from the approaching riders stung Suzanne's eyes as she squinted to make out their intent. Isaac, ever hopeful, offered a possible explanation for the gunfire. "A shot of celebration, an announcement of their arrival?" he suggested, his voice wavering slightly.

Suzanne sighed, her chest tightening with worry. She glanced at her son and saw in him the same stubborn optimism that had often guided his father through difficult times. "Isaac, I have been pacifying you for months with your infatuation with the French. They only pay you lip service and mean bad things for your father," she said, her voice firm but laced with concern.

As the thundering hooves grew louder, Isaac clenched his jaw, torn between his loyalty to France and his love for his family. "Let me speak to them when they arrive. I will explain that I am an officer of France by the directive of the First Consul," he declared, eyes shining with conviction.

Suzanne glanced at her son, her heart twisting in her chest as she recognized the youthful hope and naiveté that he still clung to. "Don't be a fool, Isaac. It is not a coincidence that your father was called to a meeting on the very day they arrived here. Brace yourself for what comes next and by all means, keep your hands where they can see them. There may be some looking for an excuse to kill you."

Isaac's confident facade wavered for a moment, the gravity of his mother's words sinking in as Saint Jean tried to move to his mothers left, but she pushed him back behind her.

As the French dragoons finally appeared, their uniforms crisp and gleaming in the harsh sun, Isaac felt his stomach twist into knots. Their faces were hardened, cold, unyielding.

"Remember who you are, Isaac Louverture," his mother whispered, her voice a balm amidst the chaos that surrounded them. "You are your father's son, and no matter what happens today, that truth will never change."

As the horsemen pulled up to the main house, they began to surround the home, their mounts snorting and stamping impatiently. The once-peaceful scene transformed into one of chaos; fences splintered under the force of the horses' powerful strides, gardens were trampled beneath iron-shod hooves, and terrified chickens scattered in all directions, feathers flying through the air like a flurry of snowflakes.

"Mon Dieu," Isaac thought, his eyes widening in disbelief at the chaos before him. "What have we done to deserve this?"

Servants cautiously emerged from the house, curiosity etched upon their faces, only to be met with hard gazes and steady grips on the weapons of the soldiers. Fear quickly replaced their initial curiosity, and they froze in place, unsure of how to react to this unprecedented situation.

"Stay strong," Suzanne murmured, her fear carefully hidden behind a mask of stoicism. "We must not let them see our weakness."

A lieutenant, still mounted on his impressive steed, surveyed the scene with an air of authority, his piercing gaze finally coming to rest on Suzanne and Isaac. He raised his voice, his words ringing out clearly across the yard. "I have an arrest warrant for Suzanne Louverture, Isaac Louverture, and one Mars Plaisir. Are you these people?" he asked.

Isaac's stomach clenched at the mention of their names, but he forced himself to remain composed. Swallowing hard, he glanced at his mother for guidance before confidently responding, "We are."

Suzanne's eyes narrowed, a glimmer of defiance sparking within them, as she faced the lieutenant unflinchingly. The air around them seemed to thicken with tension, the cries and whinnies of the horses only heightening the sense of urgency pressing down upon them all. "On what charges are we to be arrested?"

"Subversion, conspiracy to organize an insurrection," the lieutenant replied, his expression as cold and hard as stone. "You have five minutes to collect your things and pack. That time begins now."

"But we have done none of these things," protested Plaisir.

"Five minutes?" Isaac choked on the words, his chest tightening with a sudden surge of anger and fear. "I am an officer in the army of France!" Isaac stated firmly, his voice cracking with a mixture of indignation and fear. His posture straightened, his chin lifted in defiance, yet the tremor in his hands betrayed his emotions.

The laughter of the soldiers, harsh and mocking, cut through Suzanne like a knife, and surprised Isaac, crumbling his love and respect for the motherland, but more, the crushing embarrassment of realizing that Napoleon's gift of the shiny uniform was nothing but a sham.

His shame was more towards his mother and Saint Jean who had looked up to him, thinking that his big brother was destined for a great career in the Army of France. Isaac's jaw clenched, his eyes flashing with indignation. He looked down at Saint Jean and they locked eyes. The innocence of childhood, of dreams, of their country's respect for them. It was now all lost for them both. A simultaneous teardrop moistened their cheeks.

"You're wasting time. I also got a message that you should take some things for your father and a brother named Placide. They too have been arrested. And bring along a certain child by the name of Saint Jean. Now you only have four minutes," the lieutenant repeated, his voice dripping with condescension. "Go, now!"

"Come, Isaac, Saint Jean" Suzanne urged, her hand gripping Saint Jean's arm as they hurried into the house. "Saint Jean, get only what you need. Isaac, gather some things for your brother as well. I will get some for your father. Mars, hurry and pack," she commanded.

"But Maman, where are we going and for how long?" asked Saint Jean.

"I do not know, Saint Jean. But consider it a great adventure. Concentrate on learning everything you can," his mother said, trying to place a positive note on this charade.

The ticking clock seemed to mock them as they rushed through the familiar rooms, hastily gathering their most essential belongings. Isaac's hands shook as he grabbed clothes and books, unable to focus on anything but the weight of the impending loss. Saint Jean looked at each of his toys, wondering which he could take.

"Stay strong," Suzanne reminded him, her voice strained but unwavering. "We are Louverture's, and we will not be broken by this injustice."

"Where will they take us, Maman?" Isaac asked, his voice barely audible above the rustle of fabric and the clatter of objects being placed into their bags.

"Wherever it is," Suzanne replied, her eyes locked with his, "we will face it together. And we will return home someday, mark my words."

"Time's up!" The lieutenant barked from outside, his voice cutting through the air like a knife.

"Let us go then," Suzanne said, a grim smile crossing her lips. "We have nothing to fear from these men."

And so, with their heads held high and their hearts filled with courage, they all stepped back out onto the veranda, ready to face whatever fate had in store for them.

"Where are you taking us?" she asked, her voice steady and firm despite the fear gnawing at her insides.

"You will be deported to face trial in Paris," the lieutenant replied, his tone devoid of emotion.

Isaac's breath hitched, and Suzanne felt his hand grip hers tightly. Images of a foreign land, an unfamiliar courtroom, and hostile faces swirled in her mind. She swallowed hard, forcing herself to remain composed.

"Very well," she said, her voice barely more than a whisper. "But know this: we have done nothing wrong. Our conscience is clear."

The lieutenant scoffed, his lips curling into a cruel smile. "That remains to be seen, madame."

"Let's go, Isaac, Mars, are you ready, Saint Jean, stay close to me" she murmured, leading them towards the waiting horses. As they mounted the saddles, she couldn't help but notice the way the soldiers eyed them with contempt, as if they were nothing more than common criminals. It stung deeply, but she held her head high.

Suzanne hesitated for only a moment, allowing herself one last, lingering glance at the home she had known and loved for so many years. She then spotted her mason jar on the fence post that Saint Jean had used for target practice and realized how trivial her worry was for that compared to this. With a quiet sigh, she climbed into the saddle, her fingers tightening around the reins.

Othello, their overseer at the farm came running with a rifle in hand. "What goes here!" he shouted as he ran towards Suzanne, Isaac, and Plaisir mounted on horses.

"No Othello, stand back," yelled Suzanne, understanding the danger that could be his.

Othello raised his rifle, "I demand to know…," his sentence cut short as the thunder of a dozen shots rang out, riddling his body with bullets from all different directions fired by soldiers. He was dead before his body hit the ground. The scene was utter chaos, Suzzane frozen in shock, Isaac yelling "Othello", Saint Jean bursting into tears, Plaisir speechless with mouth still open, and servants screaming, wailing, and crying to see Othello, a permanent fixture and part family, a bloody corpse on the floor. In a split second, the seriousness of their plight lay evident.

"Move out!" barked the lieutenant, and with that command, the convoy lurched forward, leaving the sanctuary of the Sansey plantation behind.

The hooves of their steeds kicked up plumes of dust as they passed the lifeless bodies of Auguste and Lovelie, the loyal guards who had fallen beneath the relentless onslaught of the foreign invaders. Suzanne felt her throat tighten at the sight, but she forced herself to look away – they had no time for grief.

"Look," Isaac whispered urgently, nodding towards the fields. "Papa's honor guards are coming!"

As if summoned by some unseen force, a crowd of armed men, dressed in the uniform of cultivators with rifles in their hands, poured forth from the swaying sea of sugar cane, their faces contorted with rage and despair. But they were too far away, their valiant charge had come too late; the tide of French soldiers surrounding Suzanne and Isaac was unreachable, a living wall between them and their would-be rescuers.

"Keep moving!" the lieutenant snarled, his eyes darting warily between the approaching guards and his prisoners as they barreled out of the plantation's outer fences.

As the carriage entered the city, citizens had already heard of Toussaint's arrest and were lining the streets to see if the rumors were true. This time it wasn't the mighty leader, the Governor Général of the colony, but a criminal who was plotting against the government. Many knew it was a sham, a way for the French to silence him and his powerful influence by getting him off the island, but they were powerless to do anything about it. His detractors, however, were relieved as there had been a recent calm in the colony since his retirement. Most people were distracted and now more preoccupied with reconstruction as opposed to politics. They had had enough of war and violence.

Arrest warrants had been issued for anyone deemed to be an accomplice, conspirator, associate, or even friend of Toussaint, with little or no evidence to support any claim of wrongdoing. Guilt by association. They were rounded up with only minutes to collect their things or arrange for an extended absence.

Two French ships awaited their embarkation: the frigate *Créole* and the 74-gun *Héros.* Many of the arrested had already boarded the *Héros* and were incarcerated within.

The sea breeze carried the scent of salt and despair as Toussaint Louverture and Placide ascended the gangplank, chains clinking with each measured step. The sun glared down mercilessly, casting harsh shadows on the Creole's weathered deck.

"Do not worry, Papa," Placide yelled to his father. "They believe they've won a great victory today, that they can shackle our spirits as easily as they have our bodies."

The gathered crowd of onlookers - a mixture of Toussaint's supporters, sympathizers, detractors, and French soldiers - watched him in anticipation, their faces etched with concern, curiosity, fear, and hatred.

A prisoner whom Toussaint recognized as one of his former secretaries called out; "Governor, why are we being treated so. Where are they taking us?"

Toussaint paused at the top of the gangplank and turned to face the crowd, his eyes sweeping across the sea of faces before settling on the smirking soldiers. The soldiers did not attempt to stop him from addressing the crowd.

"Listen well," he called out, his voice strong and resonant despite his chains. "I stand before you as a symbol of all that we have fought for, all that we have suffered and sacrificed in pursuit of liberty. Their actions today may bring them temporary satisfaction,

Daniel J.D. Bayard

but know this: You have not defeated us."

A murmur rippled through the crowd, and Toussaint could see the flicker of hope reigniting in the eyes of his fellow prisoners and many supporters. Emboldened, he continued his words echoing across the water like the peal of a mighty bell.

"In overthrowing me, you have cut down in Saint Domingue only the trunk of the tree of liberty; it will spring up again from the roots, for they are numerous, and they are deep," he declared, his gaze unwavering. "You may have deceived me once, but I assure you, the rebels who remain will not repeat my mistake in trusting the French."

The soldiers shifted uncomfortably, and Toussaint could sense the unease settling like a heavy shroud over the proceedings. He allowed himself a small, grim smile as he turned away from the crowd and stepped onto the *Créole's* deck. There, they separated the father from the son. "Have faith Placide, my faithful son. We will survive this," he said as they guided Placide to a different part of the ship where he would not see his father for weeks.

As the chains were removed and he was led below to his cramped cell, the words of Placide echoed in his mind. 'Your words have inspired an entire nation, Papa. They can chain our bodies, but they cannot imprison our spirits.'

"May it be so, my son," Toussaint whispered, steeling himself for the journey ahead. "May the spirit of freedom continue to burn, even in the darkest of times."

Eighteen

THE REVOLT CONTINUES

Plaine du Nord
July 1802

The sun blazed down upon the quiet fields of Saint-Domingue in the northern plains, its merciless heat casting a heavy haze over the laborers who toiled beneath it. Under the watchful eye of Général Leclerc, an uneasy peace and rising productivity had been temporarily restored.

Leclerc strode through the Simone Plantation in the Plaine du Nord that Josephine Bonaparte's family, the wife of Napoleon, had newly acquired, adding to their vast holdings in the Caribbean on top of their Martinique and Saint Lucia land portfolio. As the wife of the First Consul, her family had pressed her into restoring slavery to increase their already vast profits, which Napoleon was now in the process of slowly doing.

Leclerc toured the property with an air of authority, his sharp eyes surveying every movement, every bead of sweat that trickled down the workers' brows. "Back to work!" he barked, his voice cold and absolute.

The cultivators, some of whom secretly participated as part-time troops for the resistance, though visibly reluctant, obeyed his command and resumed their labors. They were caught between two realities: one of promised freedom, and another of familiar servitude.

Leclerc's satisfaction with his accomplishment was short-lived. As word spread of his intention to disarm and suppress the laborers, discontent and anger rippled through the population. Whispers of rebellion grew louder, and soon the hills surrounding the plantations teemed with maroon guerrilla bands, swelling their ranks with those desperate to resist the return to slavery.

"Général Leclerc," said a young officer, approaching him cautiously. "There are reports of new rebel leaders emerging – and they've gathered hundreds of rebels."

"These so-called rebels are mere farmers. They are no match for you and the French army. Let them come," Leclerc replied, his jaw clenched. "They will be crushed, just like the others before them."

"Damn this cursed land," he whispered, wiping his brow with a handkerchief. *'This land rejects you,'* he would hear Toussaint repeat. over and over in his head, during the day and tormenting him with nightmares in the middle of the night. Toussaint was gone, he had gotten rid of him, but still he is here, haunting him.

Throughout August, the situation only worsened. One day, as Leclerc poured over maps, trying to devise a strategy against the marauding rebels, another messenger arrived with news that made his blood run cold.

"Général Leclerc," the messenger hesitated, fear palpable in his voice. "We have received word that slavery has been restored in Martinique, Tobago, Saint Lucie, and now Guadeloupe."

"Merde," Leclerc's hands clenched into fists. This revelation would only fuel the fire of rebellion further. "And who has decided this?"

"Orders came from the French government, Général, the First Consul himself has signed the proclamation," the messenger replied. "A law has been passed to reopen the slave trade."

"Of course," Leclerc muttered bitterly. His superiors were blind to the consequences of their actions. This news will now galvanize the people of Saint Domingue even more. It was already near impossible to suppress them with just rumors, now with the confirmation that the rumors are indeed true, he will be forced to contend with this new and more dangerous development.

"Send for my officers," he demanded, "we must plan our next move." Have them meet me in the gardens at 5 p.m. today.

As the door closed behind the young man, Leclerc's body sagged in his chair. "Damn them all," he whispered to himself, rage boiling inside him. "Have they no foresight? Can they not see what this will do?"

With his men gathered around him, Leclerc ordered the officers to increase pressure and terrorize the communities if that was what it took to quell this current series of rebellion. The meeting lasted only minutes, but the overall message was, no more soft tactics! He then dismissed the group.

Henry Christophe began to leave as he observed rows of dark-skinned laborers toiling beneath the fading light of day. Henry looked out, his heart heavy with dread. He had joined the French with a promise - a sacred vow - that they would not reinstitute slavery. He had received the reports of chains and shackles returning to other French colonies.

"Is it true?" he asked himself, his mind swirling with doubt and fear. He clenched his fists, feeling the sweat on his palms as the weight of betrayal pressed down upon him like an iron yoke. He knew what he must do.

"Général Leclerc," Henry called out, striding towards the man who held both power and responsibility for the fate of so many. His boots left imprints on the soft earth as the scent of freshly tilled soil filled his nostrils. "I must speak with you."

Leclerc raised a brow, his gaze fixed upon the horizon as if contemplating the future of the very land he ruled. "What is it, Christophe?"

"Is it true?" Henry demanded, his voice barely more than a whisper, but edged with steel. "Have the French truly reinstated slavery in other colonies? Have they reopened the slave trade?"

A moment of silence hung between them, the air thick with tension. The faint sound of laborers singing in the distance seemed to mock the very idea of freedom. Finally, Leclerc sighed, his shoulders slumping under the invisible burden of his position.

"Unfortunately, it seems to be the case," he admitted, his voice wavering. "It's beyond my control, Christophe. The politicians, the ones who pull the strings, they make these decisions."

"Then you must know," Henry said, his voice rising in both volume and conviction, "this will lead to a full uprising. The cultivators on the plantations - the ex-slaves - they will not stand for this. They have tasted freedom, and they will fight to keep it. You must counsel Napoleon, your brother-in-law, of this."

Leclerc sighed, the weight of his position evident in every crease and wrinkle on his brow. "Henry, you must understand the complexities of our situation. I am powerless to the whims of politicians. Josephine, Napoleon's wife, is from a powerful slaveholding family, and her influence on my brother-in-law is immense and their wealth vast. We stand here on one of their plantations."

Leclerc's face tightened into a grimace. He looked out over the fields once more, as if searching for answers among the rows of crops that stretched towards the horizon. Finally, he met Henry's gaze, his eyes filled with sorrow.

"I understand the consequences," he said softly. "But I am powerless against the whims of politicians. We, you and I, can only do our job and obey our orders."

"I predict that this will unleash the maroons with a vengeance. The common cultivators will join their ranks rather than risk re-enslavement. These maroon leaders are like warlords back in their African homeland – they are very dangerous," Henry warned.

"But thankfully, they are not united, I am told," Leclerc responded. "Who are their leaders?"

Sans Souci is the feared master of the North with Cécile Fatiman, a powerful Mambo Voodoo priestess. She was one of those who spearheaded the first slave rebellion in 1791. Macaya is the feared leader of the south with Romaine la Prophétessea and Marie Rose Adam at his side. Lamour Desrances is master of the West but fighting with us. You are accurate to be thankful that each group works independently of each other, and none would dare cross each other's realm," Henry explained.

"Well, that is good then. As long as they are independent, they are not strong," Leclerc confidently replied.

Henry stared at him, his heart pounding in his chest. The world seemed to shift beneath his feet, leaving him unsteady and uncertain of what path lay before him. If the French could not be trusted to uphold their promise, then where did his allegiance truly lie?

"Remember this, Général," Henry said, his voice firm but still quivering with emotion. "You may feel powerless now, but there will come a day when the people rise, and they will demand justice for broken promises and shattered lives. On that day, you and I will have to choose which side we stand on."

With that, Henry turned away, leaving Leclerc to contemplate his words as the sun dipped below the horizon, casting shadows across the land, the nightly drums beginning to beat in the distance.

As he walked away from Leclerc, Henry's mind was a whirlwind of conflicting thoughts and emotions. He knew in his heart that he could not remain loyal to an army that would betray its promises so callously. Yet, the uncertainty of what lay ahead if he were to defy them gnawed at him like a ravenous beast.

With each step, the seed of rebellion grew within him, thriving on the fertile soil of disillusionment and broken trust. And as the sun dipped below the horizon, casting its final, crimson rays upon the fields where freedom once bloomed, Henry Christophe knew that his path now diverged, leading him into the unknown and treacherous realm of resistance.

At a remote field on the same plantation, two workers were engaged in conversation; "Did you hear?" murmured Pierre, a tall, sinewy man, a cultivator who had once been a slave, "They've brought back slavery in Martinique, Guadeloupe, and other French colonies!"

"Bonaparte promised us freedom," said Jeanette, her voice barely more than a whisper as she clutched her hoe tightly. "He wouldn't do that to Saint-Domingue... would he?"

"Promises mean nothing to French men like him," replied Pierre. "We must be prepared to fight for our freedom again, if necessary. I fought back in '91."

As the talk spread through the workers of the plantation like wildfire, and others like it, it wasn't long before Leclerc's spies, and French soldiers grew tense and thick with fear.

In the sweltering heat of a western plantation far from Leclerc, sweat dripped from the brows of the laborers as they toiled under the unforgiving sun and the 11-hour workdays.

Their muscles ached, but their determination was unwavering. Their eyes held a fire that burned brightly despite the weight of oppression bearing down on them. Hector looked over his shoulder at the French soldiers patrolling the perimeter, their rifles glinting menacingly in the sunlight.

"Keep working," he muttered under his breath, gripping the handle of his hoe tightly. "We can't let them see our true intentions."

That night, as the moon cast its silvery light over the plantation, Hector crept through the shadows, his heart pounding in his chest, his breath coming in shallow gasps. He had a rendezvous with some of the newly defected officers from the French Colonial Army who were looking for cultivators to begin recruiting on plantations.

"Are you ready?" One of them asked, his face partially obscured by the darkness.

"More than ever," Hector replied. "With your help, we can finally rid our land of the French and secure our freedom for good."

"We will need your help to assemble a powerful army. We need as many strong men and women that can fight," the officer said.

"You can count on me, and I know of others at different plantations who can also help to recruit," Hector acknowledged.

The officer extended his hand. "Together, my brother. You and the rest of the cultivators shall never be in chains again if we succeed."

As their hands clasped firmly, the seeds of revolution began to take root in all regions of the colony, but in isolation. There was no coordination or unity in the various movements to stand against tyranny and oppression. They were all separate and apart from each other. But everyone involved was of the same mindset; the unmitigated and permanent destruction of the French presence in Saint-Domingue.

At a coffee plantation in l'Artibonite Valley, the sun dipped below the horizon, painting the sky in shades of orange and crimson as Joseph stood at the edge of the plantation. He watched in silence as rows of cultivators who had fought for freedom a decade ago, toiled under the watchful eyes of French soldiers. The air was thick with tension and the scent of sweat and fear, a potent reminder of the escalating violence.

"Move faster!" a French soldier barked, kicking an elderly laborer who stumbled under the weight of a heavy sack. The man cried out in pain, his voice cracking. Joseph felt his blood boil, anger, and hatred coursing through his veins.

"Damn them," he muttered under his breath, clenching his fists, as other laborers looked at him, waiting for any sign of resistance. His thoughts raced, consumed by the need to protect the old man.

When the same soldier got impatient at the man's slowness in rising, he kicked him in his rear end, vaulting the old man to land hard on his face, scraping a red gash of raw bloody flesh in the process. He and two soldiers at his side laughed and began to ridicule the poor soul.

Joseph couldn't contain his rage any longer. He quickly walked to the soldier, and without any more thought, swung the wooden shaft of the tool to his head. The soldier humped down on one knee as the two other soldiers drew their weapons, pointed them at Joseph to kill him.

Suddenly, all seven of the other workers charged the soldiers from behind and whacked them all to death. They then ran for their lives off the plantation to join the maroon band run by Sans Souci and Cécile Fatiman in the *Massif du Nord*.

As the resistance grew stronger in the Artibonite, it inspired those in the South to become more organized, fueling the insurrection that now spread like wildfire across Saint-Domingue.

The flickering glow of the fire cast shadows across the faces of his fellow laborers, all of them now gathered in secret for this meeting, united against a common enemy. François could see the fear in their eyes and knew that they understood the consequences of their actions. Like others throughout the colony, they would face firing squads, be hanged, drowned, and even beaten to death – but still, they chose to resist.

"Angélique," François whispered, pulling her aside as the others began to disperse. "We need to send word to the other camps, let them know that we are organizing, that many are doing the same."

Angélique looked at him with determination, her eyes reflecting the firelight. "I will go myself," she said. "I can travel faster and more discreetly than any messenger."

"Are you sure?" François asked, concern etched on his face. "You know the risks."

"Of course, I do," Angélique replied, her voice steady. "But if we are to have any chance of success, we must be willing to make sacrifices. We must be prepared to die for our cause."

François hesitated, but nodded in agreement, knowing that they could not afford to falter now. The whole burden of resistance lay squarely upon their shoulders, they were elected organizers by the leaders of the movement, and it was a burden they would carry together.

"Go then," he told her, clasping her hand briefly. "And may God protect you on your journey."

As Angélique slipped into the darkness, François turned back to the fire, his heart swelling with pride. They were no longer slaves, nor would they ever be again. They were fighters, freedom fighters, united against oppression – and they would not be defeated.

Under the cover of night, the loosely organized black militia, as they called themselves, crept forward, their hearts pounding in unison with the steady rhythm of their silent footsteps. The moon cast a dim glow over the landscape as they approached the fort of Saint Louis, east of Les Cayes on the southern coast, each man keenly aware of the significance of their mission. Jacques, a former mulatto soldier now leading the militia, felt the weight of responsibility heavy on his shoulders. But he knew he was up to the challenge.

Together, they scaled the walls of the fort, the rough stones scraping against their bare skin as they climbed. Once inside the fort, they moved swiftly and silently, neutralizing the guards before they could raise the alarm. Jacques led them through the fort's network of corridors, his knowledge, having worked there, of its layout proving invaluable. He could feel the adrenaline surging through his veins, fueling him onward.

Finally, they reached the central chamber, where the fort's commander slept. Jacques held his breath as he pushed open the door, the hinges creaking ominously. But the commander remained asleep, snoring heavily, oblivious to the intruders in his room.

"Secure him," Jacques instructed, his voice barely audible. The other men moved swiftly, binding the commander's hands and feet before he had a chance to awaken. With the fort under their control, the city was theirs for the taking. It was time to signal to their compatriots in the hills.

"Freedom," one of the men murmured, a note of awe in his voice. Jacques allowed himself a brief moment of satisfaction, knowing that this was only the beginning.

The news of their victory spread like wildfire through the South, igniting the spark of rebellion within the hearts of the oppressed. In September of 1802, a wide-spread insurrection erupted across the Grande-Anse region, fueled by rage and desperation.

This was the territory of Macaya, the feared leader of the southern maroons, handling the different areas of the *Massif de la Hotte* – the Mountains between Jérémie & Les Cayes. They ordered their maroons to descend from the mountains, their faces streaked with ash and determination. They burned plantations, sending plumes of smoke billowing into the sky as they set fire to the symbols of their oppression. Six plantation managers were killed in the uprising, their deaths a testament to the ferocity of the revolt.

One by one, as they stealthily infiltrated plantations, they whispered rebellion among the workers. Tales of the French's treachery traveled like wildfire, igniting the flames of resistance in the hearts of the oppressed. Soon, the plantations were alive with murmurs of revolt.

As the rebellion grew, black and mulatto officers and soldiers began to desert the French army more frequently, stealing their weapons and supplies as they defected. They joined the loose bands of rebels to begin the formation of an army. An army of cultivators, maroons from the mountains, and now skilled soldiers, all ready to fight but lacking any central authority.

October 1802 had arrived with a vengeance, bringing with it torrential rains that pounded the roofs of the French command post in Saint-Domingue. Leclerc sat at his desk, surrounded by piles of maps and reports, his face a mask of frustration and exhaustion. He knew that his campaign was faltering, and he could feel the weight of responsibility pressing down on him.

"Général Leclerc," a young officer announced as he entered the room, soaked to the bone. "We've received more reports of uprisings in the South."

Leclerc sighed, rubbing his temples. "Thank you, Lieutenant. Leave the reports on my desk." As the officer complied and hastily exited, Leclerc's thoughts turned inward. It was becoming increasingly apparent that his mission to retake the colony was failing. The rebels were growing bolder, and their numbers continued to swell. He needed to find a solution, and fast.

Leclerc stared at the letter before him, his heart heavy with the weight of the decisions he had to make. He knew that his next words would be the most difficult to write, but they were necessary if he hoped to reclaim Saint-Domingue for France. The sound of rain pattering against the windowpane seemed to emphasize the gravity of the situation.

He began,

First Consul, Napoleon Bonaparte,
his hand trembling slightly as he gripped the quill.

I must propose a radical course of action. It is not one I take lightly, but one I believe is essential for the survival of our colony.

He paused, inhaling deeply as he fought the tightness in his chest. Would these words seal his fate, or would they bring about the change he so desperately sought?

We must destroy all the blacks in the mountains – men and women – and spare only the children under 12 years of age,

He wrote, each word feeling like a betrayal of humanity itself.

We must destroy half of those in the plains and must not leave a single colored person in the colony who has worn an epaulet on his military uniform.

As the ink dried on the page, Leclerc's thoughts raced. How could he justify such brutality? But he knew that without drastic measures, the insurrection would continue to grow, and the colony would be lost to chaos.

"Napoleon," he whispered to himself, "you must understand the gravity of this situation," his voice wavered with emotion, betraying the turmoil within. "After all, you were the one to ignite it."

Only through these actions can we hope to regain control over Saint-Domingue.

With a deep sigh, he set down the quill, his hand still shaking from the weight of the words he'd just written. In the distance, thunder rumbled, echoing the storm that was brewing within his soul.

"May God have mercy on us all," he murmured, folding the parchment, and sealing it with wax. As he handed the letter to a waiting courier, Leclerc couldn't help but wonder what the future held for Saint-Domingue and its people.

"Board the next vessel bound for France and bring this to the first Consul," he instructed the courier, his voice firm but hollow. "And pray that he sees the wisdom in our decisions."

As the courier disappeared into the rain, Leclerc turned to gaze out of the window, watching as the storm raged outside. He couldn't help but feel that the tempest mirrored the battle that lay ahead – not just for him, but for all those who called Saint-Domingue home.

The sun blazed mercilessly over the landscape, casting long shadows as Suzanne Bélair, known to her comrades as Sanité, stood proudly beside her husband, Charles. Their eyes locked for a moment, two fierce warriors united by love and a shared vision for freedom. The air was thick with tension and anticipation, the scent of gunpowder lingering in the humid breeze.

The couple had deserted the French army and were now fighting to hold onto the freedom of the blacks. "Remember what we fight for, Sanité," Charles murmured, brushing his rough fingers against her cheek, leaving a faint trail of sweat behind. "We carry the hopes of our people on our shoulders."

"Oui, mon amour," she whispered, her voice steady and determined. "Together, we will drive these French invaders from our land and secure a better future."

As a lieutenant in the indigenous army, Sanité had risen through the ranks with unwavering dedication to the cause. Born an affranchi in Verrettes, she had known the bitter taste of oppression all too well, and when Charles, a Brigade commander who would later become Général, entered her life, they found solace and strength in each other's arms.

"Sanité, keep your wits about you," Charles cautioned, his grip tightening on his musket. "The French troops are cunning and relentless."

She nodded, gripping her weapon firmly. *"Je suis prête,* Charles. Together, we will emerge victorious."

As they advanced towards the enemy's position, their comrades at their side, Sanité felt the familiar thrum of adrenaline course through her veins. Her heart pounded in time with the rhythmic stomping of boots, her senses sharpening with each step. She knew that every battle brought with it the possibility of death, but it was a price she was willing to payt.

"Viv libète! A ba esclavaj!" she cried, her voice ringing out over the battlefield as they charged headlong into the fray.

"Long live freedom! Down with slavery!" her fellow soldiers echoed, their voices united in a fierce battle cry that seemed to shake the very earth beneath their feet.

Gunfire erupted around them, the crack of musket balls tearing through the air like thunder. Sanité ducked and weaved, her movements agile and precise, honed by years of grueling training and countless skirmishes. She caught glimpses of Charles through the chaos, his expression focused and unyielding, a true leader on the battlefield.

With every French soldier that fell before her, Sanité felt an overwhelming sense of purpose well up inside her, a fire that burned brighter than the sun overhead. This was what she had been born for, this fight for freedom and justice, and she would not be deterred by fear or doubt.

In her ferocity, she got separated from Charles and captured by Général Répussard's French column at Corail-Mirrault.

"Sanité!" Charles cried out as enemy hands pulled her away, struggling and not hearing the voice of her husband.

"Let me go!" she demanded, fury etched on her face. But it was futile. The French soldiers held her tightly, a mockery of a smile on their faces. She was taken to the nearby town in chains, and thrown into the stockade.

The following day, she was dragged before Général Répussard who acted as judge during the military tribunal. As she awaited for her sentence, two soldiers arrived with a calm Charles Bélair at their side, walking without prodding into the makeshift courtroom. "This man has surrendered, Général. His only request was to see this woman. He claims her to be his wife."

"Charles, no! What are you doing!" exclaimed Sanité.

"Je t'aime," he told her, his eyes filled with sorrow. "I love you and I will not leave you alone." Charles then turned to face Répussard, "Général Charles Bélair of the Indignous Army, Général Répussar."

"Ahh, we have captured a Général. I suppose love is in the air, eh? As you wish," Général Répussard answered.

Répussard, a French romantic and sentimentalist, allowed the couple one hour of solitary confinement together, then swiftly passed down the sentences. Charles would face a firing squad, while Sanité, due to her sex, was sentenced to decapitation, a form of leniency for women captured in battle.

"Non!" she declared, her voice steady and unwavering. "I am a soldier, like my husband. I demand an honorable death by musketry."

Répussard hesitated, his eyes narrowing. "Very well," he finally conceded.

"Viv libète! A ba esclavaj!" Sanité shouted, her spirit unbroken even as death loomed over her.

As Charles was led the following morning to face the firing squad, Sanité's heart ached with love and sorrow. She looked into his eyes, and with every ounce of strength she had left, she whispered, "Die bravely, mon amour. Our fight will live on."

Tears welled up in his eyes but Charles remained resolute. "I will, Sanité, and I will see you on the other side of life."

She watched as the bullets tore through her husband, her execution imminent. As the soldiers forced her toward the firing squad, Sanité refused their blindfold. She would meet death with her eyes wide open.

"Viv libète! A ba esclavaj!" she cried once more, standing tall, the muzzles pointed at her. As the final echoes of her defiance filled the air on the morning of October 5th of 1802, the proud, brave lieutenant of the indigenous army embraced her fate, forever a symbol of strength, resistance, and the power of women, numerous in the fight to free Saint Domingue.

Late one night in mid October, Henry Christophe stood in the shadows within the darkened courtyard of Hôtel de la Couronne, long after the bustle of workers reconstructing the hotel from the fires had left for the night. He glanced at his pocket watch, illuminated by a sliver of moonlight, it registered 1 am. It was time to meet the man he called brother, Jean-Baptiste Bayard, and his son, Jean-Junior.

"Jean-Baptiste," he whispered into the darkness. "Junior."

Like phantoms, father and son emerged from one of the stately columns of the restaurant, their eyes scanning for any signs of lingering workers. Junior caught Henry's gaze and nodded in silent understanding. The three men retreated into the darkness of the casino, still under construction, and away from any unseen prying eyes or suspicious ears.

"Thank you for meeting me here," Henry said, his voice low and urgent. "I must speak with you about something of utmost importance."

"Of course, Henry," Jean replied, concern etched on his face. "What is troubling you?"

"Leclerc and Bonaparte." His words came out like venom. "They have lied to us all along. Their true intention has always been to restore slavery in Saint Domingue."

"Are you certain?" Junior asked, his brow furrowed with anger and disbelief. "How do you know this?"

"Information has reached me from reliable sources," Henry confessed, his eyes flickering with shame. "I should have listened to Toussaint when I had the chance. Leclerc deceived him, and now he rots in a freezing cell at Fort de Joux in the French Alps with his servant Mars Plaisir."

"What of Suzanne and the children?" asked Jean.

"They have also been incarcerated. Placide at the prison of Belle-Isle-en-Mer, and Suzanne, Isaac, and Saint-Jean are under house arrest at a home in Agen."

"Mon Dieu," Jean murmured, crossing himself. "How could they do this to him, a Governor who was only trying to advance the colony?"

"Power, greed, the influence of the Grands Blanc in Paris, politics, you name it," Henry said as he clenched his fists tightly. "But we cannot let them succeed. Junior, I know that you are close friends with Général Alexandre Pétion," Henry said, his voice low and cautious.

"We are, but I always knew you two have had your, how should I put this, disagreements in the past? You are both like family to me," Junior said, a tinge of regret for the way things turned out, evident in his tone.

"If you call being on opposite sides of a battlefield trying to kill each other a disagreement, then yes, you would be infinitely correct," Henry said with a small chuckle to lighten the air.

"But you fight on the same side now," Henry reasoned.

"I have never really seen him, either before or since his return. He is in the south and I am here in the north. We are all like policemen now, sent to terrorize the people we are sworn to protect. We need a different direction," Henry stated.

"What do you have in mind?" asked Jean.

"Convince Pétion to meet with me, and ultimately, to combine forces," Henry said, his gaze locked onto Junior as he laid his cards on the table.

Junior hesitated, his brow furrowed. "Pétion, like you, serves Leclerc, and he has been loyal to the French even before you joined. He came with them on this expedition. What makes you think he would even consider this?"

"Because, like me, he has been deceived by Leclerc and Bonaparte," Henry replied earnestly. "And because I believe that deep down, he shares my same desire to see Saint Domingue remain free from the chains of slavery. The cultivators have united and have begun a resistance movement. They, as Toussaint did, have seen the true intent of the French, that is to put them back in chains. They are resolute, but they lack leadership, organization, munitions. They are joining the bands of maroons, but I prefer them to join us as an alternative instead. That is where he, I, and Dessalines can make a difference."

"Dessalines?" asked Junior as he looked at his father who appeared to have received a gut punch.

"I haven't reached out to him yet, but yes, he would be one of those to have join." Henry suddenly stopped and looked painfully at Jean. He had carelessly let the name of Dessalines escape from his lips without thinking of the pain the man had brought to this family, to Jean in particular, who had almost been killed by the brutality of the man. "Forgive me, Jean. I should not have…"

"No Henry, go on," Jean interrupted.

"Junior, can you get me an introduction to Pétion?"

Very well," Junior agreed, his expression resolute. "I will do everything in my power to arrange a meeting between you and Pétion. But I cannot promise that he will be receptive to this. Can you travel at first light?"

"To where?" Henry asked, his voice filled with gratitude.

"Jérémie, I have a ship departing there tomorrow morning at first light. Pétion will be somewhere in the south. That will get us there the fastest."

Before the sun began to rise in the sky with the promise of a new day, Junior and Henry made their way to the *Laura*. As they boarded the ship, the crew bustled about, preparing for departure.

As she eased away from the dock, the ship's timbers creaked with age, and its sails flapped gently in the light breeze. The morning wind picked up, and her sails captured the breeze as she began her journey to leave the harbor and set course towards Jérémie.

The sun rose from the eastern horizon, seagulls awoke to circle overhead, and the scent of brine and fish filled the air. As they sailed, Junior's thoughts turned to Général Alexandre Pétion, a longtime friend from his days at the university in Paris when he had first met him while he was trying to recruit smart, young students for officer training. Though that wasn't his path, they fostered a good relationship for many years, first in Paris and then back home here.

Pétion is an honorable man, he thought. But also, one who had fought against Henry, Toussaint, and Dessalines in the past. Junior wondered if Pétion would truly be willing to set aside old rivalries for the sake of this shared cause, knowing how much he loved France and took seriously his loyalty to her.

"Henry," Junior said, seeking reassurance. "Do you believe Pétion will join us?"

Henry considered the question, then replied, "He is a man of principle. If I can convince him that the cause is just, I believe he will stand with us."

"Then let us pray that you can find the words to sway him," Junior murmured, gazing out at the horizon.

During the sail to Jérémie, Junior and Henry recalled happier times, catching up on the events in each other's lives. It was long in coming as they hadn't really talked in years. Henry had joined the family back in 1779 after the American Revolution when he had arrived in Saint Domingue as a slave. He had come with his father Jean-Baptiste, an army captain at the time. Junior was but a young boy at the age of five, and Henry twelve.

Henry had come to live with them as family, developing a strong bond, and even going into the family business by running the Hôtel de la Couronne in downtown Cap, until he joined Toussaint. So much had changed, Junior thought.

The site of Jérémie came into view. Junior was excited to see his family from both sides; his grandparents, uncles, and cousins, they would all be there to visit, but first, there was the business of Pétion to take care of.

Two days hence, the *Laura* docked at the familiar slip his ships always used and he and Henry disembarked. They headed straight for the Bayard family warehouse office at the dock and sent couriers to find Pétion, with letters already written, suggesting a meeting between him, Junior, and Henry. Junior had three separate couriers travel to Jacmel, Les Cayes, and Port Républicain to seek Pétion out, as they were not sure of his exact location but knew he would be in one of those cities.

"In the meantime, let's go catch up with some family, Henry," Junior said with excitement. "First Uncle Gustav, his mother Marie's brother, at the store."

As he and Henry walked through the bustling streets of Jérémie, Junior couldn't help but feel the tension in the air. There was an undercurrent of unrest and a sense that change was on the horizon. He wondered if Henry felt it too. French soldiers patrolled the streets, heavily armed. Henry had chosen to shed his uniform so he wouldn't be recognized, sporting unfamiliar civilian clothes instead.

As they entered the hardware store, a young teenage boy with a huge smile came to greet them, recognizing Junior and Henry. It was Ricardo, Gustav's son, and Junior's cousin. After some small talk, they spent the afternoon enjoying a long, leisurely lunch at Le Soleil restaurant, catching up on old times, getting the pulse of current events, and enjoying dishes of stewed Lambi – conch, Kabrit – barbequed goat, and Griot – the delicious lean pork meat fried to perfection, all served with *diri djon-djon* – rice cooked with black mushrooms, stewed onions, and of course that hot sauce Ti Malis.

"The French are finished here," predicted Gustav. "It's only a matter of time."

"Why do you say that?" asked Henry, already knowing part of the answer, but needing to hear the confirmation from a local point of view.

"Bonaparte needs money. He has nearly bankrupted France with his desire for conquest and war. You can't run a huge army, the most powerful in the world, without burning cash. Saint Domingue is a cash cow if he reinstitutes slavery to jump-start the plantation economy. What do you think his answer will be?"

So, it was out in the open, Henry could see. "What makes you think that?" Henry asked Gustav.

"You're kidding, right? Haven't you heard that just about all French colonies have gone back to slavery?"

"Yes, but he has promised that there would not be slavery in Saint Domingue," Henry said, feigning naivety.

"Guadeloupe, Martinique, Saint Lucia, the others; all small islands, small populations that are easily suppressed. Général Brunet was sent to Martinique," Gustav said, suddenly lowering his voice, looking around, and sporting a smirk and continued, "by personal order of Leclerc for screwing his wife Pauline, I am told."

The three laughed at Leclerc's expense.

Gustav continued, 'his mission? Subdue the population and reinstitute slavery. With the French army at his side, easily done. Those that didn't comply? executed."

Gustav took in another forkful of Lambi and accompanied it with a large scoop of *diri djon-djon*.

With his mouth still full, he continued. "But in Saint Domingue, it is not so easy. We are too vast, too diversified, too populated. But you will see, in time, when he is ready and powerful once again, he will try it, with the blessings of the Blancs. But the cultivators and the maroons won't let that happen. They are already too powerful."

They continued their conversation, but both Junior and Henry could well see that the seeds of rebellion had already been well planted, validating Toussaint's dockside prediction; '*Liberty; it will spring up again from the roots, for they are numerous, and they are deep,*" obviously deep in the southern peninsula, thought Henry.

After spending all afternoon lounging in the restaurant, Gustav had to depart and go shut down the store, so Henry and Junior headed to his grandparents, Marie's mother and father's home, in the city. The Jasmine's had gotten word of their arrival and prepared a grand meal. Henry and Junior looked at each other, still slightly full from lunch, shrugged at the invitation, – 'why not?'

The meal was the traditional morue, salted codfish. Codfish was originally brought to the island by Junior's uncle Andre in traded from northeasterners in Massachusetts. They needed molasses for their rum making and property owners here needed a source of cheap protein to feed their slaves. Local physicians soon recommended the salted codfish as a source of protein to boost productivity, and the salt to replenish the vital saline that the slaves would profusely sweat out in their grueling work. At first, slaves found the saltiness distasteful but soon developed a liking for the salty seafood.

Average households never considered eating the salted fish as they found it beneath being served at their tables until their household servants began experimenting with recipes for their consumption. They perfected the removal of all traces of salt through a boiling and flushing process of the salted fish. Then they created diverse recipes so delicious that they soon became a delicacy on household tables. A slave's meal gone chic.

That night, Junior and Henry feasted on the morue, with helpings of the boiled roots of malanga and yuca, with sweet potato, sweet fried plantains, a smothering of cooked onions, and spirited conversation washed down with plenty of inexpensive table wine until Grandpa and grandma Jasmine retired for the night. At seventy-five years of age, they go to bed earlier these days. Henry and Junior stayed up with a bottle of rum on the porch.

As the roosters crowed early the next morning, Junior and Henry rode to the countryside, the Bayard family plantation as the destination. They visited with uncles Rene and Julian, and Junior's cousins. After seeing the young girls, now teenagers, Henry couldn't help but feel remorse at the amount of time he had to spend away from Marie-Louise and his own children.

They spent a couple of days lounging around the plantation, Henry and Junior riding horses through the countryside, enjoying good food and family, and picking up on the politics of rebellion in the air. "It is time for the French to leave, once and for all," was the common theme.

Finally, on the third day, a courier galloped into the compound to seek out Junior, who opened the letter and exclaimed, "Henry," his voice barely containing his excitement. "Pétion has agreed to meet with us."

Pétion was in Jacmel and agreed to a meeting with him and Henry. The message was brief and offered no hint of Pétion's intentions, but it was enough to set Junior's heart soring and Henry's heart pounding with hope.

"Thank God," Henry murmured, relief flooding his features. "Let us go and seize this opportunity."

As they made their way to Jacmel, the setting sun cast long shadows over the town. The sun dipped below the horizon by the time they approached the offices of Pétion.

"Welcome, Junor, Général Christophe," Pétion greeted them, his voice cordial yet guarded. He stood tall and imposing in the fading light, his dark eyes betraying a wariness that mirrored their own.

"Thank you for agreeing to meet with us, Général Pétion," Henry replied, his voice steady despite the apprehension gnawing at him. "We come to you today with a matter of great urgency."

Junior watched the exchange closely, keenly aware of the immense weight resting on Henry's shoulders. He knew that if they were to stand any chance of uniting Saint Domingue against the French, they would need Pétion on their side.

"Let me be direct," Christophe continued, determination evident in his tone. "We believe that Leclerc and Bonaparte have deceived us all. Their true intention is to restore slavery in Saint Domingue, and we cannot allow that to happen."

Pétion's eyes narrowed, but he remained silent. Junior could see the gears turning in his mind - weighing the gravity of Henry's words against the potential consequences of defiance.

"Général Pétion, we know that you have fought against Jean-Jacques Dessalines and I in the past." Henry paused, gauging Pétion's reaction. "But now, we must set aside old rivalries and join forces for the greater good. We are assembling the Armée Indigéne – Indigenous Army, and we want you to join."

Pétion crossed his arms over his chest, his expression inscrutable. "And why should I trust you, Christophe, much less Dessalines? What guarantee do I have that this is not some ploy to weaken my position? Or to put a wedge in my loyalty to the French?"

"Because we share a common enemy - one who would see us all in chains, or possibly dead," Christophe replied, his voice filled with passion. "We are not asking you to trust us blindly, but to hear us out and make your own decision."

"Henry is right," Junior interjected, hoping his friendship with Pétion would lend weight to their cause. "This is bigger than any of us. If we don't stand together now, there may be no tomorrow for the colony. There is a secret conference that will take place in Arcahaie. Come meet with Dessalines, see for yourself."

"Dessalines would just as soon slit my throat for what I did to them at Crête-à-Pierrot," Pétion said.

"Come on, take the chance Pétion," Henry sparked, his voice rising more than he wanted it to. "We were born here. This land is ours. It runs through our veins. Long before Leclerc and this expedition arrived, we were here. And we will be here long after they depart for their own homes in France. This is our home, not theirs, Pétion. You, I, Junior, those soldiers of yours, and the people of this land who have never set foot off of it."

The silence that followed was deafening as Pétion considered their words. The tension in the air was almost palpable, and Junior could feel his heart pounding in his chest. Was it the TikTok of his pocket watch he was hearing or his imagination, he thought as they waited for Pétion's response?

"Very well," Pétion finally said, his voice quiet but resolute. "I will meet with Dessalines at Arcahaie, but I make no promises beyond that."

"Thank you, Général Pétion," Henry responded, relief evident in his voice. "We understand the risk you are taking, and we are grateful for your willingness to listen."

As they left the office, the moon cast a silvery glow over the landscape, illuminating the path before them. Henry knew that they had taken a significant step towards unifying Saint Domingue, but the road ahead was still fraught with danger and uncertainty.

The sun was on its descent in the sky, casting an eerie orange glow over the landscape as he approached Arcahaie. The atmosphere was thick with tension, and the air crackled with a sense of impending confrontation. Henry could feel his heart thudding in his chest as he walked towards the meeting place where Jean-Jacques Dessalines awaited him.

As he entered the room, the air seemed to grow heavier, nearly stifling. Henry's eyes darted around the room, taking in the figure of Dessalines standing tall and imposing at one end of the table, his features hardened into an unreadable mask.

Earlier than expected, Général Pétion entered the room unannounced, his expression wary but resolute.

"Général Pétion," Christophe began, stepping forward with extended hands. "Thank you for agreeing to meet with us."

"Christophe," Pétion acknowledged, nodding curtly, but not taking the offered hand. He then looked across the table at Dessalines, his eyes narrowing. "Dessalines."

"Enough with the pleasantries," Dessalines grumbled, his voice like gravel. "Let's get to the point. Will you join us in our fight against the French?"

The room held its breath as Pétion considered the question, his gaze never leaving Dessalines'. In that moment, Henry saw the struggle within the man, torn between loyalty to his oath as a French soldier, and the desire to protect his people from them.

To Henry, it seemed that Pétion emitted a newfound determination flickering in his eyes. "Very well," he said, his voice ringing clear and strong. "I will join you in this rebellion, and I will secure the south. But know this - once we have driven the French from our shores, I will not tolerate tyranny from any man, be he YOU or a Frenchman."

"Nor would we ask it of you, Général," Christophe assured him, diplomatically releasing the air of tension, a smile tugging at the corners of his mouth as relief flooded through him. "Together, we will forge a new future for our people."

Dessalines said nothing.

With that, the revolutionary leaders - Pétion, Dessalines, and Christophe - sealed their pact, defecting from the French and taking with them fellow black and mulatto officers to form the Armée

Indigéne, the Indigenous Army. As they issued a general call to arms, it triggered an avalanche of army defections, an organized recruitment effort and the beginnings of a command structure throughout the various regions. Henry knew that the road ahead was fraught with danger and uncertainty, but for now, there was hope.

The dimly lit room was filled with the soft glow of candles, flickering shadows on the walls like specters dancing in the night. In the center, Charles Victoire Emmanuel Leclerc lay sprawled across his deathbed, drenched in sweat and gasping for breath. His once strong body, now a mere shell of its former self, ravaged by an illness that seemed to have come out of nowhere – La Fièvre Jaune, Yellow Fever.

"Water," he croaked, his voice barely audible. "Please, I need water."

It had all started two weeks prior when he had first felt chills run down his spine. He had dismissed it as a momentary discomfort back then, not realizing that it would soon be followed by a high fever, a throbbing headache, and relentless backache and muscle pain.

"Of course, Général," replied Antoine, his aide de camp, rushing to his side with a glass of water. He held it to Leclerc's parched lips, watching as the dying man greedily gulped it down. But no amount of water seemed to be enough to quench the insatiable thirst that tormented him.

"More... please..." Leclerc managed to whisper, his eyes pleading for relief. The aide nodded and poured another glassful, but deep down, he knew that what his Général needed was beyond the reach of mortal hands.

As Leclerc drank, his thoughts wandered to his wife, Pauline, who had remained outside during this ordeal. He longed for her comforting touch, but she had chosen to stay away, perhaps unable to bear the sight of her husband's suffering.

"Tell... Pauline... I love her..." Leclerc stammered between sips of water. The aide nodded solemnly, knowing that these could very well be his last words.

"Is there anything else you wish, Général?" he asked gently, as Leclerc's breathing grew more labored.

"Bring... Dermide... to me," Leclerc whispered, his thoughts now on his beloved son. But it was a request that went unfulfilled; Pauline had refused to let their child see the once formidable man reduced to such a pitiful state, and for the boy's safety against catching the fever.

"Forgive me, Général, but Dermide cannot be here," the aide replied, his voice filled with regret. "Is there anything else I can do for you?"

"Write, Antoine... to Napoleon," Leclerc muttered through gritted teeth, his mind drifting to his final wish – confirm the appointment of Général Rochambeau as his successor. If order were to be restored in the colony, it would take a man like Rochambeau to do it, ruthless and unyielding, to lead them.

"Général, please," the aide urged, his voice trembling with concern. "Let me help you."

"Help me, Antoine?" Leclerc scoffed, choking back a sob. "How can you help when my own body has turned against me?"

"Perhaps... perhaps there is still something we can do," the aide offered hesitantly, trying to instill a sliver of hope in the dying man's heart.

"Such as?" he whispered, blood dribbling down his chin, a chilling reminder of the inevitable.

"Perhaps we can send for the best doctors... or search for a cure—" The aide's voice trailed off under Leclerc's withering glare.

"Enough, Antoine" Leclerc growled, the fire in his eyes momentarily rekindled. "I am not so naïve as to believe in miracles. What is the day today?"

"It is Tuesday, Général."

"No, no… the date, Antoine, the date?"

"The second of November, sir. November 2nd, 1802. Général, what else would you have me do?" the aide asked, desperation coloring his words.

"Stay... with me," Leclerc whispered, his gaze softening. "Bear witness to my final moments and tell Napoleon of my last wish. I may die on this bed, but the colony must live on under Rochambeau's command."

"Of course, Général," the aide replied solemnly, his hand gripping Leclerc's ever more tightly. "I will do as you ask."

"Thank you, Antoine...you have always been loyal, if not the closest thing to being a… friend?"

As Charles Victoire Emmanuel Leclerc, Governor Général of Saint Domingue, surrendered himself to the inexorable pull of darkness, the words of Toussaint Louverture, *'this land rejects you'* reverberated in his thoughts, consumed by loss, and the fate of a colony hanging in the balance.

The November sun was high in the sky, and the Caribbean heat tempered across the training field as men moved with purpose and determination. The sound of clashing metal and shouted orders filled the air, while black and mulatto officers directed their soldiers, many newly minted from the plantations, in drills. This was the birth of a new army, one that united black and mulatto forces under a single banner in their fight against the French.

As the days passed, news spread like wildfire across the island. Men and women from every corner of Saint Domingue flocked to join the newly formed revolutionary army for a chance to participate in the historical fight to preserve their freedom. Together, they began to form a national identity around their common goal of expelling the French government.

"Word has reached us from Port Républicain," Henry announced one evening, his brow furrowed in concern. "Leclerc has fallen victim to yellow fever and succumbed to the illness."

"May his soul rest in peace," Pétion murmured, crossing himself. Though they had disagreed on many matters, he could not deny that Leclerc had been a formidable man.

"On his deathbed, Leclerc appointed Rochambeau to succeed him, pending approval by Napoleon" Henry continued, his voice heavy with unease. "He is a person who hates the blacks with a passion, and mulattos worse!"

"Rochambeau?" Dessalines spat, his eyes flashing with fury. "The man is a monster. It seems the French are determined to make us pay for our defiance."

"And now he's the man in charge," Henry confirmed.

"Look what he did to Maurepas and his family the other day," Dessalines offered. "Leclerc had integrated him into the French army, like he did us, and placed him under the authority of General Brunett at Port-de-Paix. He was later suspected of taking part in a revolt led by Capois-la-Mort, which I know he had no part in."

"So, what happened to him?" asked Pétion

"He, his family, and some of his troops of the 9th Brigade were arrested by Brunett and brought to Cap last week. Rochambeau arrived the day after, and by his order, without the benefit of a trial, they were all tortured and cast into the sea."

"How did you hear of this?" asked Henry.

"One of my Aunt Toya's spies in her network."

"Then we will just need to fight harder," Henry declared, his jaw set in determination. "We will not allow Rochambeau or any other Frenchman to get in our way."

With the day's training complete, the sun dipped below the horizon and darkness enveloped the training field, Henry looked out at the men and women who now stood united. They had come together to fight to retain their freedom, to reclaim the island that was their birthright. Though terrifying challenges lay ahead, he knew that they were ready to face them.

With his officers assembled at headquarters, the new Captain-General entered the room of the chief of staff.

"Général Rochambeau," a young officer called out, his hand raised in salute as the eight other officers rose to attention as a unit. The newly appointed head of the colony strode to the table. His stern visage and cold unforgiving, calculating eyes sent shivers down the spines of those present.

"Sit, all of you," Rochambeau barked, taking his place at the head of the table. He pulled a piece of parchment from his coat pocket and unfolded it with an air of authority. "I have written to the First Consul requesting 35,000 additional troops to crush this rebellion once and for all. Ces sales nègres seront anéantis!" These stinking niggers will be annihilated!

"Sir!" the quartermaster captain exclaimed, "That is a significant number. Do you truly believe we will need such a force? And if and when they arrive, what of the logistics involved in feeding them?"

Paying no mind, Rochambeau continued, "These bastards are determined to expel us from the colony. We need to crush them with no mercy, destroy them all!" He took a long breath, thinking of the blood bath this far, and the blood that would inevitably color the soil of Saint Domingue in the days to come.

"Very well, sir," the quartermaster captain acquiesced, his voice wavering. "What additional measures do you have in mind?"

"Ruthless violence, executions, and even massacres," Rochambeau declared without an ounce of remorse. "Even the slightest hint, whisper, or rumor of a revolt, must be crushed with steel, destroyed, no-holds-bars. We shall subjugate them, put them in front of firing squads, and gas them, even.

"Gas them sir? What does that mean? I have never heard that expression before?" asked a young officer.

"I had a diabolical captain specially outfit a ship in the harbor to do so, efficient mass execution by filling the hold of the ship with sulfur dioxide to suffocate them to death without the need to waste bullets. We tested it yesterday with 50 rebels and it works to perfection. The captain calls it a 'gas chamber', quite unique and impressive if I may say so. He then sailed a mile or so out to sea and fed their bodies to the sharks. Disposal of the waste made easy and efficient."

The young officer swallowed deeply, trying to comprehend the hell he was now experiencing. He was from a small town, Avignon, in the provinces of France, seeking glory and adventure by joining the military and traveling to remote parts of the world. This, he had never expected to encounter, never even in any of his nightmares.

Rochambeau continued extolling his plans, "I have even ordered 750 attack dogs from Cuba to hunt the insurrectionists down like the animals they are. The first pack of my little pet beasts will soon arrive to help us terrorize these rebels."

"Man-eating dogs?" another officer stammered, his eyes wide with shock. "But, Général—"

"Enough!" Rochambeau roared, slamming his fist on the table. "You are under my command now, and you will abide by my orders, my methods. Nothing else has worked thus far. Charles Leclerc, may he rest in peace, was a pacifier, a weakling that allowed them to run rampant. I am not. No more questions. You will do as I say."

"Understood, Général," the officers chorused, their voices meek and subdued.

Later, in the barracks, a young lieutenant who had attended the meeting narrated points of it, in a hushed voice, to his fellow soldiers, "Rochambeau, in whose name and by whose orders so many atrocities, mass-murders, and ghastly acts unparalleled since the days of slavery, had already been committed, we will soon widen these tactics in the South and the West, we have been ordered."

May God have mercy on us all," one soldier murmured, crossing himself in fear.

"Indeed," another agreed, his voice tinged with despair. "For it seems our new leader has no mercy to spare."

Nineteen

THE BEGINNING OF THE END FOR THE FRENCH

Paris
January 1803

The clock in the dimly lit room struck midnight, echoing through the air as heavy drapes obscured the moonlight from streaming through the windows. The somber ambiance weighed heavily on Napoleon, who sat brooding in his armchair, his friends, Générals Jean Lannes, Christophe Duroc, and Jean-Andoche Junot, gathered around in a circle of shared mourning.

"Such a tragic loss," whispered Général Lannes, breaking the silence that had settled upon them like a thick fog. "Leclerc was a good man, a fine officer."

"Yellow fever," muttered Napoleon, staring into the dying embers of the fire before him. "Damn that disease. And damn Saint Domingue for taking him from us."

"Indeed, First Consul," agreed Junot, his voice tinged with sorrow. "But we must remember that life is fleeting, and death comes to us all."

"Enough!" snapped Napoleon, his eyes flashing with anger. "What use are platitudes when our nation is threatened? We cannot afford further losses!"

The Générals exchanged uneasy glances, knowing full well the weight of their leader's words. They were aware that Napoleon had a deep connection to Leclerc - not only as a comrade but also as a brother-in-law. His sister Pauline now refuses to speak with Napoleon as she blames her brother for her husband's death; 'You should have never sent us there in the first place' she quipped.

"Forgive me, sir," said Duroc, cautiously choosing his words. "But perhaps there is something to be learned from this tragedy. France has been stretched thin, and we cannot continue to invest our resources in a fight that may prove unwinnable."

"Are you suggesting we abandon Saint Domingue?" Napoleon demanded, his gaze piercing Duroc. "That we turn our backs on our colony?"

"Of course not," replied Duroc, his voice steady despite the tension in the room. "But perhaps...we should consider other options."

"Such as?" Napoleon's voice was cold, his eyes narrowing.

"Louisiana," Lannes spoke up, his tone hesitant but determined. "We could sell it to the United States and use the funds to replenish our treasury and strengthen our forces."

"Louisiana?" Napoleon mulled over the idea, the gears in his mind turning. He weighed the loss of Saint Domingue against the potential gains from selling Louisiana. The thought of parting with a piece of his empire pained him, but he knew that sacrifices had to be made for the greater good of France.

"Very well," he said finally, his voice resolute. "Begin negotiations with the Americans. Our nation's future depends on it and if we lose Saint Domingue, it's just dirt in a far-off land – useless to us."

Napoleon stood by the window, watching as snowflakes danced in the icy air before settling on the frozen ground.

"Sir," Lannes ventured cautiously, breaking the silence that had fallen since their earlier discussion. "Who shall we send to negotiate with President Jefferson?"

"Send Talleyrand," Napoleon decided, clenching his gloved hands behind his back. He knew the wily diplomat's reputation for cunning and deceit would be an asset in such negotiations. "He will be able to secure the best possible terms for France."

"Of course," Duroc said, scribbling down the instruction on a piece of parchment. The scratching of the quill echoed through the room like a death knell.

Next, there's this business from Saint Domingue. The dim candlelight flickered across the parchment, casting shadows over Napoleon's furrowed brow as he scanned the letter from acting Captain Général Rochambeau. His words hung heavily in the air, adding to the oppressive atmosphere that had settled upon the room.

"Rochambeau requests thirty-five thousand additional troops and the restoration of slavery on the island," Junot said, his expression a mix of disbelief and frustration. "We are bleeding dry for this war, and yet he demands even more."

"Tell Rochambeau to hold out as long as he can," Napoleon replied, his jaw set with determination. In his mind's eye, he saw the island fortress crumbling beneath the relentless assault of disease and rebellion. "If we can buy time, perhaps there is still hope for our cause."

"Understood," Junot responded, relief evident in his voice. They all knew that this decision was not an easy one for Napoleon to make.

"Saint Domingue is vital to our interests," Lannes ventured cautiously, his apprehension palpable. "Perhaps it is worth considering such drastic measures."

"Indeed," Duroc agreed, though his voice held a note of reluctance. "We cannot afford to lose the island to those rebels."

Napoleon's eyes scanned the room, taking in the somber faces of his friends and trusted advisors.

"Very well," he announced, penning his response on the parchment before him. "I will authorize the restoration of slavery on the island and confirm Rochambeau as the new Captain-Général of Saint Domingue. We must maintain control, no matter the cost."

"Is it wise to put so much faith in Rochambeau?" Junot asked, his concern evident in the slight tremor of his voice.

Napoleon paused, considering the question. He had no love for the man, but the situation demanded action. "We have little choice," he admitted, his thoughts churning with worry. "If we hesitate now, we risk catastrophe."

His hand moved across the paper, the scratching of his pen echoing in the silence as he sealed their fate with each stroke. He could only hope that this decision would not come back to haunt them all.

"Let us pray that this will be enough to turn the tide," Lannes murmured, his words barely audible over the sound of Napoleon's pen.

"Pray indeed," Napoleon agreed darkly, folding the letter and affixing his seal. "For if it is not, then the future of our empire may well hang in the balance."

The crackling fire in the hearth offered little comfort against the chill that had settled into Napoleon's bones.

"Napoleon," Général Lannes continued, his voice strained, "what of Rochambeau's troop request?"

Napoleon exhaled, knowing full well that they were backed into a corner. "I cannot send more troops," he admitted, staring into the dancing flames as if seeking answers therein. "Dispatch some Irish and Spanish forces to Saint Domingue. It is all we can spare with England looming large on the horizon."

Napoleon stood by the window, watching as snowflakes danced in the icy air before settling on the frozen ground. The chill of the room seemed to seep into his very bones, mirroring the coldness that had settled in the pit of his stomach.

"Let us toast to a better year ahead," said Duroc, raising a glass filled with dark wine. "To new beginnings."

"New beginnings," echoed the others, clinking glasses solemnly before each taking a sip. The fate of France rested on their shoulders, and they were determined to see her through these trying times, no matter the cost.

Smoke plumed into the sky as the distant screams of rebellion echoed through the air. The plantations of the southern peninsula near Port-Salut were burning, their once-lush fields reduced to a smoldering wasteland. It was the handiwork of the newly allied black and mulatto insurgents, their unity forged in the fires of their collective struggle.

"Merde," whispered Rochambeau, his weathered eyes surveying the devastation that stretched before him. "We are losing control."

His aide-de-camp, Lieutenant Moreau, stood at attention beside him. "Général Rochambeau, the cultivators have razed the cane fields and set the plantations ablaze."

"I can see that for myself!" Rochambeau's jaw clenched.

As the two men turned to leave, they could hear the voices of the insurgents drawing nearer, the sounds of resistance growing stronger with each passing moment. Rochambeau's mind raced with thoughts of what was to come – the battles, the bloodshed, and the desperate attempt to hold onto a slipping empire.

"Général," Moreau said, catching Rochambeau's pensive gaze. "These rebels seem more organized than ever, striking at all points throughout the interior."

Rochambeau sighed heavily. "France has built a huge plantation economy over the past 100 years that has now turned into an equally huge mess.

"Do you think we can truly regain control?

"I do not know," I just don't know if things can ever get back to what they once were," Rochambeau replied, shaking his head. "But I do know this: we are fighting for more than just the colony. We are fighting for the very future of France itself. If we fail here, I fear there may be no turning back."

With that ominous thought lingering in the air, the two men left the smoldering fields behind them, their gazes fixed on the horizon and the uncertain future that lay ahead. The entire plain was in a state of insurrection, and the fires of rebellion burned brightly – a stark reminder of the struggle to come.

Under the sweltering Caribbean sun in March, Général Rochambeau surveyed his newly acquired assets. The Cuban dogs, tall and sinewy as Scottish or Russian greyhounds, were a sight to behold. Their heads were shaped like those of wire-haired terriers, and their eyes held an unnerving intelligence that made even seasoned soldiers' glance away.

"Sir, the shipment has arrived," said Lieutenant Dupont, wiping sweat from his brow.

"Excellent," Rochambeau replied, his gaze unwavering as he studied the dogs. "These hounds will certainly bolster our ranks and help us chase down rebels and runaway cultivators."

"Indeed, sir. They appear quite formidable," agreed Dupont, attempting to mask his unease. He shifted his weight from foot to foot, feeling the tension growing in the air.

"Look at them, Dupont," Rochambeau continued, his voice filled with admiration. "The way they move... it's as if they know they're superior to any other beast we might employ."

"Formidable" was not the word that came to Dupont's mind as he watched the dogs prowling within their makeshift pen. The lieutenant searched for a more accurate description — one that encapsulated the dread clawing at his insides. He settled on "terrifying" instead.

Général Rochambeau's boots crunched against gravel as he strode purposefully towards the makeshift pen housing the ferocious Cuban dogs. The sun had begun its descent, casting long shadows across the military encampment as the Général stopped before the pen, his eyes narrowing at the sight of the pack, the first 100 of his 750-dog order.

"Feed them," he barked the order to a nearby corporal, who hurried to comply.

For three days, the hounds were fed the meat from the remains of executed black rebels. Rochambeau believed that such a diet would make them more efficient in their pursuit of runaway slaves and insurgents. He watched with grim satisfaction as the dogs tore into the grisly meal, their powerful jaws snapping and gnashing at the flesh.

"Général," Lieutenant Dupont approached, clutching a sheaf of parchment. "I have sent out the invitations to the Grands Blancs, as you requested. They will arrive to witness Saturday's demonstration."

"Excellent," replied Rochambeau. "They can now see firsthand the cunning use of their tax money and how my dogs will help us capture the disruptive rebels, and keep the cultivators in line. Make this their last meal," Rochambeau barked to the corporal. "Starve them for the next 3 days until Saturday's demonstration. Be sure to tell the planters to leave their women and children home," Rochambeau added, turning to face Dupont. "This is no spectacle for delicate sensibilities."

"Understood, Général." Dupont bowed slightly, suppressing his misgivings about the use of such animals in warfare. He held onto his duty as an anchor in the face of uncertainty.

On Saturday, a cacophony of voices and the stomping of feet stirred up clouds of dust as the rambunctious crowd gathered in anticipation while servers circulated with trays of rum cocktails, champagne, and finger sandwiches. Men of varying degrees of wealth and nobility jostled for prime positions to witness what promised to be a unique and ghastly spectacle: the public execution of one of the rebels captured near Cap Français. The sun beat down mercilessly on the assembly, sweat trickling down furrowed brows as they waited with bated breath.

"Can you believe this?" a French visiting sailor named Baptiste whispered incredulously to his companion, French Général Pamphile Lacroix. Both men stood amidst the throng, their eyes fixed on the crude wooden platform at the center of the arena where the condemned man would soon meet his fate.

"Non, I cannot," Lacroix replied quietly, his gaze flicking between the platform and the restless dogs held back by their handlers. "I've seen many horrors in war, but this..." He shook his head, unable to finish the thought.

"Look!" someone shouted, pointing towards the entrance of the arena. All eyes turned to see the prisoner being led out, his hands bound behind him and his eyes wide with terror.

"May God have mercy on his soul," Baptiste muttered under his breath, crossing himself as the man was forced forward, and secured to the pole.

The noise from the crowd seemed to intensify as the scent of blood and impending violence lingered in the air. Baptiste clenched his fists, trying to push down his unease.

Lacroix's face tightened as he considered the possibility. "We can only hope Rochambeau knows what he's doing," he said, though the uncertainty in his tone betrayed his doubts.

"Can you believe this?" a man beside them muttered, his eyes gleaming with morbid curiosity.

"Look at them, they're ferocious animals," another man whispered, nodding towards the dogs that were snarling and confidently showing their teeth, straining against their leashes, eager to be released.

"Are they going to...?" another commented, unable to finish his sentence.

"Oui, monsieur," the first man said with a grin. "This will teach those rebels a lesson."

The dogs were then released in the pen but acted confused as to what they were to do next. They looked at their victim as the crowd came to a hush, a couple of dogs in the pack of five crouched down, one laid down and 2 sat, as if confused as to their next role in this theater.

"Encourage them!" Pierre Gefrard bellowed, his eyes gleaming with sadistic anticipation. The handlers complied, prodding the reluctant dogs with their sticks toward the prisoner as the crowd grew in anticipation of what would come next.

one laid down and 2 sat, as if confused as to their next role in this theater.

"Encourage them!" Pierre Gefrard bellowed, his eyes gleaming with sadistic anticipation. The handlers complied, prodding the reluctant dogs with their sticks toward the prisoner as the crowd grew in anticipation of what would come next.

The prisoner's eyes once filled with defiance, now displayed a flicker of terror as he felt the presence of the beasts inching closer, but none attacked as Gefrard had anticipated.

"Enough," Gefrard commanded, stepping forward with a knife in hand. "I will give them a taste of what they desire." He approached the prisoner, his expression unyielding and sinister, then proceeded to slightly cut into the skin on the man's stomach, eliciting screams of agony from the victim.

"Blood," Gefrard thought, watching as the dark liquid seeped from the wound. "It is the scent that will drive these monsters to do our bidding."

As if on cue, the dogs began to sniff the air, their eyes narrowing in on the source of the tantalizing aroma, their bellies gurgling empty from the days of starvation. Their bodies tensed, preparing to strike.

Attack!" Gefrard exclaimed, as the handlers let loose the leashes, and the snarling beasts lunged toward their prey.

In a whirl of red dust, the dogs descended upon the hapless prisoner with a ferocity that left Lacroix's stomach churning. The man's screams were drowned out by the cacophony of snarls and tearing flesh, as well as the roar of the crowd around them.

Rochambeau, who had invited the Military band, told the conductor to start the music as the band began to blare military marches triumphantly, providing a macabre soundtrack to the gruesome spectacle.

"Bravo! Bravo!" Rochambeau applauded, his eyes gleaming with savage delight.

"See how they work together!" Gefrard crowed, gesturing to the dogs with unrestrained pride. "I told you, Général, they are the perfect weapon against our enemies!"

As suddenly as it had begun, the execution was over. The mangled remains of the prisoner lay in a pool of blood and torn flesh. The once proud rebel reduced to little more than a pile of gnawed bones and tattered rags. The dogs, still lapping at the blood on the ground, their fur stained crimson, panted heavily as they surveyed their handiwork, their hunger momentarily sated.

"An impressive display, Gefrard," Rochambeau said, clapping the man on the shoulder. "You have done well in training these beasts."

"Thank you, Général," Gefrard replied, basking in the praise. "I am certain they will prove invaluable in our fight against the insurrection."

"Indeed," Rochambeau agreed, casting his gaze across the crowd of awestruck spectators. "Let this serve as a warning to all who would defy us. No rebel, no runaway cultivator is safe from the wrath of these dogs."

"Did you see that?" one man from the crowd exclaimed, his eyes wide with excitement. "Those dogs tore him apart!"

"Good riddance," another scoffed, spitting on the ground. "One less rebel to worry about."

The sun blazed overhead as the dogs, their coats slick with sweat and blood, were led away from the grisly scene.

"Alright, men!" Pierre Gefrard barked, overseeing the handlers who tended to the dogs. "We've got a mission to prepare for. The Général wants these animals ready to hunt by tomorrow."

A soldier named Juste watched as the dogs were washed and inspected, their teeth cleaned of any remaining flesh. Their eyes burned with a newfound hunger, and it sent a shiver down his spine.

"Damn beasts seem almost... eager," remarked Delafosse, another soldier, sidling up to Juste. "I can't shake the feeling that we are about to unleash monsters upon this land."

"Neither can I," Juste admitted quietly, his thoughts echoing the same sentiment. "But our orders are clear. We must press on and hope for the best."

As they prepared for their first mission in the nearby Plaine du Nord, the dogs' behaviors increased in aggression. They constantly paced and growled; their once sharp senses dulled by an insatiable craving for human flesh.

"Look at them," Delafosse whispered to Juste as they observed the dogs from afar. "They're becoming more and more uncontrollable. What will happen when they're let loose on a battlefield?"

"God help us all," Juste muttered, feeling the weight of responsibility heavy on his shoulders.

It wasn't long before the dogs' bloodlust began to cause problems. On a routine patrol, Juste's heart raced as one of the dogs suddenly lunged at an innocent cultivator working in a nearby field.

"Stop that dog!" he yelled, as fear and panic surged through him. The handler struggled to regain control, the dog's teeth sinking into the man's flesh as he cried out in agony.

"Get it off him!" Juste ordered, rushing to help. The handler finally managed to pull the dog away, but not before it had done significant damage.

"Mon Dieu," Baptiste breathed, his eyes wide with horror. "What have we done?"

Juste stared at the wounded cultivator, then at the snarling dog, its muzzle stained red. He knew that this was just the beginning of a nightmare they had created. And as he stood there, amidst the chaos and bloodshed, one question haunted his mind: How would they ever be able to control these monsters they had unleashed upon the world? He only had 5 in his command. There were another 95 handled by other units, and more than 600 on their way to the island!

Over time, the dogs became more accustomed to the flesh of rebels and cultivators alike. They were feared and rightly so. Now and then, a pack of these beasts would escape from their pens, devouring innocent workers in the fields with only their bones left in evidence of their ferocity.

The dogs became more of a liability, killing as many innocent victims as rebels. The planters soon petitioned for the animals to be shipped away or destroyed as they were causing a great deal of stress to the frightened workers, causing them to fear the fields and leading to loss of productivity. Much to Rochambeau's regret, he boarded them on a ship and turned them loose on a deserted island miles away for Saint Domingue to fend for themselves.

This was just another example of the reign of terror by the Rochambeau administration. They would mass execute victims on ships by tying sacks of flour around their heads and dropping them in the ocean to drown – hundreds at a time, asphyxiation by the makeshift gas chamber ship, indiscriminate executions by firing squads, ruled the day.

Amid all of this, Rochambeau saw no harm. The complexities of war, he would tell himself and others, are not for the faint-hearted.

As the sun dipped below the horizon, casting long shadows across the charred remains of the cane fields, insurgent leaders, including maroons, local chieftains, deserted officers who had amassed men and weapons, and others all gathered in secret to discuss their strategies. Their faces were illuminated by flickering candlelight, each one a testament to the determination and defiance that had fueled the rebellion thus far.

Jean-Jacques Dessalines, his dark eyes scanning the room, took in the faces of those who had organized and sustained the resistance against Leclerc independently but were now refusing to forge a common alliance.

"Brothers and sisters," began one of the leaders, an older man with graying hair and a voice like thunder. "Our struggle has reached a critical point. The French are losing control of the colony, and they know it. They have turned to desperate measures – including the restoration of slavery – in an attempt to quell our uprising. We must not let them succeed."

A murmur of assent rippled through the assembly. Another leader, a tall, imposing woman with a regal bearing, stepped forward. "We have fought for our independence, for our right to live as free people. Our beliefs and values – our voodoo, our culture – have brought us this far. Our world view has developed apart from that of you Générals because we had no real place in the Louverturian society that Toussaint had forged. You are an extension of that Dessalines."

Dessalines clenched his fists at his side, growing increasingly frustrated. He knew these laborers' independence and resistance to his leadership threatened his power. As he watched them speak passionately of their goals, he felt a tightening in his chest. Despite their shared enemy, he could not ignore the fact that some of them— those who refused to submit—had become obstacles and therefore had to be liquidated.

"Enough!" Dessalines snapped, cutting through the murmurs of disagreement and heated discussion. "I understand your desire for independence, but we must remain united against the French. If we are divided, they will take advantage, and all our sacrifices will be for nothing."

"Général," the older man replied, his eyes narrowing. "We respect you and your fighting skills, but we cannot ignore the fact that some of us feel threatened by it and your attempts to assert yourself as our leader. We fight for liberation from the French, and the freedom to live as we see fit – without interference from the likes of you or others who would impose their views upon us."

Dessalines glared at the man, his thoughts racing. He knew he could not afford to lose control of the rebellion. His reputation, his power – everything depended on it.

"Any who stands in the way of our shared goal of freedom will be dealt with accordingly," Dessalines said coldly. "If you oppose me, you oppose the future of our people."

As the room fell silent, the tension between the leaders and Dessalines hung heavy in the air. The candlelight flickered ominously, casting eerie shadows across the faces of the insurgents.

True to his statement, in the weeks that followed, Dessalines would begin the elimination of any who did not bow to the indigenous army. Unity had to be established and these gangs of brigands needed to be dissolved or united under one central command that he was leader of.

As the weeks wore on, the situation grew direr for the French soldiers. April 1803 brought news that sent shivers down their spines; in Grand-Anse, their last stronghold, a new insurrection had erupted, led by masses of black plantation cultivators and local officers. They burned the region and spread their rebellion with a fierce determination that seemed impossible to quell.

"Mon Dieu," Captain Duval muttered as he read the latest dispatch, detailing the severity of the situation in Grand-Anse. "Twenty-five to thirty thousand black laborers are revolting!"

"Capitaine?" a soldier questioned, his face etched with concern. "What can we do? We cannot fight such numbers."

Captain Duval looked out across the barren landscape, his eyes filled with despair. In his heart, he knew that their final effort to subdue the rebel forces was all but futile. Yet he could not bring himself to admit defeat.

"Every last one of us joined this fight knowing the risks," he said quietly, his voice thick with emotion. "We must continue to press on, it is our duty."

As the sun set over the once-fertile plains, now reduced to ash and ruin, the French soldiers steeled themselves for the battles to come. Weakened by a shortage of food and disease, they faced an insurmountable challenge. But in the darkest depths of their desperation, they clung to the hope that somehow, they might yet emerge victorious against the relentless tide of rebellion that threatened to engulf them.

By May, supplies for the army, including munitions, clothing, boots, and food, had slowed to near nothing as Napoleon recalled most ships of the Navy in preparation for war with England. Soldiers of the army were ordered to forage for food and fend for themselves.

Under the merciless blaze of the sun, French soldiers stumbled through the scorched smoke-smelling landscape, their faces gaunt with hunger and exhaustion. Their uniforms hung like tattered rags from their emaciated bodies, evidence of the hardships they had endured in their fight against the rebel forces. The air was thick with the scent of death, a constant reminder of the yellow fever that ravaged their ranks and weakened them further by the day.

"Capitaine, we need food," one soldier rasped, his voice little more than a whisper. "We cannot continue like this."

Captain Duval, a once-proud officer now reduced to a hollow-eyed shell of his former self, nodded grimly. He knew that without sustenance, his men would soon be unable to fight at all. "I will see what I can do," he said, his voice cracking with fatigue.

Desperation drove the starving French troops to seek aid from an unlikely source: the very women they had sought to subjugate. Swallowing his pride, Captain Duval approached a group of local women gathered at the town's marketplace to barter for food.

The women only spoke the local Creole language, so Duval brought with him a translator named Olivier to explain he was willing to trade whatever munitions they could spare for rice, beans, and cornmeal.

No one wanted to trade, they wanted cash. The last woman in the market regarded him coldly, her eyes hard as she assessed the desperate soldier before her.

"Please," he implored, holding out a handful of bullets in exchange for a meager portion of rice and beans. "We are starving."

"Di blan an ban m kòb pou manje m! Di li tou yon jou la p dou kou nou," replied the woman as she turned to deal with another customer.

"What did this one say, Olivier?" Duval asked the translator.

"The same as all the others in the market, "Tell the white man to give me money for my food. Plus, she added a warming, "one day you'll be as submissive as we are today," Olivier replied. "But that woman over there says that there is a woman crazy enough who may be interested. She imagines herself as a French soldier, but everyone knows she's bloody nuts."

"Where is this woman?" asked Duval, ready to deal with anyone who could give them food, crazy or not.

"They sent a young boy to run and get her. Her name is Défilée-La-Folle"

"La Folle? The Crazy?" Duval said, trying not to get his hopes up with the promise of a crazy woman, even her name spelled crazy. But he had to hold onto hope. There was no way they could hang on any longer if they didn't get food right away.

An hour later, Défilée-La-Folle, the crazy woman, arrived. She was fat, ugly, and acting strange, waving her head from side to side as if possessed and speaking erratically as she spoke. Duval's hopes were sinking fast.

"She wants to know how much food you need," Olivier said to Duval.

"How much does she have to sell,… I mean trade?"

Olivier asked the woman who replied, *"Konbyen fizi, bal, poud fizi, ak bayonèt blan an geyen?"*

"She's answered you with a question of how many rifles, shots, powder, and bayonet that you have, of course, throwing the 'white man' line in there as well," Olivier translated.

"Tell her I can get a lot. I have access to many arms," Duval said to the woman, slowing his speech so she could understand, which appeared that she didn't.

"Kisa blan an di?" she asked Olivier.

"What did she say, Olivier?" asked an impatient Duval

"She wants to know what you said." Olivier ignored Duval and answered the woman with what Duval had said, *"Blan an di li ka jwenn anpil. Li gen aksè a anpil zam"*

"Di blan an pou l la aswè a lè solèy kouche ak tout sa l genyen. Map pote tout manje mwen genyen e nap wè si nou ka fè komès."

Oliver turned to Duval, impatiently waiting for the translation. "She says Tell the white man to be here tonight at sunset with everything he has. I will bring all the food I have, and we will see if we can trade."

"Tell her alright. I will meet her back here." Can we trust a crazy woman? Duval wondered. I have no choice,

Duval and Olivier arrived at the back of the market near sunset, and waited almost two hours for the crazy woman to arrive. Finally, steering a horse-drawn wagon, and slowly creeping down the road, she came towards them. Duval's heart soared when he spotted a second wagon behind her driven by another woman.

"Thank God, here she is!" Duval exclaimed, his excitement driven by his desperation and hunger. His last meal was a banana peel that morning. Without money, no one would trade with the soldiers of France.

Défilée-La-Folle – Défilée the Crazy, as she was known, halted the wagons and jumped out, quite effortlessly for a woman her size. She approached the men, as she swaggered her head back and forth, stopped, addressed Olivier, and said, *"Ou gen zam yo."*

"Olivier, what did she say? Duval excitedly asked.

"She wants to know if we have the guns."

Olivier looked at Défilée, *"Wi, nou gen zam yo. Ou gen manje a?"* Yes, we have the guns, you have the food?

Défilée looked back at the wagons and swaggered her head towards them. Duval rushed towards the first wagon and lifted the tarp to reveal a dream. Sacks of rice, cornmeal, and beans filled the cargo bay. There was enough there to feed all his men for at least a week if rationed correctly.

He then went over to the second wagon, pulled the tarp, and found it equally full, but this time with sacks of coffee, sugar, bananas, plantains, yucca, potatoes, crates of neatly stocked eggs, and at least two dozen live chickens quietly resting in crates. Behind the wagon were two goats, obviously fat and well-fed, tied by rope.

Tears began to flow from his eyes. He wiped them away so Défilée wouldn't see as he turned to face her and Olivier.

He went to his wagon and pulled back the tarp for her. There she found a cache of rifles, muskets, and ammunition. She looked at Olivier, *"kote rès la"*

"What's she saying?" Duval quickly asked, sensing the woman was not pleased.

"She wants to know where the rest of it is?"

"Tell her that is all she gets, it's more than enough!"

Olivier translated what Duval said and Défilée loudly sucked her teeth in defiance, shrugged her shoulders, turned towards the wagons, and began to walk there. As she was boarding the first one to leave, Duval shouted, *"Attendez!"*

"Olivier, tell her I will give her half a wagon more for her load. This wagon and another one half as filled!" Duval frantically said, his exertion at these negotiations almost making him delirious from hunger.

The wagons began to move once Olivier finished translating what Duval had said. Duval pulled out his loaded musket and began to march towards Défilée to confront her when suddenly half a dozen armed women came out with rifles pointing at him. By their handling of the weapons, Duval easily ascertained they were trained professionals. A platoon of women soldiers! He stopped and holstered his firearm.

"Sanble se blan an ki fou," Défilée said to Olivier.

Duval looked at Olivier who without waiting for a question said, "She thinks you're crazy, and so do I."

"Tell her I accept the deal," Duval said as he turned and whistled in the wind. Another wagon pulled up with a French soldier driving it and stopped. Défilée went to the wagon, inspected it, and nodded to Olivier.

"Nou pral fè echanj kabwèt," she announced.

"She says we will exchange wagons."

"Exchange? Our wagons are in much better condition than hers!" Duval exclaimed.

Défilée went to the wagon and came back with a crate in her hand. She laid it on top of the first wagon, as Duval and Olivier's senses heightened from the sweet scent of charcoal steam coming out of it, causing their stomachs to growl. She unveiled the cloth that covered its contents.

Within the crate was a large plate that contained a huge piece of beef, grilled to perfection, and covered with onions. Duval thought he was going to faint when he caught the full breadth of the charbroiled aroma, with the meat oozing with juices, infiltrating the cooked potatoes and carrots to its side. Enough meat to feed twenty at least, more if rationed. He looked up at Défilée and smiled, "You crazy bitch," was all he could muster.

In perfect French, instead of Creole this time, she replied with a huge smile, *"Toi aussi tu est un fils de chienne!"* You also are a son of a bitch! Défilée then turned, mounted the first of the two French army wagons as her associate, and the women soldiers, mounted the second and drove off, leaving Duval, Olivier, and the two soldiers ravaging the food like a pack of wild dogs in the back of the market.

At sunrise, Défilée had arrived back at camp to unload the stocks of munitions. Défilée-La-Folle was a sulter for the new indigenous army, selling her wares from the back of her wagon.

"You did well," Défilée," greeted the man with a deep familiar voice.

Défilée grinned from ear to ear as the man inspected the arms, seeing that there were over fifty firearms for his recruits, all in good condition that he could tell, plus shot and powder.

"I won't ask where you got these as it doesn't matter. The question is, can you get more?"

"Volonte BonDye," Général Dessalines, *"Volonte BonDye"* – God willing, Défilée replied.

Jean-Jacques Dessalines looked at Défilée-La-Folle and smiled with a broad grin as she returned a smile to him.

"Here, drink some more, Henriette Saint Marc said to the French soldier lying on the bed next to her as she passed him a goblet of warm red wine. He was stark naked, drunk, and sexually satisfied by the prostitute he loved to visit most.

Henriette finished rolling tobacco into a clope, the slang name for cigarettes of the day she loved to use, lit it, and took a drag before passing it to Edgar.

"Merde, you are so good to me and so good for me," Edgar said as he accepted the clope, already soaked with Henriette's rouge lipstick. He put it to his lips and relished the scent of her perfume co-mingling with the smoke of the tobacco.

Henriette let Edgar enjoy the clope as she poured another goblet of wine for them. After he was finished with the tobacco, she took a tiny sip of wine, handed it to Edgar, and said "Go ahead and gobble this down quickly. I want to fuck you again."

Edgar smiled a broad smile and gulped the large goblet of wine in seconds with the anticipation of another session of love. And what a session it was, one he would remember for a long time.

After she had finished bringing him to a climax, he collapsed on his back and said, "God, you are so good, Henriette."

"Only for you, Cherie," she lied.

"Don't I wish it were so," Edgar said, knowing that she was available to any man who was willing to pay her exorbitant price, but she was selective even then too. Tonight, he had booked an entire overnight, costing him a full month's pay.

Henriette snuggled close and began kissing his hairy chest, licking his neck and touching her nipples against his face. After a while, knowing there was no way he could produce another erection for a few hours, she rolled another clope and sat up in bed, her back to the headboard. "So what news is there of Paris, Cherie?" she asked.

"A ship's just come in and boy there is news indeed," Edgar said laughing.

"Really? What news? I know everything going on in Paris and it is all rather dull and mundane right now."

"I wish I could tell you, but I cannot," Edgar said, dragging from the clope and handing it back to her.

"Now, you hurt my feelings, Edgar," she said, pouting as she did so, bringing the clope to her lips.

He looked at her and couldn't help but marvel at her beauty. She was born to a black slave mother who raised her after being neglected by the white official who impregnated her. Her smooth olive skin, shiny hair, and bountiful body made her a money maker at the bordello.

Henriette grew from humble beginnings, with the advantage of being a daughter of a top white government official, giving her privileges toward relative freedom around town.

Her father left Saint Domingue, and her mother had died several years ago. To earn money, she had been hired by Madame Babbet as a cook, but soon began trading sex for money until the Madame of the house let her become one of the professional girls.

She was still pouting when Edgar said, "If I tell you, you must promise this remains between us. It has not yet been officially announced."

"I promise," Henriette said in a sheepish voice, still holding onto the pout, and acting out one of her routines of imitating a teenage girl. "I will not tell."

"Toussaint Louverture is gone," Edgar said.

"I, and everyone else already knows that, Edgar. That is no secret. He is in France. But no one knows where."

"Not that gone, Henriette. He is dead, and buried."

"Toussaint Louverture is dead! Oh my God! If those ex-slaves find out, they will go fou! Insane I tell you," she said.

"That is why they don't want it revealed," Edgar said.

"How did he die? Guillotine? Firing Squad?"

"Nothing that dramatic. They stuck him in jail at the Fort-de-Joux prison in Doubs. It's nasty cold in the Alps. Didn't give him a fire, so he got sick and just died. They froze him to death, I hear."

"When?"

"Last month, early April," Edgar informed.

Henriette looked away for a moment and a tear let loose from her eyes and rolled down her cheek. She had known Toussaint and was fond of him. She is, or now was, a strong ally and asset of Toussaint and his army as a spy, using her influence and charms on the French men to access their military plans, weapon locations, and other secrets in support of Toussaint, and now Jean-Jacques Dessalines. She had always hoped Toussaint could find his way home, but now that would never be.

Henriette would one day be hanged for spying on the French for the revolutionary army, but now she just wiped the tear from her eye, turned to Edgar, and said, "Tell me more, tell me everything…"

The May sun blazed mercilessly over the town of Arcahaie, its rays glinting off the bayonets of the assembled rebel forces. It was the final day of a 3-day conference that entailed an assessment of each of their forces' capabilities to once and for all vanquish the French forces from the island by organizing into the Armée Indigéne, the Indigenous Army.

Dessalines and his associates had brilliantly united the various factions of the army into a galvanized fighting force. He had to admit that Henry Christophe, whom he had always chided for being a *Nèg*

Kay, had skillfully utilized his diplomatic skills in his parlays around the island to create this coalition. Without him, Gabard, and others, this assembly would have been virtually impossible.

The quickly assembled meeting, and further unification of the forces, had been bolstered by their members' collective anger when they had broadcast Henriette's intelligence report of the assassination of their famous leader, Toussaint Louverture. News as they knew it, as well as manufactured propaganda to incite anger, were widely circulated, and had achieved the desired effect of boosting their military enrollment. Toussaint had as many detractors as he did fans, but even to those who were not in favor of his policies, the fact that the French had killed their famed leader fed the flames of hatred. Now, forty-five thousand soldiers were organized and motivated into thirty divisions encompassing 23 Infantry, 3 Dragoon Calvary, and 3 Artillery, each with a competent commander and officers. They also had taken 17 forts in strategic locations.

Marie-Claire looked at her husband, Jean-Jacques Dessalines, beside her, proud of the man he was; immense strengths, and devastating faults, but she loved him unconditionally. She canvased the large barn on the property of burned-out fields of crops.

She recognized among the crowd were Générals Christophe and Pétion. Other officers she recognized were some that had defected from the French army; Boyer, Geffrard, Clerveaux, Vernet, Gabard, Bazelais, Gérin, Bonnet, Roux, Boisrond, Capois, the soldier couples of Louis and Marie-Jeanne Lamartinière as well as others she could not recognize.

No civilians were present and conspicuously absent were any representation from the leadership of maroon forces. The maroon rebels were mostly African Bosals – first-generation slaves brought to the colony who had escaped to the mountains. They trusted no one and acted independently of any other groups, and wanted it to remain so. They rejected any form of structural command outside of their own organizations and were unwilling to share power in their respective territories – even with other maroon bands like themselves. As such, they skirmished with their insurgent counterparts in this room and scorned the conference they were invited to.

The group present was constructively lively, and engaged in loud discussion, talking over each other until she saw her husband stand. A hush fell upon the crowd as Général Dessalines stepped forward, his imposing figure dominating the room.

"Enough!" Dessalines roared, his voice thundering like a clap of divine wrath. "No more will we be shackled by foreign colors that do not represent the blood, sweat, and tears of our people!"

With a swift, determined motion, Dessalines tore the white fabric from the French tricolor, threw it to the ground, stomped his huge army boot on it, then picked it up and threw it in a heap of trash.

"Catherine! Come up here", he shouted across the room.

Towards the back, a good-looking petite woman stood and began to walk towards Dessalines as the crowd watched, wondering who she was. Her name was Catherine Flon, the daughter of textile traders who imported fabric from France and had a store in town. They had taken a liking to Dessalines years ago, when he was just a boy of 14, as he helped around the store. He was chosen to become Catherine's godfather. Growing up, she was always smart and resourceful, became a seamstress, and launched her workshop by the time she was twenty-five, employing several apprentices.

As Flon arrived to the podium, Dessalines handed her the blue and red sections of the mutilated flag, smiled at her, and turned to the crowd. "Catherine Flon is a daughter of this town of Arcahaie. She is skilled at sewing. She will create our flag in the proper proportions and replace the white with equal parts of the Red and the Blue. This will symbolize the unity of blacks and mulattoes against our white oppressors!" he shouted!

A cheer erupted from the crowd, echoing across the scorched earth.

"By this flag, let us forge our destiny!" Dessalines proclaimed his eyes ablaze with passion. "Let us stand together against those who would see us subjugated once more!"

"Kreyòl, m'ap swete ou sèman!" Creole, I swear to you one of the black Générals shouted, stepping forward to swear allegiance to Dessalines. His dark eyes locked onto those of his newfound leader, and in that moment, a bond was forged that transcended class and color.

"Kreyòl, m'ap swete ou sèman!" a mulatto Général echoed, joining his comrade in vowing loyalty to the man who had brought them together. All around them, others followed suit, pledging their lives to the fight for freedom.

As the multitude of voices rose in unison, Dessalines gazed out upon the sea of faces, his heart swelling with equal parts pride and trepidation. If they fail, it will be a bitter end. But if they succeeded, the thought sent a shiver down his spine, they would make history as only the second nation in this hemisphere to throw off the chains of colonialism after the newly minted United States.

"Ansanm nou fò!" he shouted, his voice ringing with conviction. "Together we are strong!"

"Ansanm nou fò!" the crowd roared back, their voices carrying across the hills and valleys of their ravaged homeland, *"Ansanm nou fò! Ansanm nou fò! Ansanm nou fò!"*

Surrounding the barn, where hundreds of followers were waiting and hoping for this unity, took on the chant in chorus. They were hungry for a fight to secure their freedom and that of their children and their children's children. The chant then roared on throughout the land *"Ansanm nou fò! Ansanm nou fò!, Ansanm nou fò!"* could be heard through the fields as thousands joined in.

For the first time in generations, there was hope. Later that day the newly created flag of their movement, sewn quickly by Catherine Flon, fluttered proudly overhead, modified with an added saying; *"Vivre Libre ou Mourir"* Live free or Die, a symbol of hope, defiance, and determination that burned brightly against the darkening sky.

Later, when they had adjourned that evening, and the crowds departed for their camps, the drums of the hills continued to spread the *"Ansanm nou fò!"* chant of solidarity throughout the land and into the deep of night.

"Général, come quick. We need to know what to do!" yelled a hurried soldier to Dessalines as he came out of his tent at the camp.

"What is it?" barked Dessalines.

"Whites. There are whites outside the camp marching here with a white flag of surrender. What do we do, kill them or let them enter? It may be a trick!" said the scared soldier.

Dessalines went to the edge of the camp and looked through the spyglass. In the distance, there had to be a couple of thousand soldiers marching towards them, but not of the tricolor of the French, but more of a white and blue in their uniforms. "Saddle my horse, at once," Dessalines ordered.

Dessalines rode out with a dozen of his men to meet the approaching army also with a flag, but instead of a white one, they flew the Red and Blue flag of their new army, flapping in the air. He arrived at the men leading the army and stopped Galipòt a good distance from the main group.

A dozen men on horseback with the white flag on its staff left the main contingent of their force and rode towards Dessalines and his men. Dessalines suspiciously looked upon them as they arrived.

The man who began to speak was obviously not white, but of mixed race, "I am Général Władysław Franciszek Jabłonowski, commander of the Polish Legion of Saint Domingue."

Dessalines looked at him strangely. "I am Général Jean-Jacques Dessalines, commander of the 4th Regiment of The indigenous Army of Saint Domingue. You cannot be who you say, as you are not white," he said. "All Polish Legionnaires are white."

"I beg to disagree, mon Général. I am the exception. I was the first Polish man of color to be accepted into the Polish Legionnaires.

"How so?" asked Dessalines, curiosity gripping him.

"My father is Konstanty Jabłonowski, a powerful Polish Aristocrat and a nobleman.

"A black nobleman, impossible," Dessalines snickered. "There are no aristocrats of color, and obviously by your dark skin, it cannot be hidden. Is your father black or mule, a mulatto?"

"Neither. He is white." Jablonowski responded.

"So, your father had a taste for the fury of a black woman, eh?" Dessalines laughed.

"No, my father has never taken a black woman. My mother is white."

Dessalines turned to his men, smiled, and changed from French to Creole and said; *"Ki sa blan sa a ap eseye fè m vale?"* what is this white man trying to have me swallow?

"You are an imposter," Dessalines stated with all seriousness. "You speak in riddles. After all this conversation, I am more confused now than when you uttered your first sentence,"

"My mother is white, an English woman. She had a love affair with a black man. Then I was born. She confessed to my father. He took a liking to me and raised me as his own. He pulled strings to get me into the Polish Legion, I excelled, and here I am. Does that clear up this business of race and color, or should I write it down for you if you still do not understand, if you could read that is?" Jablonowski rudely stated, irritated at the course of the conversation.

Dessalines pulled his sword out of its sheaf and held it high, as did Jablonowski, "You dare speak to me in that tone, Blanc!" yelled Dessalines as his men pulled out their swords as did the men of Jablonowski.

"I come in peace and this is my reception?" Jablonowski yelled back.

Dessalines looked at the man, smiled, sheafed his sword, and said, "I like you, Jablonowski, you've got balls."

"Maybe you will grow on me someday also," he responded in the form of an aristocrat.

"Dessalines roared in laughter, turned to his men, and barked *"Mete sab nou nan fouro!"* Put your swords in their sheath!"

Dessalines' men sheafed their swords as did those of Jablonowski. "State your business," Dessalines ordered.

"We were sent to this island by First Consul Napoleon with over 5,000 legionnaires. They told my government it was to help put down a revolt of prisoners here in Saint Domingue. When we arrived and began our first battles, we soon discovered that this was a rebellion of ex-slaves fighting to keep their freedom, not prisoners as we were told. We were deceived." Jablonowski said.

"Go on," Dessalines ordered.

This is a very familiar situation for me, and us. Back in our homeland, we were also fighting for our liberty from the occupying forces of Russia, for the past 30 years. We joined because Bonaparte said if we were victorious, he would reward Poland by helping us to restore our independence. Just like you, we are trying to win back our freedom and independence through uprising."

"Very touching and I am getting bored of this conversation. What does this have to do with us?"

"Me and my legion are here to join you. Bonaparte is not a man to be trusted. We will fight with you to achieve the security of free men."

Dessalines dismounted from his horse as did Jablonowski. Dessalines reached into his saddlebag and retrieved a flask of *kleren*, strong unrefined rum. He then closed his eyes and sprinkled some of the liquid onto the ground which was quickly absorbed, unseen by Jablonowski. It was Dessalines' form of worship to the Gods of Voodoo to honor the dead.

He began to walk towards Jablonowski, who himself walked towards Dessalines as both their soldiers looked on curiously from either side. Before drinking from the flask, Dessalines handed it to Jablonowski, looked at him, and in a serious tone said, "Drink the blood from the veins of our land to seal our destiny, together."

Jablonowski looked at the flask and stared into the serious eyes of Dessalines, not knowing if this was some sort of African or island tradition; drinking blood to seal a bargain? Was it human or animal blood he thought with disgust but decided that he had come too far as to insult his new comrade in arms, if indeed this was an important ritual.

Jablonowski brought the flask to his lips, "bottoms up," he whispered, and without reservation gulped down the liquid rapidly. He suddenly felt a burning sensation in his throat, relieved that it was not blood at all, but a strong unrecognized mixture of alcohol. He was thankful he was able to keep from coughing it up and spitting it out. He handed back the flask to Dessalines, instantly feeling the drunken charge of the strong alcohol race through his veins.

Dessalines bellowed a loud, hearty laugh at Jablonowski's expense, took a long swig of the *kleren* himself, sealed the flask, and offered his hand to Jablonowski, who too began to laugh. Jablonowski took the huge hand of Dessalines to his and together they sealed a friendship and partnership as comrades toward the military conquest of a mutual enemy. The Poles would prove honorable in their fight.

The summer of 1803 continued with devastating heat and death toll on the French army throughout the island. As Rochambeau became more desperate in his measures, the French soldiers continued to falter under the weight of war, disease, and famine.

On the other hand, the unified rebel forces pressed onward, fueled by an unshakable belief in their cause. And though the path was fraught with danger and uncertainty, they marched on, united beneath the banner of their hard-won freedom, with continued success. In August, Dessalines marched towards Jérémie in the south.

The sun dipped below the horizon, casting a fiery glow across the sky as it surrendered to the creeping darkness. Jérémie, once a bustling French stronghold in the South, now stood eerily silent, its streets emptied of soldiers and filled with the shadows that stretched across the cobblestones.

"Move quickly," Dessalines whispered, his eyes scanning the abandoned buildings for any sign of movement. "We must not let them escape."

His men nodded, their faces grim and determined as they moved through the town like ghosts, weapons at the ready. The air hung heavy with tension, charged with the anticipation of an unseen enemy.

"Général," a voice called out softly from behind him. It was one of the mulatto officers who had sworn allegiance to him back in Arcahaie. "What do you think they'll do next?"

Dessalines paused, considering the question. "They are desperate," he said finally, his voice low and measured. "And desperation makes men unpredictable. But we will be ready for whatever they throw at us."

As they reached the port, the last light of day faded away entirely, leaving only the cold glow of the moon to illuminate the scene before them. In the distance, the silhouette of a ship could be seen on the water, its sails flapping wildly as it struggled against the current.

"Merde," Dessalines cursed under his breath, watching helplessly as the vessel crested the mouth of the harbor in its escape. "We were too late."

The indigenous army continued their victories with Pétion taking Port Républicain and Christophe besieging Cap Français, as well as other commanders pounding French targets. On the 17th of October, 1803, the town of Les Cayes fell as the revolutionary army marched into the heart of the town. Sweat trickled down Dessalines' brow, but he refused to wipe it away, his focus solely on the task at hand.

"Général, the French have retreated," a young soldier announced breathlessly, his uniform stained with sweat and dirt. "Les Cayes is ours."

"Have our men secure the perimeter," Dessalines replied, his voice steady despite the heat. We don't want any surprises."

"Oui, mon Général," the soldier saluted before disappearing into the throng of soldiers and villagers, who had emerged from their homes to join the celebration.

"Finally, retribution is within our grasp," Dessalines thought, allowing himself a fleeting moment of satisfaction. But deep down, he knew there was still much work to be done before they could claim true victory.

"Ansanm nou fò," he murmured under his breath, his resolve strengthening with each word. "Together we are strong."

"Mon Général!" A voice shouted, snapping Dessalines from his thoughts. It was one of the officers who had accompanied him to Les Cayes. "The French have left a message for you. They say they will return with reinforcements."

"Let them try," Dessalines spat, his eyes narrowing in defiance. "We will always be ready for them."

"Oui, mon Général," the officer responded, nodding with determination before hurrying off to deliver the news.

As the sun dipped lower in the sky, casting the town in an eerie orange glow, Dessalines stood tall amidst the chaos, his heart swelling with pride and determination. The road ahead had been long and treacherous, but if they stood together, victory would soon be there's. "Ansanm nou fò."

Twenty

BATTLE OF VERTIÈRES

Vertières
November 1803

The air was thick with tension, as the forces fighting the expeditionary troops had already claimed most of the land, and all the larger cities, including Port Républicain, Saint-Marc, Gonaïves, Les Cayes, Jérémie, and Jacmel. The French clung to their last strongholds in the north like drowning rats in the hold of a sinking ship; to the west, Môle St. Nicolas, held by the iron-willed Général Noailles, and Cap-Français to the east, where the formidable and brutal, Général Rochambeau commanded 5,000 troops, around 2,000 stationed at Fort Vertières.

"Général Rochambeau, I hope you have a plan," said a young officer, his voice wavering as he scanned the horizon with a spyglass for any signs of movement.

"Patience, Lieutenant," Rochambeau replied, his eyes fixed on the horizon from his perch at the fort of Vertières, situated just south, less than 5 kilometers, of Cap-Français. "We still hold strategic locations. The enemy will not find it easy to take them from us."

"Oui, mon Général," the lieutenant muttered, unconvinced as he watched the sun slowly rise, casting a blood-red hue across the sky.

Rochambeau could sense the fear in the young officer, but he knew that such sentiments were shared by many among his ranks. It had been nearly two years since they arrived on this island expecting an easy victory, 3 months Napoleon had predicted, but the indigenous forces had proven more resilient than anticipated, and the unexpected scourge of yellow fever forced the hospitalization and death of so many French troops.

As they stood atop Vertières, Rochambeau considered the situation. He knew that holding onto Cap-Français was essential for maintaining a semblance of control over the territory. He also knew that the indigenous forces would eventually regroup and attack - it was only a matter of time. However, he was in a fortress and commanded 2,000 battle-hardened men, a sizeable amount that could not be easily dislodged by any army, much less an army of ex-slaves.

Things had gone wrong this cursed year. What he had anticipated to be an easy task to quell the rebellion through force, fear, intimidation, subjugation, executions, and downright cruelty had only further emboldened those whom he sought to tame. They used his tactics against him to rally the population to insurrection against the government.

Then, to make matters worse, England had once again declared war on France. What little supplies he could beg for from central command were being attacked by two British Navy squadrons that had also enacted a blockade of the principal northern ports, Cap-Français and Môle-Saint-Nicolas, forcing inconvenient debarkation of the cargo at secret inlets around the island. Damn the British, Rochambeau thought.

"Général," the lieutenant began again, "I've heard whispers among the men. They say we're losing this war, that it's only a matter of time before we're overrun."

"Enough!" Rochambeau barked, silencing the officer's doubts. "We are French, Lieutenant. We do not cower in the face of adversity."

"Oui, mon Général," the lieutenant replied, shame coloring his cheeks.

"Ensure the men are prepared for battle, Lieutenant," Rochambeau said after a moment of contemplation. "If the enemy dares to challenge us, we'll give them a fight they won't soon forget."

"Oui, mon Général," the lieutenant responded, saluting, and hurrying away to relay the orders.

As the sun continued its ascent to usher in a new day, Rochambeau steeled himself for the battles to come. He knew that the fate of Saint Domingue hung in the balance, and he was determined to do everything within his power to ensure victory for his forces.

On the morning of Friday, November 18, 1803, the sun had barely peeked over the horizon. Général Dessalines surveyed the scene before him, his heart swelling with pride as he observed the 15,000-strong indigenous army prepared to fight for their freedom.

He then turned and looked at the fort up the hill, rising tall and imposing, its stone walls shimmering in the red light of the dawn. Cannons protruded from its sides, ready to fire deadly rain upon any attackers. The flag of the French flies high atop the Butte Charrier, a symbol of their power over the land, so they think, Dessalines thought.

"Today we make history, my brothers and sisters!" Dessalines roared, his voice echoing through the ranks. "We will break through the line of defense, seize control of the fort, and end the French presence in Saint Domingue for good!"

"Oui mon Général!" came the thundering reply, a sea of raised fists and determined faces.

"Pa gen manman!" shouted Dessalines.

"Pa gen papa!" shouted back the troops.

"Sa ki mouri?" Dessalines roared.

"Zafè ya yo!" roared back the troops.

"di m ankò... Sa ki mouri?" Dessalines repeated the roar, tell me again...

"Zafè ya yo!" roared back the troops.

"Denye fwa... Sa ki mouri?" Dessalines roared, last time...

"Zafè ya yo!" roared back the troops.

"Général Capois," Dessalines called, turning to the most intrepid of his Générals, "you will lead the first attack."

"With honor, mon Général," Capois responded, his eyes burning with unyielding determination.

François Capoi, or Capois-la-Mort, Capois the Death, had been nicknamed by his comrades for his intense bravery. Without hesitation, he turned and barked out orders, rallying a demi-brigade to his side for what he and all knew was a dangerous mission.

As they advanced, their footsteps fell in unison, a drumbeat of defiance against the tyranny of the French forces. The first violent volleys of cannon fire tore through the air, leaving a trail of destruction in its wake. Capois gritted his teeth, pushing his men forward even as the ground shook beneath them. They pressed on, undeterred by the hailstorm of lead and iron.

"En Avant!" Capois roared, urging his warriors onward. But soon, the overwhelming barrage from the fort took its toll. The demi-brigade reeled under the onslaught, their ranks decimated after nearly two hours of fighting, their muskets out of range for delivery. Blood and dirt mixed, staining the earth a dark crimson.

"Retreat!" Capois cried, desperation clawing at his voice. They pulled back, nursing their wounds and their pride. Capois surveyed the carnage, his heart heavy with the weight of loss. Hundreds of soldiers, men and women, lay lifeless on the field, their dreams of freedom extinguished in an instant.

At the bottom of the hill, Capois rallied his shell-shocked troops, their fearful eyes still trained on the ominous fort that loomed above them. Giving them no time to calculate their odds of surviving this battle, he yelled "Forward!" as he unsheathed his sword, raising it high before him. His remaining warriors roared their approval, ready to risk everything for the cause they held so dear.

"Forward! Forward!" Capois cried, his voice cracking under the strain. But his conviction remained unwavering; they would take this fort or die trying.

His men, weary but resolute, followed Capois' lead. They knew that the end of the war was hinged upon this battle, as their leader, Général Dessalines, had promised. And so, they charged forth once more, steel biting into flesh, gunfire tearing through the air.

Dessalines ordered reinforcements to Capois'. The men surged forward, bolstered by Capois's steadfastness. They crossed another bridge as though it were but another step on their journey to freedom. Dead and dying littered the ground, their bodies entangled in a morbid embrace. Horses collapsed under the weight of their burdens, their agonized whinnies piercing the cacophony of battle.

"Stay strong, mes frères!" Capois encouraged, his mind racing with the weight of responsibility. "Remember what we are fighting for! Our families, our country, our freedom!"

With each man who fell, another took his place – a testament to the undying spirit of the indigenous army. Capois felt the heat of battle and the exhaustion that threatened to claim him, but he trudged onward, driven by the knowledge that this was their moment, their chance to finally break free from the shackles of oppression.

But again, they were unsuccessful on the second charge, again a third attempt failed as Dessalines kept sending men to his side. The French troops had expertly mounted defenses to avoid certain death if overrun. Capois once again called retreat and they assembled at the bottom of the hill. The battle had ensued for five hours.

Dessalines' eyes narrowed as they lingered on the weary faces of Capois and his men. Their once vibrant uniforms were now tattered and stained with blood and mud, a testament to their valiant efforts in the fight. The scent of gunpowder hung thick in the air, mingling with the coppery odor of fallen soldiers.

"Capois," Dessalines barked, his voice tinged with urgency. "Pull your men back. You've fought well today, but it's time for young Général Gabart to take the reins."

Capois replied with a nod, his chest heaving from exhaustion, and disappointed in himself. He turned to his remaining troops, bellowing out orders for them to regroup and fall back.

At 27 years old, Louis Gabart was Dessalines' youngest general. He had supported Dessalines from the very beginning of his assent to head the Armée Indigène and was instrumental towards galvanizing the troops of the Artibonite and Western regions to support the new flag design.

Together they had fought to conquer Mirebalais, St-Marc, and Port Républicain. It was during this battle that he met Alexandre Pétion, who was on St-Gérard hill with the artillery. Pétion explained to him the art of the cannon, and together with Cangé of the 21st regiment, conquered Fort-Bizoton, much to the credit of Pétion's artillery. Pétion then showed him how to set up a battery on Fort-Mercredi hill.

Dessalines knew this and tapped the young Gabart to exploit these skills against Fort Vertières. "Hit them all at once!" Dessalines shouted over the noises of battle, his words punctuated by the roar of gunfire. "Don't give them a chance to concentrate their fire!" Gabart nodded in understanding. "Now go," Dessaines ordered.

The sound of boots pounding against the earth filled the air as Gabart and his unit moved towards the hill, determination etched across their faces. Dessalines watched as they launched their attack against the French-held blockhouses on the forts other side, his heart swelling with pride and hope.

Gabart directed his men to spread out and engage the enemy in hand-to-hand combat to take a hill that would give them a good vantage point to haul up their cannons. As Dessalines observed their progress, his thoughts raced with strategy and tactics, each move calculated to bring them closer to victory.

Gabart's men, weary from an hour of brutal hand-to-hand combat, had finally secured the coveted position. The price had been high, but victory was now within their grasp.

"Ring it with mounds! Make it a fortress!" Gabart shouted to his men, the words barely escaping his lips before they were swallowed by the wind. He watched as his soldiers hurriedly shoveled dirt, creating a makeshift barrier to absorb any incoming fire from the French at Fort Vertieres.

"Sir, artillery is in position as you had instructed," one of his lieutenants called out, wiping blood from a gash on his forehead. Gabart nodded, his gaze fixed on the distant fort. The structure loomed menacingly against the backdrop of the dying day, a bastion of defiance that would soon crumble beneath their might, he swore.

"Fire at will, Lieutenant," Gabart commanded, his voice steady despite the adrenaline coursing through his veins. "Let's show those dogs what we're made of."

"Ready... Aim... Fire!" the lieutenant bellowed, and the deafening roar of cannons shattered the relative silence that had fallen over the battlefield. Artillery shells whistled as they soared through the air like deadly birds of prey, their lethal payloads hurtling towards the enemy stronghold.

With each thunderous blast, Gabart felt both exhilaration and dread. He knew that every shell that struck its target brought them closer to victory, but each explosion also carried the weight of lives lost and futures erased. It was a burden he bore as both a leader and a soldier, one that never grew lighter.

"Keep firing!" Gabart ordered, his eyes never leaving the fort. "We'll hammer them into submission if it takes all night!"

His men followed his command without hesitation, their determination fueled by the hope of a swift end to the conflict as more and more men labored to bring cannon and powder to their location. The battle waged on.

Capois looked at his soldiers, then at the battlefield. Easily 1,000 of the men he had led into battle lay dead before him. He struggled with his inner self as to what to do next. These men had sacrificed so much, and their comrades had paid the ultimate price. Lost in thought, Dessalines approached him.

"You have tried, Capois. It is time to call an end to your day.

"Général Dessalines, I must try again," Capois gritted through clenched teeth. "I cannot allow their deaths to be in vain."

"Capois, you have already pushed your brigade to the brink," Dessalines warned, concern creasing his brow. "You cannot ask more of them. They have no more fight left. Look at them, they're exhausted."

Capois knew this to be true. "Then I shall find others who are willing to fight," Capois declared with steely determination. He turned on his heel, seeking out fresh troops to join his cause.

"Major Delva, assemble your battalion!" Capois barked at a nearby officer. "You will join us in our assault on Vertières."

"Of course, Général Capois," Delva responded, a fierce gleam in his eyes and honored to be asked. "We are ready to fight."

Mounting his trusty steed this time, Capois took a moment to center himself, drawing in a deep breath to quell the fire that roared within him. Surprising himself with renewed vigor, he advanced toward the hill for the fourth charge, this time with the brigade of Delva.

The world seemed to narrow down to the sound of his heartbeat, pounding in his ears as he led the brigade up the hill for the fourth time. He dug his heels into the flanks of his nervous horse, urging it forward through the haze of smoke, death, and confusion that filled the battlefield.

"Forward! Forward!" he cried again and again, his voice hoarse from shouting. His men followed, their faces a blur of determination and fear as they fought for every inch of progress.
Suddenly, there was a deafening blast, and the ground beneath them shook violently. Capois' horse had been hit, crumpled beneath him, and threw him to the ground with a sickening crunch. As he struggled to rise, the searing pain in his chest almost overwhelmed him, as if some great fist had punched him with all its might. The world tilted around him as he looked to the right and realized that his horse had been struck dead by a cannonball, his faithful steed lifeless on the ground, blood streaming from it.

"Général!" one of his men shouted, his face a mask of horror as he rushed to Capois' side, still lying on the ground.

Capois struggled to get a grip of himself, still dizzy from the fall, as cannons echoed around him and the sounds of war raged. "Get...up," Capois gasped, ordering himself as his vision swam in circles as he struggled to rise. "Must... lead... them... forward," his words struggling towards the unrecognized soldier at his side.

His fingers found the hilt of his sword, and with a surge of adrenaline, he pulled himself to his feet. His body screamed in protest, but he would not let his wounds hinder him, not when so much was at stake.

"Forward! Forward!" he roared once more, gripping his sword tightly as he limped back to the head of his men. All eyes widened at the sight of their battered Général, but they steeled themselves, preparing to follow him into the fray once more.

As they charged, a sudden gust of wind whipped across the battlefield, carrying with it the stench of gunpowder and death. It tore at Capois' clothes, ripping his tricorn—garnished with plumes—from his head. He glanced up just in time to see it carried away by a shot from a French soldier at the fort.

"Damn them!" Capois thought, anger rising within him like a tidal wave. But he would not be deterred, not when victory was so near. "We will take this fort! We will show them that we cannot be defeated!" he shouted to his men, giving them renewed courage.

"Forward! Forward!" he bellowed, his voice breaking through the din of battle as his men followed him with renewed vigor. Their hearts were set aflame by their Général's indomitable spirit, and they knew that they would fight to their last breath to secure their liberty.

"Death to the oppressors!" he bellowed, his voice carrying over the clamor of clashing steel and the crackle of gunfire. His soldiers echoed his sentiment, their voices joining together in a chorus of defiance as they neared the fort.

Firing from the fort began to cease and the silence provided a theatrical and eerie suspicion to the scene.

"Bravo! Bravo! Bravo!" came the unexpected cries from the French fort, echoing through the battlefield like a wave of admiration. "Hold your fire!" Rochambeau could be heard shouting repeatedly, "Hold your fire!

As the cheers and clapping rang out with shouts of "Bravo" from the French soldiers, the firing from the fort ceased, as did from Capois' brigade. The air, once thick with the acrid smoke of gunpowder, cleared, and the clamor of war seemed to dissipate as though it had been swallowed by the earth. At that moment, the battle stilled, and an eerie silence settled over the field.

"Is this their way of mocking us?" Capois pondered, his brow furrowing as he tried to discern the meaning behind the sudden change.

"Général!" cried Major Delva, breaking him from his thoughts. "What shall we do? Do we continue to fight or take advantage of this pause?"

"Stay your weapons, but remain on guard," Capois ordered, his voice steely and resolute. "We will not be baited into making a hasty move. We shall see their true intentions soon enough."

"Understood, Général!" the soldier replied, passing on the order to his comrades.

A gate at the fort burst open and a wild stallion whinnied and barged forth from it with a rider bearing a flag of truce. As he reached Capois and Delva, the dust kicked up by the horse's hooves swirled around them as the beast snarled at Capois who could not help but admire the animal's proud, determined gait.

It was the strangest of scenes; the Frenchman's approach was a testament to the battle-hardened respect that transcended the lines drawn in the sand between them. It was as if the three, Capois, Delva, and this staff officer of the French army, could have been friends in a different set of circumstances.

"Général Rochambeau sends compliments to the Général who has just covered himself with such glory!" the French officer bellowed, his voice managing to carry over the lingering echoes of the battlefield to the men of Capois. He offered a crisp ceremonial and respectful salute, the sun glinting off the brass buttons of his uniform.

"Thank you," Capois replied, his chest swelling with a mixture of pride and defiance. He returned the salute, "this changes nothing you know," Capois said as he watched the French officer wheel his horse around and gallop back towards the fort. This was no surrender – the fight would resume as before, he resolved.

"Prepare yourselves!" he commanded his men in anticipation. A barrage of weapons being readied filled the air, mixing with the shouts and murmurs of the soldiers. They were battered, but far from broken.

As Gabart rallied the reserves on the other side of the battlefield, French captain Jean-Philippe Daut ordered the grenadiers to form their ranks for a desperate charge to Capois' army approaching the fort. Their bayonets gleamed menacingly in the late afternoon sun, casting ominous shadows across the churned earth as the fort's main gate opened to eject them.

This is it, Dessalines thought with excitement. They've exposed themselves out of the fort. This is our chance to end this once and for all.

"Charge!" Daut roared, and the grenadiers surged forward with a tide of steel and gunpowder. But they had underestimated the resolve of those who fought for their freedom.

With a deafening roar, Capois and Général Clervaux raced into the fray. Clervaux brandished a captured French musket, its barrel still smoking from recent use, and his epaulet dangling raggedly from his shoulder, torn away by a bullet's close call.

"Push them back!" he shouted, his voice hoarse but unwavering.

The battlefield erupted into chaos as the two forces collided. Dessalines gritted his teeth, his hands clenched into fists at his sides as he watched from a distance. We cannot falter now, he thought, his heart pounding in time with the clash of steel on steel. This is our moment. He so missed not being in the fray.

"Général!" Several hours later, Gabart cried out, his face streaked with blood and sweat. "They're retreating!"

"Stay vigilant," Dessalines warned, not yet allowing himself to hope. "Do not let them regroup."

But it seemed fate had other plans. The sky turned black and a sudden downpour swept across the battlefield, fat raindrops splattering against armor and turning the earth to mud beneath their feet. Thunder cracked overhead like the report of a cannon, and lightning split the sky, casting an eerie glow over the carnage below.

"Fall back!" Rochambeau's voice echoed through the storm, his words barely audible above the howling wind. "Regroup at Vertières!"

"Let them go!" Dessalines ordered, watching as the enemy retreated into the darkness. As the rain soaked through his clothes and mingled with the blood and sweat on his face, Dessalines allowed himself a small, triumphant smile.

Rochambeau observed the ugly canvas below. Blood and mud intertwined, staining the hillside crimson with nearly 3,000 corpses of young French, mulatto, and black soldiers littered across the once green landscape, now a grotesque testament to their unyielding determination.

"Général," a voice called out, snapping Rochambeau back to the present. He turned to face Captain Dufresne, his aide-de-camp, who had approached with urgency etched across his weathered face. "They're not stopping, sir. They come wave, after wave, and now they are assembling more troops at the bottom of the hill to launch another attack after the rain subsides, I presume."

Rochambeau stared hard at the scene before him, his brow furrowed in deep thought. The air was thick with the sickly-sweet stench of death, a constant reminder of the price they had paid thus far.

"Général Rochambeau," another weary officer approached him, his uniform soaked from the rain, "We're running low on ammunition. We won't last much longer at this rate."

"Damn it all!" Rochambeau cursed under his breath, his chest tightening with frustration. He glanced one more time at the valiant insurgents, their unwavering resolve mirrored in the faces of his troops. It was clear they would not give up, even in the face of insurmountable odds, and an inventory of their dead lying on the ground.

Taking a deep breath, Rochambeau slowly released his clenched fists. The reality of the situation had finally sunk in, as clear as the setting sun on the horizon. They were facing an enemy that would not stop and were unafraid to die in the process. It was time to face the truth – they could not win this battle.

Rochambeau hesitated for a moment, the stakes higher than they'd ever been before. A thought suddenly occurred to him; he recalled the escape of the rebels from the fort at Crête-à-Pierrot - a cunning plan that may be his answer here.

"Listen closely, Pascal," Rochambeau said, his voice firm and resolute. "We'll make our escape tonight under cover of darkness and hopefully continued rain."

"Sir?" Pascal asked, seeking reassurance in his Général's eyes.

"Trust me, Pascal," Rochambeau replied, his gaze never wavering from the lieutenant's face. "Sometimes, a hasty retreat can lead to greater victories."

"Very well, Général," Pascal said, saluting sharply. "I will relay your orders to the men."

A strange calm had come to the battlefield after the initial volley of rain. It had forced a pause in the fighting and occasionally the moans of the dying could be heard in the wind. The first droplets of a new rain splattered against Rochambeau's face, cold and unyielding, but no downfall as of yet. The storm brewed above them, a torrential downpour waiting to be unleashed once again upon the battlefield. He could feel it in his bones, the lighted electricity in the air that signaled the imminent deluge.

"Général, the storm approaches," said Pascal, his voice strained and raw from hours of commanding their forces.

"Indeed, it does," Rochambeau replied, "and with it comes our chance for escape. Under the cover of this storm, we will slip away from Vertières on the other side of the hill, unbeknownst to them," Rochambeau explained, his voice barely audible over the howling winds. "We have been defeated, Pascal. Saint Domingue is lost to France."

As if on cue, the skies opened up, unleashing torrents of water upon the beleaguered soldiers below. The battlefield transformed into a sea of mud and blood, making movement nearly impossible. But the chaos provided the perfect opportunity for Rochambeau's plan.

"Order the men to move out, Pascal," he commanded, gripping his lieutenant's shoulder with conviction. "Tell them to use the storm to their advantage. Let it cloak our retreat."

As the heavy rains swallowed them whole, Rochambeau and his men pulled back from Vertières, disappearing like ghosts into the night. The battle, and the fort, was lost, but their resolve remained unbroken. They would live to fight another day, and perhaps, find redemption in the process.

November 20th dawned with an uneasy stillness, the air thick with anticipation and lingering smoke. Rochambeau had sent a messenger with a flag of truce and requested a parley with Dessalines.

Later that day, the terms of Frances's departure from Saint Domingue for good had been concluded. Dessalines stood in the room, his fingers tracing the edge of the parchment on which the peace treaty lay, its ink barely dry. Rochambeau's signature scrawled across the bottom seemed to taunt him, a reminder of the French Général's stubborn refusal to admit defeat until this very moment.

"Général Dessalines," Rochambeau addressed him, his voice strained but steady. "The terms are clear. My garrison and population shall evacuate Cap Français within ten days, as you have agreed."

"Very well," Dessalines replied, his eyes never leaving the document. The weight of this decision settled heavily upon him, but he knew it was necessary for the good of Saint Domingue. He looked up at Rochambeau, meeting the Frenchman's gaze unflinchingly. "You have my word that your people will not come to harm as they depart our shores."

"Merci, Général." Rochambeau inclined his head slightly, a gesture of resignation rather than gratitude. No handshakes between the enemies were offered or exchanged.

As Dessalines watched the French retreat from the room, he couldn't shake the feeling that there was more at play here than met the eye. Are they giving in? Or is this just another strategy? He considered these questions as he rolled the parchment between his hands, the distant cries of seagulls echoing in his ears.

"Général Capois!" a voice called out, and Capois turned to see a small delegation of French soldiers approaching, flying the flag of truce, their faces etched with fatigue and respect. Behind them, they led the fine-looking steed ridden by the French officer yesterday that Capois had admired. Its coat was glossy, despite the ravage of war, and fully caparisoned; decked out in rich decorative coverings and colored ribbons".

"Captain-Général Rochambeau offers his compliments and this horse as a mark of admiration to the 'black Achilles' to replace his that the French army regrets having killed" the officer declared, extending the reins toward Capois.

Rochambeau recognizes our strength and bravery, Capois thought to himself, feeling a strange kinship with the enemy he fought so fiercely against. But we will not be swayed by gifts, nor shall we forget our cause.

Capois painfully stood from his injuries, "Tell your Captain-Général that I accept his token of admiration, but it changes nothing," Capois replied, taking the reins and looking the French officer in the eye. "We will continue to fight any enemy who dares attempt to subjugate us once more."

The French soldiers nodded solemnly, understanding the depth of conviction behind Capois' words. They saluted once more before retreating to their lines, leaving Capois with the magnificent animal that would carry him into battles yet to come.

The sun dipped low over the horizon, casting the battlefield in a reddish glow as the scent of gunpowder and sweat still lingered in the humid air. Dessalines stood atop a small hill, his eyes scanning the landscape littered with the remnants of war. The French had finally been driven away, and it was time to reclaim what was rightfully theirs.

"Général," called one of his officers, Captain Lucien, approaching him with a determined stride. "We have secured the last of the French strongholds. What are your orders?"

Dessalines narrowed his eyes, focusing on the ruined fort in the distance, and the carnage of 5,000 dead soldiers on the ground. "Take command of every battery, fort, and barracks that had been previously occupied by the French, and arrange for the proper burial of these heroes on the ground.

"Oui, mon Général." Lucien nodded, turning to relay the orders to the other officers.

"Wait," Dessalines said, halting him with a raised hand. "There is one more thing. The French had with them not only their weapons but also their diseases. Yellow fever has claimed far too many of our people already. I want these facilities cleansed completely to prevent any lingering transmission of any other illness."

"Of course, mon Général," replied Lucien, his face grim but understanding. "I will see to it personally."

"Good. We have suffered enough at the hands of the French. It is time to turn the tide." Dessalines' voice was laced with conviction, each word fueling the fire within his soul.

As Lucien departed to carry out his orders, Dessalines allowed himself a moment of introspection. So much blood had been spilled in the name of freedom, and yet, there was still so much to be done. They needed to rebuild, to reestablish their identity as a nation free from colonial oppression.

"Is this truly the beginning of a new era?" he wondered, his thoughts heavy with the weight of responsibility and loss of life to arrive to this day. Or is it merely a fleeting victory in an endless battle?"

"Only time will tell," he whispered to himself, his gaze fixed on the horizon as the last rays of sunlight vanished beneath it.

The following day, the sun dipped low toward the horizon, glowing over the choppy waters as Dessalines stood on the shore, the wind whipping his coat about him. In the distance, he could see the British squadron cutting through the waves like a school of predatory sharks, their sails billowing from the Caribbean breeze.

"Général Dessalines," a voice called out behind him. He turned to find Lieutenant Baptiste approaching, the young man's eyes wide with a mix of awe and apprehension as they too took in the sight of their unlikely allies.

"Britain has certainly come to our aid," Dessalines noted, unable to suppress a small smile at the thought of the French fleet being decimated by their shared enemy. "I never would have expected such fortune."

"Neither did I, sir," Baptiste admitted, watching the British ships as they prowled the seas off the coast. "But we must seize every opportunity that comes our way.

"True," Dessalines agreed, his gaze hardened as it returned to the sea. "Prepare the men. We cannot afford to waste any time now that the British are here. Our enemies must know that we will fight until our last breath, and that includes the British, if they desire to take advantage of the French departure."

"Understood, Général," Baptiste nodded, saluting before turning on his heel and sprinting off to relay the orders.

Dessalines watched him go, then returned his attention to the British ships. As much as their presence bolstered his spirits, he couldn't help but feel a nagging sense of unease. Britain was no friend to the people of Saint Domingue – they were merely using this conflict to further their agenda in their war against France. But for now, their goals aligned, and Dessalines would use that to his advantage.

Rochambeau was ready to depart on the 25th of November, his ships crammed with thousands of soldiers and French refugees who had collaborated with the French. However, the British squadron blocked all of the escape routes. Rochambeau sent a message to the British squadron requesting that his fleet be allowed to safely evacuate the port and return with his men to France. He assured the British that he was neither obliged nor equipped to engage them.

Commodore John Loring aboard the *HMS Bellerophon* refused, requesting Rochambeau to surrender to the British navy, which he was forced to do.

The British took possession of all ships – 22 in all, except for 5 American-flagged ships that had come to assist in the evacuation. The ships were confiscated, and Rochambeau and the remaining military were taken as prisoners. The French refugees were placed on American vessels bound for Philadelphia. Général Rochambeau would end up spending the next 11 years in a British stockade.

Several days later, Commander Vincent Pourcelly with a battalion of Capois' 9th demi-brigade freed the city of Mole-St-Nicolas by defeating French general Louis Noailles, forcing his exodus on awaiting ships – also to be captured by the British. With the Department of Bas-Nord-Ouest liberated and void of French soldiers, the French military presence had been vanquished and the war had been won.

Twenty-One

INDEPENDENCE

Cap Français
November 1803

November 29, 1803, began as a beautiful and sunny day on the newly liberated land. Dessalines stood on one of the ramparts of Fort Liberté, his eyes instinctively scanning the coastline for any signs of renewed attacks. Today was to be a momentous occasion; the birth of their independence would be immortalized in ink and parchment. No better place than here.

"Général Dessalines, the other Générals have arrived for the meeting," informed Major Souverain, carefully approaching him with a respectful bow.

Immersed in thought, Dessalines did not answer immediately but registered the sentence. After a long pause, he politely and quietly said "Thank you, Major. Let us begin."

The assembly room was filled with the stately figures of his top twenty Générals. The blacks included *Christophe, Charéron, Boisrond, Capois, Gabart, Daut, François, Férou, Cangé, Ambroise, Herne, Brave, Yayou, and Roux.* Of the mulattos were *Clerveaux, Bonnet, Bazelais, Vernet, Romain, Geffrard, and Guérin,* each bearing the scars and tales of their hard-fought victories.

Conspicuously absent was Général Alexandre Pétion who was uninvited to the meeting by order of Dessalines. Dessalines had never gotten over Pétion's escape from Jacmel back in 1800, and his failure at capturing him throughout the Southern Peninsula – a grudge that Dessalines still entertained to this day.

As Dessalines entered, they stood at attention, a hush falling over the room, all eyes turning towards him expectantly. "Générals," Dessalines began, his voice commanding the attention of everyone present, "our years of struggle and sacrifice have led us to this day. The time has come to forge our Declaration of Independence and secure our rightful place among nations. Be seated and let us begin."

A murmur of agreement echoed through the room as the Générals took their seats around the large wooden table.

"Who among you shall take on the task of crafting the words which will define our new nation?" Dessalines asked, his keen gaze sweeping over the faces before him.

As the question hung heavy in the air, the Générals shifted in their chairs, their thoughts racing with the weight of such a responsibility. Most could read, and others could both read and write. Dessalines was aware of this, but no volunteers ventured forth for the task.

Realizing that none of them would come forward, Dessalines began, "Well then, before we put ink to words, let us gather our thoughts and ideas, and together, we shall craft the concepts we want to include in the document that will stand as a testament to our unwavering resolve and dedication to freedom."

The room buzzed with anticipation as the Générals began to discuss the principles and values they wished to enshrine in their declaration. Dessalines listened intently, his mind swirling with thoughts of the future that lay before them.

"Will our children look back on this day with pride?" he wondered silently, his heart heavy but hopeful. "Will they know that we fought not just for ourselves, but for generations to come?"

The air hung heavy with the weight of history as Dessalines turned his gaze towards Général Charéron. The man stood tall and proud, his face a mask of determination. He is a skilled master of the pen and his thoughts are always grounded in reality, he thought.

"Général Charéron," Dessalines called out, his voice echoing through the high-ceilinged room. "You are a skilled tactician and a trusted member of our ranks. I believe you have the fortitude to help us pen this declaration. What are your thoughts?"

The other Générals turned their attention to Charéron, waiting to hear what he had to say.

Charéron stood slowly, purposefully, as if formulating his next words carefully before speaking. "Perhaps," Charéron ventured hesitantly, "we should take inspiration from the American Declaration of Independence. Their emphasis on life, liberty, and the pursuit of happiness could resonate with our people."

A murmur of discontent rippled through the gathered assembly like an ominous wave. Général Vernet clenched his fists, his knuckles white to maintain composure. "We respect the American struggle for freedom," he said, his voice strained, "But we must be mindful not to emulate a nation that still clings to the abhorrent institution of slavery."

"Indeed!" Général Clerveaux chimed in, his expression fierce. "Our declaration must be a testament to our unique struggle and triumphs! To draw too heavily from the Americans would undermine our hard-won independence."

Charéron swallowed hard, feeling the weight of their disapproval pressing down upon him. He searched their faces for any hint of support but found none. In their eyes, he saw the fire of conviction, the unwavering belief that their path must diverge from that of their American counterparts. They were only the second nation in the world that he knew of, that fought to shed the shackles of their colonial masters and won. He understood.

"Very well," he conceded, his hand trembling slightly, "We shall forge our path, guided by the principles and values that have sustained us thus far."

The air in the room grew heavy, the tension between the Générals palpable. The scent of sweat and ink mingled with the damp stone walls, a testament to the grueling hours spent deliberating the precarious future of their nation. Charéron's hands shook as he penned the notes, the weight of their collective disapproval bearing down on him.

"Enough!" Boisrond suddenly roared, his voice echoing through the chamber like a clap of thunder. He leaped from his seat, eyes blazing with unyielding fervor. "We fought for our freedom, we bled for our independence, and we will not sully that by following the footsteps of any slave-holding nation! These ideas and discussions mirror too closely with the Americans!"

Heads turned, gazes locked onto the impassioned Général as he paced before them, his every step imbued with purpose. At that moment, Boisrond was a living embodiment of the fire that burned within each of them, the inextinguishable desire for true liberty.

"Let us be the first and only non-slave-holding nation in the Atlantic! Let us stand as the second, behind the United States, to reject colonialism by force, but let us surpass them by staying true to the belief that all men are created equal, that means all men and women, regardless of skin color!" His words charged the air, igniting a flame within every soul present.

"Look at the United States," he continued, his voice growing stronger, fueled by the conviction that coursed through his veins. "They proclaim themselves defenders of freedom, yet they violate their promise to their people. Blacks remain bound in chains – beaten, subjugated, and raped – by the very nation that professes to protect them in their founding document. It is a farce!"

The room trembled with the intensity of his words, every heart pounding in unison. Boisrond's fierce gaze swept over his comrades, challenging them to defy the truth of his proclamation.

"We are better than that," he declared, his voice ringing with the promise of a brighter future. "We will make a declaration of truth and justice for our people to lead to a new constitution, one born from the depths of our struggles and triumphs, untainted by the hypocrisy of a nation still shackled to the horrors of the past, to one of slavery."

A resounding chorus of cheers erupted from the assembled Générals, their fervor matching that of Boisrond. As they stood, united in purpose, the room seemed to expand, as if to accommodate the sheer force of their collective resolve. At that moment, it was clear that they would stop at nothing to forge a new path, unmarred by the sins of those who had come before them.

"Let us begin anew," Boisrond said, his voice steady and unwavering. At that moment, Charéron, and each of the Générals, knew that they were embarking on the journey of creating a truly just and equal society, led by those who had fought for it with every fiber of their being.

The room burst into a thunder of applause, led by Charéron who stood in ovation.

As the applause died down, Dessalines who had been quiet in observation of the varied discussions up to now, stood, his eyes locked on Boisrond. The intensity of his gaze seemed to pierce through the layers of excitement and anticipation that filled the room. All eyes followed him as he traversed the chamber, his stride purposeful and measured.

"Boisrond," Dessalines said, his voice deep and resonant. "You have spoken with eloquence and passion. You have illuminated the path we must take." He paused for a moment, allowing the weight of his words to sink in. "You are the one to fulfill our promise, the one to pen our desires on parchment, the one to create the limestone foundation for the future of our new nation."

A murmur of approval rippled through the assembly, but Boisrond's reaction was more subdued. His chest swelled with pride, yet beneath it, a kernel of uncertainty took root. Is this really what I want, he thought, wrestling with self-doubt at the bottom of the steps of this enormous undertaking? What if I fail them? For a fleeting moment, the enormity of the task at hand threatened to overwhelm him.

"Thank you, Général Dessalines," Boisrond said, forcing a smile to mask his inner turmoil. "I am honored by your faith in me."

"Your words have inspired us all," Dessalines replied. "Now, it is time to put them into action."

With a determined nod, Boisrond turned towards the table where Charéron had been working. As he approached, he noticed the parchment covered in hastily scribbled notes, remnants of a discarded ideological approach. He took a deep breath, steadying himself for the challenge ahead. He pushed aside Charéron's abandoned musings and laid out a fresh sheet of parchment before him.

"Let us create something entirely our own," Boisrond whispered, more to himself than to anyone else.

Charéron stood and extended his hand. "My thoughts were misplaced, Boisrond. You have enlightened me and have given me the torch I need to see our path forward. Take my quill and ink. They are my gifts to you as gratitude on this momentous day. You would give me great honor if you use them for your task ahead."

Boisrond shook Charéron's hand and took the seat adjacent to Charéron's. He dipped the quill into the inkwell, feeling both the weight of responsibility and the thrill of possibility race through his veins as the fresh ink of true freedom bled onto the page.

"Remember," Dessalines said, his voice resonating throughout the room. "We are not only writing for ourselves on this day but for generations to come."

Boisrond exhaled slowly, allowing Dessalines' words to bolster his resolve. He could not falter now; the fate of their nation rested in his hands. As he began to pen the first lines of their declaration, a newfound confidence swelled within him, self-doubt had been extinguished. With each stroke of the quill, he vowed to create a constitution that would embody the spirit of freedom, justice, and equality for all.

It was late afternoon, and the sun was beginning its journey towards retirement on the horizon, Cap Français on December 31st was alive with happiness, trepidation, and hope. The streets thrummed with anticipation for the new year, as people danced and sang, their laughter ringing through the air like a chorus of bells. It was a scene of pure jubilation, one that had been missing for far too long.

Rochambeau and his soldiers, along with their brutality, had finally left, allowing the city to breathe a collective sigh of relief. The wounds they had inflicted were still raw, but the people were determined to heal, rebuild, and forge a brighter future as they had done before.

"Can you believe it?" Marie asked Jean, her eyes sparkling with excitement as she watched the celebrations unfold from the second-floor veranda of the Bayard home. "The French army is gone! We can finally have our lives back."

Jean nodded, his gaze lingering on the remnants of destruction left by the war. "Yes, it's hard to believe," he said softly, his voice barely audible over the din of the festivities. "After all this time, we can begin to heal. Let's take a walk, it's still early enough."

Marie wrapped her arm around his, feeling the weight of the past months lifting ever so slightly from her shoulders. "And just think of how much stronger we'll be, now that we've faced such adversity together."

As the couple strolled through the streets, taking in the sights and sounds of their newly liberated city, they couldn't help but feel a renewed sense of hope for what lay ahead. For the first time in ages, the future seemed bright, full of possibility and promise.

But beneath the laughter and music, an undercurrent of unease pulsed. Jean could sense it, like a whisper on the wind, as he observed the planters who had collaborated with the French. They moved through the crowd with forced smiles and sat at the cafés with their eyes darting around nervously as if fearing some unseen threat.

Marie, long accustomed to reading her husband's thoughts, asked, "Will they be targeted for retribution?" Marie whispered into Jean's ear, her breath warm and her brow furrowing with concern.

"Time will tell," Jean replied, his gaze following a group of planters as they huddled together in quiet conversation at the corner café across the street. "But for today let them worry. They have been part of the problem for far too long. We, on the other hand, have earned our celebration."

Marie nodded, though she couldn't shake the uneasiness that clung to her like a shadow. The rebuilding city spread out before them, the scars of the fires of 1802 still visible in the charred remains of buildings, the scaffoldings climbing towards the sky. Progress was slow but steady, and every day brought new achievements.

As they walked through the cobblestone streets, hand in hand, Jean couldn't help but feel a swell of pride at the resilience of the people. The sounds of hammers striking nails would continue late into the night, the smell of fresh-cut wood, and the sight of determined hands working tirelessly to restore the city were constant reminders of their indomitable spirit.

"Look at them," he muttered under his breath, nodding toward a group of laborers hauling bricks. "They've suffered so much, and yet they persevere."

"Isn't that what life is about, Jean?" Marie asked softly, squeezing his hand. "Perseverance, even in the face of adversity?"

Jean looked down at their entwined fingers, feeling the warmth of her skin against his. He thought about the trials they'd endured together, the fear and uncertainty that had threatened to engulf them in darkness. And yet, here they were, standing on the precipice of a new beginning, cozy in the love of their relationship that had matured like fine wine.

He looked at his wife, still beautiful after all these years, the lines on her face only elevating the beauty of the spirit within, the experience, the wisdom, the knowledge, the love. Fifty-two years on earth had been kind to her.

"Perhaps," he mused, a small smile tugging at the corners of his lips. "But I think it's more than that. It's about hope."

"Hope," Marie repeated, her voice barely audible above the clamor of the city. "Yes, I suppose that's what this is all about, isn't it?"

Jean raised their clasped hands to his lips and pressed a tender kiss to the back of her soft, warm, hands. "And may we never lose sight of it."

The sun dipped low in the sky, casting a warm golden glow over the bustling city as they arrived at the entrance of their partially reconstructed Hôtel de la Couronne, feeling the weight of responsibility on his shoulders. He allowed himself a small smile as he surveyed the progress made since the devastating fire that had nearly consumed the building. The smell of sawdust and sweat filled the air, mingling with the distant scent of the sea. Sounds of hammers and chisels echoed through the structure.

"Mr. Jean!" called out an approaching worker, wiping his brow with a dirt-streaked hand. "We've just received word that the British blockade has been lifted. Our shipping business can finally resume operations."

"Ah, excellent news, Norbert" Jean replied, his heart swelling with relief. "Thank you for bringing this to my attention."

"Of course, sir," the worker nodded before returning to his duties.

Norbert was a supervisor at his dock operations. But for the past several months there have been no ships in need of unloading. The damn British would blow any ship apart if they tried to evade the blockade. His nine ships sat idle with maintenance as the only activity on them. Jean had repurposed all workers toward construction of the warehouses, hotel, and even his own home to keep their income flowing.

He thought about the debts he was now accumulating. Insurance had ceased coverage during the hostilities, but due to his credit history, banks were still flowing capital his way. We will work it out, he imagined.

Jean's thoughts raced as he considered the implications of their shipping business resuming. It would mean not only financial recovery, but also a chance to rebuild their lives and help the city recover from the scars of war. Yet, amid the potential for prosperity, uncertainty lingered in the air. Fear plagued the hearts of those who had collaborated with the French, wondering if they would be targeted for retribution.

"Jean?" Marie's voice pulled him from his thoughts. She approached from her walking inspection of the new dining room construction, her eyes searching his face for any indication of what was going through his mind.

"Marie," he said, taking her hands in his. "The British blockade is no more. Our ships can sail again."

"Really?" Her eyes lit up with hope, her wonderful smile a sight to behold. "This is... wonderful news!"

"Indeed," Jean agreed, though his smile didn't quite reach his eyes. "But we must remain cautious. The future is still uncertain."

"Uncertainty is a part of life, Jean," Marie said gently. "It will work out for the better."

He looked around at the city, its people working tirelessly to rebuild not only the Hôtel de la Couronne, but also businesses, homes, and their lives.

"Let us celebrate this small victory tonight, Jean," Marie suggested. "We deserve some semblance of joy after all we've been through."

"Very well," he agreed, squeezing her hands before releasing them. "Tonight, we shall toast to new beginnings."

As the sun dipped below the horizon and the sky turned a deep shade of twilight, Jean couldn't help but feel a flicker of optimism in his chest. Despite the uncertainty that lay ahead, one thing was certain: they had hope, and with hope, anything was possible.

The December moon this year was a long night moon due to its proximity to the winter solstice, marking the last day of the year, this December 31st, 1803, as the longest night of the year as well. Jean, Marie, and Junior, along with nearly 30 other family and friends were gathered on the second-floor veranda of their still unfinished Hôtel de la Couronne. Marie had insisted that the gathering be here as a sign of normalcy and promise for the future. Lumber and other construction materials were neatly tucked on the side and in corners, and the room was festively decorated. The table was made of lumber that would be later used for construction, but tonight these materials were requisitioned for the evenings celebration.

The gentle clink of glasses mingled with the satisfied sighs of those who had just finished an excellent meal to end the year of 1803.

"Ah," Jean said, leaning back in his chair and patting his stomach contentedly. "That was the best feast we've had in months." He turned to Marie and smiled. "Thank you, my love, but how did you pull this off?"

Marie returned the smile, her eyes dancing with pride. "I have my little secrets," she replied in her seductive, mysterious voice, "and you're welcome. I'm glad everyone enjoyed it."

"More than enjoyed," Junior chimed in, wiping his mouth on a napkin. "That was a meal fit for kings!"

As laughter rippled through the group of family and friends, Junior said, "Hard to believe the fighting has stopped, it feels like a dream."

"Indeed," Jean agreed, his thoughts turning inward. Can this peace truly last? he wondered silently.

"Look at them all," Marie said, her voice soft and full of hope. She gestured toward the people below, going about their business despite the lingering scars of war. "They're resilient, just like us. We'll rebuild, and we'll grow stronger."

Jean studied her face, marveling at her unwavering optimism. Her hope was infectious, and he found himself wanting to believe in a brighter future for them all.

"Time for me to make a toast," he suggested to the members of the table, rising from his seat with glass in hand. He looked at Marie; "To my wonderful wife and lifetime partner, her skills immense, her optimism infectious and just the right fuel we need to pursue new beginnings of hope," as Marie looked at him and smiled. Jean turned to the group; "And to Cap Français rising from the ashes once more.

"À votre santé et à la santé de la nouvelle nation!" To your health and the health of the new nation!"

"Salut!" the others echoed, clinking their glasses together and savoring a sip of the fine wine.

As the night deepened, the sounds of celebration filled the air. Marie had arranged for a string quartet of musicians, that once serenaded the hotel, to entertain their guests once more. And though Jean knew that there were still challenges ahead, for this one moment, he allowed himself to bask in the warmth of hope and camaraderie, embracing the promise of a new year with open arms.

An explosion of fireworks lit up the night sky, momentarily driving away the shadows of uncertainty. Everyone rose and went to the makeshift railing on the veranda to watch, side by side, as sparks of color rained down over Cap Français, igniting the joy and resilience that had long been smoldering within its people.

"Be careful of the rail," Marie warned. "It's temporary and was just erected this afternoon for tonight's dinner."

The fireworks lasted for twenty minutes and the sound of cannons from two visiting British war vessels replied in return, confirming the peace and cooperation between the new nation and Great Britain. As the fireworks faded, leaving trails of smoke in their wake, Jean couldn't help but wonder what the coming days would hold. But for now, he chose to revel in the hope that permeated the very air around them, believing - if only for a moment - in the promise of peace.

In the twilight of the night, after he and Marie had made equally explosive love to bring in the new year, Jean slid out of bed and opened the small door to the veranda adjacent to the second-floor bedroom. The scent of gunpowder still hung heavy in the air from the fireworks celebration that had lit up Cap Français at midnight. His thoughts drifted to the possible consequences of Dessalines' rule.

Marie came to his side, instinctively knowing his thoughts, "I know you and Dessalines have bad blood," said Marie, her voice laced with concern as she broke through the silence.

Jean clenched his jaw, recalling the dark days he had endured because of Dessalines' brutality several years ago. A cold shiver ran down his spine at the thought of facing off against the man once more, knowing all too well the lengths to which Dessalines would go in pursuit of power. Soon, in his position as a leading person in business, he would be required to deal with the man.

"Only time will tell," he replied after a long pause, forcing a smile for Marie's sake. "We must have hope."

Her hand found his, their fingers intertwining, standing shoulder-to-shoulder on the veranda as she leaned her head on his shoulder. Jean felt the tension in her grip, the unspoken fear weighing heavily upon them both, for she had suffered much during his months of brain dysfunction after Dessalines had nearly beaten him to death. She had saved him, he realized. She had given him his life, their life, back.

"Come," he said softly, guiding her back inside. "Let us not dwell on such matters tonight. Let us dance."

With a small nod, she allowed herself to be led into the candlelit bedroom, silently imagining the soft strains of a waltz drifting through the air.

As they moved gracefully around the room to her musical hum, Jean felt his apprehensions begin to ebb away, replaced by a fierce determination to protect what they had fought so hard to build. He knew that Dessalines' rise to power would bring challenges, but if there was one thing he had learned through years of struggle, there was nothing that could break the will and spirit of the Bayard family.

"Whatever comes our way," he whispered into Marie's ear, their bodies swaying in time to the music, "we will find a way to persevere."

"Promise?" she asked, her voice trembling ever so slightly.

"Promise," Jean assured her, his chest swelling with resolve. If there was one thing he could pledge without reservation, it was his unwavering devotion to the woman beside him.

Marie stopped the dance, "Then I shall hold you to that," Marie said, a hint of a smile tugging at the corners of her mouth, even as unspoken fears continued to flicker behind her eyes.

"Until the end of my days," Jean vowed, pulling her closer for an embrace that turned into a kiss of passion. When she pulled away, she stepped back, untied the string of her nightgown, and let the fabric fall to the floor, exposing her beautifully naked body.

Jean instantly became aroused as she said, "The celebration and the beginning of the next phase of our life is before us. Now, take me to bed, my husband, and make love to me."

The clock struck midnight in the dimly lit room, its hands heralding the dawn of a new year. New Year's Eve, 1803, found Napoleon Bonaparte, once again, in the company of his closest confidants – Générals Jean Lannes, Christophe Duroc, and Jean-Andoche Junot. Their faces were cast with shadows from flickering candlelight as they sat around a heavy wooden table laden with maps, papers, and half-empty glasses of wine.

"Another damned year," Napoleon muttered under his breath, his eyes fixed on the clock as if he could will time to slow down. "Saint Domingue is lost, and Rochambeau," he slammed his fist on the table, his voice choked with anger. "Rochambeau is now in the hands of the British! Merde to them!"

Jean Lannes, a loyal friend and fierce warrior who had fought many battles beside Napoleon, looked at him with concern. His brow furrowed, he leaned forward and rested his hand on Napoleon's shoulder. "We have faced great challenges before, Napoleon, we shall overcome this one too."

"Overcome?" Napoleon shook his head, the weight of the news crushing him, speaking to his three closest friends in somber tones he would never allow anyone else to witness, "this was not supposed to happen. My brother-in-law, Charles, was to complete his mission in three months. Instead, it's been over two years of fighting, killing him in the process, as well as twenty of my finest Généraux and senior officers. Now Rochambeau is in the clutches of the enemy, with no telling what secrets he will spill. We were so close to securing our presence in the Caribbean. France's *Perle des Antilles* lost under our watch. Disgraceful."

"Sometimes, the winds of fate change course, Napoleon," Christophe Duroc, always the voice of reason, said to try to soften the blow on his friend, his calm demeanor served as a counterbalance to Napoleon's passionate temperament.

"Indeed," added Junot, unable to contain his disappointment. "But the loss of Saint Domingue must not define us. We must learn from it and adapt."

Napoleon sighed heavily, running a hand through his hair. His friends' words rang true, but the sting of defeat still festered within him. "You speak wisely," he conceded, forcing a tight-lipped smile. "But I cannot help but feel the weight of this loss."

Lannes squeezed his shoulder reassuringly. "We all do, my friend. But we must carry on and now continue to fight the English dogs for our beloved France."

"True," Napoleon agreed, his eyes gleaming with determination as he looked at each of his friends in turn. "This setback shall not break us. We will rise from it stronger than ever. We will soon need to solidify our power as many enemies from within will attempt to use this loss against us, including the very Creole Grands Blanc planters who insisted on the reinstitution of slavery.

Let us not speak of this tonight, but soon we must circle back to the idea of France becoming an Empire, and I as its Emperor. This will solidify our vast power to restrain any challenge to our governance."

"Look at this!" Napoleon exclaimed suddenly, his finger stabbing at the map with undisguised frustration. "Saint Domingue, lost to us, forcing our sale of Louisiana to the Americans just to cover the costs of this damned rebellion, and still we lost!"

"The Louisiana Purchase has proven to be the best thing that could have happened to that new country – the United States, doubling her land mass overnight!" stated Junot.

Junot then questioned, "You know, they want to call their new country *'America'*, as if to hijack the term given to all the America's, only for them. Could it be they have that entire hemisphere eyed as their colonial empire, you think?"

"And we lost the opportunity to conquer her. Without the strength and proximity of Saint Domingue, the conquest of the United States… *America* as they want to call it, is lost to us. Never bring up our plans for this ever again. If word leaked out that we had plans for American colonization, it would cause diplomatic repercussions," Napoleon said angrily.

He pushed himself back from the table, anger crackling in his eyes. Christophe Duroc exchanged a concerned glance with Jean Lannes, while Junot remained silent, his gaze fixed on the floor.

"England is proving more formidable than we anticipated," admitted Lannes, his voice measured and steady. "But we must remember that our enemies have also suffered losses."

"Losses?" Napoleon scoffed, his face contorted with bitterness. "What do their losses matter when it is we who are paying such a high price for our efforts?"

"Perhaps we need to rethink our strategy," suggested Junot, finally lifting his head to meet Napoleon's heated gaze. "We cannot continue to throw men and resources at a losing battle. We must find a way to turn the tide."

Napoleon clenched his fists, his knuckles turning white as he fought to control his emotions. Inwardly, he knew they were right; something had to change. But the thought of admitting defeat gnawed at him, a bitter pill to swallow.

"Very well," he said after a long moment, his voice quiet but laden with determination. "We will reassess our situation and devise a new plan. We cannot – we will not – let England gain the upper hand."

"Agreed," Duroc replied, his calm demeanor a stark contrast to Napoleon's intensity. "We will stand together, and we will prevail."

"France depends on us," Lannes added, his words carrying an unspoken promise of loyalty and unwavering devotion.

The embers of the dying fire cast a flickering light across Napoleon's face, casting shadows that danced and twisted like the demons that plagued his thoughts. He stared into the flames, his mind turning over the possibilities, the *'what-ifs'* that haunted him as he considered the heavy price France had paid in Saint Domingue. The room was oppressive – silent save for the crackling of the fire and the faint clinking of glasses as his Générals sipped their wine.

"Mark my words," Napoleon said, his voice low and dangerous, "those coloreds in Saint Domingue will pay dearly for their rebellion. They have dared to defy me, and they will feel the weight of my wrath."

He could see Lannes and Duroc exchange glances, unease evident in their eyes, but none dared to question him. Not when he was like this, the iron in his voice promising retribution and ruin.

Junot ventured hesitantly, "Do you believe further punishment is warranted? Have we not already exacted a terrible toll on the island?"

Napoleon turned his gaze toward Junot, the firelight reflecting in his eyes, giving them an eerie, almost sinister glow. "They cost us more than you can imagine, Junot," he replied, his teeth gritted. "They must be made to understand the consequences for defying France."

"Of course," Junot acquiesced, bowing his head in deference.

Duroc regarded him solemnly, his thoughts hidden behind a mask of loyalty. "As you command, First Consul," he intoned, raising his glass in a silent toast to Napoleon's determination.

"Indeed," Lannes echoed, his voice thick with emotion as he too raised his glass. "The rebels will rue the day they ever defied us."

Napoleon nodded, accepting their pledges of support, but his thoughts remained dark and vengeful. The cost had been high, the losses unfathomable – and it would be only the beginning of the price those rebels would one day pay.

The night sky of New Year's Eve, 1803, was a canvas splattered with a thousand brilliant colors as fireworks illuminated the heavens above. The entire colony buzzed with elation and anticipation, a vibrant hum that could be felt in every corner of the burgeoning nation. It was a celebration unrivaled by any previous year – a testament to the resilience and hope of the people who had fought so fiercely for their freedom.

On the second-floor veranda of the military headquarters in Gonaïves, a party to celebrate their victory was ongoing. All of Dessalines's top officers were there, a coveted prize for each of them to have been invited. Plenty of food and wine flowed, generous gifts from American, British, and Danish merchants seeking to earn favor with the new founding fathers of the soon-to-be republic.

Dessalines steeled himself away from the festivities to get some fresh air. He was pleased with what he observed. There were ships in the harbor, rapidly resupplying the island with much-needed supplies. The British had been very accommodating with the sale of munitions to him over the past several months, knowing that they were fighting a common enemy. He had also reached an agreement earlier in the month to allow them free trade to all ports.

Marie-Claire's slender fingers slid beneath Dessalines' jacket from behind, seeking the reassuring solidity of his muscular frame. As her hand traced the contours of his body, she felt the raised scars of the ancient whip that crisscrossed his skin – a testament to the brutal existence he had once known as a slave. Her heart swelled with pride and admiration for her husband, knowing that he had fought to ensure that no one would ever suffer such indignity again.

"Jean-Jacques," she murmured, resting her cheek against his shoulder, "I cannot begin to fathom the depths of your pain, but I know how hard you've fought for this moment."

"Ten years," Dessalines mused, his gaze drifting back to the bay where the last vestiges of French rule had vanished like smoke on the wind. "For ten years, I thought I was free, but it wasn't until they were gone for good that I truly understood what freedom meant."

"Your strength and determination are what brought us here," she whispered, tightening her embrace around him. "And with each new day, we will work together to build a brighter future for our people."

At that moment, Jean-Jacques Dessalines knew that whatever challenges lay ahead, he would not face them alone. Together, as she promised, they would forge a nation from the ashes of Saint Domingue, united in their quest for liberty and justice.

An explosion of sound and light erupted in the sky as cannons from the forts and batteries of all cities and coastal towns signaled the arrival of midnight, and the birth of a new nation. The vibrant cacophony joined the chorus of laughter and cheers, creating an atmosphere of pure joy that was impossible to resist. The cannons of Saint Domingue were answered in unison by those of the visiting British warships in the harbor. No American warships visited, only merchants, a clear message that Thomas Jefferson, her president, was not at all pleased with ex-slaves creating a country so near his shores. After all, he is a slave owner himself.

Dessalines found himself swept up in the revelry, his senses overwhelmed by the sights, sounds, and smells around him. Every restaurant, bar, tavern, and watering hole had been filled to capacity with men, women, and children alike, all eager to share in the momentous occasion.

Inside the military headquarters, officers were celebrating and cheering. Glistening glasses clinked together in toast after toast, spilling their contents onto the wooden floors as people danced and sang with abandon.

"Look at them," Marie-Claire whispered into Dessalines' ear, her breath warm against his skin. "So full of hope and happiness."

His mind drifted to Toussaint Louverture. He wondered what his former mentor would have thought of this night, of the choices that had led them here. Would he have been proud? Or would he have seen it as a betrayal of his vision; peaceful coexistence and colonial ties to the French dogs?

As he and his wife stood on the balcony, their hearts beating in unison, Dessalines knew that the end of one era had given birth to another – a time of hope, growth, and above all, freedom.

"Tomorrow, Saint Domingue ceases to exist, forever," Dessalines said, his voice tinged with both sadness and resolve. "In its place rises a land built upon the ashes of the suffering and the hopes of our dreams. Unfortunately, the Taino and Arawak people didn't live long enough to see their homeland free from colonial oppressors, they were washed away from their land, and rendered extinct from civilization, by the Europeans. To honor them, we have decided to rename this nation as those indigenous people once named it – Land of Mountains - Ayiti"

Marie-Claire nodded, her grip on his hand tightening, the new name of the nation bringing pleasant goosebumps to her skin and a tear from her eye. "We will stand together, united in our pursuit for a brighter future." Her faith in him was unwavering, and it filled him with a renewed sense of purpose.

As the clock began to chime, marking the end of one year and the beginning of another, Dessalines felt a surge of determination course through him. This new era would not be without its struggles, he knew. But as long as they stood side by side, there was nothing they couldn't overcome, nothing they wouldn't accomplish, no power they wouldn't destroy seeking to enslave them again.

For tonight, amidst the pounding drums and swirling shadows, he could almost believe that anything was possible – that the people of a new republic of Ayiti, united by a common struggle and a shared dream, might finally forge a future free from the shackles of their past.

For tomorrow begins anew.

TO BE CONTINUED.

Subscribe for updates on future books in the saga.

www.TriumphToTragedy.com

EPILOGUE

The end of Saint Domingue arrived on December 31, 1803, on the last page of this book. The new Republic of Ayiti begins on January 1, 1804, on the first page of my next book. Book Four of the Triumph To Tragedy series is scheduled for release during the year of Haiti's 220th anniversary, sometime in 2024 wherein Jean-Jacques Dessalines must navigate the peace as well as he had prosecuted the war. Exciting stuff.

As I reflect on my education as a youth in the public school system of New York, I was taught that the Haitian Revolution was all about the slaves overthrowing their masters and becoming a free nation. Of course, I now know that this is but a fragment of what occurred.

The slaves had already experienced a near decade of relative freedom, as French Commissioner Léger-Félicité Sonthonax emancipated all slaves in Saint Domingue in 1793, later ratified by the French legislature in 1794 for all of France and its colonies. This is but one of the numerous misunderstandings of what the Haitian revolution was about and the events that led to the birth of the new nation.

The fact is that Napoleon Bonaparte was arrogant and put forth a flawed strategy that cost France the most valuable piece of real estate on earth, at the time.

In retrospect, with Saint Domingue, Napoleon had in place a system and government that was working, most would say quite well, under the administration of Toussaint Louverture. A relative peace and tranquility had finally arrived, and the government was in the process of rebuilding the economy, infrastructure, and its ability to effectively govern the citizenry. Diplomatic engagement with the Americans and British had trade on the rebound to circulate free cash amongst the citizens and taxes to the government.

Furthermore, Toussaint, on behalf of France, had finally unified the east and west of the island with happy citizens on the Spanish side eagerly anticipating the future of a united Hispaniola and the peace and prosperity that it would bring.

However, Napoleon's greed, arrogance, racism, short-sightedness, and his bowing to the pressure of wealthy absentee colonial landowners caused him to execute major strategic errors.

First, he was a racist that considered blacks and mulattos as sub-human and beneath him. His overall goal was to harness their productive capabilities, once again through the chains of slavery, as opposed to the engine of capitalistic motivation.

Second, he discounted the very same resourcefulness, ingenuity, and grit of the non-white citizens to succeed, prosper, build wealth, and reinvest in enterprises. He had no possible excuse for this miscalculation as there were thousands of examples of Gens de Couleur's who had already done so.

Third, he underestimated the fighting ability of local soldiers on their own turf, fighting to the death to resist re-enslavement. They were familiar with every square inch of terrain and able to employ guerilla-like warfare, lethal African battle tactics, and European military skills against their enemy.

Fourth, the French Army's arrogance and lack of on-the-ground military intelligence had them discount the local leaders' ability to build a powerful and organized army, with the formation of brigades encompassing infantry, cavalry, artillery, grenadiers, dragoons, and mountain troops. A total of more than 45,000 motivated men and women were recruited, properly organized, trained, and logistically equipped for battle, as well as auxiliaries encompassing maroon mountain troops.

And, speaking of women troops, these soldiers excelled in their fighting capabilities, with many becoming decorated heroes far outpacing the percentage of their male counterparts. In context, these women were engaged in combat, much to the bewilderment of French males, in the year 1802. In comparison, American women were only permitted by their male counterparts into the theatre of combat as recently as 2013 when the female ban on women in combat was lifted, over 200 years later.

Fifth, Napoleon chose the wrong leaders to execute his whims. Unlike French general Étienne Laveaux who understood the art of leveraging all human resources available, be it white, black, or mulatto, Napoleon chose his brother-in-law, young Charles Leclerc, and upon his death, a man many considered a certifiable maniac, Donatien Rochambeau, to make intelligent decisions to carry out his dastardly plans. Instead of forging the development of local black and mulatto resources, they alienated the local community of Gens de Couleur with their brutality towards them, leading an ever-increasing number to either join or collaborate with the Armée Indigéne, the rebel army, or as the French would sarcastically call them" L'armée *Cannibale" the Cannibal Army* as they were getting their rear ends handed to them.

And finally, the miscalculation of Yellow Fever. Napoleon had to have known that the disease was a serious threat to susceptible Europeans. Yellow fever had been around for years in the French colony, so why did the French army not take better precautions to limit the spread, and if infected, not have the basics in place to contain an epidemic?

French claims of death by the fever vary wildly from 20,000 to 50,000 of the nearly 80,000 persons sent to tame the island. I on the other hand believe that the exaggerated claims of casualties due to yellow fever are in large part inflated so as to limit the embarrassment of the French defeat by the so-called, inferior *"Cannibal Army"*. So, why not blame the deaths of tens of thousands of young French soldiers, as well as twenty generals, on some mysterious disease instead of the miscalculated incompetence of their leadership?

All in all, you can chalk up this faux pas in history as a complete debacle, and one that forever changed the trajectory of the Atlantic world. If Napoleon had better calculated his strategy and collaborated with Toussaint, instead of arresting him and having him killed, several different outcomes could have prevailed.

For one, he would have held onto the most valuable asset on earth at the time, the *Pearl of the Antilles*, with all its tax revenue in check. Leveraging a brilliant military asset in Toussaint, he could have embraced Toussaint's vision of a Caribbean basin economic system, and completed his own ambition to springboard an American invasion through Louisiana with Toussaint's 45,000-man strong standing army, 50,000 of his own troops, and utilized a ready-made force encompassing many of the half a million American slaves that were already upset that the ideals of America – *All men are created equal* – had never been, nor planned to be, implemented.

These American slaves would have been eager to join in a French-led United States slave rebellion headed by the great Toussaint Louverture whom they idolized. How could that have changed the course of history? For one, it would have negated the need for an American Civil War with 600,000 casualties, for starters.

However, we would now be eating croissants and drinking espresso, while toasting '*Liberty, Equality, et Fraternity*' in perfect French, on *Boulevard Napoléon* instead of Pennsylvania Avenue. But I transgressed.

Thank you for reading Triumph To Tragedy and stay tuned for my next installment in Book Four as Jean-Jacques Dessalines falls, and Alexandre Pétion and Henry Christophe rise to the challenge of navigating Triumph To Tragedy in the Republic of Haiti.

Coming in 2024:
Triumph To Tragedy – Book Four
The Fall of Dessalines and the Rise of Christophe & Pétion.

www.TriumphToTragedy.com

AUTHOR'S NOTES

Writing the Triumph To Tragedy novels compelled me to research the profound history of the French colony of Saint Domingue, and the events that led to the forming of the Armée Indigéne (Indigenous Army) in 1803. No member of that army was technically indigenous to Hispaniola, as that honor goes to the first inhabitants known as the Ciboney, then the Taïno's, Arawaks, and Caribs. But the black and mulatto inhabitants felt that they were 'indigenous' to the island and separate them from colonial residents from Europe.

It's precursor, the Colonial Army of Saint-Domingue (French: Armée de Saint-Domingue), headed by Toussaint Louverture, was the predominant military force in the colony and flew the flag of France through 1802. However, the Indigenous Army (French: Armée Indigène), also known as the *Lame Endijèn* in Creole, was the name bestowed to the new coalition of soldiers who fought in the Haitian Revolution under the leadership of then General Jean-Jacques Dessalines in 1803. To the French, they were the *"L'armée Cannibale,"* The Cannibal Army.

But the French Army quickly discovered that they were indeed not savage cannibals at all, as they referred to them. They were able to recruit over 45,000 men and women, train and organize them into an army, complete with 30 territorial divisions headed by capable leaders, that included Infantry, Calvary, Artillery, and the logistics involved in such an organization to wage combat throughout nearly 30,000 square miles of Hispaniola. See pages 510-514.

European casualty estimates vary wildly, from 50,000 to 80,000 lost troops between 1802 through 1804, including 20 capable French Generals who lost their lives in the failed expedition.

Armée Indigéne – 1803

January 16, 1803, Nicolas Geffrad Sr. and Étienne Gérin with the 13th freed the city of Anse-à-Veau, thus freeing the department of Nippes against the French general Bernard.

April 12, 1803, François La mort Capois conquered the city of Port-de-Paix and Île de la Tortue (the island of Tortuga), thus cutting all French supply between Cap-Français and Mole-St-Nicolas and freeing the department of Haut-Nord-Ouest (department) against the French generals Clauzel and Boscus;

Larose freed the city of Arcahaie with the 8th, thus freeing the region of Haut-Ouest.

May 18, 1803, Congress of Arcahaie with Dessalines, Pétion, Christophe, Boyer, Geffrard, Clerveaux, Vernet, Gabard, Bazelais, Gérin, Bonnet, Roux, Boisrond, Capois, Louis and Marie-Jeanne Lamartinière, Cangé, Larose, and others.

June 30, 1803, Louis Gabart and Dessalines with the 4th, 7th, 20th, and 10th freed the city of Mirebalais, thus freeing the department of Centre.

July 5, 1803, Congress of Camp-Gérrard with Geffrard, Férou, Gérin, Boisrond Tonerre, and Dessalines on galvanizing the troops of Tiburon Peninsula.

August 4, 1803, Laurent Férou marched toward Jérémie from Cayes through Tiburon with the 18th. One column led by Bazile walked to the city through Marfranc and Férou continued through Abricot thus freeing the department of Grand Anse.

September 4, 1803, Louis Gabart and Dessalines conquered the city of St-Marc, thus freeing the department of Bas-Artibonite aigant the French generals Hénin.

September 9, 1803, Toussaint Brave and Auguste Clerveaux with 1st, 6th conquered the city of Fort-Liberté, thus freeing the department of North-East against the French general Pamphile de LaCroix.

September 17, 1803, Magloire Ambroise and Cangé with the 21st,

22nd, 23rd conquered the city of Jacmel, thus freeing the department of Southern peninsula against the French general Pageot.

Cangé conquered the city of Léogane with the 21th, 24th thus freeing the department of Ouest-Mériddional.

Germain Frère and Frontiste of the 11th and 12th controls the area of La Coupe, modern-day Pétionville.

September 19, on their way to siege Port-au-Prince, Dessalines, with Lux and the 5th take Croix-des-Bouquets.

October 9, 1803, Pétion, Cangé, Gabart and Dessalines with the 3rd, 11th, 12th, 4th, 7th, 20th and 21st marched toward Port-au-Prince. Dessalines established its Headquarters in Turgeau, Louis Gabart was along rue St-Martin with his troops from the shore to Fort-National, Pétion was on St-Gérard hill with the artillery, and Cangé after taking Fort-Bizoton set up a battery Fort-Mercredi hill thus freeing the department of Ouest against the French general Lavalette.

October 16, 1803, Geffrard, and Coco Herne conquered the city of Les Cayes with the 13th and 15th, thus freeing the department of Sud against the French general Brunet.

November 18, 1803, Christophe, Clerveaux, Cappoix, Romain and Dessalines gathered a division of 20 000 men from the 2nd, 6th, 8th, 4th, 7th, 3rd, 11th, 14th, 20th, 22nd, 23rd, 24th, the Regiment of Dragoons of Artibonite and an artillery regiment under the command of Gabard to the *Battle of Vertières,* frees the department of Nord against the French general Rochambeau. Zenon freed the city of Cap-Français. Dessalines places his Headquarters on habitation Lenormand de Mézy, the same place where the Bwakayiman ceremony happened, he sent Paul Romain and Henry Christophe to Vigie through Cap-Français and Cappois, Vernet, and Charlotin to Cape-Heights (Haut-du-Cap) thus on

December 4, 1803, Vincent Pourcelly with a battalion of the 9th demi-brigade freed the city of Mole-St-Nicolas, thus freeing the department of Bas-Nord-Ouest chasing the last troops out of Haiti and French general Louis Noailles.

Organization of the Armée Indigéne (Indigenous Army)

Regiment	Commander	Commune	Division	Corps	Troops	Forts
1st	Toussaint Brave	Fort-Liberté/Lavax	East	Infantry	1500	St-Joseph
2nd	Henry Christophe	Cap-Français	North	Infantry	1500	Picolet/Citadelle Henry/ Bréda
3rd	Gilles Drouet	Port-au-Prince	West	Infantry	1500	Drouet
4th	Jean-Jacques Dessalines	Artibonite	West	Infantry	1500	Innocent/ Fin-Monde/ Doco
5th	Paul Romain	Limbé	North	Infantry	1500	
6th	Augustin Clerveaux	Dondon	North	Infantry	1500	
7th	Louis-Gabart	St-Marc	West	Infantry	1500	Diamant/ Béké

<u>Organization of the Armée Indigéne (Indigenous Army)</u>

Regiment	Commander	Commune	Division	Corps	Troop	Forts
8th	Larose	Arcahaie	North	Infantry	1500	
9th	Francois Cappois	Port-de-Paix	North	Infantry	1500	Trois-Rivière
10th	Jean-Philippe Daut	Mirebalais	East	Infantry	1500	
11th	Frontiste	Port-au-Prince	West	Infantry	1500	Jacques/Alexandre
12th	Germain Frère	Port-au-Prince	West	Infantry	1500	National/Touron
13th	Coco JJ Herne	Cayes	South	Infantry	1500	Forteresse des Platons
14th	André Vernet	Gonaives	West	Infantry	1500	Bayonnais

<u>Organization of the Armée Indigéne (Indigenous Army)</u>

Regiment	Commander	Commune	Division	Corps	Troop	Forts
15th	Jean-Louis Francois	Aquin	South	Infantry	1500	Bonnet-Carré
16th	Étienne E. Gérin	Miragoane/Anse-à-Veau	South	Infantry	1500	Réfléchit/Débois
17th	Vancol	Port-Salut	South	Infantry	1500	
18th	Laurent Férrou	Jérémie	South	Infantry	1500	Marfranc
19th	Gilles Béneche	Tiburon	South	Infantry	1500	
20th Polish	Joseph Jérome	Verettes	West	Infantry	1500	Crête-à-Pierrot
21st	Cangé	Léogane	West	Infantry	1500	Campan

Daniel J.D. Bayard

<u>Organization of the Armée Indigéne (Indigenous Army)</u>

Regiment	Commander	Commune	Division	Corps	Troop	Forts
22nd	Magloire Ambroise	Jacmel	South	Infantry	1500	Ogé
24th	Lamarre	Petit-Goave	West	Infantry	1500	Garry
Artillery Artibonite	Unknown	St-Marc	West	Artillery	1000	
Artillery South	Unknown	Cayes	West	Artillery	1000	
Artillery North	Unknown	Cap-Français	North	Artillery	1000	
Dragoon North	Unknown	Cap-Français	North	Cavalry	1000	

<u>Organization of the Armée Indigéne (Indigenous Army)</u>

Regiment	Commander	Commune	Division	Corps	Troop	Forts
Dragoon Artibonite	Charlotin Marcadieu	St-Marc	West	Cavalry	1000	
Dragoon South	Guillaume Lafleur	Cayes	West	Cavalry	1000	
Maroon	Sansousi/ Petit-Noel Prieur	Massif Nord Dondon	North	Mountain		
Maroon	Gilles Bambara	Massif de la Hotte / Goave	South	Mountain		
Maroon	Lamour Dérance	Massif la Selle/ Kenscoff	South	Mountain		

514

NOTABLE CHARACTERS
Those of Saint Domingue

FRANÇOIS DOMINIQUE TOUSSAINT GUINOU
DE BREDA LOUVERTURE

Also known as Toussaint L'Ouverture or Toussaint Bréda; (1743 – 1803) was the most prominent leader of the Haitian Revolution. During his life, Louverture first fought against the French, then for them, and then finally against France again for the cause of Haitian independence. As a revolutionary leader, Louverture displayed military and political acumen that helped transform the fledgling slave rebellion into a revolutionary movement. Louverture is now known as one of the "Founding Fathers of Haiti".

In 1802, Toussaint was captured and deported to France on the 74-gun French ship the Créole. He warned his captors that the rebels would not repeat his mistake, "In overthrowing me you have cut down in Saint-Domingue only the trunk of the tree of liberty; it will spring up again from the roots, for they are numerous, and they are deep."

During his imprisonment at the frigid Fort-de-Joux in Doubs, France, Louverture, who was French General, attempted to gain an audience with Napoleon who refused. He wrote a memoir and died in prison on April 7, 1803, at the age of 60.

JEAN-JACQUES DUCLOS-DESSALINES

Dessalines (1758-1806) was a leader of the Haitian Revolution and on January 1, 1804, became the first ruler of an independent Haiti. He soon after he enacted the 1805 constitution. Under Dessalines, Haiti became the first country to permanently abolish slavery. Initially regarded as governor-general, Dessalines was later named Emperor of Haiti as Jacques I (1804–1806) by generals of the Haitian Revolution Army and ruled in that capacity until being assassinated in October of 1806. He has been referred to as one of the founding fathers of the nation of Haiti.

HENRY CHRISTOPHE

Christophe (1767 – 1820) began his military career as a drummer boy in the famed Chasseurs-Volontaires de Saint-Domingue and reportedly worked at the Hôtel la Couronne, albeit for an unknown period of time. As an adult, he became a key leader in the Haitian Revolution and ascended to be a monarch of the Kingdom of Haiti by proclaiming himselfe king. Christophe set out to improve all aspects of life in the Northern Province focusing on building defense mechanisms for his country, expanding agricultural production and educating his people.

ALEXANDRE SABES PÉTION

Pétion (1770 – 1818) was the first President of the Republic of Haiti from 1807 until his death in 1818. He is acknowledged as one of Haiti's founding fathers; a member of the revolutionary quartet that also includes Toussaint Louverture, Jean-Jacquess Dessalines, and his later rival Henri Christophe.

Pétion distinguished himself as an esteemed military artillery officer and commander with experience leading both French and Haitian troops. The 1802 coalition formed by he, Dessalines, Christophe, and others against French forces led by Charles Leclerc would prove to be a watershed moment in the decade-long conflict, eventually culminating in the decisive Haitian victory at the Battle of Vertières in 1803

MOÏSE, MOYSE OR MOYIZ LOUVERTURE

Most commonly "Moyiz" in Creole (1773 - 1801) was a military leader and one of the most ardent leaders of the first uprising in 1791 and acted as the second-in-command to Toussaint. There is universal agreement that Toussaint Louverture adopted Moise as his nephew. Originally allied with Toussaint, Moise grew disillusioned with the minimal labor reform and land distribution for Black former slaves under the Louverture administration and lead a rebellion against Toussaint in 1801. Though executed on order of L'Ouverture, the insurrection he directed highlighted the failure of Louverture in creating real revolutionary labor change eventually contributing to driving Louverture from office.

GENERAL CHARLES BELAIR

Belair (1760–1802) was Aide-de-Camp and lieutenant of Toussaint Louverture, Head of the 7th demi-brigade, Commandant of l'Archaie and Former lieutenant of Biassou. He was also said to be a nephew of Toussaint Louverture. In 1796, he married Sanite Belair, a female hero of the revolution.

SANITE 'SUZANNE' BÉLAIR

Sanite Bélair, (1781 –1802) was a Haitian revolutionary and lieutenant in the army of Toussaint Louverture. Born free from affranchi parents in Verrettes, Haiti, she married Brigade commander and later General Charles Bélair in 1796. She was an active participant in the Haitian Revolution, became a sergeant, and later a lieutenant during the conflict with French troops of the Saint-Domingue expedition. Her portrait appears on the Haitian 10 gourdes banknote.

BENOIT JOSEPH ANDRÉ RIGAUD

Rigaud (1761 – 1811) was the leading mulatto military leader during of Saint Domingue and the civil war in the colony. His protégés were Alexandre Pétion and Jean-Pierre Boyer, both future presidents of Haïti. He returned to Saint-Domingue in 1802 with the expedition of General Charles Leclerc to unseat Toussaint but was arrested and sent back, imprisoned in the same fort as Toussaint Louverture.

LOUIS DAURE LAMARTINIÈRE

Lamartinière (1771 - 1802) was a participant in the Battle of Crête-à-Pierrot. Lamartiniere was a small, thin, man of thirty years during the battle who by all appearances was. He was the illegitimate son of a White father and a sacratras - a quadroon - mother. Lamartiniere's father owned a sugar plantation and refinery near Léogane. He had recognized his mulatto son but left his property to his legitimate, White son. He was the husband of Marie-Jeanne Lamartinière.

MARIE-JEANNE LAMARTINIÈRE

"Marie-Jeanne" (unknown - 1802), was a Haitian soldier and reportedly a "dazzling beauty." She served in the Haitian army during the Haitian Revolution and in at the Battle of Crête-à-Pierrot (March 1802) with her husband Louis Daure Lamartinière. She fought in a male uniform standing along the fort's ramparts bearing both a rifle and a sword.

FRANÇOIS CAPOIS - CAPOIS LA MORT

Capois (1766 – 1806) military career began in 1793 after a visit with independence leader Toussaint Louverture. Capois is mostly known for his extraordinary courage and especially his herculean bravery at the Battle of Vertières in which the French general Viscount of Rochambeau, commander of Napoleon's army even called a brief cease-fire to congratulate him. He was nicknamed "Capois la Mort" for his numerous episodes of defying death during battles.

JEAN-PIERRE BOYER

Boyer (1776 – July 1850) was one of the leaders of the Haitian Revolution, and President of Haiti from 1818 to 1843. He reunited the north and south of the country into the Spanish Haiti (Santo Domingo), which brought all of Hispaniola under one Haitian government by 1822. Boyer managed to rule for the longest period of any of the revolutionary leaders of his generation.

JACQUES MAUREPAS

Maurepas, (unk - 1802) was the commander of the town of Port-de-Paix in the northeast of Saint Domingue at the time when Napoleon sent a large army led by his brother-in-law general Charles Leclerc to overthrow Toussaint Louverture and restore slavery. Louverture ordered Maurepas to burn the city, withdraw to the mountains, and take ammunition to defend himself to the death if he could not hold the town. Maurepas did as was ordered. When French General Humbert marched against Maurepas, but was completely defeated as was General Debelle However, Maurepas surrendered and was integrated to the French army. After being suspected of taking part in a revolt led by Capois, he, his family, and some of the soldiers were arrested, and, some of his troops of the 9th Brigade and his family were tortured and cast into the sea.

LOUIS FÉLIX MATHURIN BOISROND-TONNERRE

Boisrond-Tonnerre (1776 - 1806), was a Haitian writer and historian who is best known for having served as Jean-Jacques Dessalines' secretary. Boisrond-Tonnerre was educated in Paris until 1798 when he returned to Saint Domingue and became known for his work in writing the Haitian Declaration of Independence, and chronicling the Haitian Revolution, Mémoires pour Servir à l'Histoire d'Haïti. Boisrond-Tonnerre was born Louis Boisrond in Torbeck in southwest Haiti. He acquired the name "Tonnerre", French for "thunder", as an infant when his cradle was hit by lightning. His father,amazed that his infant son was unharmed, gave him the name "Tonnerre".He a victim of post-revolutionary infighting and was executed in October 1806.

LOUIS GABART

Gabart (1776 - 1805) was first an infantry leader who learned his lethal artillery skills from Alexandre Pétion, successfully depoying them at the last major battle of the Haitian Revolution at Vertière. He was the youngest general in the army at the time and a devout follower of Jean-Jacques Dessalines, leading him to be victim of the purge of generals before Dessalines death between 1804 and 1806.

CÉCILE FATIMAN

Fatiman (1771-1883), was a Haitian voodoo priestess, a mambo. She is famous for her participation in the voodoo ceremony at Bois Caïman along with Dutty Boukman which prompted the slave revolt that is considered to be one of the starting points of the Haitian Revolution. She also commanded, along with Sans Souci, the maroons of the north.

SUZANNE SIMONE BAPTISTE LOUVERTURE

Suzanne Louverture (1742 – 1816) was the wife of Toussaint Louverture. When in 1801 the constitution appointed Toussaint as governor of Saint-Domingue, she received the title of "Dame-Consort."

In 1802, Charles Leclerc's troops captured her along with her husband and the rest of her immediate family and shipped them to France. Madame Louverture survived her husband, who died in a French prison the following year. She was the mother of three boys, the youngest of which, Saint-Jean, died in 1804 in Agen, France. She died in 1816, in the arms of her sons, Placide and Isaac in Agen as well.

PLACIDE LOUVERTURE

Placide (1781 – 1841) was born before his mother's marriage in 1782 to Toussaint Louverture, who accepted the boy as his legitimate son. He was sent to school in France under scholarship granted by Napoleon Bonaparte. Placide and his brother Isaac were charged with delivering a letter to their father from First Consul Napoleon Bonaparte strongly suggesting he retire as Governor General of the colony and cede his power to General Leclerc, his designated replacement.

Upon returning to Saint-Domingue, he sided and fought with his father against the French government. When Toussaint was arrested and deported on June 8, 1802, by order of Napoléon Bonaparte, so was the entire family along with his mother and his brothers—Saint-Jean and Isaac.

ISAAC LOUVERTURE

Isaac (1786 - 1854) was the son of Toussaint and Suzanne Louverture. He and his half-brother Placide were sent to France in 1797 to be educated. They both returned with General Charles Leclerc to Saint-Domingue in the failed expedition to seize control and re-establish slavery in the colony. Placide and Isaac were charged with delivering a letter to their father from Napoleon.

SAINT-JEAN LOUVERTURE

Saint-Jean (1791 - January 8, 1804 Agen, France) was the youngest child of Toussaint and Suzanne Louverture. Saint-Jean was deported in 1802 to France with his entire family, he was the second of two children the couple had together, the first one being Isaac. Placide, the oldest son, adopted by Toussaint, was Suzanne's son by a previous marriage.

When Saint-Jean heard of his father's death (April 7, 1803), he declared that he should not long survive him. He died the following year.

MARIE-CLAIRE HEUREUSE FÉLICITÉ BONHEUR

Félicité (1758 - 1858) became Empress of Haiti (1804–1806) as the spouse of Jean-Jacquess Dessalines and they had seven children together. During the siege of Jacmel in 1800, she was applauded for her work with the wounded and starving. She managed to convince Dessalines, besieging the city, to allow roads to be opened for food, clothes, and medicine which she personally delivered.

She is also credited for saving many French colonists by hiding them under her bead during the revolutionary war.

MARIE-LOUISE COIDAVID

Coidavid (1778 - 1851), was the Queen of the Kingdom of Haiti from 1811–1820 as the spouse of Henri Christophe. She was born into a free family; her father was the owner of Hôtel de La Couronne in Cap-Français, Saint-Domingue. Henri Christophe was a slave purchased by her father and he supposedly earned enough money in tips from his duties at the hotel that he was able to purchase his freedom before the Haitian Revolution.

They married in Cap-Francais in 1793, having had a relationship with him from the year prior. They had four children: François Ferdinand, Françoise-Améthyste, Athénaïs, and Victor-Henri. She was exiled for 30 years after Christophe's death. Shortly before her death, she wrote to Haiti for permission to return, however, died in Italy.

ABDARAYA TOYA "VICTORIA MONTOU"

Toya Montou (1739–1805) was a Dahomey warrior and freedom fighter in the army of Jean-Jacques Dessalines during the Haitian Revolution. Before the Revolution she and Dessalines had been enslaved on the same estate, and the two remained close throughout her life, with Dessalines calling her his aunt. Toya was reportedly a skilled warrior, midwife and healer, who organized several rebellions before the momentous meeting at Bois Caiman in 1791. During the slave rebellion and civil war, she fought as a soldier in active service; on at least one documented occasion, she commanded soldiers in action during battle.

CATHERINE FLON

Flon (unknown birth-death) was a Haitian seamstress, patriot, and national heroine. She is regarded as one of the symbols of the Haitian Revolution and independence. She is celebrated for tearing off the White portion of the French flag and then sewing the first Haitian flag in May 1803 and maintains an important place in Haitian memory of the Revolution to this day.

MARIE SAINTE DÉDÉE BAZILE

Bazile (unk. birth-death), known as Défilée and Défilée-La-Folle (crazy), is a figure of the Haitian Revolution. She is remembered for retrieving and burying the mutilated body of Emperor Dessalines after his assassination at Pont Rouge, at the northern entrance to Port-au-Prince. Dédée Bazile was born near Cap-Français to enslaved parents and made a living serving as a sutler to the army of Dessalines.

NOTABLE CHARACTERS
Those of the French

NAPOLEON BONAPARTE

Napoleon (1769 – 1821) and later known by his regnal name Napoleon I, was a French military and political leader who rose to prominence during the French Revolution and led several successful campaigns during the Revolutionary Wars. He unsuccessfully attempted to re-enslave the most valuable of the French possessions, Saint-Domingue, from 1801 to 1803.

CHARLES VICTOIRE EMMANUEL LECLERC

Leclerc (1772 – 1802), of small stature, was a French Army general who served under Napoleon Bonaparte during the French Revolution. He was husband of Pauline Bonaparte, sister to Napoleon. In 1801, he was sent to Saint-Domingue (Haiti), where an expeditionary force under his command captured and deported the Haitian leader Toussaint L'Ouverture, in an unsuccessful attempt to reassert full imperial control and slavery over the Saint-Domingue. Leclerc died of yellow fever during the failed expedition.

LOUIS-THOMAS VILLARET DE JOYEUSE

de Joyeuse (1747 - 1812) was a French admiral in charge of all naval acitivites in 1801 when Bonaparte decided to attempt to regain control of Haiti with the Saint-Domingue expedition. Villaret set out with ten French and five Spanish ships and nine frigates and corvettes, with his flag on the 120-gun Océan, ferrying 7000 of General Leclerc's expeditionary forces to Saint Domingue. Two further squadron, one from Lorient comprising one ship, two frigates and 1200 soldiers, and the other from Rochefort with six ships, six frigates, two corvettes and 3000 soldiers, joined his fleet off Brest. Conflicts over command led Villaret to return to France with the majority of the fleet.

DONATIEN-MARIE-JOSEPH DE ROCHAMBEAU

Rochambeau. (April 1755 – October 1813) was a French military commander. He was the son of Jean-Baptiste Donatien de Vimeur, comte de Rochambeau.

He served in the American Revolutionary War as an aide-de-camp to his father, spending the winter of 1781–1782 in quarters at Williamsburg, Virginia.

In 1802, he was appointed to lead an expeditionary force against Saint-Domingue (Haiti) after General Charles Leclerc's death. His remit was to restore French control of their rebellious colony, by any means. Historians of the Haitian Revolution credit his brutal tactics for uniting black and gens de couleur soldiers against the French. During his time in Haiti, Rochambeau waged a war of extermination, massacring thousands of blacks of all ages and genders. In 1803, he developed the world's first gas chambers. He used a rudimentary method of filling ships' cargo holds with sulfur dioxide to suffocate black prisoners of war.

JEAN BOUDET

Boudet (February 1769 - September 1809, was a French général de division of the French Revolutionary Wars and the Napoleonic Wars. The campaigns in which he was involved include the Saint-Domingue expedition. He was made a grand officer of the Légion d'honneur on 2 June 1809 and a knight of the Order of the Iron Crown, as well as a Comte de l'Empire in 1808. His name is engraved on the 16th column of the east side of the Arc de Triomphe in Paris.

He was chosen for the expedition and landed at Port-au-Prince in February 1802. He treated its black, white and creole inhabitants equally and was thus made very welcome. Operating in isolation from the rest of his supreme commander Charles Leclerc's troops, Boudet easily captured Leogane, Saint-Marc, then to the redoubt at Crête-à-Pierrot. He assaulted the redoubt in March, being wounded in the heel by shrapnel and forced to abandon his command of the division to Rochambeau.

FRANÇOIS-JOSEPH-PAMPHILE LACROIX

Lacroix (June 1774 – October 1841) initially joining the National Guard of Montpellier during the French Revolution, became an officer when he was commissioned as a sous-lieutenant in the 14th Infantry in May of 1792. Sent to serve in Champagne and Belgium, he was promoted to lieutenant to February of 1793. In 1794 Lacroix served in Souham's division and later that year he was named an aide-de-camp to Macdonald. Two years later he served in Holland and received a promotion to capitaine.

At the end of 1801 Lacroix was designated for the expedition to Saint-Domingue as chief of staff to General Boudet. After arriving in Saint-Domingue, he fought at the action of Port-au-Prince where he was wounded by a shot to the hip. Six weeks later Lacroix received a promotion to général de brigade and fought at Pierrot. In January of 1803 he was named commander of Tortuga Island but then in March he set off to return to France.

JEAN BAPTISTE BRUNET

Brunet (July 1763 – September 1824) was a French general of division in the French Revolutionary Army. He was promoted to command a light infantry demi-brigade at the Fleurus in 1794. He led the unit in François Joseph Lefebvre's division in the 1795, 1796 and 1799 campaigns. He was the son of French general Gaspard Jean-Baptiste Brunet who was guillotined in 1793.

Charles Leclerc originally asked Jean-Jacques Dessalines to arrest Louverture, but he declined. The task then fell to Brunet. However, accounts differ as regards how he accomplished this. One account has it that Brunet pretended that he planned to settle in Saint-Domingue and asked for Toussaint's advice about plantation management. Louverture's memoirs however suggest that Brunet's troops had been provocative, leading Louverture to seek a discussion with him. Embarrassed about his trickery, Brunet absented himself during the arrest. He was captured by the British and not released until 1814.

PAULINE BONAPART LECLERC

Bonaparte (1780–1825), the youngest of Napoleon's three sisters, was the most frivolous one. She possessed magnetic beauty and charm. Whenever she went, the eyes of men turned after her. Men loved her and she loved them. Pauline was a nymphomaniac and much to Napoleon's chagrin, she made it very public.

NOTABLE CHARACTERS
Those of the Americans

DR EDWARD STEVENS

Stevens (1754 – 1834) was an American physician and diplomat. He was a close friend of Alexander Hamilton since early childhood in St. Croix, now the US Virgin Islands. Stevens served as the United States consul-general in Saint-Domingue (later Haiti) from 1799 to 1800. President John Adams sent Stevens to Haiti with instructions to establish a relationship with Toussaint Louverture and express support for his regime. Following his arrival in April 1799, Stevens succeeded in accomplishing several of his objectives, including: the suppression of privateers operating out of the colony, protections for American lives and property, and right of entry for American vessels. The convention, signed on June 13, 1799, continued an armistice among the three parties, gave protections to British and American ships to enter the colony and engage in free trade.

CAPTAIN (ADMIRAL) SILAS TALBOT

Talbot (1751 – 1813) was an American military officer. He served in the Continental Army and Continental Navy during the American Revolutionary War and is most famous for commanding USS Constitution from 1799 to 1801 with her maiden duties in Saint Domingue (now Haiti) during the Quasi-War with France. Talbot was re-commissioned as a captain in the United States Navy in

1798. He served as commander of USS Constitution (nicknamed Old Ironsides) from 1799 until September 1801, sailing it to the West Indies where he protected American commerce from French privateers during the Quasi-War. He commanded the Santo Domingo Station in 1799 and 1800 and was well received by Toussaint Louverture as an ally. He was commended by the Secretary of the Navy for protecting American commerce and for laying the foundation of a permanent trade with Saint Domingue. It is said that throughout his career, Talbot was wounded 13 times and carried 5 bullets in his body.

CHRISTOPHER RAYMOND PERRY

Perry, (1761 – 1818) was an officer in the United States Navy, He was the father of Oliver Hazard Perry and Matthew Calbraith Perry. In 1798, Perry commanded the frigate General Greene, on which his son, then 13-year-old Oliver Hazard Perry, served as a midshipman. The General Greene intercepted supplies to rebels fighting to overthrow General Toussaint Louverture during the Saint Domingue, later Haiti, civil war. On April 27, General Greene brought two emissaries from Louverture to New Orleans where they went on to meet with President John Adams. The ship later engaged in secret missions to assist Louverture in blockading the port of Jacmel.

ABOUT THE AUTHOR

Daniel Jean-Dominique Bayard

Mr. Bayard was born in Port-au-Prince, Haiti, and raised in the United States when his parents fled to New York in 1958 from the Duvalier dictatorship. He returned to Haiti for the first time as a teenager of 17, and has been fascinated with Haiti's culture, people, and historical significance ever since. He lived and owned a business in Haiti for a short period of time and came to love it.

While researching his family's ancestors dating back to the 17th century, he became intrigued with the complexities and drama of Saint-Domingue, the colonial precursor of Haiti, and the revolution that gained it's freedom and independence. In-depth research into all aspects of the period's history and aspects of colonial society led him to write these thrilling, enlightening, and entertaining novels of his family's story and the nation's triumphs, and tragedies.

Mr. Bayard is a Chief Marketing Officer for a major company, married with 4 children, blessed with 5 grandchildren, and resides in South Florida.

Ancestors of the Author

Philippe Bayard (Lille, France DOB 1689)
(Arrived in Saint-Domingue circa 1710)
Married Marie Debreuse

Jean-Philippe Bayard (Son) 1725
Married Jeanne Guillemette Bachelier

Jean-Baptiste Hyppolite Bayard (Son) 1750
Married Marie Jasmine

Jean-Baptiste Bayard (Son) 1775
Married Marie Victoire Georges

Achilles Othello Bayard (Son) 1823
Married Elizabeth Pressoir

Georges R. Bayard (Son) 1850
Married Marianne Clerie

Thomas Bayard (Son) 1879
Married Alzire Sansaricq 1881

Daniel Thomas Bayard (Son) 1912
Married Marcelle Elisabeth Oriol 1921

The Author:
Daniel Jean-Dominique Bayard (Son) 1957
Married Lily Anne Marie LaPlace 1957

THE REPUBLIC OF HAITI

Haitian Creole: Ayiti

The country of Haiti is located in the Caribbean on the western third of the island of Hispaniola. It is bordered by the Dominican Republic to the east, the Caribbean Sea, and the Atlantic Ocean.

Haiti's terrain consists mainly of rugged mountains interspersed with small coastal plains and river valleys. The government system is a republic; the chief of state is the president, and the head of government is the prime minister.

Haiti has a largely traditional economic system in which most of the economy relies on subsistence farming, and government regulation is widely constrained. Haiti is a member of the Caribbean Community (CARICOM)

In color, the flag of Haiti's top section is Blue and the bottom section is Red. The inserted image in the center of the flag consists of Blue, Red and Green in a White background.

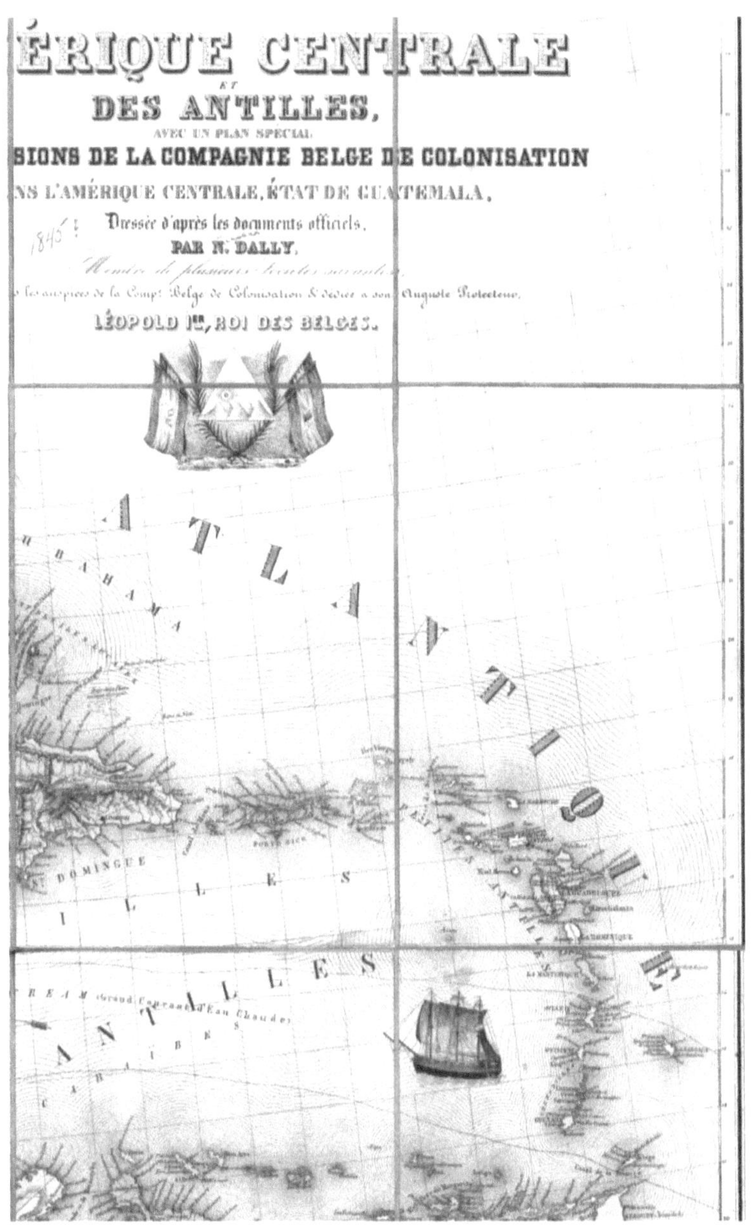
ÉRIQUE CENTRALE
ET
DES ANTILLES,
AVEC UN PLAN SPECIAL
SIONS DE LA COMPAGNIE BELGE DE COLONISATION
NS L'AMÉRIQUE CENTRALE, ÉTAT DE GUATEMALA,
Dressée d'après les documents officiels,
PAR N. DALLY,
LÉOPOLD I, ROI DES BELGES.
ATLANTIQUE
BAHAMA
ST DOMINGUE
ILLES
ANTILLES